Twirling Fire

Claudia J. Severin

TWIRLING FIRE

Copyright © May 2021

Claudia J. Severin

Published by Pella Road Publishing

Lincoln, Nebraska

ISBN: 978-1-7342-1485-7

Twirling Fire is a work of fiction. Any references to historical events, real people, or real locales are used fictitiously. Other names, characters, places, and incidents are the product of the author's imagination, and any resemblance to actual events or locales or persons, living or dead, in entirely coincidental.

Claudia J. Severin

https://claudiaseverin.net

DEDICATION

For Connie, Rickie, Pat, Jan, and MariJo, class of 1969.
I couldn't have twirled through fire without you.

CONTENTS

"Now, at the beginning of the twenty-first century, the Spoken Soul these writers exalted is battered by controversy, its very existence called into question. Though belittled and denied, however, it lives on authentically. In homes, schools, and churches, on streets, stages, and the airwaves, you can hear soul spoken every day.

Most African Americans—including millions who . . . are fluent speakers of Standard English—still invoke Spoken Soul as we have for hundreds of years, to laugh or cry, to preach and praise, to shuck and jive, to sing, to rap, to shout, to style, to express our individual personas and our ethnic identities (" 'spress yo'self!" as James Brown put it), to confide in and commiserate with friends, to chastise, to cuss, to act, to act the fool, to get by and get over, to pass secrets, to make jokes, to mock and mimic, to tell stories, to reflect and philosophize, to create authentic characters and voices in novels, poems, and plays, to survive in the streets, to relax at home and recreate in playgrounds, to render our deepest emotions and embody our vital core.

The fact is that most African Americans do talk differently from whites and Americans of other ethnic groups, or **at least most of us can when we want to.** And the fact is that most Americans, black and white, know this to be true."

—Rickford, John Russell, and Rickford, Russell John. 2000 *Spoken Soul*. Turner Publishing Company. Kindle Edition.

TWIRLING FIRE

It was the twins' birthday party, and they invited friends from their first-grade class at Eastridge Elementary school to join them at Bethany Park. They had the party on a Saturday morning to avoid the early August afternoon heat. The children played on the swings and jungle gym until their mother, Bonnie Adams, called them all to come over for cake and ice cream at a picnic table.

Debbie and Daniel sat side-by-side waiting for Bonnie to light seven candles on their cake. What would it be like to have a birthday cake all to herself? Every year Debbie could recall, she didn't finish making her wish before her brother blew out all of their candles. That had to be bad luck. This year, he was under strict instructions not to start blowing until his mother gave the signal.

Their mother lit the candles. The other children sang. Their father, Bernard, took a picture. Bonnie was about to tell them to start puffing away when a little boy ran up to their table. Not one of their guests, he had been playing with his family in the park. Debbie blinked as the cheeks of his glowing dark-eyed caramel-colored face puffed out, descended on their cake and doused the flames on her side. Her giggles erupted as her brother extinguished candles from the other side.

The artful dodger was only at their table seconds before his mother snatched him up with a profuse apology, and hauled him back to join his brothers and sisters. Before Debbie dove into her piece of chocolate cake, she sighed, witnessing his public scolding. He'd done something naughty, but she wished she had his nerve.

CHAPTER ONE

July 5, 1959
Lincoln, Nebraska

Debbie's eyes grew wide at the size of the moving van unloading in the driveway next door to her house on Mulder Drive. She pressed her nose up to her brother's bedroom window looking for the family that owned that paisley couch and two bronze wingback chairs passing into the house. Her Siamese kitten, Princess purred contently in her arms.

"Any sign of kids yet?" Daniel asked when he saw what she was doing. He tossed the comic book he had been reading on his bed and left the room. When she heard the piano, she knew he was practicing for his lesson that afternoon.

"Deborah Sue," Bonnie called. "Have you finished vacuuming?"

Debbie set the kitten on her bed and went back to the hallway and resumed her vacuuming chore. She still had to finish packing her clothes for Camp Fire camp, which started the next day. She and her friend, Janine Meeks, were going to be bunkmates. It was the first time she'd be away from home for four whole nights, and out from under the shadow of her brother. He'd had his turn at Boy Scout camp the previous week.

At dinner that evening, Daniel leaned forward. "I saw the new neighbors through my window. It looked like they had two tall skinny boys with dark hair. The younger one might be our age. They were both wearing glasses but I saw them mostly from the back."

Debbie sighed. "I was hoping for another girl in the neighborhood. Janine is the closest girl in our class and she lives three blocks away."

"What about Martha Glencocks? Doesn't she live right across

Randolph?" Bernard asked.

"Oh, nobody likes her," Debbie said. "Her dog tried to eat Janine's toy poodle when we walked by her house."

Debbie enjoyed camp over the next five days. When Janine's mother dropped Debbie off on Friday morning, she was surprised to find no one in their house. When she heard voices on the patio, she followed the sounds. Her hand flew to her mouth when she found her mother drinking iced tea with Elizabeth Taylor, the movie star. Or at least a striking dark-haired woman she'd never seen.

Bonnie jumped up to give her daughter a hug when she came outside. "You're home, Sweetie! How was camp?" Before Debbie could answer her, she added, "Oh, this is our new neighbor, Connie Edison. Connie, here's my daughter, Debbie."

Debbie twisted her blonde braid, tilting her head. The new neighbor had stood up when Bonnie did, and she was a good three inches taller than Bonnie. Tall, slender, and beautiful. Debbie couldn't tear her eyes away. She didn't look like somebody's mom.

Gleeful shouts broke the summer breeze. Over the row of lilac bushes lining the fence separating the neighbor's property, she startled when she spotted her brother flying through the air, bouncing on a newly installed trampoline.

"Go on over there, Debbie," her mother said, "Daniel has been having a blast getting to know the new kids. And he loves that trampoline as much as Clark and Vonnie do."

Debbie sighed, and slowly ventured over to the neighbors' yard. She let herself through the gate and moved cautiously toward the trampoline. When she reached the neighbor's backyard, she saw a man and the older boy installing parallel bars. The younger son was now taking a turn bouncing. She was avoiding the pieces of the apparatus laying on the grass so she wouldn't trip as she approached the trampoline.

"Look out!"

Debbie didn't see the child flip over the metal bar that formed the outer frame of the trampoline, crashing into her. The next thing Debbie knew, she was sprawled on the grass, staining her brand-new Camp Kiwanis shirt and white shorts.

"I'm so sorry," her neighbor said, and extended a hand to help her up. He had a sweet voice for a boy, Debbie thought, taking the proffered hand. And those hands were long and thin and wearing chipped pale pink nail polish. Those big doe-brown eyes and heart-shaped face must belong to a girl. Sure, she had her hair cut in very short waves like Audrey Hepburn. But her face was lovely, like her mother's.

"I'm Debbie," she said, brushing off her shorts and knees.

"I'm Yvonne. Vonnie for short." Vonnie glanced at Daniel. "Oh, you're his twin sister. I see it now."

Debbie's pale blonde hair was pulled back into braids which reached the middle of her back. She didn't think she and Daniel looked as much alike as they had a few years earlier. His blonde hair was nearly transparent in a buzz cut, and she had become slightly plump while he remained scrawny. He was more active, as was currently in evidence by the way he was learning new tricks on the trampoline.

"That's my brother, Clark, putting together the parallel bars. He's ten. He thinks he's going to be a gymnast. Your dad has been helping us at night putting in some cement to hold down the equipment. It must be swell to have a dad who can build houses."

"Oh, well yeah. His crew built these houses. How old are you?" Debbie asked.

"I turned eight in June. We'll be in the same grade. Daniel and I talked about it while you were at camp. Are you ready to try the trampoline?"

Debbie was so excited to think she had a girl in her grade living right next door, she barely paid attention to how Yvonne and Daniel were hoisting her up onto the trampoline. She had never bounced on one.

"I don't know how to do this," she admitted when she was sitting on the taut black synthetic fabric that seemed to quiver under her every move. The fabric had absorbed the sun and was hot where her skin touched.

Daniel vaulted back up on the trampoline and started jumping, gently at first, then more vigorously. "There's nothing to it. Just bounce." Debbie was still seated but his movements threw her around and she got closer to the springs.

"Get off there, Daniel! You're scaring her." Yvonne waved her hands at him until he complied. "Stand up, Debbie, nice and slow. Then when you have your balance, put your feet apart a little bit and start bouncing."

Debbie did what Yvonne asked. She appreciated that she was patient and didn't expect her to know how to do this right away. She liked the way it felt to bounce higher and higher, a little at a time.

"Once you've got that down, you can try a seat drop. Throw your legs out and go down on your bottom, then back to your feet," Yvonne said.

Debbie tried and was amazed she got right back up. "This is great!"

Daniel wandered over to watch Clark and his father working on the parallel bars.

After Debbie had jumped for a few minutes, Yvonne rolled onto the trampoline and got up and jumped with her. She showed her how they could jump together like a seesaw, when one was up in the air, the other had her feet on the surface.

"You girls have been hogging the tramp," Clark announced. "Let me show your new friend how it's really done." He climbed up on the trampoline, while Yvonne showed Debbie how to roll off gently.

"Clark, this is Daniel's twin sister, Debbie," Yvonne said. "Meet my brother. He was the biggest showoff in the Show-Me state."

Clark set out to demonstrate her claim by bouncing higher and higher, then doing some flips and twists.

"Clark, not so high now. We have to finish anchoring that thing," Harold Edison said, picking up his tools. "Once Bernard has the cement work done, we'll string some anchor ropes and stakes, to be sure it doesn't topple in a high wind."

"Wanna come over and see my room?" Debbie asked her new friend.

"Sure," Yvonne answered, picking up her black plastic eyeglasses off a box on their patio. "Lead the way."

CHAPTER TWO

April 1961

Debbie glanced at the clock and groaned. She was already tired of the exercise belt jiggling her waist, and threatening to curdle her breakfast. Her mother had a friend whose daughter lost four inches off her waist and hips, and Bonnie had become a faithful user of the Walton Master Craft Belt Vibrator. Debbie had used it three times in the past week, and couldn't tell it made any difference.

Her latest humiliation about the shape of her nine-year-old-body began when the students in her classroom sat cross-legged on the lunchroom floor waiting for the annual height and weight check done by the school nurse. She was thankful that her best friends, Yvonne and Janine were in her class this year, and her brother was not.

"Tommy Sanders, fifty-seven inches, eighty-one pounds!" Their teacher, Mrs. Hunt called out loudly enough for the nurse, Miss Benson, to hear where she sat at a desk across the room.

"Janine Meeks, fifty-two inches, seventy-three pounds." Janine scrambled back to sit with Debbie and Yvonne. Janine cringed although she was clearly within the average range of the girls in their grade.

"Martha Glencocks, fifty-four inches, 109 pounds." Debbie saw poor Martha turn bright red as she plopped back down at the edge of the group separating the boys and girls in their class. Debbie had been getting to know Martha better this year and offered her a small smile. She was the heaviest girl in their class.

"Eddie Perkins, fifty-nine inches, ninety-two pounds." Eddie grinned taking his seat.

"Yvonne Edison, sixty-two inches, ninety-three pounds." Yvonne's downcast face told Debbie that being the tallest kid in their class bothered her.

Then it was Debbie's turn to smash her backside up against the height chart on the wall and step on the big scale like the one at the doctor's office. She bit her lip as the teacher fiddled with the counterweights, willing herself to weigh less.

"Debbie Adams, fifty-three inches, ninety-two-and-one-half pounds!" Mrs. Hunt seemed to say this as though it was unlikely anyone her height and age could be so chubby. Debbie had glanced at the door briefly, wondering if she could escape. But at the moment, she felt she was so huge, there would be nowhere she could hide where they wouldn't find her. Instead, she slinked back to try to gracefully sit down next to her friends, who patted her knee in sympathy.

When she refused to eat dinner that evening, Bonnie had drawn the story out of her.

"It wouldn't hurt you to eat a little less," Bonnie suggested. You could eat just one cookie after school. And if you'd get a little more exercise, that will make you feel lighter. But you can't skip meals altogether. That isn't good for you. I haven't seen you out on the trampoline lately. And Yvonne is outside playing ball with her brother and Daniel. Maybe you should join them."

"But Mom, Vonnie's a tomboy. She said so herself. I am not. I'd rather read or play make-believe in my room," Debbie said.

But she had agreed to try the weight loss vibrating belt. It was boring. If only she could be more like Yvonne or Daniel and enjoy running around the yard. But playing ball meant she'd fall, and that hurt. Or she'd have dirt and grass stains on her clothes. At least she took their boxer, Grover, for walks. He loved her no matter how chubby she was. And Yvonne was usually eager to come along.

CHAPTER THREE

December 1967

Barry Whitaker was coming over to Debbie's house to watch television. Barry could best be described as average. He was average height, a little taller than her five foot six. He was about average build. He wore nondescript glasses and had unruly blondish-brown wiry hair. He was the guy you'd cast in a teen movie to play the awkward best friend. But he'd noticed her, and that set him apart.

She talked to him by their lockers almost every day. His locker was two away from hers. She had replayed the previous day's conversation in her head at least fifty times.

"What's happening, Blondie?" Barry had asked.

"Debbie. My name's Debbie," she laughed.

"Oh, I know. But you remind me of that comic strip, *Blondie*. You know the one with Dagwood and his huge sandwiches. You have the blondest hair I think I've ever seen. Except for maybe Marilyn Monroe."

Debbie didn't mind being compared to Blondie, the sensible wife of the bumbling Dagwood. She read about them in the newspaper regularly. And who wouldn't want to remind a boy of the late M.M. She smiled at Barry. Maybe that's what emboldened him to keep talking.

"If you aren't doing anything on Saturday afternoon, I thought I might come over. You know, to see what you were up to," Barry said. He seemed to freeze for a moment, and swallowed hard, perhaps realizing how clumsy it had sounded.

"You could come by. I'm probably not doing anything important," Debbie crossed and uncrossed her arms. "And I'll probably be done around two o'clock. Do you remember where I live?"

"Sure. I've been to your house. When I was in Boy Scouts, your brother was in my troop."

And now it was Saturday, almost two. She didn't know if she was ready. Her father had taken Daniel ice-skating. At least he wouldn't be around to heckle them. Her mom had baked cookies, so the house smelled wonderful. She had fixed her hair and put on mascara and lipstick. She rarely wore much makeup, but she had to admit, she liked the effect. Maybe if she batted her eyelashes and pouted her lips, he wouldn't care she had an extra fifteen pounds on her. After all, M.M. had been curvy and she seemed to have many admirers.

Barry was late. Debbie began pacing the floor by 2:05 p.m. A few minutes later the doorbell rang, and Debbie opened it with a big smile.

"Hey, Debs. What are you doing today? Gee, you smell nice," Yvonne said, standing on their front porch.

Debbie spotted Barry walking up the driveway before she could answer. A blush rose to her cheeks. Barry stopped in his tracks when he saw Yvonne. "Yvonne, you have to leave. Now."

Yvonne whirled around and saw Barry, who was still hesitating. "Oh. OH. Listen, I wanted to check if your folks were giving me a ride to the basketball game tonight. Six-thirty?"

"Yeah, sure. Whatever," Debbie motioned with her head for Yvonne to retreat to her own house. Debbie never wanted a boy to compare her to Yvonne. She loved Yvonne, but she had morphed into someone closely resembling a fashion model, once she had started wearing contacts and grew her luxurious reddish-brown hair past her shoulders.

Yvonne backed away, turning in time to see Barry's cautious approach. She waved at him and left without another word.

"Did your plans change?" he asked. "Were you and Yvonne supposed to—?"

"No, it's nothing. It was about tonight. Come in, Barry."

They settled on the sofa in the basement with a plate of cookies. *King Kong* was showing on the afternoon movie. Debbie had seen this 1933 black-and-white film a few times, but it always made her jumpy when the monster gorilla roared or thundered through the jungle.

"You aren't scared, are you?" Barry asked.

She gave him her best wide-eyed look, like the movie's lead actress, Fay Wray. "It doesn't scare you, Barry?" she asked.

He put his arm around her shoulders.

Debbie was encouraged. This was going well so far.

"You're as bad as my little sister. She always wants to cuddle up on the couch when we watch scary movies," Barry said, grabbing another cookie with his free hand.

Debbie was about to put her head on his shoulder when she got an image of him sitting with his sister. Had he been thinking about kissing her or had she imagined that? She took a deep breath.

When she did, she caught him suddenly looking at her chest. She was wearing a mohair sweater but she didn't think it was unladylike. She supposed it did show off her generous breasts. It wasn't like she could hide them completely, although she'd been looking for a way to do that since she was thirteen and she caught a boy in class snickering at her.

Barry suddenly leaned away from her, moving his arms around to hug his sides.

Just when Debbie thought things couldn't get worse, Daniel came bounding down the stairs. Debbie heard her mother calling after him, to try to stop the interruption of her date, but it was too late.

"Are there any more cookies down here, Deb? You didn't eat

them all, did you? I am starving!" he said bouncing off the last steps and launching himself toward the plate with two cookies left. "Oh, hey, Barry. What are you doing here?" Daniel sat down next to Barry on the couch and glanced at the console T.V. "*King Kong*. I love this part where he climbs up the Empire State building."

"Daniel Morris Adams, didn't you hear me calling you? Come back up here right now," Bonnie hollered down the stairway.

Daniel stood up. "What's her prob—oh. I see. Sorry," Daniel said, grinning knowingly. He started laughing as he climbed the stairs, polishing off the last cookie.

"I suppose I should go," Barry said, getting to his feet.

"But the movie isn't over," Debbie protested.

"Would you like to go to a movie at the theater next weekend? I think the basketball game is out of town."

Debbie's face brightened. "Sure. That'd be swell." She stood close to him, not wanting their time alone to end.

He stared into her eyes then kissed her on the cheek. Not what she had been expecting, but maybe a step forward. She could still hear her brother making noises in the kitchen, so she didn't follow Barry upstairs to say good-bye. She stayed on the couch and watched Kong battle the dive-bomber biplanes. Just once she wished the big ape would win.

CHAPTER FOUR

February 1968

"Debbie, we have a surprise for you," Bernard announced at breakfast the next Saturday. "Uncle Bob has found a good car for you. A pretty little Volkswagen Beetle."

It was a toss-up whose face registered more surprise, Debbie's or Daniel's. Daniel found his voice first.

"Wait. Why is she getting a car? What about me? Do we have to share?"

"Debbie's getting a car first because her car insurance rates will be cheaper," Bonnie said. "If we wait until you're seventeen, your insurance rates will be lower than they are now. You'll be able to ride with her, of course."

"I'm a much better driver than she is! She only got a B in driver's ed last semester," Daniel protested.

"I'm really getting a car? That's wonderful! Thank you!" Debbie gushed. She had visions of her popularity soaring as she chauffeured all of her friends around town.

"You'll have to earn money to put gas in it, and oil. I think you have some in your babysitting fund. The car will be in our names, but you'll be the principal driver," Bonnie told her. "Uncle Bob's expecting us this afternoon."

Daniel pushed his empty plate away and stormed out of the kitchen. They heard his bedroom door slam.

"He may not be going along if he keeps that up," Bernard said.

"He'll come around. It's only six months until they are seventeen, and he can probably get a car in the summer. Surely, he'll want to check out the cars on the lot," Bonnie said.

Daniel sulked in the backseat all the way to the used car lot in

Omaha. He left the others in order to look around the lot while their uncle showed her the 1962 turquoise Bug with only 30,000 miles on it. Bob said he'd adjusted the drum brakes and replaced the tie rods, and he thought it was niece-or-nephew-road-ready.

Debbie couldn't believe her eyes when she slid onto the silvery vinyl seats. It looked as much like a dressing table as a car interior. The exterior paint color gleamed like a robin's egg. She never thought she'd care about a car, but she was instantly in love. Then she spotted the white-handled gear shift lever.

"I don't know how to drive a standard transmission," she admitted. "I've only driven Mom's car and the school cars. They had automatic transmissions."

"You'll learn, Kitten," Bernard assured her. "If you want this car, I'll have to teach you to drive a stick." His truck was a standard transmission. "Let's take it for a spin, Bob."

Bernard got into the driver's seat, and Debbie sat beside him. Bonnie stayed behind to look at cars with her son. Bob handed the keys to his brother and told them the route they had test drivers take through the neighborhood.

"One of the first things you need to learn when driving a stick is to listen to your engine. That means no radio until you've driven the car for several weeks. You start in neutral, to go slow you use first gear. If you have to back up, you'll go to reverse, of course. Every time you change gears, you have to depress the clutch, an extra pedal on the floor. You'll have to use both feet some of the time. As you accelerate, the engine will get noisier. Do you hear that? That indicates you need to shift to a higher gear."

Debbie felt her insides vibrating as her father gave her the first lesson in driving this car. Her car. She couldn't believe it. In their whole lives, this may have been the first time her parents seemed to favor her over her twin brother. She was going to enjoy it.

14

CHAPTER FIVE

Debbie had been taking her car out for some small jaunts. Her parents wanted her to practice driving with a manual transmission before she started driving to school every day. They knew she'd be driving Daniel or Yvonne often, and wanted to be sure she was comfortable before adding those distractions.

One of the errands she was assigned was to transport Daniel to and from Youth Symphony practice. He played the French horn in the symphony and they were having weekly practices in preparation for their spring concert in a few weeks. She arrived about fifteen minutes early to pick him up and strolled into Lincoln High School since the door was propped open to the warm spring air. Debbie had played clarinet in the band there the previous summer as part of a summer school program open to all Lincoln student musicians, so she knew where the music rooms were.

She stood in the hallway for a few minutes waiting as kids poured from the room before Daniel and another boy came walking out laughing about something.

"Oh, hey Debs. You didn't have to come in," Daniel said.

"Daniel, my boy. You didn't tell me you had such a smokin' hot girlfriend!" his companion said, moving in a little closer than Debbie had expected him to. He was taller than Daniel, who was a few inches taller than Debbie. His curly dark brown hair and black glasses gave him a studious look, and he apparently wasn't shy.

Daniel chortled. "She's not my girlfriend, she's my sister, Debbie. My twin sister."

"Your sister?" his friend asked, leaning closer to Debbie. "I'm Keith. Keith Pritchard. I guess your brother has no manners."

"You're right. I am the cultured one in the family," she smiled warmly at Keith. He may have been a flirt, but she'd never had a boy flirt with her in front of her brother. This might be fun.

"And considering you're twins, how is it you got all of the good looks, and he got—? Well, I don't know what he got but it wasn't musical talent or brains or—" Keith went on with a wicked grin.

Daniel rolled his eyes at both of them and started walking down the hall toward the exit.

Keith put his hand gently on Debbie's elbow and steered her to follow. He was carrying a violin case.

"You know what else I got?" Debbie asked. "The car. Would you like to see it?"

"I'd like to see anything you want to show me, Honey Bun."

When they got outside, Keith walked around the VW admiring it, but he kept glancing up at Debbie. Daniel was already seated in the passenger seat with his arms crossed.

Debbie strolled up to the driver's door and opened it. For some reason, she couldn't stop smiling.

"If I call Daniel's house tonight, what are the chances you might answer the phone?" Keith asked.

"It depends. Would you be calling for him or me?" She deliberately slid slowly into her seat.

"Oh, I'm not speaking to him. He didn't even tell me he had a sister."

Debbie laughed and tried to start her car without stepping on the clutch. It made a grinding noise and the car lurched. Daniel gave her a dirty look. She watched Keith get into a Ford Thunderbird which appeared to be new. He pulled out of the parking lot like he was in a race.

"Tell me about your friend, Daniel," she said.

"I thought he was my friend. Now he seems to have lost his marbles. I can't believe all those phony lines he was using to try to impress you." Daniel tapped his foot on the floorboard.

16

"You don't think boys should like me, is that it? I am so hideous no guy should look twice?"

"That isn't what I said. God, maybe this is what Dad meant. He told me once when we got older, I was going to have to watch out for you, like to protect you. I didn't expect someone like Keith Pritchard to try to put the moves on you." Daniel's lips twitched and he wrinkled his nose. "I admire his talent. You should hear him play the violin. It's amazing. He's a senior at Southeast and I think he has a music scholarship."

"That should give me something to talk to him about when he calls."

"You're not thinking of going on a date with him?" He turned to look at her, blinking.

"I can't say. I just met him. Why shouldn't I?"

"Well . . . because you don't date, do you? You haven't been on a date."

"I went to the movies with Barry. And he came over to see me and we took a walk."

"The idea of you going out with boys, especially boys I know, is weird. Do you even know how to defend yourself if they try anything?"

She laughed. "Why would I need to defend myself? I don't think I'll go out with anyone who might get into a knife fight with me."

"You know what I meant. What if some guy tries to kiss you or something?"

"Then I think you should stay out of my love life and I'll stay out of yours."

"Hmmm. I still can't believe he said you were smokin' hot." He squinted at her. "Maybe he needs those glasses cleaned."

17

She shook her head and beamed. She felt smokin' hot now.

Debbie and Keith went out the next weekend. He took her to dinner at a nice restaurant called Eddy's. Keith seemed to have money at his disposal, as he bought them steak dinners.

"What are your plans after high school, Keith?" she asked.

"Well, I've been playing the violin since I was about eight. I am going to study music and maybe play in an orchestra. What I'd like to do is be a concert violinist or travel around to different symphonies and be a guest violinist. I'd consider the top musical school to be Julliard, and there are others near New York City, but I plan to attend Rice University in Houston. It will still be a long way from home, but not so crowded."

"That is a long way," Debbie said. She could see their relationship had an end date already, but it wasn't like she had set her expectations very high.

"What do you want to do after high school, Debbie?"

"I hope to go to nursing school. I always wanted to take care of people who can't do for themselves. When I was ten, my mother's brother, Morris, developed cancer. He was a concert pianist. But my mother, brother, and I stayed with him or sometimes he stayed with us. Near the end, he needed someone to help him quite a bit, and I found I didn't mind caring for him. Of course, it was hard when he died, but we were lucky we spent so much time with him. Daniel was named after him, and he became more serious about the piano after Uncle Mo got sick. He always wanted Daniel to play for him." She smiled at the memory.

Debbie thought Keith was a perfect gentleman and didn't even try to kiss her that first night. He did look at her in a way that made her uncomfortable sometimes as though he was checking out her body. Maybe she was being naive thinking that boys should always look her in the eyes. After all, he had told her she was attractive.

CHAPTER SIX

Debbie and Yvonne were the junior twirlers for the Capital High School band. As such, it was their job to train anyone who signed up to audition for the two twirler vacancies for the next year. One of the senior class twirlers, Joann Walters, had been helping, but the other senior, Barbra Simpson, seemed to be too busy with her boyfriend, John Anthony.

Once these afterschool practices started, Debbie started falling behind in American History. The student teacher, Mr. Gibson, offered to help her after school for a few days.

"Yvonne, I am going to have to miss the practice today, and maybe tomorrow. Can you and Joann handle it?" Debbie asked her friend after band class.

"What's going on?" Yvonne took her flute apart and put it in the case.

"I got a bad grade on my history quiz, so I am going to have the student teacher help me after school."

Yvonne raised her eyebrows. "Is he a hot college guy? Oh, the one I saw in the hall with long dark hair?"

"No, this one's pretty ordinary looking, but I appreciated his offer to help me. I'll come over here when I am done and give you a ride home."

At the afterschool session, she sat at her usual desk which was in the back of the room and opened her history book. The student teacher took the desk next to hers.

"What gave you trouble on the last test, Miss Adams?"

She laughed, "I know you like to call the kids by their last names in class, but you can call me Debbie now. Miss Adams sounds so formal."

"All right then. Call me Jerry." He smiled at her, and she

19

realized he was better than ordinary looking. And he was staring at her a little more intently than she expected. He kept looking at her mouth.

Debbie licked her lips nervously. "To tell you the truth, I don't think I spent enough time reading the chapters. I've been busy lately. Maybe you could tell me if there are certain things I should be looking for when I am reading the book. You know, like how to figure out what is most important."

"Sure, let's look at the chapter we're reviewing now: Chapter Twenty-one."

She found the chapter in her book and opened it. He stood and moved behind her looking over her shoulder. He pointed to the subheadings in the chapter and the boxes which showed related material on some pages. He ran his finger over those while he was talking, and seemed to be moving closer to her as he did so, and she felt his breath on her neck. She could even smell his aftershave.

"History is partly about dates, places, names, and events. Sometimes it makes sense to try to memorize things. But it's also important to understand why people took the stands they did. Why were these abolitionists and slaveholders so passionate? In these boxes, it gives you some concrete examples which may make more sense to you. These subheadings are a guide through the chapter. It might help you to say those aloud. Go ahead and try that," he suggested.

Debbie squinted. "You want me to say the . . . okay." He put his finger on one of the subheadings. "*The Underground Railway.*" Her mouth went dry. She looked over her shoulder and his face was nearly touching her. Then she felt his hands reaching around her, grabbing her breasts. Time stood still as her mind froze. She jerked forward. The desk wobbled and scraped the linoleum when she lurched out of it, and her book flew to the floor. As soon as she was on her feet, he grabbed her upper arms and pushed her against the back wall, crushing her mouth with his.

Debbie couldn't believe this was happening. No one had kissed her before, not on the lips. What did this teacher think he was doing? He had caught her off guard, but she regained her equilibrium and pushed him away from her. She was shaking but the adrenaline propelled her forward, snatching her fallen book and bag, and running for the door. He let her go.

She ran to the nearest girls' bathroom and flew into the stall farthest from the door. She slammed her bag and book on the floor, dropped onto the toilet fully clothed, and started hyperventilating.

She didn't want to talk to Yvonne about what had happened. After about twenty minutes, she emerged from the bathroom and went to the music alcove where the twirlers practiced. It appeared they were wrapping up the practice session.

"All done?" Yvonne asked when Debbie approached. After they waved off the other girls, Yvonne studied her. "Are you okay, Debbie? You look like you've been crying."

Debbie shook her head. "I think I might be getting some allergies. I have been blowing my nose." They piled into Debbie's slug bug. Yvonne droned on about the practice, but Debbie felt like she couldn't focus on what she was saying. They were nearly home when a collie dashed into the path of her car.

"Stop!" Yvonne shouted.

Debbie slammed on the brakes and missed hitting the dog. But she froze with her hands locked on the wheel, shaking like a leaf.

Yvonne's brows knit together and she turned her body toward Debbie. "You'd tell me if something was bothering you, wouldn't you, Honey?"

Debbie nodded but didn't meet Yvonne's gaze. She had killed the engine when she'd hit the brake without the clutch, so she started the car and slowly drove the remaining blocks to her house. "I think

I am just tired. I might be coming down with something," she tried to explain as she got her things out of the car.

Debbie locked herself in her room. She thought Yvonne had accepted her story. She didn't like lying to her, but she needed to sort this out for herself. She'd been waiting for her first kiss for years, expecting it to be so romantic. She had started to think it might be with Keith. She liked Keith, and he seemed to like her, even if he was leaving in the fall. But now, it felt like it had been ruined. Jerry Gibson, student teacher and predator, had stolen her first kiss. It wasn't sweet or exciting. It was violent. It was unwelcome. It was against the rules.

And she wasn't going to think about the other thing, how he'd groped her. She shuddered at the memory.

She tried to do her homework then, but her concentration was pitiful. She'd break into tears as soon as the events of the afternoon broke back into her thoughts.

Daniel knocked on her door. "Debs, it's your turn to set the table. Mom says to get a move on."

"I don't feel like eating. I don't feel well," she said hoping he'd leave.

"Open the door. You know Mom will want to check on you," he insisted.

She opened the door and he walked into her room.

"What's wrong with you? Your eyes are all red."

She tried to think of something to minimize his questioning. "I have cramps. You know girls get weepy during that time of the month."

He frowned. "That's what you said last week when you didn't want to take out the trash. I think it's something else." He folded his arms and stared at her.

She sat back down on the bed and looked down, trying to will away the tears.

He sat down next to her. "Debbie, I am getting a bad twin vibe here. There is something wrong. Tell me."

Her eyes overflowed. "I can't tell you. I can't tell anyone. I just have to forget it happened."

"I'm not leaving until you tell me." Daniel stuck out his chin. "I am the only person who's known you since before we were born. Didn't we agree not to lie to each other?"

Debbie went to the door and locked it again. "If I do tell you, you can't tell anyone else. Not Mom or Dad. No one at school. None of our friends. Nobody."

He frowned as she returned to the bed and sat facing him. He covered her hand with his. "This sounds serious."

She tried to summon her courage, tried to find the words. He sat waiting until she spoke. "I got a bad grade on my last history quiz."

He exhaled, "Oh, is that all? I can help you with history."

She shook her head and held his gaze. "I spoke to Mrs. Cummings, my history teacher. She said she was having the student teacher, Mr. Gibson, help some of the students who were having trouble and he could review some things with me after school."

Daniel scoffed. "That Gibson guy is the student teacher in my history class too, fifth period. There's something a little creepy about him. Did he help you?"

"He kissed me."

Daniel blinked. "Who kissed you? Are you talking about Keith Pritchard now?"

She shook her head. "No. Keith hasn't kissed me. No one has ever kissed me until today." She pulled a Kleenex out of the box on her nightstand.

Daniel stared at her, as though it was slowly sinking in. "You aren't saying . . . Mr. Gibson kissed you?"

She saw the storm clouds gathering in his eyes and waited for the thunder. Her lips started trembling. "Yes," she whispered.

Daniel jumped to his feet and walked around the room raking his hands through his hair. "What exactly happened? Were you like flirting or something?"

"Flirting?" Debbie jumped up and fisted her hands on her hips. "No! There was no flirting. He was showing me something in the textbook. Then he grabbed me like this and pushed me like so!" She demonstrated this by taking Daniel's arms and pushing him up against the wall, showing him the kind of force that had been used by the teacher. "And then he plastered his mouth all over mine like something he'd seen in an R-rated movie." She released her grip on Daniel and saw only shock in his eyes.

"Holy Macaroni. What did you do?"

Debbie sat back down on the bed and blew her nose into a tissue. "I ran. I grabbed my book and bag and split. I don't know if I can go back to school. I can't go back to history class. Not with him there."

Daniel let out his breath slowly and approached her. "I know you don't want to hear this, but you have to report him. You can't let someone like that become a teacher."

She jerked her forefinger in his face. "No! You promised. You can't tell anyone!"

"That was before I knew how serious this was. Debbie, this is assault. It's a crime. He'll probably do this again. Maybe he's done it before."

She shook her head. "I am done talking about it. It's too painful. Tell Mom and Dad I am sick. Don't say a word about this to anyone!"

He started for the door. But then he turned back and pulled her to her feet in an embrace. She'd expected anger from her brother, not support, not understanding. It made it twice as hard to hold her tears at bay. She was glad he only hugged her a moment before he was back on the far side of her locked door again. Her crying jag erupted anew. Telling someone hadn't made it easier. Not even a little.

Debbie didn't go to school the next day, claiming she was ill. By Monday morning, her anxiety level was slightly lower. When she arrived in her third-period American history class, she tried to bury her face in her book. She had forced herself to study the text since she had time off from school and did feel more prepared.

Mrs. Cummings leaned on her desk at the beginning of the class. "I'm sorry to report Mr. Gibson won't be in class all week because he has mononucleosis."

Thank God! Debbie wouldn't have to see him for a while. Uh-oh! What if he gave her the "kissing disease?" She had known a few girls in her grade who had been diagnosed with mono over the years. They missed school for three or four weeks, with sore throats, fevers, and general fatigue. She couldn't miss the twirler auditions next week. And she was going to prom with Keith the following Saturday. Suddenly her throat ached and she was flushed.

When she got home, she found the thermometer and swabbed it with alcohol. Bonnie saw her taking her temperature.

"Are you feeling sick again, Sweetie? I thought your headache and runny nose had gotten better," Bonnie said.

Debbie regretted taking a fake sick day since she might need real ones soon. "I heard about someone I sit by in class having mono, and I wanted to check to see if I had a fever. I feel pretty good right now though."

Bonnie looked at the reading after Debbie had the thermometer under her tongue for three minutes. "It looks normal. But maybe you should take it easy tonight. Your prom dress is ready to try on if you want to do that. Yvonne should try hers on too. There's still some tacking and hemming to be done, but we need to check the fit."

Bonnie was an excellent seamstress and she had made both Debbie's and Yvonne's dresses using different views of the same pattern, and the same fabric. Yvonne came over and they both tried on their dresses.

Debbie's dress had a light blue bodice and full lace-covered white skirt and sleeves while Yvonne's had the white lace on top with a narrower blue skirt. At the time they picked out the fabric, Yvonne asked to have Bonnie follow the pattern. Her gown was cut lower in the front and back. Debbie thought she should have her gown cut a little higher to conceal her bust. But now when they compared the dresses in the full-length mirror, Debbie had second thoughts.

"I like the way your top looks better," she said. "I think mine is too high."

"I tried to tell you to show off a little cleavage. You're lucky to have so much to spare," Yvonne said.

Debbie turned to her mother. "Is it too late to lower the neckline more like Yvonne's dress?"

"You know, I think I accidentally followed the pattern with the blue fabric the first time I cut your bodice out. Then I remembered it was supposed to be higher. Let me see if I still have the first version." Bonnie went back into her sewing room and came back with some blue fabric scraps which looked like the bodice pieces. She had Debbie pull down the front of her dress and replaced it with the pieces she had pinned together.

"Okay, so now the seam will take it right to about here. I don't think you could wear this bra though; it would show. You'd have to buy a push-up bra or whatever they call that style."

"This sounds like a shopping trip!" Yvonne said.

Debbie pursed her lips. "Would it be too much trouble to rework the top, Mom?"

"No, we have time. But you should try to find a bra that works by next weekend, so you aren't scrambling around for something at the last minute."

CHAPTER SEVEN

Keith took Debbie to a movie on Saturday. Since they were going to prom, she was glad they'd a chance to become better acquainted. Keith's prom was scheduled for the same date, and she was touched he had agreed to go to hers instead. Of course, she wondered if he was embarrassed to have his friends see him with her, but he hadn't given her any reason to believe that.

They settled in their seats before the opening credits of *2001: A Space Odyssey* flashed on the screen. Keith had been excited to see this show, but Debbie didn't know much about it. He bought a big box of popcorn and soft drinks for them. She had her hand in the popcorn when it occurred to her that she might be infectious. She pulled her hand away.

"I thought you said you wanted some popcorn." Keith gave her a sidelong look.

"I do. But I just remembered I was exposed to mono this week. I don't want to get you sick, in case I have it."

"You think you're coming down with mono?" His brows shot up. "Don't you feel well? My brother had mono for a month last summer, but I didn't get it. I am probably immune." Keith took another handful of popcorn.

"I feel fine. But what if I am contagious? I'm worried about coming down with it before prom."

"I understand. Let's get this over with, then you can relax." She didn't know what he meant. Then he put one hand under her chin and kissed her on the lips right in the middle of the movie. Right in the middle of the movie theater.

He tasted like salt. Like salted popcorn. Well naturally, that's what he was eating. And a little like Coca-Cola. He hadn't given her time to think beforehand, but his kiss was soft and gentle and it only lasted a few seconds. Exactly what a first kiss was supposed to be like. Nice.

He smiled. "Now eat your popcorn. If you get mono, so will I."

Debbie had no idea what the movie was about. She was flying through space herself.

After the movie, they were walking back to his T-bird, and he took her hand. "Did you like the show?" he asked.

"Oh, um, it was very . . . um—"

"Strange. Wasn't it? Kind of scary to think the computer could take over the ship," Keith mused.

Was that what happened? She'd take his word for it.

"Oh, what are you wearing to the prom?" he asked.

"A dress. Why?"

"Something sexy?" he grinned at her.

Her brows rose and her eyes widened. "I dunno. It's blue and white. You know, a prom dress." She was beginning to think it was a good thing she had her mother lower the neckline.

"Well, I was going to ask about the color for the corsage."

"You're getting me a corsage?" She hadn't thought of that and felt the color rise on her face.

"I went to the prom at Southeast last year. Everyone had corsages and boutonnieres, and I think they are supposed to match the dress," he said.

"Oh, well mine is blue and white."

"Yeah, you said that."

She laughed. "Sorry, I guess I am tired." She dipped her head feeling flushed again. And it didn't help when he squeezed her hand.

CHAPTER EIGHT

Debbie had been looking forward to the junior-senior prom for months. She and Yvonne had worked on a committee months ago that made crepe paper flowers for the Garden of Ecstasy theme. They must have made two hundred flowers. She'd cut and pasted flowers together while picturing the event itself. Who was going to take her to prom?

Yvonne had nothing to worry about. She had a steady beau, Dick Dunn. Yvonne never seemed to have trouble attracting boys. Sometimes Debbie took advantage of that. The two of them would go to skating parties or dances and stand next to each other. Someone always asked Yvonne to skate or dance right away. And once the boys trained their eyes on Yvonne, one of them usually picked up the consolation prize, Debbie. At least that was how she thought of it. Occasionally the shorter boys preferred her. Yvonne was still taller than most of the kids in their junior class.

The week before prom, Yvonne broke up with her boyfriend, and now she was going to prom with Debbie's brother, Daniel. There had been so much drama going on that week with Yvonne, Debbie hadn't even told her Keith had kissed her. She rather liked keeping that secret to herself. *Keith had kissed her.*

"Where do you girls want to go eat dinner before the prom?" Daniel had asked a few days before.

"Oh, I know Tony & Luigi's is Yvonne's favorite," Debbie said. "I've only been there twice, but it's a perfect place for prom."

Debbie and Yvonne had been to the hairdressers, and Debbie's hair was swept up in teased waves resembling Dairy Queen's swirly vanilla soft serve. She looked like a movie star. The dress looked better after her mother had revamped it. She was showing cleavage, but it was still conservative enough for a school dance. She could pass for twenty-five. Maybe they'd offer her a cocktail at the restaurant.

When Keith arrived after five o'clock, Daniel went next door to Yvonne's house.

Keith's face brightened when she walked into the living room. "Whoa, you look great, Debbie. Gorgeous and sophisticated,"

Debbie beamed, walking up to him, trying not to lose her balance in her new high-heeled dyed-to-match blue shoes. Bernard turned on the movie camera immediately.

"Oh, wait, Daddy. We don't have the flowers on yet."

She smothered a chuckle watching Keith's ears turn red as he fidgeted trying to pin on the blue-and-white carnation corsage near the neckline of her gown. "Is there a problem?" She batted her thickened eyelashes.

"I don't want to poke you." She saw a gleam in his eyes when he looked back at her. The flash of interest surprised her when he ran his fingers under the side of her neckline, too close, much too close to her décolletage.

Bonnie came to his rescue and attached the corsage with the expertise that comes with practice.

When they arrived at Tony & Luigi's, Keith recognized several friends from his high school, Lincoln Southeast, as they passed their tables.

"Oh, hey there, Martin, Gabe, Jack. Oh, and Mary Jo. You all look spiffed up," Keith said, rubbing the back of his neck. "This is Debbie Adams. We're headed to her prom tonight at Capital."

Martin, Gabe, and Jack all halfway stood when they were introduced. Martin said, "Keith, these are our dates, Sharon Stern and Sylvia Wright. They're sophomores."

Lucky girls. To be asked to prom by older boys. They looked young, cute, peppy, and petite. Keith could have asked a girl like them to prom. Debbie felt several eyes scrutinizing her and her dress, but Keith seemed to be happy to be showing her off.

"They're all in the orchestra with me," Keith explained to Debbie as they sat down with Yvonne and Daniel. "I guess I should have introduced you as my date."

"Wasn't it obvious?" Yvonne smirked. "I think you get points for not defining her as your property."

Keith raised his brows until Yvonne and Debbie burst into laughter. Daniel rolled his eyes.

"So, what do you like here?" Keith asked, "Steak or pasta?"

"They have steak here?" Debbie asked.

"Yes, of course," Keith broke out an Italian accent, "They have Veal Scalopine ala Marsala, Veal ala Parmigiano, Sirloin ala Parmigiano, Italian Beef Roll, Chicken Cacciatora, Spaghetti with large meat balls, raviolis, lasagna, mostaccioli and steak."

"I'm usually full by the time I finish their relish tray, cheese spread and crackers, soup, and salad," Debbie admitted.

"But tonight, *Mi Amore,* we shall feast!" Keith hefted his water goblet in the air.

"We feast!" Daniel clinked his goblet with Keith's, and they all laughed.

The meal was delicious. Debbie had been eating very lightly all week, in anticipation of the big night and the form-fitting dress around her middle. Keith had steak and she tried the ravioli. She was afraid she might get sauce on her pretty dress if she tried to swirl spaghetti around her fork. She knew her brother would be too budget-conscious to have anything besides the cheapest entrée, and Yvonne ordered pasta as well.

The prom was already going full blast when they arrived.

"C'mon snake, let's rattle," Keith said, pulling her onto the dance floor soon afterward. She was surprised he knew how to jitterbug and wasn't shy about trying any of the popular dances, like

The Jerk, or The Watusi. He was a bit eccentric, to her surprise. Or maybe he didn't mind being the center of attention since he didn't attend school there.

They were dancing to Steppenwolf's *Born to Be Wild* when Keith bounced down to the floor and did the splits. Debbie shielded her face with her hands, thinking everyone would be watching them afterward, but he only did it once.

"Let's go get some punch," Debbie suggested, and he followed her to the refreshment area. She was pulling Keith along by his hand when she nearly ran into her friend Barry Whitaker in front of the cookie table.

"Blondie?" Barry's eyes widened as he pivoted and dropped his plate of cookies right in front of her. He immediately squatted retrieving the broken cookies. Debbie started to bend over to help. When Barry rose, he was looking down the front of her dress. Barry let out a low groan.

Debbie thought she'd never seen a boy turn quite so red. He turned and scurried away without a word. Debbie frowned and tried to tug up her dress in the front.

Keith laughed and draped his arm around her waist. "Don't be so surprised boys are freaking out seeing you in that dress. You're a knockout."

Debbie opened her mouth then closed it without speaking. She glanced back in the direction Barry had gone. That's unfathomable. Boys were attracted to tall thin girls like Yvonne or cute little Gidget types. Not someone like her. Never her.

A few minutes later, the prom king and queen were announced. One of the senior football players, Ted Rumsfeld, was named prom king, and Barbra Simpson was named prom queen.

"That's Barbra! She's one of the twirlers! I voted for her, but I can't believe she won!" Debbie said to Keith. "I have to find Joann, the other twirler. And what happened to Yvonne? I haven't seen her for a while."

Debbie found Joann Walters, up by the stage, and hugged her. Ted was her prom date but he was called up on stage for the crowning and afterward, he and Barbra were asked to dance one number alone. Debbie stood next to Joann watching the dance, while Keith moved in behind Debbie, wrapping a hand around her waist as they swayed to the slow song. Debbie realized they had placed themselves so they were facing most of the other students at the prom, and it was nice having a view of the room.

Later, Debbie was in the restroom, trying to fix her hairdo. Some of it had come loose when she had done The Pony. Marcy Bellmore strode up to the long mirror next to her and smeared lipstick on her mouth.

Marcy met her eyes in the mirror. "Well, you certainly got everyone talking."

"Me? What'd I do?" Debbie squinted at her.

"It isn't what you did, it's what you're wearing. You're finally giving the boys an eyeful. You have power with those knockers. You just need to learn to harness it. Don't be surprised if your phone starts ringing, but hold out for what you really want." Marcy smiled and breezed out of the bathroom.

Debbie looked to see if anyone else was in earshot or sight. She thought she was alone. What kind of girl did Marcy think she was? Marcy was at best a loose cannon and had a very bad reputation. But she couldn't deny some of the boys had been acting weird around her and stealing glances at her tonight. She tugged her dress up higher in the front, then debated. Maybe she should show off a little more. She leaned forward and pulled her breasts together in the middle. Power? That seemed silly. But why shouldn't she look as pretty as she could? Looking good was the very essence of prom.

When it was time to leave the prom, Keith helped her into the backseat of her father's Cadillac, then he and Daniel had a discussion she couldn't hear. Apparently, it had to do with how they planned to say good-night to their dates because when Debbie and Keith got out of the car at her house, Daniel and Yvonne stayed in the car.

The front porch light was gleaming through the warm spring darkness. Before Debbie could think about whether her parents were still awake and might spot them, Keith had pulled her into his arms, kissing her eagerly. His enthusiasm seemed to be a big leap from the sweet kiss he had given her at the movies. She liked Keith, and they had been having fun together, but why was he trying to stick his tongue in her mouth and moving his hands down her back?

"Whoa," she said, breaking away, but he still had her in an embrace. "Slow down, Buster."

"Oh, but Debbie. You feel so soft and nice, and—" Keith pulled the side of her dress away from her shoulder as far as he could and kissed her skin.

She murmured and let her head touch his. "I'd better go inside. Thank you for taking me to the prom."

Keith smiled and moved his hands up behind her head and kissed her lips again, more gently this time. "Okay, we'll say goodnight for now."

Why is my pulse racing like I've been running? Something must be wrong with me. Debbie let herself into the house and slipped into her room quietly. As she changed into her pajamas, she looked out the window and saw Yvonne's bedroom light go on. She could call her and rehash the wonderful evening again. But they'd have time for that tomorrow.

CHAPTER NINE

Debbie was feeling more confident in her American history class. The student teacher hadn't returned, and she had made an effort on her own to spend more time reading the textbook. Since twirler auditions were over, she could spend the last few weeks of school concentrating on studying for the final tests.

Mrs. Cummings had a substitute a few days after prom. Debbie was surprised when the substitute called her name and asked her to come forward at the beginning of class.

"Are you Debbie Adams?" the substitute teacher asked. When Debbie nodded, she handed her a pink note, often called a class pass, which teachers used to excuse a student for part of a class. The note asked her to meet Mrs. Cummings in the east study room in the library.

Debbie's mouth went dry. Her history grade must be worse than she thought. Maybe she was in serious academic trouble. She picked up her bag and made her way to the library. She felt like her feet weighed fifty pounds each. She found Mrs. Cummings and the guidance counselor, Mrs. Baker, in the designated room, sitting at a table. They motioned for her to sit on a chair facing them.

"Debbie, I am sorry to pull you out of class like this," Mrs. Cummings began.

Debbie took a shallow breath. "Is it my history grade? I thought I was doing better."

"Oh, no. It isn't about that. This is probably a false alarm."

Debbie looked from Mrs. Cummings to Mrs. Baker and sensed they were reluctant to explain why they were there.

Mrs. Baker sat up primly. "Another student has filed a complaint against Mrs. Cumming's student teacher, Jerry Gibson. He has missed teaching here for a couple of weeks because of illness, but this other student said he behaved inappropriately around her. Several other students had appointments with him for tutoring, and so we're asking all of them if there were other incidents of inappropriate behavior on his part."

Debbie felt her eyes grow into saucers. She was instantly back in that classroom with Jerry Gibson, the memory she had tried desperately to block.

Mrs. Cummings scrutinized the look on her face and got up took a seat right next to Debbie. "Something did happen, didn't it, Honey? Can you tell us what it was?"

Debbie's lips were trembling, and her mind was suddenly going blank. "Daniel. Can I have Daniel come in here with me?"

"You want your brother to join us to talk about this?" Mrs. Cummings asked. "Does he know what happened?"

Debbie nodded and looked away toward the door. She pressed her knees together to keep them from bouncing.

Mrs. Baker picked up the phone on the wall and called back to the office. "Would you please locate Daniel Adams and send him to the east study room in the library at once?"

Waiting for Daniel gave Debbie time to think. What would happen if she told them the truth? Daniel had said before she should report him so he wouldn't accost other girls. But would she have to tell her story to anyone else besides these two women? Would her parents have to find out? They'd be furious she hadn't told them right away.

What if she said nothing happened or revised what happened? What if she said he said something dirty to her? But she'd asked for Daniel to come. She wanted him to back her up, but he already knew about the kiss. She'd have to tell that part now.

Daniel burst through the door frowning. "What's going on? Debbie?"

Debbie looked down at her sweaty palms.

Mrs. Cummings moved back to where she had been sitting near Mrs. Baker and indicated Daniel should sit by his sister.

"Debbie asked us to include you in this meeting. We asked Debbie if she had any problems with Mrs. Cummings' student teacher, Jerry Gibson. Another student has filed a complaint."

Daniel's brows drew together as he slid onto the chair and studied Debbie's face. "Tell them."

Her eyes rimmed with tears as she looked into his eyes. "Mr. Gibson was showing me the history textbook, then he pushed me against the wall and kissed me. I don't know why; it was out of the blue."

"He kissed you?" Mrs. Cummings repeated.

Debbie took a breath and nodded.

Mrs. Cummings looked at a calendar she had with her. "Was this on April 18? It looks like I had you scheduled after school that day."

"I guess so."

Mrs. Baker frowned. "I'm not sure I understand exactly. You said you were looking at the history book. Where were you and where was he?"

Debbie sighed. "I was sitting at my usual desk in the back. He was sitting next to me, then he stood up and stood behind me pointing to things in the book, talking about them."

"Then how did he kiss you if he was standing behind you and you were seated?" Mrs. Baker asked.

Daniel scowled at Mrs. Baker, then turned back to look into Debbie's eyes.

Debbie knew she hadn't explained this part to him, and now he was wondering too.

"I was seated in one of those desks, you know how they wrap

around you. I had the book open on the desk surface. He was right over my shoulder, and he kept getting closer and closer to my face, to the side of my face. He was making me nervous."

"Did he grab your face to kiss you?" Mrs. Cummings asked.

Debbie closed her eyes debating whether she should say more. When she blinked them open, she said, "No, not while I was seated. He put his hands around me, on my . . . breasts."

"What?" Daniel jumped to his feet. She saw his eyes bulge and his nostrils flare.

"I know, Daniel. I didn't tell you that part. But after he did that, I jumped out of the desk, or I tried to, but I was hung up on the desk thingy hitting me in the stomach and I nearly knocked the desk over." She stood up awkwardly, trying to demonstrate. "Then he grabbed my arms, as I was trying to escape. He whirled me around and slammed me against the wall and pushed his mouth and body against me." She reached her hands out trying to reenact his actions. "As soon as I could, I pushed him away and ran out the door."

Debbie took a deep breath and sat again, and let the tears slide down her cheeks. She couldn't look at her brother. He must be disgusted and furious at her.

Daniel huffed out his breath and glared at the two older women. "What are you going to do to this creep?"

"Daniel, I imagine you're almost as upset as your sister about this. We're gathering information right now," Mrs. Baker said. "Mr. Gibson won't be coming back here before the investigation concludes, and since school will be out soon, he likely won't be back at all. Beyond that, I don't know what the consequences will be for him. It's an ongoing matter."

"Just don't ask her to go through this again." Daniel stood up and reached out to Debbie, indicating she should come with him.

"You don't have to tell my parents, do you?" Debbie rose,

looking at the teachers.

"I don't see why we need to. But you should tell them yourself," Mrs. Baker said.

Once they were back in the hallway, Daniel put his hands on Debbie's shoulders. "That was worse than I thought. Are you okay to go back to class?"

She nodded, sniffing. "Thank you." If she had tried to say more, she knew her tears would return. He turned and walked back toward his class. Why was it so hard to tell him how much he meant to her? *He's my twin. I hope he knows already.*

CHAPTER TEN

Keith Pritchard invited both Debbie and Daniel to his graduation party. He lived in a section of town near the country club, and his mansion had been completely remodeled by his parents, including their swimming pool.

"Yvonne, this is a shopping emergency!" Debbie told her friend on the phone. "You have to help me find a killer swimming suit. Keith practically told me he's having a pool party just so he can see me in a bathing suit. This could be a disaster."

"I'm sure we can find a cute one, don't worry. Let's try Gateway Mall first. We can check at Miller & Paine, Hovland-Swanson's, and Montgomery Wards. If we don't find anything there, we can go downtown to Penney's and Gold's."

It was easy for Yvonne to find a swimsuit, Debbie thought. She watched her try at least a dozen in the junior department at Miller's, and Debbie thought they all looked great on her. They looked like they were designed for someone with long lean legs, no hips or stomach, and hardly any bust. Like a life-size Barbie doll. But the two Debbie tried on didn't cover her up enough.

The saleslady poked her head in the dressing room. "That one looks cute on you, Dear," she told Yvonne. She looked at Debbie and sighed. "You should probably look in the Misses section, though. Those suits are designed for full-figured gals."

Debbie thought that sounded like "beached whales" but looked through the racks anyway. They certainly had more fabric. Some of them seemed matronly, but she found a few worth trying.

"You know they'd sell more bathing suits if they had special mirrors in these dressing rooms. You know, mirrors that made you look thinner, or at least better lighting," Debbie said as she struggled to pull up the bottom half of a two-piece suit. Yvonne was still prancing around in bikinis, and it was becoming demoralizing.

"I'd buy four suits, but that would be dumb. I have to wear the one-piece Eastridge Pool supplies when I am lifeguarding. And I can only afford one suit anyway. But I don't know which to pick."

"Look at this one," Debbie said. She opened the dressing room door and showed Yvonne a two-piece pale green and blue suit with a skirted bottom. The top at least provided support and kept everything in place. "I feel like Annette Funicello in a beach party movie. She always looks like a thirty-year-old housewife and all the other girls look about fourteen."

Yvonne studied her. "Well, I like the colors. It does seem to flatter you."

"Except for this part here where my thighs stick out. Oh, and the back. That doesn't look very good. We'd better keep looking." Debbie sighed and dressed again.

They decided to go downtown to J.C. Penney's. This time Debbie tried on both one-piece and two-piece suits. "You know I might be able to get away with wearing a scarf over the swimming suit bottom at the pool party. Then I wouldn't worry about cellulite on my thighs. If I got in the pool, I'd remove the scarf. Then I could just find a top I like." After trying on about a dozen more suits, she bought one. Yvonne bought two, despite her budget.

Debbie knew the bathing suit trauma wasn't over. She still had to wear it in public, in front of her boyfriend, which was probably worse. She had been out with Keith a couple of times since prom. They had gone miniature golfing with a couple of his friends. Another time, they went out for pizza. She had also seen him at the Youth Symphony concert. They had enjoyed each other's company but they didn't talk every day.

"I probably won't stay at Keith's party for too long. I don't know if I'll even get in the pool," Daniel told her when she parked the Bug on his street. "Another Youth Symphony buddy, Joel Hansen, is going to a different party after this one, and he said he'd give me a ride if I wanted to go along."

"No problem. As long as I have a car I can stay longer or leave. Let's see how it goes."

It was crowded in the Pritchard's backyard. Debbie ditched the shirt she'd worn over her swimsuit top and went looking for Keith. She found him on an inflatable raft in the shallow end of the pool. There were six girls in bikinis trying to launch him into the water.

She fisted her hands on her hips and grinned at him. "Looks like you have a harem!"

"About time you got here, Debbie. I almost sent out the Coast Guard," he blew out water when the girls pulled the raft out from under him. He hoisted himself onto the side of the pool and stood up and gave her a wet hug.

"I graduated! No more high school!" He pulled her back to look at her bathing suit. "Nice. Maybe a little too nice. Too much fabric, not enough skin." He teasingly slid one strap down her shoulder an inch or two.

"Stop that. I figured this was a G-rated party," she laughed.

"Well, we can take it inside and make it R-rated if you want." She shook her head and he laughed. He introduced her to his parents and brother, and they had some food. There was rock music playing, and she thought they might dance, but his friends kept pulling him back into the pool for some rough-housing.

When he didn't get back out, she sat on the edge of the pool and watched. Daniel left and she didn't know anyone else to talk to. She began to resent the fact she'd spent hours shopping for the perfect suit, and he had stopped paying any attention to her. She knew he had invited all of these kids, but she felt out of place.

"Keith, I'm going to go," she called. One of the bikini-clad girls had climbed on his shoulders and he was engaging in a chicken fight with another couple.

"Oh, no wait!" he said. Keith got down in the water and slid the girl off his shoulders. He got back out of the pool and grabbed a towel.

"I hardly saw you today. I'm sorry." He steered her over to the patio furniture. About half of the kids had left by this time.

"It's okay. You had to entertain everyone," Debbie said.

He dropped down on a padded redwood chaise and pulled her into his lap. She could feel his cool wet suit under her and watched the droplets of water shimmering on his chest. "You didn't even get in the pool, did you?" She shook her head and he pulled her into a kiss. She wrapped her arms around his neck. It was brazen of him to kiss her in front of his friends. "That suit is pretty sexy. But I think I know what would make it even sexier," he said when he pulled back.

"What?"

"Water." She squinted. Then he leaped to his feet with her in his arms. She started screaming as he ran down to the deepest part of the pool and jumped in. He let her go when they went underwater. He came up laughing but she squinted, pursing her lips.

"You never even asked if I could swim!" she said treading water.

"I'd have pulled you out if you sank. But I figured you had built-in life preservers."

Debbie swam to the ladder and climbed out of the pool. She was still wearing the scarf around her waist, but it was clinging to her butt and legs now. And her top was riding a little lower than it had before. She imagined her hair and makeup was a mess. She found her bag and pulled out a towel. When she turned, he was behind her.

He took the towel from her and patted her chest with it. "I was right. It's even better wet."

She narrowed her eyes at him, but a smile crept across her face.

"Now I am leaving." She put on her button-down shirt over her suit, and slipped on her sandals, dripping on them. But she was happy he stood there long enough to watch her walk away.

CHAPTER ELEVEN

July 25, 1968

Debbie had organized an outing for the new Capital High twirlers who had been selected in the spring. She went over to Yvonne's house and met up with the two juniors, Linda Bridges and Nancy Evans.

The girls ate pizza and soft drinks and styled each other's hair and makeup. Afterward, they were going to the Keentime dance at Antelope Park.

Debbie was brushing Nancy's long red hair. "Your hair is amazing, Nancy. Do you want me to put it in a high ponytail?"

"I suppose, it's so hot tonight. Who do you think will be at the dance, Debbie? Is there a special guy you're looking for?" she answered.

"I think there may be younger guys who'll be sophomores and juniors, but at least they will be in high school, not graduates. My last boyfriend was a senior and now he's looking forward to college. I think he forgot about me. But we weren't serious. It's time for the next one to come along. One of the best things about Keentime is that kids from all of the high schools are there. You might meet someone from Pius, for example."

"I know a lot of boys who go to Pius X. They're in my parish. I could have gone to Pius, but my sisters didn't so I didn't. I'd rather meet a rebel." Nancy's eyes shone.

"A rebel?" Linda asked. "Now that sounds more like me. What would you do if this rebel boy comes up to you and made a move? You'd freak out, wouldn't you?"

"No, I wouldn't. I'd be like, 'What's happening, Man?'" Nancy flipped her wrist loosely trying to show a casual attitude. The other girls all laughed.

"Linda, what do you want me to do for your hair," Yvonne asked, running her fingers through Linda's very short dirty-blonde tresses.

"It's hard to do anything different with it, but it's easy to style. Put a little goop on it and it stays in place. Just think of Twiggy." Linda pulled out a jar of Dippity Do from her purse.

Yvonne's face brightened. "That's it! We'll do the full Twiggy with the eye makeup. You could be a dead ringer for her. Debs, where's the photo of Twiggy we pulled out of the magazine when we were looking for prom hairdos?"

Debbie looked in Yvonne's nightstand and found the photograph. Yvonne went to work on Linda's makeup.

"So, we know Nancy is looking for a rebel, Linda who are you looking to ride shotgun through your life?" Debbie stood behind Nancy to get the right angle for her tail.

Linda laughed. "Oh, I doubt I'll find someone to be with the rest of my life. I get bored easily. Hmmm, but Mr. Right would have to be handsome and easy-going. I don't like those bossy types."

"I want a guy to be romantic. How can you identify that right away?" Yvonne said.

"If he is carrying a bouquet? Not much chance of that. Maybe he'll whisper sweet nothings in your ear while you're dancing," Nancy suggested.

"So, Linda wants Mr. Easy-to-get-along-with, Nancy wants Easy Rider, Yvonne wants Pepé Le Pew. I don't know what I want now. I am keeping my options open." Debbie surveyed her handiwork and put the brush away.

Hundreds of kids were at the Keentime dance. Debbie knew some from Capital High, but most of the faces were unfamiliar. After a few minutes, they were approached by one of their classmates, John Anthony Turner. He asked Yvonne to dance.

Debbie clenched her teeth and crossed her arms. She was the one who used to have a crush on John Anthony, and Yvonne knew it. She couldn't help it. Even when he was fourteen, he'd had classic good looks, shaggy blondish-brown hair, broad shoulders, brown eyes, and long lashes. He was a dreamboat and she had been smitten. She'd been caught by the teachers staring at him in class in eighth grade. But they had never been more than casual friends. Last year, he had dated Barbra Simpson, the twirler who was prom queen. She had graduated and left town so she supposed John Anthony was up for grabs. And of course, he was falling right in Yvonne's lap. Like every other boy in school.

"You wanna go outside, Nance? I can't watch this anymore." Debbie shook her head.

Nancy nodded and they wandered out into the cooler park area.

Debbie approached a uniformed policeman with his back to her. "Excuse me, Officer. Do you have the time?"

The police officer turned around. "It's almost nine-thirty, Miss. You might want to go inside the pavilion. That's where the dancing is."

"I know but it's so loud and hot in there, we're taking a break."

She felt his eyes on her before she saw him. The middle-aged stocky police officer moved sideways revealing a handsome young man. His dark chocolate eyes seemed to drink her in. For a second, she felt like she was rooted in place. She'd never seen anyone with such dramatic eyes. Then they sparkled as he broke into a wide grin. He had perfect white teeth and full lips.

"Ya look like ya wanna make a run for it," he laughed.

"No," she felt her ears burning red and hoped the twilight would conceal them. She tossed her pigtails tilting her head. "I don't want to run. Should I?"

The policeman had walked away, speaking with some other kids. The boy moved into a spot directly in front of her. She looked up at him then studied his features. He had high cheekbones and a broad nose. His dark eyebrows didn't overpower those spectacular eyes. When he moved in front of the light, there seemed to be a halo around his kinky hair. He was wearing black pants, a vest, and a long-sleeved white shirt, while most of the kids, including her group, were dressed in T-shirts and shorts for a hot summer night.

"Haven't cha read the papers? Dey say dere are gangs of Negro kids causin' fights at dese dances." His eyebrows winged up and a smirk crossed his lips.

Debbie glanced around. "I don't see any gangs. Or any fights."

"You feel safe wid me?" His smile faded as he scrutinized her.

"Yes," Debbie said. She glanced back at Nancy to see if she was still with her. Then she turned back to her admirer. She realized he *was* admiring her. "My name is Debbie Adams. This is my friend Nancy Evans. We go to Capital High School."

The young man nodded. "Robert. Robert Washington. I go to Lincoln High School. I'll be a senior in the fall." A couple of other boys, overhearing the introductions, came forward and stood by Robert. "Oh, now I found some pretty girls, you two wanna get in on the action?" Robert put a hand on one of the other boy's shoulders. "Dis here's Wayne Johnson, and de other's Leon Gaines. You probably heard dere names are Debbie and Nancy."

"How do you do?" Nancy said. Leon extended a hand to Nancy and they shook.

Robert put his hand on Debbie's arm, moving her slightly away from the others. "So, Debbie, wha'da ya do at Capital High?"

Debbie giggled. Where had that come from? She never giggled. She cupped her hand over her mouth. "I'll be a senior too. I'm a twirler in the band. You know one of those—" She put her hand up and twisted her wrist mimicking the motion of baton twirling. "Oh my gosh, I don't know why I did that. Of course, you know what twirling is. I also play the clarinet. And I have a twin brother. Everyone knows me because of him."

Robert's eyes swept the surrounding area. "Your brudder here wid you?"

"Oh no, tonight is a girls' outing. I left two of the other twirlers inside dancing."

"Now the cop moved on, I'm going to go smoke. Wanna come?" He started moving toward a cluster of trees that wasn't well-lit. Debbie hesitated, then followed him. He walked for about thirty yards, stopping before he got too close to the brighter parking area.

Robert lit a cigarette, then held his pack out to Debbie. "Want one?"

This night is about trying new things. "Sure. My father smokes. I snuck one of his two years ago." He lit her cigarette for her.

Robert chuckled. "I don' think my father'd approve of any of his children smokin'. He's an ordained Baptist minister. Some of the police officers here even know him. I don' think they'll rat me out though."

She took a tentative drag on her cigarette, trying to replicate what he was doing. "What did you mean when you said there were fights?"

Robert leaned on a tree. "Couple of weeks ago I'se here for Keentime wid friends. Some kids I know got into an argument wid Whitey. He claimed he was hit with a chain, but I didn' see that. 'Bout the time we's leaving, somethin' went down. Saw a bunch of guys runnin'. The newspaper said fifty or sixty Negro boys were chasin' a police officer. Dat was bull. Weren't even many Negros at the dance. I guess the cop sprayed one of the boys wid Mace, supposedly in self-defense. A girl came to the boy's side to help him and she got Mace in her eyes too.

"I went to a meeting at the Quinn Chapel las' week. Dere was a different side of the story. Dey say there were a bunch of White guys in cars looking for trouble afterward. And den dere was trouble at Muny pool where all of the staff quit. I guess some of them came back, but dere was a lot of bad information wid dat too. What people need to do is to talk it out, hear from both sides. Dat's what I heard. But some of yo' White friends might not approve of you talkin' to me tonight."

"I can make up my own mind. I think it's high time I made some friends who aren't so much like me. Take Nancy there. She's Catholic. My parents were raised Lutheran."

Robert laughed. "Bein' a different Christian religion ain't the same as bein' friends with someone like me."

"Are we going to be friends, Robert?" Debbie straightened her back and gave him a playful grin.

"You really wanna find dat out? C'mon inside and dance wid me." He threw his cigarette on the sidewalk and took hers, tossing it next to his. He crushed them both with his shoe and held out his hand.

She slid her fingers into his and he pulled her toward the pavilion. There was something mysteriously wonderful about this boy. She didn't understand it, but he made her pulse race.

The dance floor was crowded. Robert pulled her into a spot near the stage but off to one side, close to one of the speakers. Her eyes widened and he gave a devilish smile as he started moving and grooving his hips and shoulders around to the rhythm. She'd never seen a boy dance that well. Usually, they merely shuffled their feet around. It was like the music and beat were controlling his body.

"I don't know how you do that!" she shouted since it was so loud where they were dancing.

Robert chuckled, and moved next to her. He put one hand on her hip, and gently pushed on it as he moved his hips to the beat.

She was able to imitate the motions he was making, at least with her hips. She felt like she was spinning a hula hoop. She didn't even try to get her arms involved. Debbie noticed one of the chaperones was giving her dirty looks as though they shouldn't be touching when they were doing a fast dance. Robert moved back away from her and tried to show her what to do with her arms and shoulders. She tried, but she didn't think it looked as good as when he did it.

When the band slowed down, he didn't try to pull her into a double-clutch, he placed one arm on her back and took her other hand. Debbie was instantly nervous he meant to try something complicated, but he only did some side-to-side swaying and stepping she could follow.

"Are you ready to try a spin?" Robert asked.

"What?" Debbie shouted.

He released his hand from her back and twisted his other hand putting her in a turn, then returning his hand to her back. "See, like baton twirling." He grinned and she laughed.

Who knew dancing could be so much fun? And challenging?

When the band took a break, they dashed into the cooler air outdoors. She'd seen some of the kids squinting at them, but she was happy to ignore them.

"Where did you learn to dance like that?" she said, finding a bench to sink onto. He put one foot on the bench and leaned over to talk to her.

"Three older sisters," he said. "An' my aunt teaches dance in St. Louis." He took out a cigarette but didn't light it. Keentime was for age fourteen through nineteen and that most of that age group couldn't legally smoke.

She beamed at him and couldn't think of a thing to say.

He tugged on one of her pigtails. "You have the blondest hair . . . maybe in the whole world."

She laughed. "Oh, I think one of my cousins in Sweden might have me beat."

"Gimme your phone number, Debbie," he said, pulling a pen out of his shirt pocket.

"I don't have any paper."

He unbuttoned his cuff and pulled his sleeve up slightly, rotating his arm.

She wrote her phone number on the inside of his wrist. "You may sweat this off. Bernard Adams on Mulder Drive. You have a phone book at home, don't you?"

He smiled and moved closer. "I want to kiss you. But we have an audience!"

She laughed and glanced around. They were being observed, by the police, by some other kids she didn't know. *I want you to kiss me too.* "Maybe another time." She couldn't stop smiling and her mouth was starting to ache.

The band played one more set, and they found a better spot on the dance floor. Some of the crowd had thinned out as it was approaching eleven o'clock. When Robert was gliding her around during a slow dance, she noticed Yvonne was dancing with a tall red-haired boy she didn't know, and Nancy was with a boy she didn't recognize either. Linda Bridges had reappeared dancing with John Anthony Turner. Debbie sighed. She couldn't have planned this night any better if she'd tried.

CHAPTER TWELVE

"Adams' residence," Daniel said the next afternoon, answering the kitchen phone. He squinted and glanced at his sister. "Yeah, just a sec." He set the phone down. They were clearing the dishes from their Saturday lunch. "Debs, there's some guy on the phone for you."

Debbie's eyes widened. "I'll take it in my room. Hang it up after I answer. Please." She bolted down the hall leaving him with the dish chores.

"Hello?" she said breathlessly.

"Debbie? This's Robert. From last night."

She smiled again, and those muscles in her face still hurt. "You must not have washed my number off."

He chuckled. "I lost the first two numbers, so I had to go through all the Adams in the phone book to see which last six numbers matched. Adams is a popular name!"

"Well, I am glad you found me." She didn't know what to say. It was as if she'd never spoken to a boy on the phone before.

"Maybe we could do somethin'," he began. "But I dunno what you like ta do. I have to work at six tonight, but I could come to pick you up before if you're free."

"Where do you work?"

"I'm a dishwasher at Valentino's on Holdrege Street. Nothin' fancy, but it puts gas in the car, and I get leftover pizza," Robert said. "Do you wanna go somewhere? We could go for a drive and talk."

"Okay, that sounds nice." Debbie gave him directions to her house. She sighed. Robert had called her. He wanted to see her. She jumped up and looked in the mirror. She had to get ready.

What was she going to wear? If they were driving around, she supposed it didn't matter. But he seemed to like to dress up since he wore fancy clothes the night before. Did she have a decent dress? She scoured her closet and found a sundress she hadn't worn since the previous summer. She shook the dust off and tried it on. It was a little tight on top, but at least it minimized her hips.

Then she dashed to the bathroom to check her hair. It had dents in it from the pigtails the night before. She didn't have time to wash it, but she could at least wet it down. She bent over the sink and splashed water on her hair, then brushed it. It gave it an unusual sort of effect, the wet part looked darker, and the ends still had some wave in them. She pulled part of her hair into a barrette where the dents had been. At least she could wear it down today. Her hair was now past her shoulders and looked pretty good when she was done.

She hadn't worn much makeup the night before, so she decided to stick with that. If they were outdoors, it was still a hot July afternoon, and she didn't want her eye makeup running. She used a little mascara and lip-gloss.

She didn't know when he was coming over. He implied he'd come at once, but she didn't know where he lived. She hadn't even checked with her parents yet. They expected her to ask if she was going out.

"My, don't you look nice!" Bonnie said when she walked into the living room. Debbie's mother was doing some hand-sewing and Bernard was working on some papers at the dining room table. "Are you going somewhere?"

"Yes. That was the phone call I got. A boy I met last night at the dance. He's coming to pick me up and we're going to drive around."

"Drive around? Drive around and do what?" Bernard asked.

"I dunno. I guess we might stop if we find something interesting. It's sort of spontaneous," Debbie said, pacing back and forth to the front window.

"You only met this boy last night? What do you know about him? Does he go to Capital?" Bonnie put her sewing down in her lap.

"No, he goes to Lincoln High. Um, he's a very good dancer. Oh, and his father's a minister. I'll probably find out more today." When the doorbell rang, she felt her heart in her throat. She had forgotten to mention one thing. What will they think about that?

She gulped. The doorbell rang again. She strode into the foyer. She could see him through the three staggered glass panes in the front door.

"Hello Robert," she said brightly, hoping to hide her nerves.

He was wearing a short-sleeved button-down orange shirt and blue jeans. Not worn-out jeans, these might have been new. She thought the color of the shirt looked great on him.

His brows jumped up as he surveyed her from head to toe. "You ain't lookin' like Lil' Miss Pigtails today." His wide grin broke out. "Very nice. You look very nice."

She wanted to run out the door and get into his Buick Riviera. But she stepped aside to let him in. "Sorry. You're going to have to meet my parents."

Robert stepped in next to her and waited for her to lead the way. Heat radiated off his body and he smelled like tropical hair cream. She sighed and walked into the living room and he stood next to her. His gaze settled on her parents' faces.

Bernard stood up. His head jerked back slightly as his mouth opened. Then he blinked.

Bonnie seemed to freeze. Her eyes darted from Bernard to Debbie to Robert as though she didn't know where to look.

Debbie closed her eyes then opened them. "Mom, Dad, this is

Robert Washington. Robert, these are my parents, Bernard and Bonnie Adams."

Robert glanced at her, then strode forward extending his hand to shake her father's. Debbie noticed he seemed to look Bernard in the eye, although her father was clearly surprised. Then he turned to Bonnie, "Pleased ta meetcha, ma'am."

Bonnie's eyes were as big as sunflowers, but she managed a small smile. "It's nice to meet you as well. Robert, was it?"

Debbie took a quick breath. "Okay, so we're going to go then." She started to turn away.

"Debbie!" Bernard said. "Where is it you're going?"

She looked at Robert.

"We thought we'd go for a drive. Maybe stop and get a Pepsi at King's," he said.

Bonnie stood. "You don't need to do that. It's warm outdoors. Why don't you go out on the patio, or if it's too warm, you can talk in the basement. We have soda here, and I baked a cake this morning if you'd like some."

"Well, we kinda wanted to ..." Debbie began, but then she caught her father's look. He wasn't at all sure this was a good idea; she could see that. She may have to compromise until they get used to this. She turned to Robert. "Would you mind if we stayed here?"

He put up his hands palms out. "I'm easy. We can stay in, no problem." Debbie noticed when he raised his hands, he still had her phone number on his wrist.

Debbie took him into the kitchen where they retrieved bottles of Pepsi-Cola from the refrigerator and used the bottle opener attached to the kitchen wall. She took him through the walkout basement and out to the patio where they sat on wicker chairs.

He started laughing. "You didn' tell 'em. You see their faces?

Like, oh my God!"

She squirmed and looked at her feet. She'd put her pink Keds on because they matched her dress. "I'm sorry. I ran out of time."

"It's okay. Once they get to know me, it'll be fine." Robert took a sip of Pepsi.

Debbie would have thought the same thing before she saw her parents' faces. Maybe it was what he was talking about the previous night, there had been things reported in the newspapers that worried them. "Robert, have you ever dated a White girl?"

He studied her. "Guess not. I've danced wid White girls. Ain't dated many girls. I've taken girls to movies, church events, and prom. Mostly been to group things, like parties at somebody's house, or basketball games, baseball games where people sorta mingle. Since my father's a minister, we socialize wid the other kids at church. Haven't wanted to go out wid girls much. But dere was somethin' different 'bout you. I'se still trying to figure dat out."

She smiled at him, lowering her lashes. "There's something I like about you too. When you figure it out, let me know." She took a sip of her soda. One of the things she knew she liked was he seemed to always meet her eyes. He didn't make her uncomfortable by letting his eyes wander.

"You said you had a twin brudder. He's not home? Any other siblings?"

"Daniel was home earlier. He might be in his room. No other brothers or sisters. I have a Siamese cat named Princess and we have a dog named Grover. I think he's napping over there in his doghouse. Grover!"

Slowly one fawn-and-white paw emerged from the doghouse and the big boxer rose and stretched and ambled over to sit at Debbie's feet. She leaned toward him, petting his head, and he stuck out his long tongue, panting in the July heat.

Robert's eyes bulged. "He seems friendly enough."

"Oh, he is." She went to turn on the hose and sprayed water in the nearby dog dish, "Are you thirsty, Boy?" Grover followed her and began lapping water. "What about your family, Robert? You said you had sisters."

"Three older sisters, and two brudders. My parents had three girls then three boys. I'm number five on the list. I share dat car out dere wid my nineteen-year-old brudder, Donald, and the youngest, Truman, will be sixteen next spring, so we'll be fightin' over it. My oldest sister is married and lives in St. Louis. The second-oldest is teaching in Omaha, and gettin' her master's degree, and my third sister is attending Baptist Bible College in Springfield, Missouri. Donald is working as an orderly at Lincoln General Hospital. He thinks that'll help him get into medic training in the army. Truman's going to be a sophomore at Lincoln High."

"And what do you want to be when you grow up?" She returned to where she had been sitting on the patio. Her father was looking out the big window in the living room above. Had he been watching them?

Robert smiled ruefully. "Somedays I just hope to be able to grow up. It can be a dangerous world out there. I plan to study mechanical engineering in college. I like designing things. I am a member of the science club and even—" he lowered his voice to a whisper, "the chess club."

Debbie moved closer to him and pushed on his arm playfully. "No! I don't think I know anyone who plays chess. That's scandalous!"

He grabbed her hand before she could move back to her chair. He pulled her over to the picnic table so they could sit next to each other on the seat.

"Dis's better," he said, entwining their fingers. "Just don't aks me to play ball. Donald played football and basketball and Truman likes baseball. Me, I'd rather take apart the lawnmower or washing machine and see how it works. Or go dancin'. We should go dancin' again."

Debbie looked at his long fingers, and how they contrasted with hers. His hands were strong and soft at the same time. *Why does that take my breath away?* Holding hands had never seemed so sensuous. She looked back into his eyes as he looked at her mouth. She looked back up to the living room window. No one was there now.

But he followed her gaze, then rose and pulled her next to the house, leaning her against the siding, and pressing his mouth to hers, ever so gently. It wasn't tentative. It was like warm liquid; his mouth flowed onto hers deliciously. When he slipped his hands on her back, she felt the July afternoon sun heating up. For once, she had no desire to retreat to the shade. Then as she wrapped her hands around his neck, Grover started barking.

While they were kissing, Grover had come up next to them, as though he was guarding Debbie. Robert jumped back and Grover began sniffing him suspiciously.

"Nice dog," Robert said, putting his hands out for Grover to inspect.

Debbie laughed, "I've never seen him do that before. Maybe he thought you were threatening me somehow."

"My mother was bitten by a dog once when she was growing up. She'd never let us have one. Maybe he smells our cat on me."

Daniel burst through the patio door then. "What's wrong, Grove?" He started when he saw Debbie and Robert, still standing next to the wall of the house. "What's this?"

"Oh. We were checking the paint. You know to see if the house needed repainting. I think it's okay for now, don't you, Robert?"

"Yeah. Looks fine to me." Robert glanced back at the cadet-blue siding, then back to Debbie and Daniel.

Daniel knit his brows, turning his back to the sun to see them better. "Who's your friend?"

"Oh. Daniel, this is Robert Washington. My twin brother, Daniel," Debbie said, gesturing with her hands, as though they wouldn't know who was who.

Daniel shook Robert's hand, then dropped to a squat to ruffle the dog's ears. "So where did you meet him?"

Debbie walked back to the picnic table, which was partially in the shade of a crabapple tree. She felt the perspiration running down her forehead now. "We met last night. At Keentime. Robert is a great dancer."

"I'm sure." Daniel set his jaw. "Are you in high school?"

"Yes. Lincoln High. I am going to be a senior too." Robert sat down next to Debbie but kept his eyes on Daniel.

"Wasn't there some sort of fight at Keentime last time? The paper said a bunch of Negros were chasing down a cop. Did anything like that happen last night?" Daniel stood up but kept Grover heeling next to him.

Robert wiped his brow with the back of his hand. "Nothin' happened last night. But I was der the night dat other thing happened. I wasn't in the group chasing the cop. Dere were only about a dozen kids doing dat. Maybe two dozen. I've been to several meetings about it since. I'm on the Keentime Council. We're trying to get everyone to cool it."

"You are?" Debbie smiled at Robert. "You do like to fix things. Let's go get some cake. Do you want burnt sugar cake, Robert? It's cooler inside."

She took Robert back up to the kitchen, and Debbie started cutting the cake. Fans were running which cooled the house down, and the kitchen was on the east side of the house.

"I don't have time to eat a whole piece of cake, Debbie," Robert said. "I need to leave in a few minutes to get home in time ta go to work. My brudder might need the car tonight."

"That's okay," Debbie said. "You can try mine." She forked a bite of cake for him and put it in his mouth while they were standing by the counter. She watched as he licked his lips slowly.

"It's excellent cake. Compliments ta your mom."

"Do you want more?"

"I want mo'."

The intense look he gave her made her think he wasn't talking about the cake any longer, but she fed him another bite. Then she put some in her mouth and scraped her teeth over the fork.

"I'm goin' now. But I'll call you probably tomorrow night." He gave her a big smile and winged his brows.

She stood on the front stoop and smiled at him as he drove away. Holy smoke! She'd never fallen for anyone that fast. What was going on?

She was still floating on air when she poured herself a glass of iced tea. The pop bottles had been left on the patio.

Then she saw her mother standing in the kitchen doorway. "Deborah Sue. We need to talk about this. Come into our bedroom."

She gulped some tea. At least her parent's room had a window air-conditioner. As she expected, Bernard was in the bedroom too, propped up on the bed. Debbie took a seat at her mother's dressing table.

"You like this boy," Bonnie began.

Debbie nodded. "Yes, why shouldn't I? He's nice."

Bernard cleared his throat, "Kitten, I don't think you understand the ramifications this could have, dating a Black boy."

"Why should it have any ramifications? All men are created

equal and all."

"That's true. But I am talking about what's been going on in this country, even in this state and this town, right now. Martin Luther King and Bobby Kennedy have been assassinated. Both were fighting for civil rights in different ways. There have been riots in Washington, Baltimore, Boston, Cleveland, Detroit, and Pittsburgh. After George Wallace came to Omaha, there were riots. One person was killed, others were wounded, businesses, schools, and cars were damaged. There's a racial war going on in our country and it could land on our doorstep any time."

"And there have been fights right here in Lincoln," Bonnie said. "Right after Keentime dances. So, don't think this can't affect you."

"But Robert is one of the people who's trying to fix things. He said he's on the Keentime council and he's been to some church meetings about the events at Keentime. He said the reporting wasn't completely accurate. He saw some things himself," Debbie rose and fisted her hands on her hips.

"If he was close enough to witness something, he could've gotten swept up in it. Anyone you're dating, or even hanging around with, needs to be able to keep you away from dangerous situations."

"I think you're assuming things about him because he's Black. His father is a minister, he does things at his church, he's not a troublemaker. He plays chess, for goodness' sake! He has a sister who's a teacher, and one who's at a Baptist college. His brother works at a hospital. For a seventeen-year-old boy, he's practically a saint!"

"Robert may be a perfectly nice boy. The problem is he could put you in risky situations." Bernard got off the bed and put his hands on her shoulders. "It might not be his fault. Trouble might find him. Especially if he's dating a White girl."

"I didn't think my parents were prejudiced." Debbie's eyes were filling with tears, and she backed away.

"We aren't against you dating him, Sweetie. It's what other people might do that concerns us. You need to be very careful out in public. You need to pay attention to how other people are reacting if they're objecting." Bonnie put an arm around Debbie's back. "There may be times you need to leave if people are looking at the two of you in a hostile way."

Debbie looked at her mother, then her father. "So, you're saying I can go out with him? Do I just need to be observant? I'd like to think we could be part of the solution, not part of the problem."

"You said his father is a minister. If you decide to continue to date Robert, it might be smart to go to church with him sometime, to see how his family and the church members react. That might tell you if you're going to have a problem there," Bonnie suggested. "The bottom line is we don't want you to be hurt, not physically or emotionally."

Debbie drew her brows together, studying them. "Sure. We can be careful. I mean we haven't even been on a real date yet. But he has a car. And a job. I do like him and I think he likes me. Is that all?"

She went back to her room and changed into shorts and a sleeveless top. She laid down on her bed, and Princess curled up next to her. They'd given her a lot to think about. *But right now, I only want to think about that kiss.*

CHAPTER THIRTEEN

Debbie and Robert had gone on a few dates. They had gone to Keentime dances, and out for milkshakes at the northeast King's restaurant. There were King's burger restaurants in various parts of town, and students in each high school had informally claimed the one that was nearest the school's neighborhood.

They were sitting on the swings at Bethany Park a few days before school started.

"When are you going to invite me to come with you to your church, Robert?"

He tilted his head. "You wanna come to my church? You mean wid me? I thought you said you were Lutheran." Robert pulled out a cigarette and lit it.

"Well, I don't think I am anything. My parents were married in a Lutheran church, but we haven't gone to church much. I've been to the Presbyterian Church with my friend, Yvonne. I thought it would be nice to see your church."

He sighed. "Um, dat would probably be a bigger deal than ya think. I mean anybody's welcome in church, but if you show up wid me, well everybody'd be staring at us. Because my father's the minister."

"You don't want to do this."

"Huh. Well, if you wanna see the building, we could go there sometime when it's not being used. I have a key. I have to help clean sometimes. Maybe you could come 'n see it when I'm cleanin'." Robert dug the toe of his shoe in the dirt under the swing.

"Did you tell your family about me?" Debbie asked.

"Sure. They know I am datin' someone. I take the car." He opened his mouth to let the smoke waft out, then inhaled.

"Do they know my name?"

"Uh, no. If I told them dat, dere'd be all sorts of questions. Right now, I'se keepin' dat to myself."

"Hmmph. Maybe I should come to one of the church services myself, maybe with my brother, and see if you'd pretend you don't even know me."

"No, Debbie. You don' understand."

"You're right. I don't understand. You don't want your family or church friends to know about us." She walked back to the car, but he'd locked it, so she leaned against it.

He walked up and leaned next to her. "It ain't whatchew think. My sister, Janel, didn' bring her boyfriend to our church 'til they was engaged. I'm afraid people would start getting notions about us."

"Notions? What does that mean? Are you sure you just don't want your little girlfriends at church to find out we're dating?"

Robert looked skyward nearly hitting the back of his head on the car. "Let's wait. Lemme talk to my dad and see what he thinks about it."

Debbie frowned and huffed out her breath.

"It's his church!" Robert took another long drag on his cigarette.

Debbie shook her head. "You know my mother suggested I go to your church to see how people would react to us. Now I understand what she meant. You're even afraid to see how people will react to us."

"I wanna take things nice and easy. We not trying to stir things up. We not making a statement. Dis's about you and me. Nobody else."

"I think I want to go home now." Debbie turned around and put her hand on the car door handle.

Robert slammed the driver's side door and put his cigarette in the ashtray. Debbie picked it up and took a drag.

She gave him a teasing smile. He pressed his lips together and shook his head. He pulled her head to his and kissed her quickly.

"Please be patient, Baby."

The weekend before Homecoming, in October, Robert picked Debbie up on Sunday afternoon.

"Where're we going?" she asked.

"It's a surprise." He drove for about fifteen minutes until they were in a section of the city called T-town.

All Debbie knew about this part of town was her father had told her to avoid driving through it because he thought there were more crimes committed there. He pulled into a driveway and stopped the car. She looked at him expectantly.

"This is where I live. C'mon."

Debbie studied the large two-story white house with a wrap-around porch on S Street. There was a small garage at the end of the long driveway, and another car was parked in front of them. She was so busy gawking, she didn't open her door, so Robert opened it for her and took her hand to help her out.

"Who you got there, Baby?" a woman called out from the porch.

Robert chuckled and turned to Debbie. "You sure you ready to meet the Washingtons?"

She smiled as they approached the porch.

"I told you, Mama, I was going to bring my girl over to meet you. This is Debbie Adams." Debbie stuck out her hand to Mrs. Washington. She was a plump, agile woman in her forties, Debbie guessed, with large dancing brown eyes and a bountiful smile as big as Robert's.

"No Child, we hug around here," Robert's mother insisted, pulling her into a tight embrace. "You okay wid dat?"

Debbie yelped, "Oh!" when she was squeezed, but then started laughing.

"My mother, Thelma Washington," Robert said. "We all afraid of her, so be careful."

Thelma shook a finger at him, "Now don' be telling her tales. As long as you all do as you're supposed to, there's nothing to fear. God's watching!" Thelma sat back down on the big porch swing and patted the seat next to her for Debbie to sit.

The screen door opened, and a tall burly bald man in a suit appeared. He scowled at Debbie.

"Dad, this is my friend, Debbie Adams. Quit trying to scare her," Robert said. "This is my father, Reverend Donovan Washington."

Donovan broke into a grin and pulled her into a hug too. He was a bear of a man, at least a head taller than she was, and he had four inches on Robert.

"Did I scare you? Sorry. I hardly ever gitta scare anyone now that the kids have grown. All's I can do now is threaten people wid hell and damnation. And that don't always work."

He let out a boisterous roar of a laugh that had Debbie's eyes popping.

"She's a pretty one, Robert. I guess you did all right," Donovan told him.

Debbie smoothed down her sweater. If she'd known they were meeting his family today, maybe she'd have worn something nicer than denim pants. And she might have thought of something smart to say. As it was, she was at a loss for words.

"Is the party out here?" Another younger man came through the door. He was about the same height as Robert, but he wore a baseball cap backwards on his head, a sweatshirt with the sleeves cut out, and long shorts.

Robert sighed, "And this is Donald, my older brudder. My girlfriend, Debbie Adams."

Donald raised his brows and took her hand, and ran his thumb across the top of it. "Now when you git tired of playin' wid boys, you come find me, Sugar. I'll show ya what real men're like."

Debbie's mouth fell open. Donald's voice was full of a baritone sweetness that probably knocked the girls flat. She could see the resemblance between the brothers, but Donald's face was fuller, and his brows were more pronounced, with a little scar running through his right brow. Compared to his brother, Robert was almost pretty. That might have been hard to handle.

"She's never gonna be that desperate, Brudder," Robert said.

Debbie sat on the swing with Thelma, while Robert and Donald plopped down on the wide concrete sill that topped a stone wall instead of porch railings. Donovan lowered himself into a large wooden rocker.

"There's a lot of you," Debbie said smiling.

"Oh, Honey. You jus' wait until the whole kit 'n caboodle is here." Thelma patted Debbie's hand. "Janel's about ready to have a baby, so she isn't coming up here for a bit. We see Ruthie about once a month, and Shaunda comes down every few weeks from Omaha. I don' know where Truman run off to."

"He said he was goin' to study over at Rockford's. I am amazed Rockford knows how to open a book," Donovan said.

Robert's father seemed to be funny. Debbie always thought ministers were so serious.

"What about your kin, Debbie? You have a big family?"

Thelma asked.

"Maybe Robert didn't tell you. I have a twin brother, Daniel. And my parents, of course."

"Daniel. There's a good Christian name," Donovan said. "Your name Deborah? Like in Judges?"

"Um, yes it's Deborah. Is there a Deborah in the Bible?"

"Sho' 'nuff," Robert said. "She a judge in Israel. Kinda a cool chick wid great faith who inspired udder folk."

"Sweet," Debbie said.

"Boy knows his Old Testament," Donovan said.

Robert rolled his eyes. "Like I had a choice."

"So whad it like to have a twin?" Donald asked. He leaned back on the porch column and put one foot on the stone sill in front of him.

"Hmm. It's hard to explain. He's been there since before I was born; before I had a conscious thought. Sometimes it feels like he's literally part of me, and other times, it's a real pain having to share everything. It used to bug me when people kept talking about how I was part of this set of twins like we were duplicates. I guess we don't resemble each other so much now. His hair is darker and he's taller than I am. And smarter, and he has more musical talent. But what can I do?"

"We all have gifts. Sometimes we's blind to our own," Thelma said. "Some people has a bushel full of one talent, but dey's lacking in most everything else. Other folks, they have a lil' bit of everything all neatly spread out. You might jus' be one of dem."

Debbie's eyes sparkled. "You may be right."

They chatted for a bit longer, and Thelma brought out a big pitcher of lemonade and some glasses. They heard a blue 1958 Edsel Citation with a noisy muffler rumble up the street. The driver looked at Robert's Buick in the driveway, which was extending nearly to the sidewalk, and scowled. She continued down the street and turned around, returning to claim a parking spot across from the Washington's house.

"Robert Seymour Washington! Why can't you park that dumb eyesore of yours closer up to the garage? Other folks want to park in the drive too, you know," the driver hollered while walking up to the porch.

"Maybe I wanna be able to escape when I hear your noisy-ass contraption coming!" Robert fired back. "Look out, Debbie! Here comes trouble."

When the newcomer got up the porch steps, she heaved a sigh. "What 'cha all doing sitting out here? Didn't nobody clean the house again? You gots newspapers piled on all the chairs? An' who this? Some lil' White girl got lost selling encyclopedias?"

Debbie blinked. She wanted to hide behind Thelma. Instead, she crossed her arms clenching her elbows.

"Shaunda! There ain't no cause to be rude!" Thelma said. "Debbie's a friend of Robert's and she visiting. Debbie, this our second oldest daughter, Shaunda. Ya might not guess from her behavior, but she teaches eighth-graders in Omaha."

Shaunda looked at Robert frowning. "He ain't old enough to be chasin' after girls. He barely old enough to drive." Then she turned to Donald, "Get yo' lazy self up and go fetch me a chair from the house. Don't you boys have manners no more?"

Debbie's eyes widened when Donald jumped up and went into the house and brought back a dining chair. Shaunda settled her ample backside onto the chair and turned her attention back to Debbie. Debbie would've described her as pear-shaped, bigger on the bottom half than the top, probably topping the scales at seventy pounds more than was healthy. Her shiny black hair was pulled neatly into a stylish beehive hairdo, and she wore a snug burgundy print dress with flat shoes.

"What's the matter with dis girl, Robert? She can't talk?"

"I'm pleased to meet you, Shaunda." Debbie took a deep breath. "I was waiting for you to get comfortable."

"Serious now. What she doing here?" Shaunda said.

Robert walked over to stand by the swing next to where Debbie was seated. "Mama tol' you, Shaunda. I'm dating Debbie. Been hangin' out wid her for nearly three months."

"That ain't right, Robert. Why don't you have a Black girl? Aren't there plenty of nice Black girls in our church?"

Debbie's mouth flew open again. She fought the urge to run.

"Debbie aksed to meet my family. Everybody been nice 'cept you," Robert said. "Why you trying to scare her off? I don' see you bringin' yo' boyfriend home."

"An' I won't be bringing my man home, thank you. That would scare him off," Shaunda said. "Don't mind me, Miss Debbie. I've been battling know-it-all thirteen-year-olds all week."

Debbie found her voice again. "What do you teach?"

Shaunda helped herself to the rest of the lemonade. "I try to teach those dimwits some etiquette and common sense. But I tell you, some days it ain't worth the trouble. I'm paid to teach French, typing, and shorthand."

"You speak French then? Have you ever been to France?" Debbie asked.

"Ha! I'm still waiting fo' a Sugar Daddy to foot dat bill. But I'se been to New Orleans and Lafayette, Louisiana. Took some kids down there in June. Dey speak a different type of French there, more Cajun." Shaunda squinted at Debbie. "I suppose yo' rich White folks took you all over Europe?"

Debbie felt the blush rising to her cheeks. "We're hardly rich.

My father builds houses. I've never been out of the country. Oh, but you know if you live in Omaha, you might have heard my Uncle Bob's advertising on television. 'Adams Auto sells Bargain Beauties.' I think that's his slogan."

"Adams Auto? Maybe I see him when it's time to trade in my Edsel."

Donald hooted, "It sounds dead already."

Debbie glanced up at Robert. Maybe she was winning Shaunda over. He still was looking grim.

"Let's go into the kitchen," he said to Debbie. "I'm gonna see what's keeping Truman."

She followed him into the house. She had wondered why his parents didn't have them come into the house earlier. She didn't see any mess, other than a few books stacked neatly on one chair. The walls were lined with family portraits, and the wood floors shone. One room held a large dining table and the other had a couch and a few overstuffed chairs. They seemed to have more furniture than space, but she assumed that was normal for large families.

In the kitchen, Robert picked up a black wall phone. He opened the nearby cupboard door where there were at least forty phone numbers scrawled in pencil. She spotted hers near the top of the disorganized list. Robert dialed one of the numbers he found.

"Hey, dis's Robert Washington. My brudder Tru there? Yeah? Can you aks him to git on home? Somebody I want him to meet. Yeah. Thanks." Robert hung up.

"They said he come along soon," Robert said to Debbie. "But in the meantime, we all alone here." He pushed her up against the counter, placing his hands on the counter on either side of her, and kissed her.

Truman arrived about five minutes later. By then, the rest of the family members had migrated into the dining room. Thelma was serving coffee and leftover cinnamon rolls from the morning church service.

"Hey Shaunda," Truman said as he walked in the door. "I see dat box-a-salvage-parts you call an Edsel made it down here again."

"Don't you start sassing me, Boy," Shaunda said. "Come give yo' sista a hug." Truman hugged Shaunda and sat down by her at the table. Donovan had gotten a jigsaw puzzle out and they were trying to pick out corner pieces.

"Truman," Robert said. "I want you to meet Debbie Adams."

Truman looked up as though he hadn't noticed Debbie before. "Oh, you the Debbie? All week it's like Debbie did dis and Debbie did dat. I'se beginning to wonder if you was real."

Debbie gave Robert a sidelong look. He was looking daggers at his younger brother. "Are you saying Robert talks about me?"

"He never shuts up. Like you his main squeeze, dat's fo' sure." Truman laughed at Robert's expression. Debbie saw that familiar toothy grin she admired on Robert.

"What grade are you in, Truman?" she asked.

"I'se a sophomore at Lincoln High. Last of the Washingtons to rule the school."

"He da runta the litter, ain't you, Monkey?" Donald said, trying to ruffle Truman's Afro.

"Leaves da hair alone! Man! Debbie, you have five brudders and sistas?" Truman asked.

"No, just one."

"Want some of mine?"

"No. Just one." She smiled at Robert. "But I'd better be heading home. It was lovely to meet all of you."

CHAPTER FOURTEEN

The previous summer, Yvonne and Debbie had decided they were going to try something more ambitious for the homecoming performance.

"You know how Joanne and Barbra did a traditional patriotic show for homecoming? Apparently, that has been the pattern for years," Yvonne had said, as they had practiced twirling together in her backyard.

"Boring," Debbie had rolled her eyes. "Can we change that?"

"Believe it or not, Mr. Humphreys said the band is playing 'Light My Fire.' He asked if we wanted to twirl fire batons. I could've kissed him!" Yvonne had laughed. "Let's do a whole variety of batons and make it fabulous."

Debbie remembered how Linda's and Nancy's eyes sparkled when she first explained the concept. "We're not doing safe. We're not in our comfort zone. I know this is only going to be your fifth performance, but let's have fun. Make the show unexpected, maybe a little sexy. Go for it."

Putting the show together was nerve-racking. Yvonne had taken on the fire baton routine, but Debbie had to design the flag routine herself, and Linda and Nancy were working together on the hoop routine. If they ran out of time to prepare, it could be a disaster. Debbie kept reminding herself it was their chance to show how good the twirlers were. They had to focus. If the pressure to perform using different batons wasn't enough, she had invited Robert to come to watch their show for the first time.

Twirling fire was scary. Who knew what would happen if the flames got too close to their clothing, or if they dropped a lit baton on the grass field? Debbie could picture the headline: *HOMECOMING TURNED INTO BONFIRE WHEN FOOTBALL FIELD SET ABLAZE.*

75

The first time they tried to light one of the batons, it was windy, and they couldn't keep it going. It was calmer the next day, and by the time they got to the Friday practice, they were excited about twirling fire.

Debbie sighed, "I don't think I'll ever get tired of listening to Jim Morrison of The Doors singing "Light My Fire." It's romantic and a little taboo. The minor-key melody is haunting. Makes me want to get my groove on."

"You know it's about sex and drugs, don't you?" Linda said.

"Sure, but my brother insists there is a little Bach in the beginning. I only know I like it," Debbie said.

Despite a mist that canceled the pre-game show, the half-time homecoming performance went on as planned. The hovering residual dampness in the air made the fire batons seem to glow eerily. Yvonne was starting the routine, then at sixteen count intervals Linda, Nancy, and Debbie would join. Debbie waited her turn to have her baton lit and watched as her friends' faces seemed to be glowing in the reflected light. They had sequined headbands around their tightly wrapped hair to reflect more shimmer.

Once that fireball was whirling around her, she didn't want the song to end. The twirlers all started laughing a little when they got to the last sixty-four counts and started a hip-rocking rotating step. The crowd whistled and hollered its approval. Daniel had been drafted to take home movies of their performance, and Debbie hoped he'd gotten some good shots.

The hoop routine and the flag routine weren't as showy, but certainly different from the usual batons. Debbie blamed her excess adrenaline when she botched a few counts of the flag routine she had designed. She had let her mind wander, wondering where Robert was sitting in the stands.

By Saturday night, the show was a proud memory and she was

getting ready for her first homecoming dance. She had a shiny satiny red dress Yvonne had insisted she buy, saying it accented her in all the right places. And she had strappy black patent leather pumps that would stand up to any crazy dance step her boyfriend threw at her. Her long blonde hair was curled and sprayed into submission.

Daniel was taking his new girlfriend, Andrea, to the homecoming dance. Debbie finished getting ready in time to see him leave in the new brown tweed sports jacket and brown pants he'd bought for senior pictures.

When Robert rang the bell, she was a little surprised to see him dressed in a navy pin-striped suit, which hung loosely on his thin frame. Debbie had noticed Robert had a certain polish in whatever he wore. His shirt was always pressed, his dress pants were creased, and his leather shoes were shined. She'd never seen him wear a necktie before.

"Holy cow!" Robert said when he saw her red dress. "You look like you could start a fire." Debbie's bright red lips curved, as she rotated around.

When they got into the Buick, he started the engine to warm the car back up. "Are you ready for this?" he asked.

"What homecoming? Dancing? I can't wait."

"No, I wonder if anyone's gonna give us any trouble. You said you didn' have any Negros in your class. I'll stand out. I'm used to it, but I dunno if you are."

"I think it'll be fine. We've been together at several Keentime dances."

"But ya know these kids. I don' want you to be caught off-guard."

"Don't worry, Robert."

He shook his head and chuckled at her naiveté.

When they got to the dance, Debbie knew she was right. They met up with Yvonne and her boyfriend, Randy Sparks. Linda was there with John Anthony Turner and Nancy was with another band member, Peter Thompson.

"I heard this combo was supposed to be very good," Yvonne said. They were soon all dancing and stayed near each other as long as they could.

When the band switched to a slow number, the twirlers were all delighted it was a slower tempo version of "Light My Fire." Debbie was surprised when Robert didn't take her hand as he usually did to do a more formal ballroom step. He pulled her hands around his neck and put his hands on her waist.

"You dig this song, don't you? I could tell that last night," he said pulling her face closer to his.

"Mm-hmm. I do. Jim Morrison. Unbelievable keyboards, kind of jazzy even."

"Oh, I thought it was the words you liked."

"Mmm. That too, Baby." Debbie smiled when he pressed his forehead to hers.

Over his shoulder, Debbie recognized Nancy's uncle, Mason Evans, frowning at them. He made a motion with his hands indicating they should move apart. She started to pull back, then looked around and saw other couples in a double-clutch.

"I guess there's one chaperone who doesn't like our dancing style," she admitted.

"Ol' Beef Face over there you mean? He's been evil-eyeing me since we walked in. Let's try something else. You may need to put those swivel hips to work." Robert took her hand in his and put his other hand on her hip. "Remember those cha-cha moves we practiced?'

Debbie didn't remember exactly how to do it, but he coached

her in a soft voice and after a few tries, they were rotating around rather impressively. She still marveled at how his every action seemed instinctive, while she was focusing on every muscle she moved. Soon, the kids dancing next to them stopped and backed up and watched. Debbie wasn't used to being the center of attention, but she hadn't bought that bright red dress for nothing.

When the dance ended, several couples clapped for them. Then Debbie saw Daniel and Andrea about twenty feet away. He put his hands out palms up as if to say, where did you learn that? Hmm. Maybe there was something she could do better than her twin.

She couldn't help but notice a few couples were leering at them. The girls looked away, but the boys shook their heads in disapproval.

When the tempo picked up, they started doing the Watusi. She leaned into Robert and said loudly, "You're going to make me a star." Her classmates were starting to watch them out of the corners of their eyes.

"You already a star, Baby. Look whatchew did last night."

When they were thirsty, they got glasses of punch and sat at one of the round tables. They had their hands entwined on the tabletop.

A couple of junior football players walked by their table and bumped it, spilling their punch slightly on the linen table cloth. Debbie heard them making chimpanzee noises as they walked away.

Mr. Evans walked by them and glared. He didn't speak but continued walking to observe other dancers.

"What's his problem?" Debbie said. "That must be Nancy's cousin Marilyn's father. She's a sophomore. I think I saw her here too."

"We could go out to the courtyard. I think I saw Yvonne and Randy heading that way." Robert said.

"Good idea. Before he comes back."

The courtyard was strewn with leaves, and illuminated with dim floodlights. Withering vines were crawling up a brick wall, and Robert leaned her on that. His kiss was more potent than she expected. "Debbie, you know a good place to park?" His lips were trailing heat behind her ear.

"What's wrong with where we parked the car?"

He chuckled. "No, after the dance. We could park somewhere. Be alone."

Her brows winged up. "Um, I guess I don't know anywhere. We could drive around and find someplace."

"Have you parked somewhere before in your neighborhood?"

She glanced to the side without shifting her head. "I've never done that."

He frowned. "You've never necked in a car before?"

A slow smile spread across her face. "I guess that's another thing for you to teach me."

He kissed her again, and she wrapped her arms around his neck. Debbie suddenly felt a strong arm on Robert's shoulder.

"You can't do that, Boy. What's wrong with you?" Mr. Evans snapped. He pushed Robert away from Debbie. Debbie stumbled forward in her heels, catching herself against Robert.

"Nothin's wrong wid me. Don' you see all the rest of dem kissing?" Robert retorted.

"Don't give me any backtalk, Boy, or I'll have you both thrown outta here. You keep your hands, and your mouth off of these White girls."

Robert narrowed his eyes but didn't say anything else to Mr. Evans. Debbie stared at him wide-eyed.

"All of you kids, come back inside. You'll only get in trouble out here," Mr. Evans announced.

Once they were inside, Randy asked Robert to show him some steps, and they were soon having fun again. Debbie felt like she had danced her legs off, and she was ready to sit down when the homecoming dance ended. Mr. Evans seemed to be watching them putting on their coats and walking out the door. Debbie noticed there were some uniformed guards outside the school building and there was a police cruiser in the parking lot, but she didn't think it was unusual.

Robert had driven down one row in the parking lot when he turned to her and said, "I think we're gonna have to postpone the necking portion of this date."

"What's the matter, are we too close to curfew? I think my mother gave me a thirty-minute extension since the dance was a late one."

"No, it's not dat. I think we're getting an escort. Look behind us."

Debbie shifted around where she was sitting in the middle of the front seat to look through the back window. The police cruiser was following them.

"Debbie, listen to me. If they stop us, do whatever they aks. Mr. Evans was one thing. This's the police. You gotta trust me. They do dis to Negros a lot. I know what to do."

She gaped at the back window, then at Robert. Her forehead crinkled. "Why . . . what do they—" She saw beads of perspiration pop out on his face. It wasn't from dancing. His fear was contagious. It had never occurred to her to be afraid of the police. They were supposed to protect the citizens.

CHAPTER FIFTEEN

Robert kept one eye on his rearview mirror watching the police car, while he slowly drove to Debbie's house. He was under the speed limit and obeying all traffic laws.

Once he was on the straightaway on Randolph Street east of Cotner Boulevard, the police officer turned on his flashing lights and Robert pulled over to the curb. Keep cool. It'll be fine. He'd never been stopped but Donald had. His father had many times. They'd been schooled.

Robert rolled down his window. "Good evening, Officer."

"Get out of the car, Boy," Officer Comstock said. He looked at the officer's nametag before opening his door. He glanced back at Debbie who regarded him with wide eyes.

Robert waited for the policeman to request his license and registration, but that didn't happen. He stood patiently against the car looking into the officer's eyes. His father had told him to avoid eye contact with cops. But this was 1968. Surely things had changed since Donovan was a young man in St. Louis.

"Whatchew looking at?" the cop snarled.

"I'm waiting for you to tell me why you stopped us. I figured you wanted something."

"You figgered—"

"Lookee what we got here, Chester," the second officer said in a sing-song voice. He was looking in the passenger side of Robert's Buick Riviera shining his flashlight on Debbie. "A cute little blonde bombshell. Maybe we ought to get her out of the car and frisk her."

Robert whirled around glaring at the other policeman. Before he had a chance to speak, Officer Comstock pushed Robert's chest against the car. "Git yer hands up on the car, Boy." He pulled out a nightstick and pushed it between Robert's shoulder blades. "Come back over here, Harry, and frisk this sonabitch. He's probably carrying."

Robert sucked in a breath and put his hands on the hood of the car. Harry came back around to the driver's side and patted Robert down for weapons.

"Okay, now. Turn around nice and easy," Comstock said. Robert turned back to face them and squinted at the cop who'd been called Harry. He noted the officer's nametag said 'Baines.' "Don't look at him, look at me, Boy. I'm talking to you. Didn't that whore mother of yours teach you manners?"

The tightening in his chest made it hard for Robert to recall the lessons Thelma had taught him about turning the other cheek. The calm he tried to summon didn't make it to his eyes, which were full of stone-cold fury.

Baines spoke up again, "Look at those purdy clothes this boy is wearing. He must like his fancy duds. He looks like a pimp. Is that whatcher doin'? Rounding up whores? Yer kinda young for a pimp, ain't cha? Maybe he's a junior executive pimp!" Baines laughed loudly at his own joke. "Oh, and she must be your junior whore. Maybe we should get her out of there and run her in."

He saw the game Officer Baines was trying to play. He hoped insulting Debbie would make Robert lash out at them.

"What's the matter, Boy? Nuttin' to say?" Comstock sneered, pushing his Billy club perpendicular against Robert's Adam's apple.

Robert felt the cold wooden nightstick threatening to choke his airway. "May we go, officers?" Robert asked evenly.

"What are you doing in this neighborhood?" Comstock's lips curled.

"I am taking my date home. She lives on Mulder Drive."

"Okay then, you go on ahead. We'll give you an escort in case there's any trouble," Comstock said. "You're liable to scare White folks in this neighborhood. There was a report last week of some colored man sneaking around the backyards, peeking in windows. That wasn't you, was it, Boy?"

"No, sir."

"What was that, Boy?"

Robert spoke louder, "No, sir."

"All righty then, get her on home. We'll follow."

Robert got back into the driver's seat and started the car. He took a deep breath. When he braced his arms on the steering wheel, the tension in his forearms ached. A muscle in his jaw twitched. Heat spread up to his face, flaring his nostrils.

"What was that all about?" Debbie asked. She had moved back toward the passenger door after Officer Baines had reprimanded her.

"Harassment." Robert hissed. He pressed his lips together to keep them from trembling. He drove slower than the speed limit again, partly to give himself time to regain his cool. "Debbie." He glanced at her briefly. "When we reach your house, get out of the car. Don't say a word. Don't look back. Go inside as quickly as you can."

"But we can't let them—"

"Do it. Just like I said."

Debbie's lip quivered and a tear rolled down her cheek, as he pulled into her drive.

"I'm sorry you had to see that. I'll call you tomorrow."

She looked back at him and sniffed. Then she opened the car door and strode inside as he had asked.

Robert closed his eyes and sighed. He looked in his rearview mirror and the police car was waiting for him. They followed him all the way home, but when he pulled into his parents' driveway on S Street, they continued down the street.

CHAPTER SIXTEEN

Debbie hadn't yet heard from Robert after the encounter with the police. On Sunday morning she had gone over to Yvonne's and told her all about what had happened. Yvonne told Debbie to tell her parents about that encounter if she wanted to report the police officers for harassment.

After lunch Sunday, Debbie saw her chance to speak to Bonnie and Bernard. Daniel had gone to the library to research a paper he was writing.

"Mom and Dad, may I talk to you?" Debbie began.

Bernard and Bonnie settled on the sofa in the living room. Debbie sat on the adjacent armchair. "What is it, Kitten?" Bernard asked.

"Something happened last night when Robert was driving me home. I can't imagine this is typical of most of the policemen in our town, but their behavior was completely rude and I think we should report them to the chief of police or whoever handles complaints."

"Report who? What are you talking about, Sweetie?" Bonnie asked.

"I don't know their names. But a police car followed us from school. When Robert got to Randolph Street, they turned on the flashing lights. Robert pulled over and they asked him to get out of the car. They didn't tell him why they stopped him, they frisked him and pushed him with that club thing, and called him names. I think they insulted me too, but it was hard to hear inside the car. He was completely cooperative and he hadn't broken any laws. It was to harass him. He did tell me that much. They acted as though he didn't have a right to drive through Eastridge because he was Black. Do you know who to call to lodge a citizen's complaint?"

Bernard's brow furrowed. "Didn't you tell us his older brother also drives that Buick Riviera? Maybe they have him mixed up with his brother."

"They probably checked the license plate on their radio," Bonnie said.

"I met his brother. He works at Lincoln General Hospital. He's not a hoodlum either." Debbie cocked her head. "These two cops were out of line."

"The police are here to protect us. Maybe there was something about Robert or his car which made them suspicious. Just because you don't know what it was doesn't mean they didn't have a reason to stop him."

"I'm sure they stop many teenagers." Bonnie patted Debbie's knee.

"I'm sure they stop many Black teenagers!" Debbie stood up and fisted her hands on her hips. "You don't think we should report the cops? What if they had decided to hurt Robert or arrest him on some trumped-up charge? Where would that have left me?"

"I believe you're blowing this out of proportion. You know, I think I did hear one of the men on my crew talking about a peeping Tom that was spotted on Margo Drive. They may have been patrolling Eastridge looking for him," Bernard said.

"Aren't you listening to me? These cops followed us home from the dance! All they were looking for was a Black guy who dared to drive into our lily-white neighborhood!"

"You're getting too wound up about this, Debbie," her father said. "You go on to your room now and let your mother and I discuss this. I'm not sure I approve of your attitude."

Debbie huffed out a breath, and fled from the room, catching her foot on the hassock, nearly losing her balance. She slammed the bedroom door and flung herself on her bed and sobbed.

After about ten minutes, Bonnie knocked on her door. "Deborah. Come back into the living room," Bonnie said.

Debbie had stopped crying and had been thinking of other tactics she might pursue to convince them the police were in the wrong. She slumped back in the chair she had been sitting in before.

"Your mother and I have reached a decision," Bernard said. "I know you're young and new at this dating business. Sometimes we're attracted to people who aren't a good fit for us. We have seen a change in your behavior since you started dating Robert. You aren't going to see him again."

Debbie blinked. This couldn't be happening. This was worse than what the police had done. "You can't . . . you aren't serious? I'm crazy about Robert! He's been a perfect gentleman. He —"

Bernard put his hand up as if to silence her. "You're probably blinded by your feelings. That's common at your age, Honey. But we have a responsibility as your parents to protect you. What happened last night could happen again. Negro men are always going to be suspect, and teenage boys are suspect. You're putting yourself in danger even if he's as nice as you think he is."

"But that isn't right. He has rights like everyone else. The police, no one should treat him like he's a suspect. Even at the dance, there was a chaperone who was mean to him and us just because he's Black." Debbie's eyes were filling with tears again.

"That is what we're talking about. You're going to be subjected to hateful behavior because of your association with him," Bonnie said. "You're too young and inexperienced to deal with that. We're going to have to stop it before you get hurt."

"Before I get hurt? You're the ones hurting me! Don't you see that? I am trying to fight back against injustice, and you want me to abandon him? That doesn't help anyone!"

"I know it seems harsh now, but you'll find another boy at school to go out with. And Robert is a good-looking young man. I'm sure there are other girls of his kind that would be happy to date him. He probably would be left alone if he was with a Black girl."

Bonnie's hands shook as she picked up a sofa pillow and plumped it up.

Debbie shook her head. "No, I am not going to do this. It's wrong of you to ask me to break up with him. I should never have confided in you about the police. You're on their side, not mine."

She stormed back out of the room, but this time she grabbed her coat and went outdoors. She felt hot tears running down her cheeks as she pulled her coat around her and hiked up the sidewalk. She didn't know where she was going, but she had to walk. She wanted to jump in her car and drive to see Robert, but she couldn't even talk to him now. She felt too out of control. How would she ever explain this to him? He thought her parents would learn to like him. Wasn't that what he had said? No, no, no. She wasn't leaving Robert. She'd have to come up with another way. She headed back and spent the rest of the afternoon in her room.

It was almost supper time when Robert called her. She listened woodenly while he explained how the police had followed him home but didn't bother him after that.

"Debbie? Are you okay? You sound funny," Robert said.

She took a ragged breath. "I don't know what to do. I told my parents we should report those cops. You know they must have some internal complaint department. My parents went crazy. That's all I can think. They told me we can't date anymore."

"What?" Robert's voice wasn't much more than a whisper. "They told you to break up wid me?"

She started to cry again. "I said I wouldn't do it. You were in the right, not those terrible cops. But I don't know how we can see each other without them knowing about it."

He didn't say anything for a few moments. "I can't aks you to disobey your parents, but it'd be possible. We both have cars. I'd hate lying to dem though."

She sniffed. "You're right. They wouldn't have to know. We're supposed to be going to Lincoln High's homecoming on Saturday night."

"Oh, gosh, yeah. I forgot. But we couldn't . . . wait. You probably don't know anyone else who'd be dere. No one is likely to tattle on you. Maybe I could get someone else, another friend of mine to pick you up. Dey didn't say you can't date anyone, did dey?" Robert asked.

"No, but I think they were ruling out dating Black boys."

"I have White friends. Heck, most of Lincoln High is White, you know. If I aksed one of my friends to pick you up, would you come wid him?"

"And meet you there? Yes. That might work. But I need to see you before then. Can you come by after school sometime this week? Come to the school, not to my house. The twirlers will probably be outside practicing for the halftime show."

"Let me work on it. We'd better hang up before your parents get mad. If you give me Yvonne's number, maybe I could get a message to you through her."

"No, I am mad at Yvonne too. It was her dumb idea to tell my parents what happened with the cops. If I hadn't done that, they wouldn't have tried to break us up. Maybe I'll give you Linda's number. She has a teen line so her parents can't listen to her calls. For now, show up at school when you can."

"All right," Robert said. "And Debbie, try not to worry. We'll work somethin' out."

The lump in her throat rendered her unable to speak, so she just hung up.

CHAPTER SEVENTEEN

Robert had a plan. He hoped he could persuasive enough. After chess club on Tuesday, he stopped his friend, Lester Gibbons.

"Lester, I wonder if you could help me out," Robert said.

"You want to know what move you should have made in the last match?" Lester asked.

"No, this isn't about chess. It's more of a girl problem."

Lester raised his bushy eyebrows.

"I've been dating this terrific girl who goes to Capital High, Debbie Adams. But her parents made her break up with me because the cops stopped us last Saturday night. They're worried about her dating a Black kid now."

"Sorry to hear that," Lester said, putting his jacket on.

"Well, Debbie and I already planned to go to the homecoming dance this Saturday, I hate to disappoint her. I wondered if you might pick her up and bring her to the dance if you don' already have a date," Robert said, holding his breath.

Lester pushed his glasses up on his nose and stood taller. He was an inch or two shorter than Robert, and slightly pudgy. His greasy light brown hair fell over his forehead when he moved. His thoughtful green eyes studied Robert. "You want me to go out with the girl who broke up with you?"

"You'd just hafta bring her to the dance. You have a car, don' you, Lester?"

"Sure. I got a car last year. It's nothing fancy but it runs."

"Well, if yer sure you don' mind doing this. Here, I'll write down her name and phone number. I'll tell her about the plan tomorrow, then you can call her about the details." Robert jotted down the information and handed it to Lester.

"Tell me something about her so I can plan out topics of conversation," Lester said.

Robert scoffed. "This ain't a chess match, Egghead. It's a date. But okay. She's a baton twirler, likes to dance. She likes old movies like *Gone Wid the Wind, The Wizard of Oz, A Star is Born,* anything with Judy Garland. She has a twin brudder." Robert looked at the floor. She likes to kiss. He wasn't going to tell him that though. No point in giving Lester ideas.

The next day, Robert was able to convince his brother, Donald to let him have the car to drive to school. Donald had made several jokes about dating some of the nursing students at Lincoln General Hospital and how they had enjoyed the big back seat in Donald's car. Robert shuddered when he looked in the back seat as he got into the car, and didn't want to think about his brother making time.

The whole reason he wanted the car was to go visit Debbie after school. She was right where she said they'd be, on the outside of the music wing, tossing up batons with her friends. He parked the car on the drive circling the school near the majorettes. By the time he got around the car, Debbie was running up to greet him.

He pulled her into an embrace. "I missed you, Doll. Are you okay?"

"Oh, Robert. It's been awful. Can we sit in your car and talk?" Debbie asked.

They got into the car and she leaned in for him to kiss her. He wasn't sure that was smart right in front of the school, but he hadn't seen anyone patrolling the grounds.

When he moved back away from her, he said, "I think I have a plan for Saturday night. My friend, Lester Gibbons, will call you. He's going to pick you up instead of me and bring you to the dance. I don't know which one of us will take you home, it depends on how long he sticks around at the dance. Do you think your parents wait up and see you when you come home from a date?"

"Not usually. I suppose they watch the clock in case I'm late. But you're saying we can still go to the dance?"

"Yeah. I told Lester what happened and he seemed fine wid the plan. Don't be surprised if he's a little nervous. He's probably never been out with a girl."

"I am grateful he's helping us. I missed seeing you though." Debbie put one hand on Robert's cheek.

"Me too, Baby. But we'll have plenty of time on Saturday night. The dance is from seven-thirty to eleven. I wanna be there early."

Robert was feeling more confident now that he'd put his plan in motion. He wasn't even upset to find his sister, Shaunda, at their house when he got home.

"Whatchew doing here on a school night, Shaunda?" he asked.

"I am here for a little visit. No school for the next two days. Some sort of training but I went last year so I am excused. I came home to sing at church on Sunday. I'm going to choir practice with you tonight. Make sure you boys are behaving."

Shaunda and Truman rode to choir practice with him. He had to admit his sister had a powerful singing voice, and the church was happy to have her participation when she was available. After practice, he was waiting for Shaunda and talking with some of the other high school kids when Nina Johnson, his friend Wayne's younger sister, came up to him.

"Robert, I was so sorry to hear you broke up with your girlfriend," Nina said.

Robert blinked. How had she heard that? He must've mentioned it to Wayne. Robert shrugged. "It happens."

"Your sister, Shaunda, was worried you had to break your date for homecoming."

"Huh?"

"Oh yeah. She said you were too shy but you wanted to aks me to go to homecoming wid you. I thought someone else was goin' to aks me but he didn' so I can go wid you." Nina batted her impressively long eyelashes.

"My sister said I wanted to aks you to the homecoming dance?" Robert's brow furrowed.

"I know that sounds weird, but if we're both available, we might as well go together."

Robert's mind was racing. Would that work? Could he switch girls with Lester once they all got to the dance? Would it be better to have Nina as a pretend date to make the whole thing seem more legitimate? Was there a chance Nina might get upset and then Wayne would be mad at him too?

"What time you wanna pick me up?" Nina persisted.

"Um, seven. No seven-fifteen, I guess."

"Good 'nuff. I'll see you Saturday, Robert." She gave him a sweet smile as she walked away.

What the heck just happened? Had he agreed to go on a date with Nina Johnson? He was already meeting Debbie at the dance. There was nothing wrong with Nina. She was a cute little junior. She used to be a pest when Robert went over to help Wayne set up his Citizen's Band radio or listen to music at their house. But now she had long straightened hair, and big eyes, and even had a little booty. But kinda forward. Did she ask him on this date? He sighed. He was going to have to make it all work.

CHAPTER EIGHTEEN

Debbie was pleased Lester showed up on her doorstep at seven-ten on Saturday night. Her parents had been surprised when she told them she had agreed to go to Lincoln High School's homecoming with Lester since she couldn't go with Robert. They seemed to think it was a good sign she could get over Robert so easily. As if that was possible.

Debbie had picked out a baby-blue cashmere sweater and dark blue skirt to wear to this dance. Robert had told her this event wouldn't be as dressy as the dance last week. She liked the way the blue sweater brought out her blue eyes and eyeshadow. And it skimmed her body gently in the right places. Of course, it wasn't Lester she was trying to impress. She didn't even know what Lester looked like.

He was standing under the light in the foyer when she first saw him. Lester was very pale, was about three inches taller than Debbie, and had his brown hair slicked back. His mostly frameless glasses looked like he bought them ten years earlier, and she wondered how he saw through the smudges on the glass. But she tried to be positive. His navy sweater and matching slacks suited him. She appreciated the fact he was stockier than she was.

"So, tell me, Lester. What interests you in school?" Bernard said when Debbie introduced them. "You don't look like you are an athlete."

"No, sports are a waste of time from my perspective. I like a good math problem. I've been reading about multidimensional parabolic equations, for example. Are you familiar with those?"

"Say what?" Bernard sputtered.

"Don't forget your gloves, Debbie. It's supposed to be cold tonight," Bonnie said.

"It's forty degrees Fahrenheit, with a wind from the northeast at fifteen miles per hour. The humidity is thirty-three percent. Expect a cold front to arrive around two o'clock tomorrow morning," Lester straightened his shoulders and helped Debbie into her coat.

Her mind was on Robert, but Lester kept talking, once they got into his car. "Robert told me you were a majorette, Debbie. I play the alto saxophone in our school band," Lester told her.

"Oh, that's nice. I play clarinet when I'm not twirling. I think I used to be better at it but I haven't devoted much time to practicing the clarinet lately."

"I'll bet you have a good embouchure," Lester said.

Debbie blinked slowly. The only person she'd ever heard talk about how a reed instrument player uses her mouth was the band director. She pressed her fingers to her lips in response. Was that a backhanded compliment about her mouth? "I guess," she said.

"Have you ever learned to play chess?" he asked.

She nearly snorted. "Oh no! Robert threatened to teach me once. I don't think I have the right kind of brain for chess." Then she worried she'd insulted him. "But you enjoy playing, don't you, Lester?"

"Yes, I find it very stimulating. To be strategic you have to memorize your past moves and your opponent's moves. It can be exhausting."

"Good for you. You must be very smart."

"I had my I.Q. tested last year. It was 158. Genius is considered to be 160. Robert said he tested at 150 so he's pretty smart himself."

Debbie's mouth flew open. It wasn't a surprise Lester was so smart, the way he spoke, but she had no idea how smart Robert was. Robert was always using slang. She didn't even know whether he got good grades. Somehow this information made Robert more appealing. He hadn't even bragged about it.

When they got to the school gymnasium, it was quite dark. The overhead lights were off, and there were strings of white lights winding around the pillars at regular intervals across the room. The combo was lit on the stage but it was hard to pick out the dancers in the large crowd. Debbie expected Robert would be near the entrance to meet her, but she didn't see him.

Once they hung up their coats, Lester asked, "Are you ready to dance?"

"You want me to dance with you?" Debbie said. She hadn't planned on that. "Do you know where Robert is?"

"I think I saw him dancing over there with Nina Johnson. Are you trying to avoid him?"

Debbie crinkled her brow. "Why would I be avoiding him?"

"He said you broke up with him, so I assumed you might not want to see him."

Debbie shook her head. "Lester, what exactly did Robert tell you to do regarding bringing me to this dance tonight?"

"He gave me your name and number. He said you were disappointed you couldn't go to homecoming since you two had broken up. He thought I might want to take you instead. I thought it was nice he wanted to set up his ex-girlfriend on a blind date."

"A blind date? Is that what you thought this was?" Debbie could feel her temper crawling up her neck.

"Yes. I mean we haven't met before. Isn't that called a blind date?"

"It is. But Robert told me I was still going to the homecoming dance with him. He said he asked you to pick me up to fool my parents. And now I see him dancing over there with another girl. I don't know what to think."

"Fool your parents? He never mentioned that."

"I'm sure he didn't. C'mon, Lester." Debbie said, taking Lester by the hand and pushing her way through the crowd until they were next to Robert and Nina.

Robert saw them approaching and watched her face. She started dancing very close to him. "What is your plan, Robert? Did you bring another date to this dance?"

"I can explain. Um, Debbie, this is Nina Johnson. She's Wayne's sister. You remember Wayne from the first night we met?" Robert said.

Debbie watched Nina gyrate around the dance floor. She looked like a petite bouncy cheerleader. She wouldn't have been surprised to see her start turning cartwheels, except she was too smoothly coiffed, too polished, and pampered-looking for that. Nina gave Debbie a faint smile as though she knew there was no comparison between them. Nina may not have heard the introduction over the music. If she did, she didn't acknowledge it.

Debbie turned on her heel and started walking away. By the time she reached the edge of the dance area, Robert grabbed her arm, spinning her to face him.

"Where you going?" he said.

"What are we doing here? I thought I was your date, not that little twit."

"She's a nice kid. But I don't think I explained this well enough. She thinks we're on a date."

"Did you go to her house and pick her up?"

"Yes. But I told her my ex-girl, uh, my girlfriend was going to be here and I'd be dancing with her. I mean you."

"Well, if you explained it like that, she's bound to be confused. Did you say I was your girlfriend or your ex-girlfriend?"

"Jeez. I don't remember now."

Debbie raised her brows. "Here I thought I was still your girlfriend. But maybe I am about to be your ex." She started to move away again but he wrapped an arm around her.

"Let's go outside."

She didn't have much choice when he pulled her along. She saw him looking around for a place to talk, but adults were keeping watch at the entrance to the building. He took her hand and they walked to his car in the school parking lot. He surprised her by opening the back door and ushering her onto the backseat.

She folded her arms waiting for an explanation. Instead, he took her head in his hands and kissed her. His warm mouth seemed to melt her frustration away. He hadn't kissed her quite like this before like he wanted more. She wrapped her arms around him.

"Not my ex-girlfriend," he said. "You look more beautiful than ever." She let his tongue slide into the kiss, and his hands were inching under her sweater. They hadn't stopped to get her coat, and she was chilled. She remembered he'd said he wanted to park last week, but they hadn't been able to because of the police following them. But here, they were surrounded by a hundred other cars. At that moment, the rest of the world was a million miles away.

He kept kissing her over and over. Those amazing lips were tracking down the side of her neck. She wasn't sure what he was doing with his hands, but his fingers were spreading across her ribs. She liked the way it felt. Hmm. Until he put his hands on her bra. He filled his hands with her breasts the way that creep Jerry Gibson had done.

She gasped and jumped back.

He frowned when he looked into her wild eyes. "What's wrong?" he asked.

She shook her head. Reality slapped her hard. "We shouldn't be out here. Can't we go back and dance?"

"Debbie, something happened. Did I scare you?"

She shook her head more rapidly this time, but tears filled her eyes. "It's just once before somebody . . . never mind. I want to go back." She stared at the bottom of the door.

He lifted her chin and saw the tears. He kissed her once again tenderly, then opened the door and they walked back to the dance.

Debbie estimated they had been gone about forty minutes. She tried not to think about how they had been rude to their alleged dates.

Robert seemed to be emboldened by the necking in the parking lot. The combo was singing "My Girl" by the Temptations, and he pulled her into the swaying side-step they had improved over several dances. She kept her eyes on his, as though they were the only two people in the room. Before the dance ended, Lester was standing next to them.

Lester spoke loud enough to be heard over the music, "Robert, what's going on? Didn't you set me up on a date with Debbie?"

Robert stopped dancing and looked at Lester. "I didn't mean to give you the wrong impression. I wanted you to pick Debbie up so the two of us could keep our date for tonight. If you want me to help you find a girl to go out with, I'd be happy to. Go ahead and dance with Nina if you want to."

"That isn't copasetic," Lester said, crossing his arms. "If you had asked me to pick up Debbie under some pretense, I would have refused. I think you know that. So, you chose to deceive me and her parents. And it looks like little Nina was misled as well."

Robert sucked in a breath through his teeth and averted his gaze from Lester. Debbie knew Lester was right. She couldn't blame him for being indignant. But she followed Lester's eyes and turned the other direction. Nina was standing behind Robert, and Wayne Johnson was right behind her.

"What you trying to pull, Robert?" Wayne was slightly taller than Robert, and about thirty pounds heavier. Wayne looked like he'd played football. "Whad'ya bring Nina to homecomin' fo' if you already had a date? Ain't right. We'll settle dis outside."

Debbie saw Robert's brows wing up looking from Lester to Wayne, then to Nina. Nina had her jaw set and her eyes narrowed. She wasn't looking quite so cute now.

Before Robert could respond, he was being manhandled out to the parking lot again by Wayne. Debbie was surprised to see Lester grab Robert's other arm, and help Wayne take him out.

Nina chuckled mirthlessly. Debbie turned to her. "I thought Robert and Wayne were friends."

"They be friends. But I'm Wayne's family. He needs to get the word out. Nobody better mess wid' me."

Debbie suddenly felt her stomach lurch. She retrieved her coat and went outside to see what was happening. It wasn't hard to find them. There were at least twenty kids gathered watching Robert and Wayne sparring. Lester was holding Robert's suit jacket. She could tell Robert had already been hit in the eye, and Wayne had a split lip.

In a flash, Wayne lunged for Robert and they were wrestling around in the wet grass.

Debbie sighed and approached Lester. "Are you going to take me home?"

He shrugged and handed Robert's jacket to another guy watching the fight. Debbie and Lester headed back to the parking lot, as police sirens were heard approaching the school.

CHAPTER NINETEEN

The next day, Debbie found her father watching a home movie. He was projecting it on the wall in the family room. She sat down to watch when she saw that the homecoming twirling show appear.

"This is the footage your brother took of your homecoming performance. I assumed he would know enough to shoot movies of you," Bernard said, shaking his head.

Bernard ran the projector backward until he reached the part where the show began.

"That's it," Debbie said. "The fire baton performance started with only Yvonne in the beginning. I was the last one to come in."

"I remember when we watched it in person. But let's see what happens when you come in," Bernard chuckled.

She couldn't imagine why he was laughing. She thought she had done that routine perfectly. They watched Yvonne for the first segment, then the camera zoomed back to show Linda and Yvonne. Then it went back to a close-up shot of Yvonne. A little too close; you couldn't even see her feet. And the camera seemed stuck like that. Just on Yvonne. The rest of the fire baton routine showed just Yvonne. The other twirlers, including Debbie, weren't in the frame.

"Isn't there any footage of me twirling the fire batons?" Debbie asked.

"I don't think so. This is as far as I got. Maybe there's some of you later," he said.

Bernard let the movie play. It was clear Daniel had made Yvonne the star of the show, although he did back up and pan over a few times to the other girls and stayed on Debbie most of the time when it got to her flag routine. He captured her perfectly when she made a mistake.

"I can't believe it. Why on earth did Daniel take so much

footage of Yvonne?"

"It seems clear enough to me, but you'll have to ask Daniel yourself."

CHAPTER TWENTY

Debbie didn't hear from Robert until Tuesday afternoon. So far, they hadn't had problems with calling each other on the phone. If he had to leave a message with her mother, he said he was Lester, but gave his own phone number. Debbie knew Robert's number by heart.

"I've got a black eye!" Robert told her.

"How can you tell?" Debbie chided him. She meant it as a joke but she wondered how a black eye would look on someone with dark skin.

"Oh, you funny. Ain't you ever seen pictures of Sugar Ray Robinson or Sonny Liston after a fight? I don' look quite that bad, but Wayne had a little mercy on me. I got my licks in too."

"I'm surprised the cops didn't haul you off to jail."

"Oh, the other kids stopped us before the police showed up. But after the fight, I couldn't find you. Someone said you left with Lester. He didn't give you any trouble?"

"I like Lester. He has integrity and manners. I don't know what to think about you."

"I think you do. You in love with me. That's what you think about me."

"What?" This wasn't something that should be discussed the first time over the phone.

"You heard me. I'se in love with you too. We're stuck now. In this together."

Debbie sighed. How was she supposed to be angry with him now? "Robert?" She opened her bedroom door to be sure no one was eavesdropping. When she found no one except Princess, she let her in and locked the door again.

"Yeah, Baby."

"You may be right. But what are we going to do? I don't think Lester is going to help us out again."

"Do you ever go do things with your girlfriends? You have a car. Say you are meeting another girl for a coke at King's, and I'll meet you instead. Somethin' like that. Or drive your car to a church parking lot or school and I'll meet you there, and you can get in my car. I'll try to find some other boys who will pick you up the next time we want to go to a dance or somethin' that requires a date. This time I'll level with them though."

"You've thought about this."

"Believe it or not, I talked to Lester about it. He's a whiz at strategy. He was mad I didn't explain myself before and he didn't want to lie to your parents."

"Lester told me something interesting about you. He said you have a very high I.Q. Almost genius. Do you get good grades at school?"

Robert chuckled. "I'm not a genius. Lester is very close. But I've always been on the honor roll. Didn't I tell you I wanted to study engineering in college?"

"But sometimes you talk like—"

"Oh, I know. Dat's jus' fo' fun. You know, to fit in, like a Southern accent. I can say *AaaaSsssssKssss* when I want to, jus' like yo' White boys."

She laughed. He was clever. Maybe she hadn't realized it until now. And she was in love with him. He had her there. "All right, so when can we see each other?"

"How about Saturday night? I don't have to work. I think my friend Leon and I have an idea. He has a girlfriend now and you can meet the three of us somewhere. I'll get the address. You come up with a story about meeting a friend somewhere or going over to a friend's house."

By Saturday night, he had given her an address to meet him in Bethany, a neighborhood north of Eastridge. She spotted his car on the street and another car in the driveway of the house.

Leon answered the doorbell. "Is this where you live, Leon?" Debbie asked.

"Nah. This is my grandma's house. She in a nursing home right now, but I think she be back when she gits better. Nobody home but us tonight."

Robert appeared behind Leon. "You made it." He put an arm around her and guided her into the living room and they sat on a flowered couch. Leon disappeared down the hall.

"This is Leon's grandmother's house? What are we doing here?"

"Ain't it obvious, Baby? Our own little passion pit. We've got hours," Robert said.

"Where did Leon go?"

"He went back into Grandma's bedroom with Sally."

If she hadn't understood initially, it was pretty obvious once Robert started kissing her and laid her down on the couch. Debbie wasn't sure this was a good idea.

"Robert?" she said, trying to catch her breath. "Did you mean it when you said you loved me?"

He sat back up. "Of course, I love you, Debbie. Don't ever doubt that."

She smiled. "I love you too."

"Then it's time to take some clothes off."

"What?" She sat up then. "What do you mean? Leon is in the other room. Don't forget."

Robert laughed. "What do you think Leon doing? He got a girl in there."

Debbie wrapped her arms around her chest. She had on a sweater and a pair of slacks. It wasn't very warm inside Grandma's house. Robert slid his hands up her back under her sweater and kissed her again slowly. She relaxed a little bit and kissed him back. She closed her eyes tightly and took a deep breath.

When he touched the front of her bra again, she stiffened. *Yikes!*

"What is it? Don't you like that?"

How long is some lecherous student teacher going to haunt me? Maybe I should find out what it is like with a boy I want to touch me.

She took a chance. She pressed her mouth to Robert's instead of answering. She felt his hands trembling when he unhooked her bra. She slipped her fingers between the buttons of his shirt. He unbuttoned the first three then pulled it off over his head.

She tried to keep her body plastered against his chest so he couldn't look at her, opening her lips for him and teasing him with her hands in his hair. But he kept stroking her in ways that made her blood simmer. This must be what Yvonne and Linda had been talking about. It was so easy to relax and enjoy the undertow. But when he unfastened the waistband of her slacks, she pulled away and put her hands across her chest.

"I don't want you to take off my clothes. Not unless it's dark."

"You want me to turn out the lights? Why?"

She pulled her sweater down to cover the front of her. "I wish I was a skinny little thing like some of the other girls we know. But I'm not. I'll probably never be. I don't want you to look at me."

"You joking, right? Debbie, you's gorgeous. I don' wanna cuddle up to some bony-ass girl. Curves make women appealing. Dontchew know dat? Your body is soft and sensuous. I can't keep my hands or my eyes off you. I wouldn't want you skinnier."

106

His words drove heat right through her core. *Oh Lordy.* She couldn't imagine what he could have said that would have made her surrender herself more readily. He was telling her the opposite of what every fashion magazine had taught her the past five years. Did all boys believe that? Or was this a Black thing? She let him leave the lights on, and he let her leave her panties on.

Debbie and Robert didn't have an opportunity to be alone for weeks. They went to see *Romero and Juliet* at the theater and parked afterward. But it was getting colder and the idling engine didn't retain enough heat and wasted gas. But Debbie was glad for the time they had to spend together. It was getting harder to come up with new cover stories to tell her parents.

In early December, Robert called her an hour before they were supposed to go out on a date. She had told her parents she was going over the Linda Bridges' house.

She felt her muscles tighten when she heard his voice. Her gut warned her it was bad news. "What's going on, Robert?" Debbie said when she could be sure no one else picked up a phone extension.

"Debbie, I am glad I caught you. I wasn't sure you'd be home tonight," he said in a formal tone.

Debbie noticed right away Robert didn't sound normal. He was talking loudly and enunciating more for one thing. Her eyebrows drew together. "Are we still meeting at King's tonight?"

"No. Um, here's the thing. I just had a discussion with my parents. My father is rather adamant we stop dating. He thinks we're too young to only date one person. So, I guess that means I have to go out with some other girls. You might want to think about dating other guys too."

"Oh my God. Are you serious?" Debbie suddenly couldn't breathe. "They are standing right there in the kitchen, aren't they?"

"Yep. We only have one phone," Robert sighed. "I guess there isn't anything else I can say. I just called to let you know." She thought she heard a catch in his voice. "Goodbye, Debbie."

She sank on her bed, a whimper forming in her mouth. Her hand was shaking on the phone receiver but she couldn't seem to put it back on the base. This was it? His parents gave him a little flak and he went along with them? She thought she should be crying. He'd broken her heart, why wasn't she crying?

Oh no. She'd told her parents she was going to Linda's tonight. She'd have to pretend Linda had gotten sick or something. No. Maybe she should go talk to Linda for real. She had to go somewhere tonight. She might start screaming if she didn't get out of her room.

She dialed Linda's number. Thank God she answered.

"Linda, are you busy tonight?"

"Debs? What's going on?" Linda said.

"I'll explain when I see you. Can I come over?"

"Sure. John Anthony was here this afternoon." Her tone went sarcastic. "But he has something else going on tonight. I was going to stay home anyway. I might go get some pizza. You want pizza?"

"We'll see. Thanks, Linda. I'll see you in about forty-five minutes."

Debbie started getting dressed and fixing her hair. She couldn't stop shaking though. It felt like her nerves were all tied in knots. And there was a chill in her bones, even though she was wearing a heavy cardigan.

Then the phone rang again. She almost didn't answer, but maybe Linda had to change her plans.

Robert sounded frantic. "Debbie, I'm so sorry! I didn't know what to do!"

She frowned at the phone receiver, holding it away from her ear. Her first thought was to hang up on him. Instead, she waited and huffed out her breath.

"As soon as I could leave the house, I went to a payphone. Told 'em I was outta cigarettes," he said. "This whole mess started with Leon,"

"Leon? What do you mean?" Debbie asked.

"Leon's mother goes to our church. His father ain't around much, but his mom and my mom are tight. You remember Leon's girlfriend, Sally? She's P.G."

"Sally's having a baby? Leon's baby?"

"Yeah, dat's why my parents're freaking out. They assumed because Leon and I hang out, I'm doin' what he doin'. And I never had sex with any girl. I told 'em dat. Dey jus' said, 'good you jus' keep it dat way.' Then they started talking about boys and girls shouldn't go steady. I said, 'we ain't going steady' but dey didn't care. Dey thought we should see other people, try not to get serious in high school. Plenty of time for dat later. I dunno what to do."

"I think it is obvious what you have to do. I just don't want you to do it," Debbie said. Her candor even surprised her. "Look, I decided to go over to Linda's. She's expecting me now. You can get messages to me through her or Yvonne. I gotta go." Debbie hung up.

At least she knew now what had prompted this, what his parents were reacting to. It was the same kind of thing her parents had done. They wanted to protect their child. Their parents didn't want them to complicate their lives while they were still in high school. But parents had to let their children grow up and make their own mistakes at some point.

Linda lived in the nearby neighborhood of Piedmont, where the homes were generally older, but grander. Her house could easily be called a mansion. When she tried to pull into Linda's massive driveway, she slammed on her brakes because a new wine-red Lincoln Continental was backing out of the garage. Linda's father, Michael Bridges, looked startled to see her as he pulled away but gave her a brief wave. As the adrenaline drained from Debbie's body, she felt a part of her crumbling.

Debbie lit up a cigarette as soon as she got to Linda's room. Linda joined her in solidarity.

"Okay, lay in on me," Linda said.

"It's Robert. Of course, what else? He broke our date tonight because his parents think we are seeing too much of each other. They want him to date around."

"Ain't that a bite? He can't go out with you or he can go out with you along with dating other girls?" They were sitting in facing overstuffed chairs by a dormer window bordered with lace curtains. Linda pulled some psychedelic ashtrays out of the top drawer of her dresser, and put them on the antique coffee table between them. Linda's room was an eclectic mixture of tasteful early American furnishings contrasted with posters of hard rock bands and home-made batiks taped to the walls. The floral elegance of Laura Ashley designs meets Steppenwolf.

Debbie knit her brows. "I'm not sure. Maybe you can ask him if he calls here. I did give him your phone number to get a message to me if he even wants to." She crossed her legs. "He called me twice. The first time to break our date and his parents were standing right next to him. About ten minutes later he called back from a payphone all apologetic for making the first call. He felt bad, but the fact is he's stuck. His parents are trying to stop us from dating and my parents have been doing that for almost two months now."

Linda tucked her long thin legs into the chair seat. "Are you planning to go out with someone else?"

Debbie looked out the window at the pine tree bending in the wind. "I dunno. I thought about calling Robert's friend, Lester, but I don't want to take advantage of him. I think I should go out with another guy so Robert won't think I am waiting for him to figure things out. And maybe so I don't feel so helpless."

"Sounds to me like you are both powerless in this situation. Sometimes I can't wait to grow up. But then I remember I might not have Daddy's money if I was on my own!" She laughed at herself. "The smart thing would be to let him put me through college and dental school first."

"How are things with John Anthony?" Debbie asked.

"Well, I'm not sure. I suspect he is seeing Barbra Simpson again." Linda took a long drag on her cigarette.

"What? I thought she went to Colorado to have Dick Dunn's baby." Debbie sighed remembering the drama Dick had caused when he broke up with Yvonne, and it turned out later he'd been sleeping with Barbra Simpson.

"She came back a few days ago. Rosemary Atkins called me. She found out I was now dating John Anthony and thought I should know." Linda rolled her eyes.

"Do you think he could forgive her? Get back together with her?"

Linda shook her head slowly. "She hurt him. But some people are gluttons for punishment. The funny thing about John Anthony is that he likes to make out, but he's never tried to push it further. He seems to have a tight rein on his libido. It makes me wonder if that was what drove Barbra to sneak around with Dick."

Debbie chuckled. "I don't think boys have any idea what to do with their libidos. Robert's friend, Leon, apparently found out he is going to be a father. That was what set Robert's parents off, I guess. And they probably don't know about the night Leon, Sally, Robert, and I went to Leon's grandmother's empty house for a make-out party."

Linda's brows winged up. "Sounds juicy, what happened?"

Debbie felt the blush creeping to her ears and wished she hadn't mentioned it. But it might be the last time she ever did something like that with Robert. "Oh, it was getting juicy, but we haven't gotten as carried away as Leon and Sally did. And now we may never have another chance."

She felt the tears backing up in her eyes when it sunk in that she and Robert might be through. They still loved each other but couldn't be together. Just like *Romeo and Juliet*. Damn.

CHAPTER TWENTY-ONE

Debbie didn't hear from Robert for almost a week. She was beginning to think she wouldn't talk to him again. Then Linda gave her a letter that Robert had mailed to her house.

DEAR DEBBIE,

I AM SORRY I HAVEN'T BEEN IN TOUCH, BUT I'VE BEEN DOING A LOT OF THINKING. MY BROTHERS AND I HAD A LONG TALK WITH MY PARENTS AND THERE ARE THINGS WE SHOULD TALK ABOUT THAT I GUESS I AVOIDED. IF YOU NO LONGER WANT ANYTHING TO DO WITH ME, I'LL UNDERSTAND. PLEASE ASK LINDA TO TELL ME. HOWEVER, IF YOU 'D LIKE TO TRY TO WORK SOMETHING OUT, MEET ME AT THE MAIN LIBRARY DOWNTOWN ON SUNDAY AT 2:30 ON THE FIRST FLOOR. I KNOW SOME PLACES WHERE WE CAN TALK THERE.

LOVE, ROBERT

Debbie sat in the school bathroom stall reading the letter over and over but it still wasn't clear at all. Was he saying his parents changed their minds? The letter gave her a flutter of hope in her belly even as she swiped tears away. At least it was Friday and she only had two more days to wait to find out more.

When she got to the library, she looked around for Robert. He came up behind her and gestured for her to walk toward the staircase. They went down to the basement where there were fewer people. He found a table in a quiet corner and put his book bag on it then sat. Debbie took a seat facing him.

He stacked his fists vertically on top of his bag so he could rest his chin on them and study her. She met his eyes and tried to read his expression. He looked uncertain, dropping his gaze before searching her eyes again. Then a smile dawned on his face.

"I really missed you," he said finally. "I was afraid you wouldn't come."

Debbie sighed finding it hard to hold his compelling stare. "Was there something you wanted to say? Has anything changed at your house?"

He leaned back and opened his book bag. He took out a spiral notebook and opened it to a page near the back. She could see he had written nearly a page.

"You have notes?" She narrowed her eyes at him.

"Yeah. I told you. Lotsa thinking." He tapped his index finger to his temple. "My dad had some concerns about me datin' you. Ya know he's one of the leaders of the Black community, being a minister and all. He thinks the White city council is depending on him to keep a lid on things. They don't want riots like they had in Omaha or Detroit. He's nervous that me crossin' over might stir up trouble. Some folks wanna keep things separate. Segregated."

"So it wasn't that your parents wanted you to date other girls? They don't want you to date a White girl?"

Robert tapped his long fingers over his lips. "I dunno. They seemed fine wid it for a while. Then they freaked out about Leon and thought we might get too close. I may have to convince them we's just friends." Robert continued looking at his notes. "One of the things my parents said was that you and I could have fun together, but never truly understand each other. And I realized we've never talked about our differences."

"I didn't think we had a lot of differences. I considered you exactly like my White friends. You're still talking about race?" she asked.

"Race, culture, religion, history. It all runs together. We never talk about anythin' important. Even the night when the cops pulled me over. We talked about those two cops were wrong to do dat. But what about police in general? You realize they're trained, they're conditioned to look at Black people as much more likely to commit crimes? I'll bet police cars go down my street at least four times as often as they do your street. Jus' looking to see who be out of line."

"I've never heard you talk like this." Debbie bit her lip.

"I know. And maybe I ain't been real enough wid you. I was tryin' to impress you, to get you to like me. But talkin' to my dad, even wid my brudders, it made me see the problem with datin' a White girl is you have to explain how your life is impacted. Black girls know all dat, they see it as clear as Black guys. It has been shoved down their throats all their lives."

"I don't understand," Debbie shifted in her chair.

"I know you don't. Dat's my point." Robert glanced skyward. "Try one easy example. Whaddaya think God looks like?"

"God? I told you I don't go to church. But I guess I've always pictured God with long white hair and maybe a white beard. Sort of like Jesus with a long white robe. Maybe like the painting on the ceiling in the Vatican."

"The Sistine Chapel, Michelangelo? You think God is White?"

Her brows shot up. "Well, sure."

"What if I said he was a Black Jew? The Bible supports this theory. You go back into Jesus' family tree and there were lotsa Black folks. But somewhere along the way, he was depicted with wavy dark blonde hair and blue eyes and that image stuck. So, if Jesus was Black, it follows God's also Black. Son of God created in His own image and all."

"You believe that? Does your church believe that? You have pictures of Jesus with dark skin?" Debbie didn't know whether she was fascinated or horrified.

He laughed. "No. All of the pictures are the same as you see all over America. Even Black people were taught to worship a White Jesus, a White God. But that just tells everybody that White people are superior. Holy. Destined to be in charge. It's all a crock."

"Are you accusing me of being prejudiced?" Debbie blinked rapidly.

"I'm sayin' everyone is prejudiced. America needs to wake up and examine its own culture and institutions. Dis is so pervasive, it's hard to know where to begin. You were raised on the same kind of propaganda I was. Dis is the way White people were and dis is the way Black people were. The difference is dat you've been taught to reinforce the stereotypes while I was taught to avoid being a victim. I don't know if we can get across a divide like dat."

Debbie shook her head. "This all sounds like theory or politics. It doesn't much matter if none of our parents will allow us to date each other anyway."

"I may have found a way to change my parents' minds. And possibly your parents as well," Robert said. He pulled out a printed brochure from his bag and handed it to her.

"My father is takin' Wayne and me to this seminar in Chicago over Christmas break. It teaches about community organizing and how to bring White and Black volunteers together. Dad is attendin' too, as a pastor. So, I think he'll be open-minded to havin' you participate in some discussions once we start our work back home."

Debbie pressed one knuckle to her lips. "But you don't want to go out with me?"

He took her hand, glancing around to see if others were observing them. "Yeah, I do. But I think this is goin' to help if we're going to have a future together. Whatchew thinking?"

"I'm still trying to picture God being Black. Does he have an Afro?"

Robert laughed. "I never pictured God with an Afro. But I did talk to my dad about having you attend a church service sometime. He said it'd be okay, as long as we're not datin' anymore."

"Now you want me to go to your church? After all of this? I don't know if I could clear it with my parents. Maybe if I went with one of my friends or Daniel. I'll have to think about how to make that work."

CHAPTER TWENTY-TWO

Debbie and Daniel walked into the sanctuary at Northern Baptist Church looking around. She clutched her small purse fiercely like a talisman. Debbie had convinced her parents to let them come as an experiment in social awareness. Debbie promised to write a paper on it for her civics class, how it felt to be in a minority. She wanted Daniel's impressions too, and he said it was better for him to go than for her to go alone.

Although Robert had issued an open invitation, she hadn't gotten word to him they were coming on this specific Sunday morning. They arrived early enough to sit in the middle of the large sanctuary. She immediately began looking for Robert or his brothers and mother. She'd only met his family members once several months ago, and she wasn't sure how they'd react to seeing her since they thought she wasn't dating Robert.

"Do you see Robert?" she asked her brother.

"Are we looking for Robert? I've only met him a few times, I'm not sure I'd spot him. We're probably the ones who stand out."

She saw a woman sitting near the front who looked like Thelma from the back, but only one son was sitting with her. She realized it was very hard to distinguish them from the other church members, everyone looked so similar from the back. Many of the women wore hats. And almost everyone was Black. Some people had light complexions so she wasn't sure, but their hair made her think they were Black. And there were a few long-haired young White couples, and older White couples.

Right before the service, Reverend Washington entered the raised altar area from a room to the side. Then about twenty choir members followed in purple robes. Debbie spotted Robert and Truman in the choir. As soon as he sat, he spotted her face when he looked out at the pews. She was wearing the blue sweater she wore to his homecoming dance. He broke into a wide grin. She wondered how many other girls in the congregation thought that dazzling smile was meant for them.

"Isn't that Robert in the choir?" Daniel asked. She saw her brother studying her. It would be hard to hide her feelings.

"Yes, I think so," she said casually. "It looks like his younger brother next to him. I didn't even know he could sing."

"Hmmm. When was the last time you saw Robert?" Daniel squinted at her.

"Oh, Gee. It's been a while. I think Mom and Dad told me not to date him right after homecoming. When was that, October sometime?" She chose her words carefully, not wanting to lie in church. That Black Jesus might strike her down in her pew.

"But you talked to him about this community organization he's working on?"

"Oh, I've spoken to him on the phone, sure. I think he said the community outreach program might start in January. I think Mom and Dad are okay with me going. You could probably come if you wanted to."

They were caught up in trying to follow the church service. A family next to them helped them find the attendance card to pass along. Once the service was underway, the other congregants stopped looking at them.

Debbie startled the first time someone in the pews shouted. Members of the congregation waved their hands up and said, "Praise Jesus!" or "Amen!" Around them, people were clapping and nodding. Debbie and Daniel tried to copy the others.

Reverend Washington began to pray, but when he started singing the prayer. Debbie looked at Daniel wide-eyed. *What's going on?* One-by-one people stood up and started swaying.

"Thank you, Jesus, thank you, Lord," Reverend Washington began. "Thank you for giving me this day to come and share with my congregation. Thank you for staying with me every step of the way. Much obliged, Sir. I am grateful for the times you kept me in my right mind despite the challenges of the day. Thank you for the clothes on my back and the roof over my head, the food on my table. Thank you for being my burden bearer, for shielding me, for lifting me. Thank you for our families who can come together today and worship. Thank you for giving us that sweet baby Jesus that he could come and save us all."

By this time, the entire congregation was on its feet, as Reverend Washington seemed to be getting more passionate about his message. This was not like Yvonne's church. The emotion filled the air.

The choir performance was more animated than she expected too. She slapped her hand to her mouth to suppress laughter when Robert and Truman started swaying and clapping to the music they were singing. They didn't have music books in front of them, they must have memorized the song. *Boy, this church has a lot of energy!*

"Please come downstairs for coffee and cookies after the service. Are you new in the neighborhood?" The lady sitting in their pew asked when the service ended.

"Oh, no. We don't live around here. We're just visiting." Daniel shook her hand. "My sister wanted to come to see this church after meeting the Washingtons. It's quite something!"

"We like it," the lady said. "I hope you'll come back."

Debbie smiled at her. How would she ever find Robert in the basement? They'd have to follow the crowd.

Debbie felt the weight of people's stares when they were waiting on the stairway surrounded by the church members. She swiped her sweaty palms on her skirt more than once. The minister was greeting the faithful at the bottom of the stairs.

Would Reverend Washington recognize her or even be happy to see her if he'd told Robert to date other girls? To make matters worse, Thelma was standing right behind her husband.

Thelma spoke up first with twinkling eyes. "Debbie, how nice to see you at church. Donovan, you remember Debbie, dat nice White girl who came by selling encyclopedias?"

Donovan let out one of his booming laughs. "Of course, Robert's friend. Looks like you already got yo'self another beau."

Debbie was sure her face was bright red by then, as Reverend Washington held her hand. "Oh no. This is my twin brother, Daniel Adams. Daniel, this is Donovan and Thelma Washington, Robert's parents."

"When did you try to sell encyclopedias?" Daniel asked when they had gotten past the minister and his wife.

Debbie started to explain the inside joke, but then she spotted Robert. He must have put his choir robe away and he and Truman were holding court among a bevy of teenage girls. They all seemed to be hanging on his every word, and he looked to be enjoying their admiration. When he saw her, he smiled and beckoned them over.

"Hey, you made it," he said offhandedly. "Daniel, how you doing, Brudder?" Robert offered his hand to Daniel, and he shook it. "Oh, Daniel, this here's my brudder, Truman. He's a sophomore." Daniel shook Truman's hand too.

Robert slipped his hand around Debbie's back. "Debbie, we've got a lot of girls here today. Don't know where the guys are, maybe stayed home to watch football. But these girls are Tamira, Latoya, Deneice, Velinda, Nisha, Ronnell, and JaVonda. Wayne and Nina are running around somewhere, probably getting something to eat."

Daniel introduced himself to each of the young women. Debbie wasn't sure how his girlfriend, Andrea, would like the way he was lavishing attention on them, but the girls were easily distracted.

"How did you like the service?" Robert said, leaning in to try to have a private conversation.

"It was very uplifting. Almost emotional. People seemed to be into it." Debbie glanced around at the roomful of congregants.

"Might be a little hard to get used to the "praise" part. You need to let the spirit move you. Let yo'self go. You know how to do that, doncha, Baby?"

The look he gave her made her blush again. She couldn't believe he'd say that in church. "Um, I dunno. I might have forgotten."

"I guess we'll have to work on it then, won't we? Maybe I can get you to say 'Amen' if you get excited." Robert glanced around, then pulled her into one of the rooms on the outer edge of the large assembly area. When no one seemed to notice, he pulled her behind the door and kissed her.

That Black Jesus is definitely coming after me now. But she smiled.

"Can you meet me at King's at three this afternoon? I need to talk to you," Robert said.

"All right. But I have a lot of homework to finish."

Robert was already drinking hot chocolate when she slid across the table from him in the booth at King's.

"I think I got dis plan worked out. Found me the perfect girlfriend." Robert grinned with a gleam in his eye.

"I thought I was your perfect girlfriend," Debbie squinted at him.

"No, I mean the perfect fake girlfriend. Her name's Gianna. She's in my class and she's dating an older guy. I think he's twenty. And he's White. Her parents don't want her to go out wid him cuz he's older. Gianna is Mexican and Black, I think. She's very pretty. I can pick up Gianna and Sam will pick you up and then we can switch."

"You think that'll work? Will Sam call me, or will you?" She picked up the phone in the booth ordering a vanilla Pepsi.

"I dunno, maybe both. Your parents won't mind you dating Sam, will they?"

"I guess I'd have to meet him."

"He's right over there." Robert pointed to a young man with long hair pulled back into a tail, working the line assembling food at the restaurant. He was wearing a paper soda jerk hat to keep his hair neat, a white King's shirt, and a green apron.

Debbie shrugged. "He looks harmless enough. At least I know he has a job."

After a few moments, Sam looked up and saw Debbie had arrived. He hollered something at his manager, then appeared at their table with her drink.

"Debbie, this's Sam Swenson. This's my girlfriend, Debbie Adams." Robert skated his hand across the table to claim Debbie's.

Sam smiled at Debbie. He was tall and had broad shoulders and a slight growth of beard that made him look more mature than boys her age. She might have trouble remembering he was the decoy.

"N-nice to meet you, Debbie," he said. "Why don' chew give me your fa-fa-phone number?"

"Sure," she said, writing it on a paper napkin for him.

"I better get back to—" Sam gestured toward the kitchen with his head, then returned to his post.

"He doesn't talk very much," Robert said. "I don't think Gianna minds."

Debbie raised her brows. He was probably right.

CHAPTER TWENTY-THREE

The plan worked like clockwork. The following Friday night, Sam Swenson came to pick up Debbie to go to a play at Lincoln High School. He had graduated from that school two years earlier, and Debbie asked him to try to dress as he did in high school.

When she opened the door, he was wearing his LHS letterman's jacket. It did look a little snug. He was clean-shaven and his hair hung loose past his shoulders.

After Debbie introduced him to her parents, Bernard asked, "What did you letter in?"

Sam looked at his jacket, as though he'd forgotten. "Fa-football. Um, and b-b-basketball."

"Basketball season is going on. Don't you have a game tonight?" Bernard said.

"Oh, yeah. I played basketball last year," Sam scratched his face. "But I had an injury last m-month, so I can't play now."

"Oh, how sad. Were you injured playing football?" Bonnie asked.

Debbie watched Sam's eyes glaze over and he stuffed his hands in his pockets. "Sam, I think we'd better get going if we're going to be there in time for the start of the play."

She hustled him out the door, and they got into his Plymouth Barracuda.

"Y-y-your parents are scary," he chuckled.

"Oh, they can be. You don't want to know."

Nearly every Saturday night, Sam picked Debbie up and they met Robert and Gianna a few blocks from Debbie's house, and switched dates.

A few weeks after Debbie brought Sam home, her father was

reading the prep sports section of the newspaper when she came into the kitchen for breakfast.

"I see Lincoln High's doing well in basketball," Bernard said.

"Yeah, I guess. Northeast is the team to beat," Debbie said as if she knew something about sports.

"You know, Kitten, they list the players on the teams in the paper." Bernard studied her face.

"They do?" Debbie hoped her hand wasn't trembling as she poured milk on her cereal.

"I haven't seen Sam's name. It is Swenson, right?"

"I think he might still be on the injured list. He may've been dropped from the team," Debbie improvised. "I think he's embarrassed to talk about it."

"It seems like it would be obvious if he was playing basketball." He folded the paper he'd been reading. "All those practices and they usually have two games a week."

"That's why I think he was dropped. I know he works at King's quite a bit. I don't know how he has time to do it all," Debbie let out an exaggerated sigh.

"Well, you need to have an honest relationship. He might be embarrassed, but whatever it is, he should tell you the truth," Bernard sipped his coffee.

Debbie stirred the milk around in her bowl, not wanting to look at her father.

Bernard mused, "He doesn't look like a basketball player, more like a hippie. He's not one of those pot smokers, is he?"

"Huh? Oh, I don't think so. He doesn't smell like pot. He smokes normal cigarettes though. I have smoked with him," she added hastily, not sure if that was helping.

After talking to Sam, Debbie announced to her parents Sam had quit the basketball team. "He said he wasn't playing because of his injury then when he was cleared to play, he wasn't playing as well, so he was benched. He decided he'd rather work and be paid." Her parents accepted this explanation.

Debbie and Robert had another narrow escape in January. Robert had been bringing Debbie home, but they usually didn't park in the driveway. They parked on the street so his car wasn't visible from her parents' bedroom window. They were kissing goodnight in the Buick when Daniel drove past them coming home from his date with Andrea.

Daniel parked in the driveway, got out of his Fury, and walked back to where Robert was parked. Fortunately, Debbie saw him coming.

"Let me talk to him," Debbie told Robert. They didn't have time to get their stories straight. She opened the passenger door, then turned back around to speak to Robert as she got out. "Thank you for giving me a ride home, Robert. I appreciate it."

Robert pulled away from the curb and waved at Daniel like it was perfectly natural he was there.

Daniel scrutinized his sister. "What was that all about?"

Debbie jerked a shoulder and hurried toward the house. "Sam's car battery died. We were all at King's and Robert saw we were having trouble in the parking lot. He offered to bring me home while Sam waited for someone to jump-start his car."

"And you were grateful?" Daniel smirked as he caught up with her.

"Yes, of course."

"So grateful you kissed him."

Debbie swallowed hard and pulled her collar tighter. "That was sort of an accident. He said he missed me and the kiss just sort of happened."

"I thought you were seeing Robert once a month at those community racial relations meetings."

"Yes, he's conducting the teen sessions. We don't have time to talk privately at those," Debbie said. She stood blocking the front door. She didn't want their parents to hear their conversation. "Daniel, forget what you saw. It isn't important. I am going with Sam. Robert has a new girlfriend too."

Daniel locked eyes with her and nodded. He pulled out his key and unlocked their door.

On most of their dates, Robert had taken Debbie to activities like movies, plays, or Keentime dances after basketball games. She was required to attend Capital's basketball games to play in her school pep band, so at least one of her weekend nights was taken. But when he drove to his father's church one Saturday night, she looked at him with raised brows.

"Why are we here? Is there a church event tonight? I don't see any cars in the lot." Debbie couldn't read his expression in the dim light.

"We have to be quiet. Come wid me, I have to go find da key to da manse." He closed the car door quietly and took a flashlight from the back seat. He opened the church with an antique-looking key, and they found his father's office using the flashlight. Robert went right to the oak desk in the center of the room and fished out a key marked "manse."

They retraced their steps and got back into the car after locking the church. Robert drove down an alley across from the church, parked behind a house, and pulled out the flashlight again.

"C'mon. Dis is it."

"This is what?" Debbie asked.

"Shhh!" he answered. "Don't talk 'til we inside." He reached into the backseat and pulled out a bed pillow and a rolled-up sleeping bag. He handed her the flashlight and pulled the key from his coat pocket. He stopped and appeared to be listening to the neighborhood sounds.

Debbie winced as the porch steps creaked leading to the back door. Robert fumbled the key but managed to enter the house. It was in the middle of some sort of renovation. The kitchen cabinets were missing, and so was the stove. It looked like new drywall had been installed in the front two rooms. Debbie was used to being in houses that were under construction since her father was a builder. Bernard had even tried to teach her how to frame walls the previous summer.

Robert took a deep breath. "Dis's da manse. The church owns it and da minister and his family are supposed to live here as part of da salary. But there are only three bedrooms in dis house, and it was too small for us when all six kids were home. So, the church rents it for income. Right now, dere's a crew remodeling it, so no one's living in it."

He looked around until he found a space heater and turned it on. He put the heater in front of an old couch that had been left there. The only other places to sit were on drywall mud buckets. "It isn't fancy, but it's private."

Debbie's eyes darted from Robert's face to survey the room. She ran her tongue over her teeth. Someone might see Robert's car, even though it was off the street. They hadn't turned any lights on, but maybe the glow from the space heater could be seen from outside. Those sagging window shades and busted blinds might not be enough to hide them.

Robert dropped onto the couch and drywall dust poofed into the air. He sneezed. "Careful, it's a lumpy one."

Debbie sat slowly and felt what he meant. She could almost see the springs trying to pop through the worn cushions. She pulled her coat around her tightly. "Doesn't this place have a furnace?"

"They might be replacing it. They're working during the day when the sun is shining so the space heater might be enough. Let me warm you up."

He started kissing her, and she had to admit things did heat up. She wasn't sure if the space heater began to handle the cold air or if it was the romantic sparks, but they took their coats and gloves off pretty quickly. The last time she felt like this—

Debbie pushed back to catch her breath. "Robert, what happened with Leon and Sally?"

He shook his head. "You wanna talk about Leon? Now?"

She nodded.

"Well, they're having a kid," he said. "I guess Sally's about four months, maybe five months along. You can't tell, she so skinny."

"Are they married?"

"Married? Leon? Ha. No, I don' think they're gettin' hitched. Dey still in school, though I guess Sally will drop out. My mom has calmed down some about it. Not giving me the third degree every time I go out. She thought I was dating Gianna too much too, so now I have to tell her I am goin' out with one of the girls from church. I dunno what's gonna happen if she compares notes wid' dere mamas."

"I don't know why this has to be so hard. I wish we could date openly." Debbie pressed her lips flat.

"I dunno, Baby. I guess da world's against us. We jus' need to make each other happy." He pulled her back into a kiss, and tried to lay her down on the couch, but it wasn't comfortable, and had drywall dust on it. "Do you want to try the sleeping bag instead?" he asked.

When she didn't answer he unrolled and unzipped the sleeping bag. After slipping off his shoes, he put the pillow at the top and crawled into it, like they were at a slumber party. She'd never shared a sleeping bag before. Once she got in, and he zipped it partway up, their body heat seemed to ward off the cold air. And when she couldn't see what he was doing, she didn't mind so much that clothing was being discarded. It was comical trying to get undressed in the confines of the sleeping bag as their elbows and knees were destined to clash.

"Robert?"

"Yeah, Baby."

"Did you lock the door after we came in?"

He scoffed. "I ain't getting' outta here now! It is too cozy. You worried, you go check."

That first night in the manse, getting cozy was as far as they got. But on each subsequent visit, it was apparent Robert was planning to push the boundaries a little further. Still, Debbie was confident Robert had heard enough about the consequences Leon and Sally were facing, and he'd resist going all the way.

CHAPTER TWENTY-FOUR

Donald couldn't fool Robert. It was plain his big brother had changed his tune. Last summer he'd made Robert cringe talking about how many eager nursing students had developed a serious case of jungle fever. Donald seemed to have a rolling clinic in the back of his Buick Riviera to treat their obsession. Robert thought he should spray disinfectant on the seats every time he used the car.

But that had all changed. Donald was no longer playing the field. There only seemed to be one girl for Donald: Darla. Whatever Darla had; Donald wanted it. He was in love. Robert was amused.

"Guess what I'm getting Darla for Valentine's?" Donald said as he was shaping his hair in the bathroom mirror.

"Whatchew getting Darla?" Robert asked. Buying gifts for girls was a new dilemma. He'd bought Debbie a pair of mittens for Christmas, he figured a girl couldn't have too many mittens in Nebraska.

"Valentine's Day, you gotta turn it up. Serious romance, man. I got this giant heart-shaped box of chocolates and two dozen red roses. Roses cost a fortune this time of year. She sure is worth it though."

"That must be expensive." Robert frowned as their eyes met in the mirror.

"I'm a grown man now. Twenty years old. Darla twenty-one. What else should I spend my hard-earned dough on if not my queen?" He winked. "You's lucky I has to work Friday night so you can have the car. We be doing our own Valentine celebration a day early."

Robert's stomach lurched. He had less than a week to pull off something impressive or he'd totally fail as a boyfriend. The way he and Debbie had been getting closer, she probably expected something grand. No idea what that might be.

"Gianna, what should I get Debbie for Valentine's Day?" he asked his fake girlfriend a week before the big day. "I want to get something she'll like, but I can't spend much money."

"Jewelry is the best bet. Flowers or candy won't last. But if you find something you can afford at one of the jewelry stores, or even Kresge's or Wards, she'll be over the moon." Gianna gave him a friendly pat on the shoulder.

Robert dragged Leon to several inexpensive jewelry stores with him. He figured Leon owed Sally something major for Valentine's Day since she was having his kid.

"Can I see that one?" he asked the saleswoman.

She laid out a shimmering silver necklace with a filigree heart. The price was affordable.

Robert looked at Leon, who shrugged non-committedly.

"I'll take it." Robert pulled out some bills.

Debbie will love this. She can wear it even though she's pretending we're not dating.

Robert had planned to take Debbie to her school's Sweetheart Dance at the Cornhusker Hotel. They were using their usual routine of having Sam pick up Debbie. Robert told his parents he was going to shoot pool with Leon that night. Three days before the dance, Gianna told Robert she and Sam had a fight, and they wouldn't be going out on Valentine's Day. No Sam and Gianna meant Sam wasn't picking up Debbie.

Robert called Yvonne after school from a payphone. "Yvonne, you've gotta help us work this out. You know Sam has been picking up Debbie for our dates. He was supposed to pick her up for the dance on Friday but now he can't. Gianna said they may have broken up. Is there any way you can bring Debbie to the dance?"

Yvonne didn't answer for a moment. "Doesn't Debbie need a boy to pick her up like a date? I mean I suppose Randy could do that, and you could pick me up but we do live right next door. It seems like one of our parents would think this was fishy."

"I don't know who else to ask. Can you get a message to Debbie telling her to find another guy to get her to the dance? We had this nice evening planned. I hate to ruin it."

There was only one other thing bothering Robert, and he figured his skirt-chasing big brother could help him. And Donald would never be the wiser. When Donald was at work, Robert searched his room. *If I were Donald, where would I hide my rubbers?* As it turned out, not in any of his drawers, the closet, under the bed, not even in his shoes.

Robert scratched his head. Time to check more devious hiding places. Under the mattress, he found a couple of issues of *Playboy* and *Penthouse.* That slowed down the search. He found some weed taped under the surface of the desk. But still no rubbers. He thought he could count on Donald.

The night of the Sweetheart Dance, he paced the lobby of the hotel. He was dressed in his suit, and one elderly lady tapped his arm, apparently mistaking him for a bellboy.

"I'm sorry, ma'am. I don't work for the hotel. I am waiting

for someone."

The White woman squinted at him as though he was joking.

"Look, here's a luggage cart, let's get your things on here. Maybe one of the staff can help you from there." He lifted the woman's luggage onto the cart before a man in his forties appeared, who seemed to be her son.

"Henry, this boy doesn't want to help us to the room," she complained. The man winked at Robert and rolled the cart toward the elevator.

"Looks like you're hitting on older women now," Debbie said when he turned back toward the door. "I guess I'd better not be late again."

Robert beamed at her. "Boy, am I glad to see you. Happy Valentine's Day, Baby." He took her hand and they went up the stairs to the ballroom.

"Nancy wasn't happy when she got into Peter's car and saw me in the back seat," Debbie said. "For a minute, I thought she was going to refuse to come with us, or somehow blow the whistle on us." They hung up their coats and began walking toward the dance floor. "I don't know if she thought Peter was dating me or what she was so angry about."

"Maybe you'll have to show her you only have eyes for me." He pulled her onto the dance floor laughing as the band started singing "I Only Have Eyes for You" as recorded by the Flamingos. Debbie was wearing that figure-hugging red dress she had worn to her homecoming. He had to give her credit that she had become much better at swiveling her hips to the music under his coaching. But damn! She must've been practicing on her own because she was making his heart race and they were just getting started. He was afraid to look around and see how many other boys were eyeing her.

Robert took a deep calming breath when Randy and Yvonne approached.

"Why is it I only see you at dances, Robert?" Randy asked.

"It's the only time they let me outta the house," Robert quipped. "I guess I am good for something."

The band played some faster songs and they danced to those. But the theme of the night was romance, and there were more slow-paced songs than normal. When Robert pulled Debbie in close it seemed like the heat was radiating off her reminding him of the space heater. He wasn't sure how much time they should waste at the dance when he knew they could be skin sliding over skin in the sleeping bag. It was getting harder to ignore his desire.

"Debbie, how long do you want to stay at this dance?" he said softly in her ear.

"Hmmm. I dunno. Did you have something else in mind for Valentine's Day?" She smiled as he nuzzled her.

"I wanna be alone wid you." Debbie didn't object when he pulled her back toward the cloakroom. "Wave goodbye to your friends."

Once they arrived at the manse, they turned on the transistor radio the renovation crew had left. They slow-danced while they waited for the heater to warm the room. The night was balmy for February, and it didn't take long. Robert could feel Debbie's pounding pulse in her neck when he planted soft kisses there. Her breath hitched when he took her mouth possessively sliding his tongue over hers. The flowery cologne she wore made his mind spin. This would definitely be off-limits at a school dance. Thank God, no chaperones to stop them here.

Can't rush it though. During the second song, he unzipped Debbie's dress. He put his suit jacket, tie, and her dress on a plastic bag he brought with him. He'd never seen her wearing a girdle. He supposed she'd mostly worn slacks on their dates. But something about those garters and black stockings made his heart flutter. Maybe it was the thought of undoing them very slowly, one at a time.

"Oh, I almost forgot to give you your Valentine's gift." Robert pulled back and reached into his suit jacket on the couch. He pulled out a small box tied with a red ribbon.

Debbie's eyes lit up. "I wasn't expecting this." She sighed when she pulled off the lid and picked up the delicate silver pendant. "Oh, Robert. I love it! I love you." She put her arms around his neck and kissed him before he could put the necklace on her. Working his clumsy fingers on the tiny clasp, he managed to drape it around her neck.

The heat she'd poured into that kiss told him all he needed to know. Her reservations had faded away. They didn't have to hold back anymore. It was time to get busy.

"I don't have a gift for you," she murmured into his neck.

"I think you do. If you're sure." He trailed his lips from her neck to her shoulder pushing her straps down as he went. "I love you too, Baby,"

He'd unzipped the sleeping bag all the way so it was twice as wide. He wished he'd thought to bring another blanket to cover them. But he wanted to be the only thing covering Debbie tonight. The rest of their clothes came off in a flurry. So much for undoing those sexy garters.

Robert furrowed his brow. He was still working this out in his mind. He'd fantasized, sure. But nothing beat systematic directions. For a guy who always wanted a schematic or a blueprint, this was flying blind. God, couldn't he have cracked an anatomy book before trying this? He wouldn't have attempted to play a chess match without more preparation. He understood how male and female parts interfaced when they were talking about connectors and receptacles. This was going to be a trial run.

Later when they were breathless on the sleeping bag, he wasn't sure he knew how they had gotten there. Neither one of them had any expertise at this, after all. But it had happened, he knew that much for sure. Somehow in the throbbing hot slippery jumble of bodies and intentions, he'd managed to reach the target. They'd overcome their nerves and started following their instincts.

He turned on his side to look at Debbie. Her ivory skin glistened as she lay naked beside him. The heart necklace shone in the light streaming in from the window caressing her throat and breasts. "I guess this's one Valentine's Day we won't forget. I can't even describe how beautiful you look."

She smiled. He wrapped the sleeping bag around them like a burrito and snuggled close.

"Robert, wake up! What time is it?" Debbie sounded frantic. She was already yanking up that girdle and rolling on her stockings.

He sat up and blinked. He hadn't taken off his watch, just everything else. Jesus, it was twelve-thirty. Her curfew was midnight. He was supposed to pick Donald up from the hospital at twelve forty-five. He scrambled to his feet and began throwing on his clothes.

When he saw the flashing red and blue police lights, he groaned. He didn't think he was speeding, although he certainly was close to it. They didn't have time to go through a song-and-dance of police harassment right then. Debbie automatically scooted to the passenger side of the front seat as he pulled to the curb. They stopped on an incline but he thought it was still safe.

He rolled down his window and put his hands on the steering wheel as the policeman approached.

"License and registration, please," Officer Kenneth Dodd said, shining his flashlight in on both of them.

Robert let out a sigh of relief. He leaned over to the glove compartment in front of Debbie and popped the lid open. He couldn't believe his eyes when a large box of Trojans flew out and landed in Debbie's lap. He knew Donald had some! Why hadn't he checked the car? He fished out the registration paper and handed it to the officer, then pulled out his wallet and gave him his driver's license. Robert gripped the steering wheel to keep his hands still. *Jeez, dis ain't awkward.*

Officer Dodd was clearly trying to suppress his laughter. Debbie had covered her mouth with her hands but seemed incapable of touching the box of condoms.

"It looks like you had more fun on Valentine's Day than I did." Officer Dodd grinned, handing Robert back his paperwork. "Your left taillight is out, that's why I stopped you. I'm not going to give you a warning tonight, but you get it fixed right away, Young Man."

"Yes, sir. Thank you, sir." Robert said. He could hardly believe the difference in how this cop had treated them. He turned to Debbie and shoved the registration and box of condoms back into the glove compartment. "Donald," he said as if that was all the explanation she needed.

When they approached Debbie's house, they could see lights on inside. It was twelve-fifty by then, she was almost an hour late. "Do you want me to go talk to them wid you?" Robert asked.

"You can't. They think I am out with Peter Thompson. Since Nancy got so upset about him picking me up, I guess I can say I got into a fight with Peter. He probably won't be able to pick me up again anyway."

"I hate all this lying, Debbie. Let's come clean with them," Robert said, not sure where that had come from.

"Oh, yeah. Mom and Dad, I was with Robert against your orders. We had sex and fell asleep. Sorry." She shook her head. "I'll probably be grounded for a week or so as it is. I'll ask Yvonne to call you."

He winced as he watched her walk toward the house. But he had to go try to find Donald outside the hospital and face his tirade for being late.

CHAPTER TWENTY-FIVE

Debbie had been grounded for two weeks for breaking curfew. She had only been allowed to go to school, basketball games, and to babysit for a neighbor. The babysitting gig allowed her to talk to Robert over the phone at least. During the two-week period, Sam and Gianna had patched things up, and Sam was once again available to pick Debbie up for dates.

Linda came over to hang out with Debbie one Saturday afternoon in April. They were sitting on Debbie's bed. "Have you been able to see Robert lately, Debs?"

Debbie felt more comfortable confiding in Linda. If she told Yvonne she'd lost her virginity, she was afraid she wouldn't be as understanding. "We've been seeing each other, but most of the time we go to this house his church owns. They're renovating it, but I think it will be finished by May. Then I don't know what we'll do."

"You need to get an apartment like Tom," Linda said. "Then you have complete privacy."

"Your parents let you go to Tom's apartment?" Debbie's eyes widened.

"I haven't mentioned it, but they know he lives in one," she smirked. "Of course, he had a roommate. My parents don't know the roommate moved out in January." Linda moved closer to look Debbie in the eyes. "So you and Robert, are you saying you . . . ?"

"Yeah. The first time was on Valentine's Day. It was romantic, sort of. But awkward. We didn't know what we were doing. There was a lot of fumbling that first night," she said. "But since then, it has gotten easier. He is always asking me if I like it when he does this or that. He says quality improvement is important in everything. He cracks me up."

"I think that sounds sweet, in a scientific sort of way. I wish Tom would be a little more sensitive. He seems to think I should tell him if I want him to change anything."

"So, you and Tom are um, doing that too?"

"You mean sex. Yes. But he isn't the first guy I've been with."

"Really? Who was the first?"

Linda sighed and hugged Debbie's study pillow to her chest. "The first time wasn't so great. Last summer. Not someone you know. I'll tell you about it sometime. It's better with Tom. He's had some experience at least. So, changing the subject, is Yvonne coming over to talk about the twirler auditions?"

"Yeah, let me call her."

"Robert, we need to talk about prom." They were sharing a milkshake at King's.

"I said I'd take you to prom, no problem. I even reserved my tux yesterday. Did you change your mind?" He studied her.

"Oh no. I'm all set. My mom bought me a dress where she works. But I think there could be a problem with Sam picking me up."

"He knows he doesn't actually have to go to the prom," Robert said. "We'll meet somewhere and switch."

"But he would have to look like he's going to the prom. He'd need formal wear."

"Oh. I didn't think of that. I don't think I would want him wearing my tux first, that'd be kind of gross. Besides, I think he's still larger, although I have gained fifteen pounds since September."

She brushed her hand across his hair, which was getting bushier. "I think you've grown a little taller too. Hard to tell with this Afro." Debbie smiled, "I've lost ten pounds since February." I started walking around the school halls or outside to get some exercise. I guess it helped. Plus, my stomach has been kinda blah lately. I can't eat much."

"Have you asked Sam about this problem? Maybe he has a suit he can wear." Robert took a sip from his straw, draining the milkshake glass.

"I have another idea. I want to ask my parents if I can go to prom with you."

"Why would they change their minds now?"

"Well, they let me go to your church once. They let me go to the community racial relations sessions, and they knew you'd be there. They know we've spoken on the phone sometimes. I think it is worth asking."

"Won't they expect Sam to take you? Don't they think he's your boyfriend?"

"The thing is, he doesn't act like my boyfriend, he acts like my friend. And Lord knows, he has been a great friend to keep doing this pretense. But we never get cozy or flirty or anything around my parents, so I think they know we aren't in love."

"Well, he'd better not be acting flirty or cozy around you," Robert narrowed his eyes.

"But if they agree we can go to prom that opens the door for dating again. And we'll soon be graduating and I'll be eighteen in August. I think they might start giving me more leeway. They're letting my brother go to Kansas for school. He'll be able to do whatever he wants."

"You think they'll go along with this?"

"Only one way to find out."

Debbie decided the best course of action was to be bold, so she broached the subject that evening at dinner, hoping Daniel might be on her side. "Mom and Dad, I decided I want to go to prom with Robert instead of Sam. Robert asked me a few weeks ago. He said he has only been stopped by the police once since homecoming, and the cop was very professional. He had a broken tail-light on his car. The cop didn't even give him a warning. And he said he has met some influential people since he has been working on that racial progress thing. Like he knows the mayor and the chief of police now. I think he's in a better position than he was."

Bernard laughed. "He is hobnobbing with Mayor Schwarzkopf? He may be out of your league, Kitten."

Debbie furrowed her brow, "What's that mean?"

Bernard sighed, "Do you have any concerns, Bonnie?"

Bonnie pursed her lips. "You know one way you might avoid trouble is if you drove. You could take the Cadillac. If someone saw a White girl with a Black boy as a passenger, they might react differently."

Debbie's face lit up, "You're right. And that way we could take Yvonne and Gary with us. That might be even better."

"Yvonne's going to prom with Gary? Who's Gary?" Daniel scowled.

"Oh, you know. She went out with him last summer. He goes to Northeast." Daniel rolled his eyes. "Can I tell Robert it's okay then?"

"What about Sam? Won't he be heartbroken?" Bonnie raised one brow.

Debbie shrugged. "I think he'll be relieved. He's a little old for prom."

Bonnie and Bernard exchanged glances. Debbie's face turned red when she realized her mistake. "What I meant was, he's been to prom a few times and it's probably getting old. He was pretty popular last year."

"N-n-nobody likes him now?" Daniel teased.

"Daniel, that was mean. He only stutters when he's nervous. I hardly ever hear it," Debbie said. She knew that was because she was only around him for brief periods.

"I think you're old enough to decide who to go to prom with. At least you've dated several boys this year and haven't had any real disasters. As long as you aren't going with that Peter fellow. He can't tell time," Bernard chuckled.

"Oh, thank you, thank you!" Debbie jumped up and kissed Bernard and Bonnie both on the cheek, then ran to her room to use the phone. Her dinner was half-eaten.

CHAPTER TWENTY-SIX

Debbie caught herself dancing around her room. It was like she was in a scene from a movie, Cinderella waiting to put on her magical ball gown. She had a beautiful sleeveless yellow dress she was wearing for prom, and her Grandma Lake had loaned her long white gloves that came above her elbows. She had even lost a few more pounds so the dress hung loosely around her waist and hips. It was only tight in the bust, which surprised her because it fit fine a month ago. At least this dress wasn't as low-cut as the one she wore last year.

Her hair even looked nice. Yvonne and Debbie didn't get their hair done this year and were wearing it long and loose. What had she been thinking with that crazy updo last year? Tonight, she looked like herself. The best version of herself.

Yvonne had a lovely pink dress with a tulle overlay. Yvonne confessed she was nervous about dating Gary again since she hadn't seen him in months. But Debbie knew the night was going to be perfect.

When Robert rang the doorbell, Debbie had to calm the butterflies in her stomach. Maybe that was why she'd been nauseated the past few weeks, just nerves. She was humming "My Cherie Amour" by Stevie Wonder, but she didn't know all the words. She checked her hair one last time and pulled on the long elegant white cotton gloves.

Debbie clutched her hands to her chest when she locked eyes with Robert. She'd never seen him look more debonair in a white jacket and shirt with a yellow ruffled placket and black bow tie and pants. He even had a yellow pocket square. His face was nearly glowing as he was smiling from ear to ear. She was flat-out crazy for him. How was she supposed to hide that from her parents?

"Wow. I mean seriously, wowee!" Robert said. "Can't think of another word."

Debbie was pleased he was a little tongue-tied. She took a deep breath, "Robert, I am so glad you could make it. I haven't seen you for a little while. You look very nice."

Robert nodded catching her hint to be more formal. "Thank you, Miss Debbie. Shall we put the corsage on?"

After Yvonne and Gary arrived and endless photographs were taken, Debbie got them all into the Cadillac.

"You do look spectacular, Baby," Robert said when they were out of earshot of her folks. "Even this pretty yellow rose you're wearing can't outshine you. In fact, it might be cruel to show up at prom. All of the other girls will be jealous." He smiled, running the back of his hand down her bare arm until it reached the glove.

Debbie batted her thick eyelashes at him slowly. "Thank you. Now how am I supposed to drive with my dress down around my feet?" His brows winged up when she hiked her dress up to her knees.

They went to Linda's house for a pre-prom party. Robert had never been there. Before they even got through the front door beyond the pillared portico, his mouth had dropped open and his head was swiveling around to take it all in.

"You know someone who lives here? This ain't some damn movie set?" Robert took a deep breath, releasing it slowly as he surveyed the lavish setting.

Debbie laughed, "Yes, Linda Bridges lives here. You've met her. Looks like Twiggy. Her father runs an insurance company. Wait until you see the pool."

"Dey gotta pool? Of der own? Holy moly."

The party was on the deck surrounding the pool, and they munched on shrimp cocktail, pigs in a blanket, cheese puffs, and pizza bites. Linda had hung Japanese lanterns in tree branches around the pool area and candles were floating in the pool.

Debbie and Robert sat at one of several glass top tables, as Linda brought around "mock-tails" made with punch and ginger ale.

"I wish my Mama and Dad could see this." Robert eyes were still huge. "This must be what heaven looks like."

"I think this is how the other half lives," Gary laughed. "That must be Linda's folks over there by the bar. Her dad will probably frisk us when we leave to make sure we haven't pilfered anything."

Robert glanced to where Gary was looking at a tall middle-aged man with gray hair and a pretty brunette woman.

"No, they won't. Her folks are nice," Debbie said. "Her bedroom has antiques in it. And Linda puts cheap ashtrays and her Birkenstocks on what is probably a two-hundred-year-old coffee table."

Playing hostess, Linda circulated among the two dozen guests. Linda had told the other twirlers earlier in the week she thought she was pregnant, but she looked very slim in a dark navy gown. She must have been mistaken. In a few minutes, Linda came over to their table, holding out a fourteen-carat gold cigarette case to Debbie.

"Virginia Slims anyone?" she offered.

"You even dressed up your cigarettes for the occasion?" Debbie picked out a cigarette from the case.

"No Marlboro's?" Robert grinned.

"Hmmm, Tom might have one," Linda said.

"Kidding, I'm good," he said, pulling a pack from inside his jacket. He lit his and Debbie's. Tom Case, Linda's boyfriend, sat down with them to smoke after Yvonne and Gary went to take their empty plates to the kitchen.

"How do you like the patio, as Linda calls this?" Tom asked chuckling.

"I've never seen anything like it," Robert said. "I suppose you have a place like this."

"Oh no. I am a poor student trying to pay my college tuition," Tom said. "My folks have a ranch out west, but nothing like this. Our money is in livestock."

"I'll be in college next year. At least I should be able to save money living at home. It isn't far from campus." Robert rolled his ashes around the crystal ashtray on the table.

When they arrived at the prom, Debbie was still feeling the magic in the air. The theme this year was Starlit Nights and the cafeteria shone like the Milky Way between the twinkling white lights and the candlelit tables.

Both her brother, Daniel, and her best friend, Yvonne, had been nominated for prom royalty. She didn't have to wonder who to vote for. She wasn't sure what had changed since homecoming, but she didn't notice anyone scrutinizing her and Robert anymore. The chaperones ignored them, and the other kids seemed to be cool with her date. Maybe it was because they were seniors and about to graduate. They no longer had to prove anything to anyone in high school.

And none of their parents were around to object to their relationship. Robert barely let go of her hand all evening, and most of the time they owned the dance floor.

When he held her in his arms and she looked into his eyes, she knew she was lucky. She could talk to him about anything. They could laugh, share secrets, even in the most intimate ways she could imagine. Hardly anyone here has had that level of closeness. Oh sure, some of her classmates must have had sex, but so many of them treated it like a casual thing, a joke. It was special to Debbie and Robert.

Once when she came back from the restroom, she found Robert on the sidelines talking to Randy Spears. Randy stood several inches above most of the crowd and his carrot-top made him easy to identify. Randy and Yvonne had broken up on Valentine's Day. It was ironic considering she and Robert had gotten even closer that night. Randy had brought a junior girl to prom, Lauren James, but here he was talking to Robert while his date stood pouting watching her friends dance.

Debbie smiled broadly as she walked up to Randy's date as though they were old friends. "Lauren, you're looking fah-bulous, Dah-ling," Debbie said in her best Zsa Zsa Gabor voice, and linking her arm through Lauren's. "I love the dotted Swiss dress. Is Randy talking your ear off yet?"

Lauren rolled her eyes. "I wish. He hardly talks to me at all. I don't know why he invited me if he didn't want to get to know me."

"Have you asked him about basketball? Or baseball? He loves his Cardinals." Debbie stole a glance back to their dates.

"No, I don't like sports much." Lauren shook her head slowly and puckered her mouth.

"Well, you'll have fun cheerleading next year then," Debbie said under her breath. "How about cars? Randy helped my brother when he was working on his Fury." Lauren looked blank. "Ever played Fight in the Skies?"

"Sure. I used to beat my little brother all the time."

"There you go. Randy's a fanatic about that game. Ask him." With that, she patted Lauren's hand and walked over and took Robert's, dragging him back to the dance floor. When she looked back over Robert's shoulder, she saw Randy smiling talking to Lauren animatedly.

"What the heck was that all about?" Robert asked, pulling her in closer.

"I want everyone to be as happy together as you and me," she smiled.

After a few minutes, the president of the student council, Ed

Perkins, stood on stage announcing the prom royalty. Debbie and Daniel had known Eddie since they were children, and he was still one of her brother's pals.

Debbie thought she was hearing things when Ed said, "Our 1969 prom king is Daniel Adams."

Debbie and Robert were standing in front of the stage next to Yvonne and Gary. She exchanged shocked looks with Yvonne, then started cheering and clapping.

But Ed wasn't finished. "We have a tie for prom queen, Daniel. You have to decide the winner between Mitzi Mason and Yvonne Edison."

Debbie felt like she was frozen in place, along with Yvonne and Daniel. The rest of the group seemed to fade into the background. She looked at Daniel's face. He looked away, and sighed, then seemed to focus his gaze on Yvonne.

Come on, Brother. There's no question here. You have to pick Yvonne. I know how much you care about her, even though you won't admit it. Don't do something stupid because of your pride.

Debbie looked at Yvonne. The color was rising in her cheeks. Tears were forming in Yvonne's eyes. Debbie knew Yvonne so well; she saw how much she wanted him to pick her. Debbie could see it even if Daniel pretended not to.

It was like a thunderclap when she heard her brother, her own twin brother say, "I'll say Mitzi." Debbie's head whipped back to him.

How could you be so stupid? I thought you were such a smart guy? I know you're sweet on Yvonne. Now you blew it.

And poor Yvonne, she must be—but Yvonne was gone. Debbie looked where Yvonne had been and she wasn't there. She spotted her dashing out to the courtyard, with Gary on her heels. Debbie moved to follow Yvonne, but Robert grabbed her hand.

"She be okay. You should stay here. Watch your brudder." Robert pulled her back to where they had been in front of the stage. Debbie nodded. She'd almost forgotten Robert in the last couple of minutes. But he'd been watching out for her, watching the drama unfold in Debbie's eyes. She'd tried to be there for Daniel and Yvonne but Robert was there for her. She squeezed his hand and nodded again.

After Daniel danced with Mitzi, the rest of the crowd resumed dancing, including Robert and Debbie. About ten minutes later, Gary tapped Debbie on the shoulder.

"Have you seen Yvonne?" he asked.

Debbie looked around the dance floor. "No. Did you lose her?"

"I went to the john, and I haven't seen her since. It's been quite a while now."

Robert said in her ear, "I saw Daniel leave the cafeteria about five minutes ago."

Debbie scrutinized Robert, unsure what he was implying. Then her eyebrows shot up. "Um, Gary. Let's go outside."

Robert, Debbie, and Gary all went out to the courtyard. It didn't take Robert long to discover if they went around the corner of the building, kids were smoking.

"We could get kicked out," Debbie admonished when he lit up, leaning against the building.

"Prom is nearly over, ain't it?" Robert smiled. She took his cigarette and treated herself to a drag.

"Can I bum one?" Gary said.

Robert pulled his pack out again and Gary took a cigarette and the lighter from Robert.

"I didn't know you smoked, Gary." Debbie studied him for the first time that night. She supposed she'd been too busy looking at her date. Gary had gotten better-looking since she'd met him last summer. More mature, rugged maybe. Something darkened his expression.

"I only smoke when I'm stressed out. Like when my date ditches me in the middle of prom." He squinted at Debbie. "She's with your brother, isn't she?"

Debbie shrugged. "No one tells me anything." Then she smirked. "But I'll bet she'll wonder where you went when she comes back and can't find us. She might even think we left her here."

Gary scoffed and crushed the gravel under his shoe. "I bet she'll find a way home. Girls like Yvonne always do."

"Yep," Debbie agreed, taking Robert's cigarette again. "Sometimes I hate her too."

"That's no way to talk about your best friend," Robert folded his brows. He put out his cigarette as they made their way back indoors.   Gary   stayed   behind   to   finish   smoking and sulking.

"Maybe you're my best friend now," she said.

"Oh, I think we're much more than friends." He planted a quick kiss on the side of her head before they came into view of the chaperones. Robert steered her to the far side of the dance floor when they spotted Yvonne slip through the entrance door.

Prom ended fifteen minutes later. Yvonne had found Gary, but Debbie hadn't heard them speak to each other as they walked to the parking lot. There was a stony silence hovering over the backseat as Debbie drove back to her house. When she pulled into her driveway, Gary got out and went to his car without a word.

"I don't know what he's in a huff about," Yvonne said. "I told him I was talking to Daniel about why he didn't pick me for prom queen."

"Nothin' else? You and Daniel were talkin'?" Robert turned around to look at Yvonne.

She blushed and shook her head. "Not just talking."

"Then you know why he's pissed," Robert said.

Yvonne shrugged and got out of the car, "Thanks for the ride, Debs. See you, Robert."

Robert turned back to Debbie. "Whatchew grinnin' fer?"

Debbie put the keys in her bag. "Yvonne and Daniel. I have to be happy for them. They've been denying their feelings for a year. But I knew this day would come."

"Zat right, Miss Know-it-all? So, tell me, what're we gonna do now dat the manse is finished and the new renters are moving in?"

Debbie leaned her head back on the seat. "Try out that big backseat in the Buick your brother's always bragging about?"

CHAPTER TWENTY-SEVEN

Robert was surprised the next Friday afternoon when he and Donald drove up to their house and saw Debbie's VW parked on the street. When they approached the porch, they saw her sitting in the swing, and her eyes looked red. He and Donald both stalled facing her on the porch. Before Robert could speak, the front door opened, and Donovan stuck his head out.

"Debbie wanted to talk to you, Robert. Donald, your mother and I need to see you inside. Now."

Donald followed his father through the doorway, closing the door. Robert sat next to Debbie. She appeared to have been crying.

"What's wrong? Your parents crack down on you again?"

She shook her head. "I don't know how—I've been feeling nauseated for several weeks. I went to the doctor Monday." Debbie unfolded a letter from her lap. She took a deep breath. "Robert, I'm pregnant."

Robert felt a giant sinkhole opening under his feet and he was being sucked into a swirling vortex. His jaw dropped and he simply stared blankly at her. "No, dat can't be right," he croaked. He looked at the paper in her trembling hand which gave her pregnancy test results. "I got condoms. We used a condom last time." But he could read the results as clearly as she could. It said she should come in for an exam.

He furrowed his brows. Could this be real? Was this happening? "Couldn't it be a false alarm?"

She shook her head, "It's probably right. I've missed two periods."

He studied her letting his eyes drop slowly from her face to her lap. "You mighta mentioned dat before." He scraped his hand down his face. "Two? What zat mean in terms of—how many months or whatever?"

She shrugged but the tears overflowed her eyes. "I guess two already, two to three."

"But we figured dis wasn't very likely to happen. What 'bout all those married folks probably have sex every night, and don't have babies for years? We only did it 'bout six times, maybe seven." His breath was ragged. "If you're two months along, dat means it had to happen after only three times. How zat even possible?"

"I don't know. All I know is this!" Debbie shook the piece of paper in her hands. "Robert?" her voice dropped to a whisper. "What are we going to do?"

"God. I dunno. Can't think. You saying we having a baby." The last words were wedged behind the lump in his throat. He swallowed hard but that didn't help. "We need time—my brain doesn't seem to be workin' right now. I don't even think I can breathe."

She put her hand on the back of his head as he leaned forward putting his face in his hands. "I felt the same way when I opened this letter. As soon as I could drive, I came straight over here. Your mama tried to get me to come in and have some pie, but I just needed some air. I said I'd wait for you out here."

He sat back and looked in her eyes again, then pulled her into an embrace. She started crying softly, and he held her until she stopped. "Don't say nothin' to nobody. I'll call you tomorrow. We graduating in a coupla weeks. We can figger it out then."

He took Debbie out to her car and slowly staggered back to the porch. How did he get himself in this kinda trouble?

He heard raised voices from inside the house, so he went in. Donald was sitting on one end of the dining table, and his mother was seated at the opposite end. Donovan was standing pointing a finger at Donald.

"What's goin' on in here?" Robert asked.

"This don't concern you, Robert, go on up to your room,"

Thelma said.

But he hesitated. He needed a distraction right then in the worst way. And Donald was glaring at him.

Donovan simply ignored him and turned back to Donald, "Are you going to lie to my face and tell me you've never been in that house?"

"What house?" Robert asked.

Donovan grumbled. "I got a report today somebody has been breaking into the house the church owns across the street. It's been under renovation for six months. The first crew stopped working, had to get new workers. One of the neighbors kept seeing the same car parked in the alley at night, and they finally saw some people. They got a license number. Guess what? It was Donald's car! And he dares to deny it."

Robert clamped his mouth shut, but the words flew out. "It was me."

Three sets of brown eyes bored into his. For a moment, the silence hung in the air like a drifting leaf in the autumn breeze. Then the rage on Donovan's face rippled like molten lava down from the veins in his bald head. Thelma stood up and planted her arms on the table as though she might topple. Donald's smug smirk turned to a genuine smile as he shook his head assessing his younger brother.

Donovan's booming voice sounded more like a growl to Robert. "Donald, you may go now."

"No, Dad. I'll stay. You might need my help."

Donovan looked at Donald with pure fury.

"Who else gonna stop you from killin' him?" Donald said calmly. "Mama can't save him."

Donovan snarled, turning his roiling anger on his second son.

Robert closed his eyes. He'd heard his father and Donald go

many rounds. He thought Donald liked baiting his father sometimes. Robert had never wanted to. But he had to be honest now, no matter what the consequences.

"You've been going to the manse?" Donovan crossed his massive arms.

"Yes." He tried to keep looking at his father's face but he felt his pulse pounding all the way to his temples.

"How did you get the key?"

"I let myself into the church office and borrowed the key. Then we had one made."

"You had a key—" Donovan turned and paced back into the kitchen to try to calm down. Everyone held their breath. He came back and started again, "Have you been going to the manse with girls? Is that what you're saying?"

"Girls?" Robert winced. "No, not girls. Just Debbie."

"Debbie?" Thelma cried. "I thought you'd stopped seeing Debbie. I was surprised to see her today; it had been months. I thought you were dating Gianna."

Robert looked at the floor and shook his head. "No, I've only been dating Debbie."

"And why would you take Debbie to an empty house?" Donovan thundered, "There hasn't been any furniture in there. The heat wasn't even working."

God, they were going to make him spell it out? "I had a sleeping bag. There was a space heater."

Thelma strode over and put her face up right in front of his. He thought she was going to slap him. But the tortured expression on her face hurt more. And the lump in his throat was back big time.

"What in God's name do yo' have to say fo' yo'self, Robert Washington?" his mother's voice was raspy.

He was blinking back tears now. "There's more." He felt them all eviscerating him with their eyes. "She's pregnant."

Robert really hoped the neighbors didn't call the cops when they heard Thelma scream.

CHAPTER TWENTY-EIGHT

Debbie barely made it six blocks before she had to pull her Bug over on a side street because she started crying hysterically.

What had I expected? He was in shock. Heck, I'm still in shock.

She was sure the doctor's office would assure her she wasn't pregnant. Maybe a stomach bug. Of course, they should have used birth control. Once he found those rubbers in the car, she thought he'd want to use them. She didn't know much about birth control. She didn't want to make sex any more difficult. She'd gotten better at making herself relax and she wanted to please him.

She found a tissue in her purse and wiped her eyes in the rearview mirror. She'd wanted to go to a clinic. Wouldn't that have been more confidential? But she found out they had closed the county free clinic on February 1, a few months ago. Would the doctor's office be obliged to tell her parents since she was only seventeen? At least her mother hadn't opened her letter.

How will I ever break this news to my parents?

Her parents didn't even know she was dating Robert. Could they force her to have an abortion or give up the child? She wasn't going to let anyone else decide. Only Robert had a vote. He seemed as anguished and lost as she was. But he had a point. They should wait. Think about it and wait. But how could she hide her feelings? She couldn't.

She wrapped her arms around herself to try to stop the shaking.

Write it down. One of her teachers had talked to them about that. Connie Edison, Yvonne's mother, maybe, when she substituted for their health teacher. She said when you have an emotional decision to make, list the pros and cons, or the steps you have to take. That makes it feel more logical as if you have control. Then you can deal with it. She'd try.

When Debbie got home, she was surprised to find Bonnie and

Bernard had gone out to a dinner party hosted by one of the developers Bernard worked with. Daniel was eating a hot dog and a milkshake he'd made with the electric mixer.

"You want some of this?" he asked her. "We have more milk and ice cream, and chocolate syrup if you want chocolate." He laughed, "Or maybe you've had enough chocolate for a while."

She didn't even bother to dignify his rude comment with a response. "I'm not hungry."

"Well, you ought to eat something. You've lost too much weight. Anyway, Yvonne and I are going out, so I guess you'll have the house to yourself for once."

She made it to her room before the tears fell again. She had hoped to talk to Yvonne if her parents weren't home, but Daniel had ruled that out. Maybe she should call Linda, but she wasn't sure if Linda was dealing with her own pregnancy. No, she'd stay in and be glad no one was questioning her. She lay down on her bed on her back. Before long, her hand was resting on her flat belly. Princess joined her and snuggled her head on Debbie's hip.

The next morning, she had to drag herself out of bed. Who knew pregnancy made you so tired? She put on some pants she hadn't been able to get into for a year or more and smiled at herself in the hall mirror. At least she was thinner for the moment. She threw on an old baggy sweatshirt and pulled her hair into a sloppy ponytail. Today she was probably going to have to clean her room.

She padded into the kitchen barefoot. And found Robert coming in the front door. She had no makeup on, dressed like something the cat dragged in and hadn't even brushed her teeth.

"Robert! My gosh, what're you doing here?"

"I was about to ask him," Bonnie said.

Robert met Debbie's eyes. He avoided holding Bonnie's gaze. "Oh, kinda a surprise. I had some things to do this mornin', so I stopped on impulse. I need to talk to you, Debbie. Let's go out for breakfast."

"Breakfast? Now?" She didn't know why she said that. When else would you go to breakfast if not on a Saturday morning? She was starving. She hadn't eaten dinner the night before. "Mister Donut?" she asked.

Robert and Debbie both looked at Bonnie. Robert scratched his cheek.

"Don't be gone too long, Sweetie. We've got some work to do today." Bonnie returned to the kitchen where she was washing the dishes."

Debbie wanted to go change her shirt and put on her face, but she was afraid Bonnie might change her mind if she thought about it longer. So, she slipped on her Keds she'd left right by the door and went with Robert.

She felt Robert's nerves jangling as they waited in line at the donut shop. He was blinking more than normal and he shook his hands loose a few times as though to release tension. He nearly dropped the five-dollar bill he pulled out before handing it to the clerk. But how could she blame him? She'd dropped a bombshell on him yesterday afternoon. She hadn't recovered either. But she was touched he'd come to see her this morning.

When he didn't start the car right away, she picked up her donut and started eating. She was so hungry and that chocolate-covered Bismarck with the Bavarian cream filling was delicious even if it stuck to her fingers. She knew she had gotten it on her nose when he laughed at her. She took a sip of hot cocoa.

"I told my parents everything last night," Robert blew on his hot coffee.

"What?" Debbie's brows shot up.

"Dey was blamin" Donald for goin' to da manse. Dey didn't believe him when he denied it. I had to tell them we were the ones who'd been goin' there. And after that, I told them about the pregnancy."

"Oh my God. What did they say?"

He grunted and looked back toward the donut shop. He pursed his lips. "Dey was pretty darn mad. Have you ever had anyone stand right in front of you and scream at da top of dere lungs? My ears are still ringing. And dat was just Mama. My dad wanted to tear me to pieces. He kept pacing back and forth and making dis awful growling sound. I wanted to tell him to go ahead and swear, he'd feel better. Thank God Donald was dere. Dad told him to leave but he said he would stay to keep my dad from killing me. If looks could kill, I woulda been dead ten times over. But then Donald suddenly said something even I hadn't thought about."

"What?" Debbie had turned in the seat so she was facing Robert.

"He said, 'I can't believe you's so angry when you just found out you's having another grandchild.' Dat stopped 'em cold."

Debbie's eyes were as big as saucers. "Then what happened?"

"Then they were like, 'whatchew gonna do?'"

"I said I had to talk to you again. So dat's why I'm here now." Robert reached into the backseat and pulled out a paper-wrapped bouquet of red roses. He handed them to Debbie.

"Roses? How sweet! You've never given me flowers. No one has ever given me flowers." She plunged her nose into the midst of them and inhaled.

"I want to marry you, Debbie. Say yes."

She gasped. "Married? We're so young. They won't let us get

married. You're going to college to be an engineer. I can't ruin that for you."

"You won't. I have scholarships and a Pell Grant. I'm going to college next fall even if we get married. But you the one wid a baby growing inside. You may have to delay your plans."

She took a breath, then studied him. "We could do that. I could get a job, you could go to college. Then when you're done, I'd go. That might work. Do you really want to get married?" Her eyes were getting water-logged again.

"I do. I thought about nothing else all night long. I wanna marry you and have the baby."

Suddenly she was in his arms, getting chocolate icing and Bavarian cream on his shirt and in his hair. They were crying and kissing and laughing all at the same time.

When Debbie got back home an hour later, she put the roses in a vase with water.

"Robert gave you roses?" Bonnie frowned.

"Yes, wasn't that sweet? Mom, where is Dad this morning?"

"He had a meeting with several crews. He promised he'd be home before noon. I want to work on cleaning the carport today."

"Okay. I'm going to take a shower, then I'll start cleaning my room." Debbie started to walk away with the vase of roses.

"Wouldn't it make more sense to shower after you're done cleaning?"

"Maybe, but I feel like I need it right now."

She went into her room and looked at the clock. In a half-hour, she'd call Robert and tell him to come back after one.

Robert showed up for the second time that day promptly at 1:30

p.m. The Adams family was finishing lunch. This time Debbie had on denim trousers, a nice T-shirt, and makeup. When Debbie brought Robert into the dining room, everyone looked surprised. Her hand started twitching so she tucked it behind her.

"Robert, you're back again? Debbie didn't talk you into helping with the cleaning, did she?" Bonnie asked.

"No, I'm back because Debbie and I have some things we need to tell you," Robert bit his lip and looked at Debbie.

Bonnie and Bernard exchanged glances.

"I guess that's my cue to leave." Daniel started to rise. He motioned to Grover, who had been sitting under Daniel's chair waiting for table scraps.

"It might be better if you stayed, Daniel," Robert said, thinking of how his brother helped to diffuse the reaction of his parents. He turned to Debbie, "Do you want to start?"

Debbie took a breath, then looked back at Robert. She pushed her hair behind her ears.

Robert plunged ahead. "First we should tell you we've been dating since the day we met last July. I know you were worried about Debbie dating me after the police harassed us. My parents also objected because dey thought we should date other people instead of getting serious at our age. But we wanted to see each other, so we . . . lied. We pretended Debbie was dating Sam, and Lester and what was his name? Oh, Peter. Dey picked her up and den I met 'em. I told my parents I was dating a girl named Gianna, who was actually Sam's girlfriend. None of dat matters. The point is, we were just dating each other."

Bonnie and Bernard were staring at them mouths ajar. Daniel frowned and put his head on his hand with an elbow resting on the dining table.

"You weren't going out with Sam? Who wasn't on the

basketball team?" Bernard scratched his head.

"No, Sam is twenty," Debbie explained. "He played basketball at Lincoln High two years ago. Gianna's parents didn't want her to date him because he was three years older than she was, so Robert was her fake date."

"Robert, I think it was gallant of you to come to help Debbie tell the truth, but it's time for you to go so we can deal with our daughter. I hope you're prepared for the consequences. We won't tolerate any more deception." Bernard waved his arm at Robert as though he was shooing him away.

"No, no, Daddy. We're not done talking about this." Debbie reached out and clung to Robert's arm.

"You're right, Kitten. We're certainly not done talking about this. But it no longer involves Robert. You'll never see him again."

Tears sprang to Debbie's eyes. "No Daddy. That isn't for you to decide. Not anymore. I'm pregnant!"

"You're what?" Bernard roared springing forward and shoving his end of the dining table four inches off the floor. Plates danced on the surface while two glass tumblers rolled and shattered on the floor. Bonnie sprang from her chair as the table bounced toward her, and Daniel leaped up and grabbed her arm to keep her from falling.

Robert and Debbie instinctively stumbled back. Debbie began to shake. She'd never seen her father so angry. Robert stuck out his chin and held his ground.

"Did he force you?" Bernard roared.

"No!" Debbie cried.

"I'm gonna give you five seconds to get outta my damn sight, Fella! Then I ain't gonna be responsible for what I do to you. And I got witnesses here who will testify I gave you fair warning!" Bernard's face and neck were flushed, and spit was flying from the sides of his mouth. He pounded one fist into the palm of his other hand as he lumbered toward Robert.

"Daddy, stop!" Debbie wailed.

Daniel moved toward Debbie and Robert to try to ward off any blows. Grover started barking and growling.

Robert's eyes went wide showing the whites more than normal. But he didn't move. He pulled Debbie under his arm. "He ever hit you?" he asked her.

That seemed to enrage Bernard even more. "NO! I don't hit my kids! Jesus Christ! You, on the other hand, come in here telling me you have ruined my daughter?" Bernard had his finger in Robert's face. The veins in his neck were popping out and his nostrils flared. "There's no reason I shouldn't beat you to a bloody pulp!" He shoved Robert with both hands knocking him against the wall, causing Debbie to stumble against the china cabinet. Bonnie grabbed Debbie's arm, pulling her to her, and wrapped a protective arm around her from behind.

"Bernard, Bernard, no!" Bonnie gasped. Grover kept barking at Robert and Bernard.

"Don' think you want to do this, Mr. Adams. Won't solve anything." Robert put his hands up defensively.

"Debbie, take Robert into the other room for a few minutes," Daniel said. "Everyone, calm down."

Debbie moved toward the living room and Robert followed. She fell into his arms and burst into tears.

Bonnie put her hand on Bernard's arm. "Sit a minute. Relax."

"You want me to calm down, Bonnie? Didn't you hear what they said? Don't you get it? He defiled our daughter. We could probably have him arrested! She's only seventeen for God's sake. They have been lying to us for months! Now she's pregnant with a bastard Negro child. Is that what you want for your only daughter?"

"Can you at least lower your voice? The whole neighborhood can hear you!" Bonnie said.

"I don't give a damn who hears me! You need to hear me! Why aren't you screaming at them too?"

"Because I can't scream louder than you!" Bonnie retorted. She took a deep breath. "Of course, I'm angry. But we can't banish her to her room like she was ten years old. We have to be able to talk this through. And I worry about your blood pressure."

"What the hell are you talking about? My blood pressure's fine. My daughter is not." Bernard strode into the living room. He pulled himself up to his full height of six feet two and crossed his arms, glaring at Robert. "You're still here?"

"Yes. Yer wife's right. We needa talk this through. I understand yer emotions. Debbie and I were blown away ourselves when we found out about the baby but—"

"You don't understand nothin'. You ain't a father. Screwing an innocent teenage girl doesn't make you a father. There's no baby. It's probably no bigger than a peanut. She can get rid of it and get rid of you."

Bernard lunged for Debbie and had one hand on her before Robert broke his hold, pushing Debbie behind him. "Git yer hands off her!" Robert's eyes blazed menacingly. "Don' touch her again 'til you ready to embrace her, to forgive her." Debbie stood behind Robert with her hands on her mouth weeping.

Bernard turned back to Bonnie throwing his hands up in the air, his voice ragged. "You hear this, Bonnie? Now he's trying to tell us how to treat our own child!"

Daniel walked up to his father, putting a hand on his upper arm. "Would you let me talk to them a minute? You take a breather."

Bernard squinted at his son, then nodded. He walked back into the dining room and took a seat.

"What the hell is wrong with you two?" Daniel shook his head looking from Robert to Debbie. "You must have known this would happen. Do you think this is some kind of romantic fantasyland where love conquers all? What are you going to do about it now?"

Robert licked his lips and answered in a low voice. "I aksed Debbie to marry me."

"Marry you!" Bernard erupted again. Debbie leaned her forehead on Robert's arm and continued crying. Bonnie walked toward Debbie but Daniel put his hand up stopping her.

Daniel gritted his teeth. "You think you can get married? And then what? Get a job to support your new family? I thought you were gung-ho to go to the university, to become an engineer."

Robert nodded. "You can be married and go to college."

Bernard stood up and swept his arms apart. "You're going to have your pregnant wife work so you can get a nice education? That isn't how the real-world works, Boy."

"Daddy, that's enough!" Debbie surprised them all by emerging from Robert's side to stand facing Daniel. "These are our decisions now, Robert's and mine. Not yours, Daddy. Not Mom's or yours, Daniel."

Daniel took ahold of Debbie's arms, briefly glancing at Robert to see if he would interfere. Then he locked eyes with his sister. "Debbie, I love you. You can't throw your life away at seventeen years old. You're in trouble, but it isn't the end of the world. Let your family help you before it's too late."

Debbie gasped. "You want me to get rid of my baby too? No! That's wrong!" She shook her arms free and backed away.

"You could put it up for adoption. It would be the best thing for the baby. Then you could go to nursing school afterward," Daniel continued.

"No!" Debbie covered her ears with her hands. "Stop saying

that! Leave us alone!"

Daniel leered at Robert. "I tried, Dad. I'm not stopping you anymore. You do what you need to. I don't want any part of this!" Daniel marched toward the front door and snapped his fingers. "C'mon Boy." When Robert looked up, Daniel sneered. "The dog," he spat out.

Grover followed Daniel outside. His Plymouth Fury squealed out of the driveway.

Bernard stood up again. "Robert, what's it going to take to get you to leave? Do you want me to call the cops?"

"No. I'll leave if Debbie aks me to."

"If he leaves, I'm going with him," Debbie fisted her hands on her hips.

"Do you think you can run off and get married? You can't. Not without our permission. You haven't even graduated from high school! You're still a child, Deborah!" Bernard smirked.

"Where are you going to go?" Bonnie asked. "Where are you going to live without money? You need to have a job to live on your own. That's why children have parents to support them until they're old enough and capable enough to be on their own."

"You can't take the car, it's in my name. We bought all your clothes. What do you even own that you bought yourself?" Bernard raised one brow and tilted his head. "And he's probably in the same boat. Doesn't that car out there belong to your father or older brother?"

Robert pursed his lips and nodded.

"You're trying to turn this into some fairytale, Kitten. This isn't your knight in shining armor. Maybe he will be someday if he gets that engineering degree under his belt. You have to deal with reality. And the reality is you both made a very bad choice. We're trying to help you fix it." Bernard slumped back into the chair again and put a hand on his chest.

"Bernie, what is it?" Bonnie was at his side in a flash.

"Nothin', just heartburn. It'll pass."

"I think you're opposed to this because Robert is Black," Debbie stuck her chest out and set her jaw.

"No," Bernard continued massaging his chest. "This isn't about race. But we can make it about race if you want. You marry a Black man and there's a good chance he'll be dead or in jail before he's thirty. Maybe before he gets that fancy degree. Then that baby you insist on having will have no daddy, and you'll have no degree. And if he's lucky enough to survive, he won't have a chance to be as successful as any of the White engineers, even if he's twice as smart and works twice as hard. It isn't fair, or right, but it is reality. You'd be much better off marrying that Lester character. He may not be good-looking or have the tiniest bit of charm, but he'll probably make a boatload of dough."

Debbie erupted into tears again. "I can't believe you would say something so hateful!"

Robert put his arm around her. "Let's go outside a minute." They went out onto the driveway, and stood there, locked in a tight embrace.

"I can't stay here. But we have nowhere to go. What're we going to do?" Debbie tried to dry her eyes.

"I didn' think we'd be able to live together right now. But if you stay wid your parents, I'm afraid dey won't let me near you again. Is dere any place else you could sleep tonight? Dey's so upset and it might be better tomorrow." Robert stroked her hair.

Debbie sniffed. She looked over at Yvonne's house and thought she saw Yvonne move past her bedroom window. "Yvonne's house is like mine. She has an older brother who's in college and lives in the dorm. I don't think he's back home for the summer yet. I might be able to stay in his room. Even if I have to sleep on the floor in Yvonne's room, it would be better than being at home tonight."

Robert nodded, and they headed back inside Debbie's house. When they got back to the living room, it was deserted. They heard Bonnie pounding on the bathroom door, shrieking at Bernard inside. They rushed to her side.

"Mom, what's going on?"

"I don't know! He locked himself in the bathroom and I could hear him crying hysterically. I was afraid he was having an attack. He won't open the door, and now he won't answer."

"Daddy! Answer me! Are you okay?" Debbie screamed.

They heard sounds of sobbing from within.

"Do you have another way to open the door? Should we break it down?" Robert asked.

Debbie leaned on the door. "Come out, Daddy. You're scaring us. I love you. You know I do. But I love Robert too. And I want to have this baby. Don't make me choose." She rapped softly on the door until they heard the lock click.

Slowly Bernard opened the door. Tears streaked down his ruddy whiskers. "I'm done discussing this with you tonight. If you want to leave, go."

Debbie sniffed and nodded.

"Wanna go to Yvonne's?" Robert asked.

"I'll go pack a bag for tonight," she said.

Robert wandered back into the living room. Bonnie remained with her husband. Debbie came into the living room after about five minutes.

They walked outside. "I can't believe how much we have upset both of our families in two short days. Your father hates me. Your mudder and brudder will never forgive me. My parents are ready to throw me out, and my sisters haven't even heard about it yet. Dat'll be hell to pay." Robert shook his head. "You still think dere's a chance for us?"

"Remember Romeo and Juliet? Don't drink the poison yet." Debbie was surprised she could find dark humor in their situation.

Debbie stayed the night at Yvonne's, and Robert went home.

CHAPTER TWENTY-NINE

Debbie wasn't sure what to expect when she returned home on Sunday morning. Both of her parents eyed her cautiously when she walked into the kitchen.

"Robert called for you already this morning. I told him you were still at Yvonne's. You need to call him back," Bonnie told her.

"We need to have another meeting," Bernard said. "Ask Robert if his parents can come over here with him sometime this afternoon. I'm sure Sunday is a busy day for preachers but I hope they'll be available."

Debbie blinked. "Why do you want to talk to his parents?"

"I can't imagine they were happy to find out what's been going on without their knowledge. Robert has told them, hasn't he?" Bernard asked.

"Yes, he told them Friday night. And they were pretty angry too." Debbie lowered her eyes.

"Well, then we'll have that in common. We need to know what view they have in this situation. Your mother and I have come up with some ideas, and I think we should lay the options out and see what's the most agreeable for everyone."

Debbie frowned. "Robert and I are the ones who have to make decisions about us."

"I know you want to believe that. But you can't change the fact you're seventeen and both of you are dependent on your parents. We're prepared to make some compromises and maybe Robert's parents will agree, maybe they won't. That's why we should meet and have an understanding. Ask Robert if they can come over."

"Robert thinks you hate him, Daddy," Debbie pursed her lips.

"I can see why he thought so. I was very upset. You're my pride and joy, Kitten. I guess you had to grow up, but I didn't think it

173

would happen like this." Bernard sighed and his gaze darted away when his voice began to catch. "I'll apologize for some of the things I said."

What did they have in mind? They wouldn't go into any detail until they'd met with Robert's parents who agreed to come over mid-afternoon.

Thelma, Donovan, and Robert Washington arrived at the Adams' house and Debbie went to the door. She was surprised when both Thelma and Donovan hugged her. She nearly started crying again, but she was beginning to blame her emotions on her pregnancy. Robert kissed her on the cheek.

After introductions, Bonnie asked the guests to be seated at the dining table and she served iced tea and chocolate cake. Debbie and Robert sat together at the opposite end of the table from her parents.

Thelma laughed, trying to break the ice. "You know that chocolate cake makes me think of a day a long time ago, gosh, maybe ten years now. I had the kids at Bethany Park playing on the swings, and Robert got away from me. The little devil ran right up to some child's birthday cake and started blowing out the candles. We didn't even know them! I had to scold him good, but inside I was laughing. You remember, Robert?"

Bonnie's mouth fell open. "That was Robert?"

"It was my cake. Mine and Daniel's. It was funny!" Debbie covered her mouth.

"You were there?" Robert asked.

"Was I there? It was my candles you blew on. I remember thinking you were pretty bold."

"Well, after ten years, you finally get to have some of my home-made chocolate fudge cake, Robert," Bonnie laughed.

"It's fabulous. Just like the burnt-sugar cake was," he said.

"That's quite a coincidence. And the cake is wonderful, Dear, as always," Bernard broke in. "But we're here to discuss something more serious. Tell me, Donovan and Thelma, what was your reaction to this development?"

Donovan shook his head, "Oh, we came down on Robert like a ton of bricks. We didn't even know he was dating Debbie. Then to find out they were sneaking into the church manse . . . well, needless to say, I don't want the congregation to hear that story."

Bonnie squinted at Debbie, then at Robert. "I don't think we heard about that."

Robert cleared his throat, "We spent some time in a house across from our church which was being renovated. No one was living there, and I had a key."

"I don't want to think about the details. Only going to make me mad all over again." Bernard asked, "Tell me, what do you think of this pregnancy, Donovan?"

Donovan raised his brows. "As a minister, I can't condone premarital sex between teenagers. As a father, I know it happens. One of Robert's childhood friends is in the same boat. If you're going to make adult choices, you have to deal with your responsibilities. Robert says he wants to marry Debbie. I'm not sure that's the smart choice, but at least it is an attempt to take responsibility."

Bernard nodded. "And I understand he was planning to attend the university this fall?"

Thelma answered, even though the question seemed to be directed at her husband. "Robert has always been a good student. Dat's one of the reasons dis's been so difficult for us. He has several scholarships dat should pay his way."

"Why are they talking about us as if we aren't here?" Debbie whispered to Robert.

Bernard sent her a warning glance. "You'll have a turn." Bernard looked back at the other set of parents. "So, is it your expectation he should still attend college as planned?"

"That depends. I mean for him, it would be best, but he has to think about two other people's needs first. He doesn't want to desert Debbie and we wouldn't expect him to," Donovan said.

"Okay. Well, let's look at other options. Debbie doesn't even want to talk about having an abortion, and even though I think it might make some things easier, I do think a mother should have the final say on that. Despite what she thought yesterday, I would never force her. But giving up the baby for adoption is a reasonable and unselfish choice. My wife has relatives near St. Louis and I believe Debbie told us you have a daughter in St. Louis."

"No, Daddy—" Debbie started.

"I am asking the Washingtons' opinion now, Kitten. Just wait."

"We do have a married daughter in St. Louis. She had a baby last fall. Little Natalie is cute as a button," Thelma said. "I'm sure if dat is what was decided, Debbie could stay dere."

"Mama—" Robert started, but his father cut him off with a wag of his finger.

"All right. So that's a reasonable option. Debbie could go to St. Louis for maybe four months and come back after the baby was born. Robert could go to school this fall. When Debbie returns, she can enroll in nursing school as she planned. Did you write this down, Bonnie?"

Bonnie had a tablet and pen in front of her. "Yes, I've got it."

Debbie sniffed. They were making a list of their life choices? Hers and Robert's?

"Then, that takes us to the option the kids seem to prefer, getting married. Bonnie and I discussed this last night. We may be able to go along with that if they agreed to certain conditions. But I wanted to know how you felt about it first." He gestured to Donovan and Thelma.

"If they get married, Robert has to put his wife and child's welfare first. He can't let them go on public assistance, even if it means he has to delay his dreams. That's how we feel, Mr. Adams." Donovan pressed his lips tightly and glanced at his wife.

Bernard nodded. "Here's what we're proposing then. They get married in August, sometime after Debbie's eighteenth birthday, shortly before her brother goes to college in Kansas. Until then, they each live at home. They can see each other, but we expect them to be truthful. Once they're married, they move in with us. We'll have another room since Daniel will be gone most of the year, and they could make his room the nursery. We have room in the basement to make our son another bedroom, or we might even expand the basement a bit. I built this house; I could do it in my sleep." Bernard paused examining the sea of shocked faces. "Robert would attend college as planned. But he'd also have to work, whether it is at his current part-time job or something that pays more. This way we could keep an eye on the two of them to make sure they're doing okay. And when the baby comes, Bonnie could help Debbie."

"Debbie would have to get a job too, as soon as school is out. She probably wouldn't be able to go to nursing school for several years, but we could decide that later," Bonnie said. "Robert and Debbie would have to start paying for their expenses such as for their cars, some of their food, but at least they would have a safe rent-free place to live while they get started. We'd want them to stay here for at least the first two years, then it would be up to them if they wanted to move out. It's sort of a push-them-out-of-the-nest-slowly plan. Of course, you and the rest of your family would be welcome anytime."

Debbie looked at Robert with wide-eyes, then at her mother. She got up off her chair and pushed herself into Bernard's lap, draping her arms around his neck, with her head on his shoulder, like she did when she was a child.

Robert watched her with tears looming in his eyes. "I think dat's a 'yes' vote from her. But what I don't understand is why you changed your mind. I thought you were ready to kill me yesterday."

Bernard chuckled, patting Debbie on the back. "Oh, I was. But cooler heads prevailed." He gave Bonnie a crediting look. "Besides, I know how stubborn this girl can be when she wants something. And Lord help her, it seems to be you."

"Thank you, Daddy. You won't be sorry. You're gonna be a wonderful grandpa." Debbie got up and hugged her mother next.

"Grandpa!" Bernard choked. "I don't know if I am quite ready for that!"

Donovan and Thelma laughed.

Bernard cleared his throat. "Robert, I said some cruel things yesterday. I hope you'll understand I was in shock. I was angry. But I'd have been wiser to bite my tongue until my temper cooled off. I apologize."

"Oh no, sir, I understood even then. But just so I'm prepared, do you get that mad very often?" Robert smirked.

Bernard let out a raucous laugh and Donovan joined in. "Well, here's one thing I understand today that mystified me yesterday. This skinny kid of yours wasn't intimidated when I stood up threatening to pummel him or even call the police. Now I get why. He's had to face off with a father who is bigger and probably louder than I'll ever be. Plus, you always had God on your side, am I right?"

Donovan laughed so hard and loudly he was slapping his knees. And that had everyone else laughing heartily too. "You think you can keep this boy in line then?" Donovan smiled at Bernard.

"If I can't, I know who to call for reinforcements!" Everyone laughed again.

Debbie had gone back to sit by Robert and held his hand. This was happening. They were getting married. They were all figuring out how to become one family.

CHAPTER THIRTY

October 1973

Debbie tapped her foot waiting for the doctor to come into the examining room. She didn't even know why she had to change into a hospital gown. She was looking for some professional advice to lose weight. It used to be easier when she was a teenager. She assumed her metabolism had slowed down after having two children. Or maybe there was something wrong with her.

She hadn't gotten down to her pre-pregnancy weight after having Jamal a year ago. She had been trying to juggle two children and a job, along with her marriage. Her mother had been a big help, but in May they'd moved to South Carolina when Robert graduated. The stress of looking for a new job and daycare for her boys was too much, and she knew she was eating poorly. She had no time for exercise. She hoped the doctor had a quick fix.

"Good afternoon, Mrs. Washington, is it? I'm Dr. Quackenbush. What seems to be the problem?"

"I've been trying to lose weight on my own. I want to get down to where I was before I had my second baby. But I haven't had much luck. I was hoping you could prescribe something. I know my neighbor lost about twenty pounds taking some sort of pill."

"How much weight are you trying to lose?" The doctor looked at her weight the nurse had recorded.

"Well, twenty or twenty-five pounds would put me back where I was. Maybe a little more."

"Hmmm. Seems reasonable. How old are you?"

"Twenty-two." Debbie shifted on the exam table. He probably thought someone her age shouldn't need help losing weight.

"All right. We'll do a quick exam. Then I'll have my nurse bring in some pills and a recommended diet plan. Come back to see me in sixty days, unless you're having any problems, then call sooner. Now, I should caution you, it may be a little hard to sleep for the first few nights as your metabolism speeds up. But otherwise, these pills are to help your thyroid, and vitamins and minerals."

The doctor listened to her heart and lungs, took her blood pressure, pulse, ran his hands down her neck, and checked her knee and ankle reflexes. "Everything seems fine. Just take all of the pills as directed."

She was leaving the office within fifteen minutes, armed with nearly 200 pills in various colors, and a 1200-calorie-a-day diet plan.

On her way home, she stopped by Robert's office. Robert had been recruited a few months before graduation to work for a growing aeronautics firm, and he was excited about the work he and his team were doing. Debbie had been nervous about leaving the security of her family and friends to move across the country, but she loved the climate in South Carolina. She had been to his office a few times with the children, and the chief engineer had invited the team to his house in the summer for a barbeque.

Robert worked with ten male engineers, all of them older than he was and White. In an effort to look a little older, Robert had grown a goatee when they moved to Columbia. There was also the chief engineer, who reminded Debbie of Bernard, as he was near the same age. The team was supported by a clerical staff of two, a middle-aged gray-haired grandmotherly type, Mary Ann Wilson, whom Robert confided ran the office, and another young hire, fresh out of a local secretarial school, Shelly Tamlin.

Shelly looked like she'd stepped off a Jamaican beach. She was tall and thin, the epitome of the "Black is Beautiful" slogan. Debbie had only seen her wearing skin-baring tops and mini-skirts hovering above mid-thigh. Her wide-spaced eyes and high cheekbones made her exotically stunning, and her close-cropped natural black curls seemed to glimmer in the lights, showcasing her elongated neck.

Debbie absolutely hated that Robert had to look at her every day. And there she was, leaning over Robert's desk, smiling at some little joke they probably shared. Debbie knew she must have stopped short looking at the two of them.

Then she realized Mary Ann was speaking to her. "Mrs. Washington, how y'all doing today? Where's those sweet darlin's, André and Jamal? You didn't bring them?"

"What? Um, no. I had an appointment so they're at the babysitter. I thought I might speak to Robert for a moment if he's free." Debbie's gaze drifted back from Mary Ann's to Robert's glass-topped cubicle. "Please call me Debbie."

Shelly strode back to her desk next to Mary Ann's and sank slowly into her chair, as though it was an exercise designed to tone her thigh muscles.

"I reckon you remember Robert's wife, Debbie, doncha, Shelly?" Mary Ann rolled two sheets of paper sandwiching a carbon into her typewriter.

Shelly smiled. "Of course. I forgot you were blonde."

Debbie plastered on a smile she knew didn't reflect in her eyes and ran a hand through her bangs.

What did that mean? Does she think I dye my hair? She forgot I was White? She thinks I am a dumb blonde? "Always have been," Debbie said.

"When's your next baby due?" Shelly stretched her long neck and tilted her head.

Debbie clenched her fist until her nails dug into her palm. She wanted to hit this girl. She was so glad she'd gotten those diet pills today. "I'm not pregnant now. But we're always working on it." She flounced into Robert's office as he seemed to be watching them through the glass, unable to hear the exchange.

"What's wrong, Baby?" He drew his brows together studying

her face. He looked so elegant in his white shirt with his sleeves rolled to his elbows. His tan sports jacket hung neatly on a hanger on the door.

"Kiss me," she said.

His swallowed and dropped his voice. "Debbie, I'm at work, that would be inappro—" She leaned in and planted a kiss on his mouth when he hesitated. He put his hand on the back of her head and gave back what she was offering. "What brings you by?"

She glanced over her shoulder to see if Miss Jamaica was watching, but she was typing away. "I went to see a doctor. He gave me some diet pills. I thought it would help give me some energy and to lose the rest of the baby weight."

"Or you could push the stroller around the block every day. Enjoy the South Carolina sunshine," Robert said. He shuffled some papers on his desk. "I need to finish this before the end of the day. Did you need me for something?"

"Oh, I need you, Baby." She raised her brows. "But I guess it'll have to wait until tonight."

CHAPTER THIRTY-ONE

May 23, 1969

Debbie was excited about the graduation ceremony that night. But she wasn't looking forward to sitting through a baccalaureate service on Sunday, and Robert's high school graduation on Wednesday. It was too much pomp and circumstance. And she had more important things on her mind, namely planning a wedding and getting a real job.

Daniel was going to be giving a speech as the valedictorian of their class. He hadn't been home when the parents had all agreed to let Robert and Debbie marry in August and move into the Adams' house. It was clear he wasn't happy about it.

"Debbie, would you let me practice my speech for you?" her brother asked her as she was toweling dry her hair.

"Haven't you practiced it a thousand times already?" she rolled her eyes and sighed.

"Not in front of a live audience. I had to make some changes since I gave it for the principal and speech teacher."

"All right. But first, tell me why you're still mad at me." She picked up her comb and started working her way through her long tresses.

"I don't understand how you and Robert could have made such a mistake. And after you did, how could Mom and Dad change their minds so quickly? I can't believe they're letting you get married, then use my room for a nursery. It's the story of the prodigal son, the one who screwed up got the fatted calf feast and the son who obeyed the rules got squat."

"You didn't get squat; you're going to college away from home. You can do whatever you want there. I'll be under our parents' watchful eyes and so will my husband."

"I have to maintain my grade point average to keep my scholarships, so I think that rules out skipping classes and going on week-long benders. The only reason they want you to live here, is they don't think you will know how to handle a baby. You'll have to figure that out. But for some reason, they're still spoiling you."

"Spoiling me? You were always the golden boy. I was just the other twin."

"You're kidding, right? If I had anything golden, it was because I had to work for it. You were Daddy's little princess. You even got a car and didn't have to buy it. I had to save my hard-earned dough to get a car which wasn't as nice as yours."

"I'd have paid for my car, but I didn't have a job."

"There's another example: you've never even had a real job. I hope this whole marriage and baby thing forces you to be more responsible cuz I don't think you see how easy you've had it so far."

"Well, I hope your speech to the rest of our class doesn't sound so self-righteous. They might boo you out of the auditorium. But sure, let me hear it. I'll try not to fall asleep."

"You know, never mind. I'll read it to Grover. He won't give me any trouble." Daniel stalked out of her room. She heard him later on the patio reciting the speech to the dog.

Despite their argument, Debbie did enjoy his speech at commencement, and she was proud of him. She sat by Yvonne and wondered if their friendship would last. Daniel and Yvonne had started dating again, but Yvonne would be moving to the university campus in August, about the time Daniel left for college in Kansas. Their lives were moving in different directions now. That was the gist of Daniel's speech; how they would be tackling different challenges, but they all had a solid base growing up in a Midwestern city with traditional values.

There was an unsanctioned graduation party at an acreage east of town right after the ceremony. Only graduates of their class were invited, so she couldn't bring Robert. After they had changed into casual clothes, she rode to the party with Daniel and Yvonne. Daniel brought the girls plastic cups of beer from a keg in the barn, then went to chat with some of the other classmates.

"Have you told anyone else you're getting married? Or that you're pregnant?" Yvonne asked.

"I only told Nancy and Linda about the baby. But several people have asked what I planned after graduation and I told them I was getting married," Debbie said. "It was pretty awkward telling Linda. She knew she was pregnant already at prom. Now she thinks she might get rid of it. I could never do that. I don't know where her head is at."

"Linda has different ideas than you do, Debs. She's pretty independent. I think she might like rebelling against her parents and her older sister. It's a tough situation for anyone."

"Daniel probably still wishes I'd do that, or at least give up the baby," Debbie said, as Daniel came back up behind them.

"You probably shouldn't talk about that subject if you don't want everyone here to know," he said, slipping his arm around Yvonne.

"I was telling my friend here you're still mad at me. What's it going to take for you to forgive my sins?" Debbie could feel the beer was starting to relax her.

Daniel studied his sister in the dim lights of the torches burning around the barn and stable where the party was held. He was drinking his second beer. "You lied to me. You even told Yvonne the truth while lying to me."

Yvonne shifted away from his grasp. "Well, I only knew they were dating, I didn't know—"

Debbie gave her brother the side-eye. "I couldn't tell you. You'd have spilled the beans."

"You don't know that. Now we'll never know. I thought I could always believe what you told me. Did you tell me the truth about Mr. Gibson?"

Debbie gaped. Why had he brought that up? Yvonne didn't even know about that.

"What about Mr. Gibson?" Yvonne knit her brows.

"Yes, I told you the truth. Never mind, Yvonne. It was a long time ago."

"Mr. Gibson, the lecherous student teacher, made a pass at her. Not just her, as it turned out."

"Daniel!"

"Oh my God, Debbie. Why didn't you tell me?" Yvonne sputtered.

"I wonder if that had something to do with your current problem. Were you trying to prove to yourself you weren't scarred for life?" Daniel smirked.

"This's why I didn't share my secret with you, Dear Brother! You'd want to throw it in my face!" Debbie marched off in the direction of the keg, which was where most of the kids had gathered. Standing near the barn door all alone was her old friend Barry. For once, he didn't appear awkward or embarrassed to stare at her. He did look a little glassy-eyed though. She refilled her beer and went to stand by Barry. He was still ogling her unapologetically.

"Are you having fun tonight, Barry?" she asked tossing her head. She was still steamed at Daniel.

"I could be," he said. "How about you? Do you want to have some fun?"

Debbie scoffed, and let her gaze return to where she'd left

Daniel and Yvonne. "So far I can't say—" Barry cut her off by pulling her into a torrid kiss. She had no idea he could kiss like that. But what was he doing? What was she doing? She was getting married in less than three months!

"C'mon Debs. No more beer for you," Yvonne pulled her friend back out of Barry's clutches and forced her to walk beside her back to another area of the party. "I distinctly remember you telling me Barry didn't think of you that way. I think you were wrong. Barry must be shy. Until he starts drinking."

Debbie's head was spinning. She wasn't doing very well at this engaged thing. Then suddenly her stomach turned over. She made it to the outer edge of the party space before throwing up in a bush. A little someone was telling her they didn't like beer. She sank onto a nearby hay bale, and Yvonne patted her shoulder. After a minute or two, she was aware that someone else was standing by Yvonne.

"Yvonne says I owe you an apology. I'm sorry if I insulted you, Sis." Daniel said, pulling her up. "I think we'd better get you home."

CHAPTER THIRTY-TWO

August 9, 1969

"It was a lovely wedding, Dear," Thelma Washington said hugging her new daughter-in-law. "Even though the reception was a little warm."

Debbie pushed back the tendril that fell on her forehead. "It was beautiful, but I could have done without the fainting!" She'd gotten so overheated in the minutes before she walked down the aisle, she had passed out about two minutes into the ceremony. Fortunately, her maid of honor, Yvonne, and the best man, Donald, had been watching her and helped to keep her from taking a hard fall.

"That will just be a funny part of the wedding story you'll tell your grandchildren," Bonnie assured her.

"Are you 'bout ready to leave, Debbie?" Robert asked. The wedding reception at Bethany Park was winding down with mostly family left to clean up. "Daniel and Yvonne left a while ago."

The remaining guests, including Nancy and Linda, threw rice at them when they piled into his Riviera, strewn with streamers and a "Just Married" sign. Empty tin cans tied to the bumper broadcast their relationship status to traffic and pedestrians nearby. Their parents had chipped in to get them a nice room at the Clayton House hotel downtown.

"This is nice," Debbie said as she stood in front of the window over-looking the street below and enjoying the air-conditioner blowing on her face. "Do you want to change clothes and go find some dinner?"

"Not very hungry after eating cake," Robert said, taking her head in his hands and kissing her. "But we should getchew out of that heavy dress, Mrs. Washington. Don't want you passing out on me again." He unzipped the back of her dress and pulled it off her shoulders. She stepped out of the dress and went over to open her suitcase wearing her full slip over her bra, girdle, and white nylons.

"Oh no!" she said. "I forgot to pack my negligee. I bought it just for our wedding night."

He shrugged. "It isn't the first time we're having sex. Although," he sighed, "it's been months now. Ever since we admitted it to our parents. Almost like we're starting over."

"Maybe I should call my mom and have her bring it down here." Debbie moved toward the phone and sat on the bed.

"What? That's silly. You can wear it tomorrow or some other time. You aren't going to be wearing it long."

"But tonight, we have some privacy. Once you're sleeping with me in my room, I think it's going to be a little weird. You know, with my parents right on the other side of the wall."

"What?" Robert tilted his head. "Are you saying your parents' room is right next to yours?"

She bit her lip. "Sorry."

"How 'bout we take Daniel's room? Zat farther away?"

"Well, it is on the other side of my room. But my mom said it would be better to put the baby there because it will cry at night and it was less likely to wake my dad if it was farther away."

"Then maybe we'll just have sex in Daniel's room. There's a bed in there, right? Maybe dis was the whole idea behind their generous offer to let us move in with them. Your parents thought they'd stop us from ever having sex again." He scratched his head.

"Don't be ridiculous. I think you're required to have sex when you're married. But we don't have to do it too often. I mean, I'm already pregnant."

"Wait a minute!" Robert took her by the shoulders and looked into her eyes. "What zat mean? You just said married people are required to have sex, but not very often?"

"I mean, pretty soon, I'll be too big and——"

"Don't you want to have sex?" His brows folded.

She looked toward the window and scooted back. "I suppose I'll get used to it. But I do get tired since I'm pregnant."

"Get used to it? You not supposed to get used to it, you supposed to enjoy it." Robert dropped next to her on the bed. "Haven't you ever had an orgasm?"

Her eyes grew wide. She twisted her new wedding ring on her finger. "I don't know. I wasn't sure that was a real thing."

He jumped off the bed and lowered his voice. "A real thing?" Robert's hands raked his hair as he walked around the room. "Oh my God."

"Don't be mad. I'm sorry." Debbie clutched her arms around her body.

He shook his head slowly. "We not ready to be married. What were we thinking?" He opened the door, then turned back to grab the key.

"Robert! Where are you going?" Tears spilled over her cheeks.

"I need some air."

Robert sat at the bar, drinking coffee and smoking. He'd never been in a bar before. At first, he mistook it for a lunch counter, but then he noticed all the liquor bottles.

"You look like you've got the weight of the world on your shoulders, Sonny." A man about his father's age with a thick stock of gray hair moved to the stool next to him and shared his ashtray. He had two short glasses sitting in front of him with lime wedges garnishing them.

"Looks like you thirsty," Robert said looking at the drinks.

"Happy hour. Two for the price of one. You want a vodka gimlet?" the man asked.

Robert shrugged, "Not actually old enough—"

The man laughed. "I'm Mike. Bartender, give me two more. We're gonna sit over here in this booth." His gaze returned to Robert's face. "And you're gonna tell me why you're wearing a monkey suit and a long face." Mike got up and moved to a nearby booth that wasn't well-lit, and Robert followed him. "My girlfriend is late; I might as well let you entertain me."

The bartender put the second set of drinks in front of Mike. When he walked away, Mike pushed them toward Robert.

"They can't serve me, told you I'm underage."

"They didn't. They served me. Try it. You don't work here, do you? Maybe in the band or something in that getup?"

Robert looked down at his tuxedo. He took a gulp of the drink and grimaced. "Oh, no. I got married today."

"Married? Where's the bride?"

"She upstairs. Probably wondering if she jus' made the biggest mistake of her life."

"What's yer name, Kid?"

"Robert. Robert Wash—"

Mike held up his hand, "First name's fine. Here's my first tip. Don't be giving people your whole name in a bar. It can work against you."

Robert chuckled. "Dis the first time I ever been in a bar."

Mike took a long drag on his cigarette and eyed Robert. "So, you got married this afternoon and you're already fighting on your wedding night? That isn't what couples usually do on their wedding night. You know that, right?"

Robert pursed his lips. "I know. They're supposed to be . . ." he made a vague gesture with his hand, then took another big drink.

"Are you worried about having sex for the first time?"

Robert's brows winged up. "Not our first time. She already pregnant."

"Oh. That's why you got married before you could legally drink."

Robert lit another cigarette and wondered how he was having such a personal conversation with a honky he didn't know. Maybe that was why people came to bars. They both drank for a minute in silence. The vodka gimlet was a little sour, but it seemed less so with every sip.

"Okay, so what were you fighting about?" Mike asked.

Robert raked his hand over his face. His head was starting to buzz. What was that about? "We weren't 'xactly fightin'. She said somethin' about not wantin' to have sex and I had to get out of there. Don't know why."

"She didn't want to have sex on your wedding night?"

He squinted. "She was planning to, but then she forgot her negligee." Mike laughed heartily. "Dat seemed weird to me too. But then she said somethin' about not plannin' to have sex very often."

"It sounds like you might need more experience. It takes women longer to warm up to the idea. They have to overcome all those old wives' tales telling them good girls don't want sex." Mike leaned back in the booth.

"Yeah. I think that's part of it. She hasn't figured out how to enjoy it."

"Okay, Sonny. Robert, right? I'm gonna give you some advice.

I've had experience with quite a few ladies, so I know a little about it. But didn't your father ever talk to you about women?"

Robert smiled. "My dad's a Baptist minister. So, no."

"It's up to the man to find out what the woman wants. Like so many other things, it comes down to supply and demand."

"How you supposed to do that? I mean I've aksed her before if she likes dis or dat, but it doesn't seem to make a difference."

"No, no. Don't ask, just explore her body. Everywhere you can put your hands, your lips, your tongue. You'll find out what she likes. Then you'll find out what she really really likes. And when you find out what she really really likes, don't stop. Believe me, you won't be sorry."

Robert felt beads of perspiration forming on his forehead as the heat seemed to rise up his face. He swallowed. Then took another gulp of his drink. The first glass was empty. "Explore? Everywhere?"

Mike smiled. "With some women, the more taboo they think it is, the better they like it."

Robert couldn't believe what he was hearing. Was this guy on the level? He supposed he had nothing to lose.

"I'll tell you what. I'll walk you out to the elevator. You take this second drink up to your bride and make her drink it. It will help, trust me. I have to call my girlfriend from the payphone in the lobby anyway. I don't know what's keeping her."

"I don't even think I thanked you for the drinks. Want me to pay for part of it?" Robert reached for his wallet.

"No, my treat. A wedding present, we can call it. Maybe thirty years from now, you'll be giving the advice." Mike signed the tab the bartender had left and placed some bills on the table. He picked up his drink and the one Robert hadn't started and headed toward the lobby. When they got to the elevator, he handed Robert the full glass. "You enjoy your wedding night, Robert. Good luck."

Debbie was lying in bed under the covers when he got to the room. Her hair was brushed out and damp as though she'd showered. He set the drink down on the nightstand. "You should drink this," he said.

Debbie sat up. She was only wearing the slip now. Maybe it wasn't as revealing as her negligee but he had trouble breathing eyeing her abundant cleavage when she leaned forward. He'd nearly forgotten how great it had felt to run his hands across her velvety body. What was he waiting for? They were married now; they should be rolling naked between those expensive sheets.

"Where did you get this, is there alcohol in here?"

"Definitely. I ran into a guardian angel named Mike. He helped me see things differently." Robert began stripping off his tuxedo jacket, vest, and shirt as Debbie took a tentative sip. Was that the alcohol hitting him or his libido making demands? He somehow felt much bolder.

"It's strong. Vodka, is that what it is?" Debbie swirled the ice around in her glass.

He nodded, "Keep drinking. I downed a whole glass." He continued taking off his rented clothes and piled them in a chair. When he got down to his shorts, he sat on the bed. "I'm sorry I ran out on you earlier. Guess I freaked out. Thought we were in over our heads. But we can take it slow . . ." After she drank most of the vodka gimlet, he pulled her into an impatient kiss wrapping his arms around her. She laughed softly when he freed her mouth. Then he moved his hands and mouth down her jaw and neck, sliding the slip off her shoulders, and kept touching and kissing his way down her body as they reclined.

Explore, huh? That's what the man said. He could get off on this kind of adventure. He'd let his hands wander over this landscape before but he'd been more reticent with his mouth. His grumbling stomach tried to tell him they'd missed dinner, but he only hungered for her. When his tongue ran across her silken skin, he found localized flavors he hadn't expected. Sweet, salty, some of it floral like her favorite lotion. Venturing farther south the scent was more musk and heady desire. All of it twisting him into a dizzying fervor.

She was full of divine terrains. He'd swear the twin peaks had gotten more grandiose, giving way to lush valleys and golden plains. But the wetlands smoldered under his touch as her moans of pleasure encouraged his quest to go further inland. But unlike the earth's topography, there was nothing but softness here. He sank into the cushions of her feminine curves. Making love in a bed under a down comforter certainly was luxurious.

Heat spiraled through him and it was hard to ignore his throbbing loins, but he had to concentrate on what his bride was feeling. She was warming up to this, pushing the bedcovers and slip away, and pulling his mouth to hers. Her ragged gasps were music to his ears. Sweat glistened on her body as she arched like a flower opening in the morning dew. He put aside what he thought sexual coupling was supposed to be. This was a different level of need, part madness, and part explosive pleasure. He was pretty sure some of the wild groans he heard came from him. Her eyes grew wide with shocked delight when he advanced with a primal greed, he didn't know he had. She cried out when she seemed to abandon the rein on her control and let him carry her over into bliss.

By the time they were ready to sleep, Robert knew Mike wasn't an angel. He was a goddamned Grandmaster of sex.

The next morning, they were checking out at the registration desk. While he was waiting for his receipt, Robert glanced back toward the elevator and saw Mike emerge with a leggy blonde woman who looked to be about twenty-five. They stopped while he lit her cigarette. Robert didn't see any luggage. The couple walked up to the desk, and Mike glanced at Robert and Debbie. Then he squinted at Debbie.

"Good morning, Mike," Robert said. How could he begin to thank him?

Mike furrowed his brow and looked the other way.

Robert grunted, picking up their luggage and he and Debbie walked toward the garage. "How rude. The guy was a buddy-buddy in the bar last night. In the light of day, he wants nothing to do wid me."

Debbie glanced back. "That was Mike? The guy who bought you drinks at the bar?"

"Yep."

"It's not you, Baby. He recognized me. That's Mike Bridges, my friend Linda's father. And that certainly wasn't Linda's mother."

CHAPTER THIRTY-THREE

November 26, 1969

"Mrs. Washington, would you stop by my office at the end of the day?" Dr. Carrington asked.

"Certainly, Doctor," Debbie said. She liked Dr. Carrington. He was everyone's grandfather at the medical practice where she'd been working since late June. The other two doctors in the practice were younger, but Dr. Carrington's family medical group had started to feel like home. Working with the nurses and another clerk there had made Debbie even more interested in pursuing a career in the health field.

She was excited about Thanksgiving tomorrow. Robert would be finished with classes this afternoon, and she and her husband were spending part of the day with each set of parents. She hadn't spent as much time with him as she hoped, as he was often busy with his study group or holed up in the basement doing homework when he wasn't at class or work. Daniel would be home later tonight too, and she hadn't seen him since summer.

Debbie settled into a guest chair in Dr. Carrington's office at the end of the workday. She hadn't been in his office before, and she looked around curiously at the old charts and knickknacks. He had a brass microscope, some clouded bell jars labeled "Arsenic," "Belladonna," and "Hemlock." Posters on the walls showed operating arenas from the nineteenth century. He had an ancient-looking doctor's bag with a skull and crossbones on it. Mixed in with these collectibles were modern landscape paintings and drawings by his grandchildren.

Dr. Carrington sighed. "Do you have family plans for Thanksgiving, Debbie?"

"Oh yes, of course. My husband and I'll probably have to stuff ourselves twice. We're going to his parents' home for a noon meal and then eat again in the evening. I suppose that's part of being married," Debbie chuckled.

"Good, good. Then you'll have a nice weekend I'm sure. The thing is ... I've been waiting for you to ask about leaving your job. Your baby is due when? Next month already?" Dr. Carrington put his elbows on his desk, steepling his fingers.

Debbie's hand instantly went to her abdomen. "Uh-huh." She felt a knot forming in her stomach.

"Well, you may not realize this, but pregnant women aren't normally allowed to work once they are showing." Dr. Carrington wet his lips.

Debbie picked up a paperweight on his desk. It had some sort of sea creature enclosed in it, and she put it back down at once. She took a deep breath. "I planned to work as long as I could. We need the income."

"The thing is, if I let you do that, the other women will expect the same thing." Dr. Carrington glanced at his watch.

Debbie glanced around at the decorations in his office. Dr. Carrington clearly appreciated the historical artifacts. But someone in the distant past must have discarded them because they had outlived their purpose. Someone had decided they were replaceable.

"I can still do my job. I've been at work even when I didn't feel well." It was no use, she knew. He had let her work past the six-month mark when most pregnant women were considered inappropriate in the workplace.

"We've enjoyed having you work here, Debbie." Dr. Carrington cleared his throat and stood up. "I wish you all the best with your new family. I don't want to cut this short but—"

Debbie stood up as quickly as she could tipping the chair by its arm due to her extra girth. She managed to spit out, "Thank you, Dr. Carrington," before the lump in her throat made talking difficult.

Her hand on the door handle seemed frozen in place. But escape was the only path forward.

She leaned her head back on the car seat trying to stretch out her torso. It'd be nice to stop working but they needed the money. Her parents had agreed to pay for some of their necessities, such as their room, and most of their food. Debbie and Robert were paying for all of their car expenses, clothing, and medical bills.

Her income and what Robert earned from his part-time job had to stretch as far as possible and she couldn't afford to forfeit weeks of earnings because she was visibly pregnant. It wasn't like she had to stand up all day. Her job at the doctor's office involved checking patients in, making phone calls, typing. Most of the people she saw probably couldn't tell she was pregnant when she sat behind the counter. But it was done, out of her control. Now she had to break the news to Robert.

A few weeks later, she was trying to read some library books she had gotten on childbirth and caring for a newborn. She'd wanted to take Lamaze classes, but they were too expensive.

"Women have been having children as long as the human race has existed, and most of them didn't take classes," Bonnie told her. "Take this time you have left to do some reading, and you can ask me anything you want."

How could a baby that looked the size of a basketball under her navel squeeze out of her body, unless the baby somehow got smaller or the exit got a lot bigger? She read the descriptions in the books, and this still seemed impossible, or at least unbearably painful. But she wasn't going to ask her mother about her private parts. Bonnie had never talked to her about anything sexual. She'd learned much more from Dear Abby. Her ignorance was one reason she found herself pregnant at eighteen.

But the romantic notion of a child back in May was all too real now. How was she supposed to rest at night with this thing kicking repeatedly? Her feet were always swollen, and it seemed like she'd just settled down with them elevated when she thought she had to use the bathroom again.

"Robert, I'm beginning to wonder if I can do this baby thing," she said that night when they were trying to get comfortable in her old double bed.

He chuckled, "We're doing this baby thing. Just don't go into labor before my last final, that's all I aks."

"When is that?"

"Monday, December 22," he said. "You can hold out until then, maybe even until Christmas. Then I have a couple of weeks before classes resume, so our timing could be perfect."

She took his hand and put it over her baby belly. "The closer this gets, the scarier it is. What if something goes wrong?"

"Nothin's going to go wrong." Robert rubbed her expanding abdomen. "It's under control thanks to your parents mostly. Your dad and I put the crib together. After the baby shower, you have most of the necessities. I imagine we'll get more supplies and clothes for Christmas. You need to relax."

Men should have babies. Then they could tell her to relax. She tried to muddle through the next week or so, doing as little as possible.

CHAPTER THIRTY-FOUR

On December 22, Yvonne called her early in the morning shortly after Robert left for his exam. "How are you feeling? No baby yet?" Yvonne asked.

"No, but my back hurts today. I am getting very tired of being pregnant."

"I thought I'd check on you. I'm going with Linda down to Kansas for Nancy's wedding today. She's already about six months pregnant, and I don't think either her parents or Peter's are coming. We knew it wouldn't work for you to come along, but we'll be thinking about you."

"You can stop and have a Chinese fire drill in my honor," Debbie said, remembering the times they did that in her VW bug.

Yvonne had no sooner hung up than Debbie felt something odd. Sharp pains in her back seemed to radiate to the front. When she got off the bed, it seemed worse. She walked into the kitchen looking for her mother. She found a note saying Bonnie had gone to do some Christmas shopping. She looked out the front windows and saw Linda's car in Yvonne's driveway next door. Yvonne jumped in the car, and Debbie watched as they pulled away.

"Help!" she said in a weakened voice as she gripped the edge of the counter. She leaned on the counter and panted. That's what she had read about Lamaze, you were supposed to pant to minimize the pain. It didn't seem to work.

The pain subsided then. She had read that even if she was starting labor, it'd likely take all day. She made toast and poured coffee from the pot on the stove. When the pain came again, she leaned on the counter. That seemed to move the pressure off her back. Couldn't sit down. Might not be able to get up. Who could she call? Her dad was at work and had no phone at the construction site. Her mom was shopping. Daniel hadn't come home for Christmas break. Robert was down on campus.

Oh boy. Wait, Yvonne's mom. It looked like her car was in the Edison's carport. She could call Connie Edison.

But maybe it was too soon. She leaned on the counter eating toast and drinking coffee. She dialed the Edison's phone number next door. It rang ten times and no one answered. Fear gripped her with the next more powerful contraction.

No one can help me. She began screaming and sobbing at the same time.

Thelma, she thought. She should call Robert's mother. She's probably home. But it would take her at least fifteen or twenty minutes to get there. What was her number? She used to call Robert there frequently. Why wasn't her memory working? She tried Connie Edison's phone number one more time.

"Hello?" Connie sounded rushed.

"Mrs. Edison, it's Debbie. I need help. Please come over here."

"Honey, what's wrong? I just got out of the shower. Let me grab a towel. I'm all wet."

Debbie's grip on the receiver slipped when the pain began again and she started screaming.

Connie was pounding on the door within five minutes, dressed but with her hair wrapped in a towel. She tried the knob and let herself in. Debbie was slumped over the kitchen counter whimpering.

"My goodness! Where's everyone?" Connie demanded. She helped Debbie sit in a dining room chair. Connie took a seat beside her and began toweling off her hair while they spoke.

Debbie swiped at her eyes. "Dad's working. Mom went shopping. Robert's taking his last final. My due date isn't for three more days."

"It's okay now. When did you start having pains?"

Debbie shook her head. "An hour ago. Do you think it's time to go to the hospital?"

"Let's time your labor pains first. Tell me when you have another." Connie looked at her watch. She could tell by the panting and crying Debbie was starting another contraction.

The next time a contraction came, Connie said, "We're going to the hospital. Have you packed a bag?"

Debbie told her where to find the bag, and scribbled a note to whoever came home first. It had snowed lightly the night before, and Connie's car fishtailed through the first intersection.

"Aaaah!" Debbie cried. "I don't know if we're going to make it."

"Whatever you do, Debbie, don't push! I don't want to deliver your baby."

They made it to the hospital, and she was wheeled upstairs to the maternity ward. Once Debbie was settled into a room, the contractions seemed to slow down. A nurse stayed with her to monitor her progress.

"How far apart did you say the contractions were?" the nurse asked.

"When I timed them, they were a little over four minutes," Connie reported.

"Well, they're a good five minutes now. We'll see what Dr. Hanson has to say." The nurse left abruptly.

"Is that bad? The contractions are farther apart instead of closer together?" Debbie rubbed the sides of her arms.

"It isn't unusual, I'm sure. Are you cold, Honey?" Connie asked. She found a blanket in the closet and draped it around Debbie's chest and shoulders. They'd had her change into a lightweight hospital gown.

"Mrs. Edison, tell me a story to distract me. How did you decide what to name your children?"

Connie sat down on the chair and pulled it next to the bed. "Well, let's see. Clark was my mother's maiden name. My mother didn't have any brothers, so no males to pass on the last name. That one we had decided ahead of time. Yvonne was more impulsive. Yvonne De Carlo was one of my favorite actresses, and she became even more popular in the fifties. She had such a beautiful exotic look. People used to tell me I looked like her. I know that's silly."

"No, it's not silly. The first time I saw you, I thought you looked like a movie star too," Debbie shifted in her bed as another contraction started. Connie held her hand and tried to help her breathe through it.

Connie leaned back after Debbie did. "When Yvonne was born, her father kept going on and on about how beautiful she was. He was just in love. But he agreed to call her Yvonne. I hope you have names picked out."

Dr. Hanson walked in. "Miss Debbie, how are you doing?" He immediately pulled his stethoscope from around his neck and checked the baby's heartbeat on her belly. "Baby's heart rate is good. Contractions five minutes apart, right? It will probably be hours, but you never know. Good thing Mom got you here. It's supposed to snow more this afternoon."

"Oh, this isn't my Mom—"

"I'll come back to check on you in an hour or so. I have another mother ready to go down the hall, so I'll be close." The doctor waltzed out of the room humming to himself.

In about thirty minutes, Bernard and Bonnie came rushing into the room.

"Oh, my goodness," Bonnie cried. "I had no idea this was going to happen. I'm so sorry. I should've been home!"

"It's okay, Mom. Mrs. Edison was great. Where's Robert? He wasn't home yet?"

Bernard shook his head. "He must still be at school. He's probably waiting for a bus. You left him the keys to your Volkswagen, didn't you?"

Debbie's eyes rounded before the next contraction hit her. When it was over, she said, "Did we bring my purse, Mrs. Edison?"

"Sure. You said all of the doctor information was in there, and phone numbers if we needed them." Connie picked up Debbie's purse and fished a hand down to the bottom. "Are you talking about these keys?"

"I can go back and wait for Robert and bring him," her father said.

"Why don't I go home, and I can take him the car keys?" Connie said. "She needs family here."

Debbie was getting discouraged, as nothing seemed to be happening except for the labor pains about five minutes apart. Dr. Hanson returned after about an hour. Debbie introduced her parents.

"We've got a new contraption which helps us monitor the baby's heartbeat. Since your labor isn't moving quickly, we're going to try it on you. This will help us catch any problems if the baby's having trouble, such as if the cord is wrapped around his or her head. Any sign of distress in the baby, and we can do a cesarean section." Bernard and Bonnie left the room when he inserted a catheter and attached a clip to the baby's scalp that would monitor the heart.

The doctor also ordered some pain medication for Debbie and told her she might start dozing between contractions. The nurse came in periodically to check the printout from the baby's heart monitor.

CHAPTER THIRTY-FIVE

Robert felt like he'd been running on pure adrenaline all morning. The bus was late due to an overnight snowfall and he barely made it to his final exam in time. Heading home, the bus was running further behind. When he walked in the door of the Adams' house, Daniel had hustled him into his car to head for the hospital.

"How long has Debbie been in labor?" Robert looked at his watch for the tenth time in the last twenty minutes.

"I dunno. Mom's note just said that we should come to Bryan Hospital as soon as we got home. Connie Edison brought over Debbie's keys to the bug. But I knew you'd be a nervous wreck. So, I waited." Daniel spun his wheels in the slush trying to take off from a stoplight.

"Thanks. But you should slow down. I want to get there in one piece." Robert felt the knot in his stomach getting tighter.

Three hours after she had been admitted to the hospital, Robert and Daniel walked into Debbie's room. Robert rushed over to her side immediately and planted a kiss on her forehead. "You wanted to have this baby before Christmas, didn't you?" he asked.

Debbie moaned. "It's about time you showed up. You might have missed it."

"My final went well, thanks for asking," Robert grinned.

"You seem pretty calm, Debs. I thought having a baby was all about screaming." Daniel moved across the bed from Robert. "What are all these machines for?"

She gripped both of their hands when the next contraction came. She wasn't ready with the breathing that time. "AAAAAhhhhhh!" Bonnie moved in closer and started doing Lamaze breathing the way she'd seen the nurse do. Debbie tried to start mid-scream, but it came out more as a combination of screaming and panting.

"Holy smokes! I think you broke my hand!" Robert said. "Is it that bad every time?"

Debbie clenched her jaw. Beads of perspiration were running down her face. She had long since abandoned the blanket Connie had draped over her. "Yes, it's that bad every time and I hope I did break your hand. I'll trade places with you!"

Daniel backed up laughing. "This may be more fun to watch than I thought."

"Come on, Baby. What can I do?" Robert stroked her abdomen. "You want something to eat? Daniel and I can go get something in the cafeteria."

"She isn't allowed to eat. Nothing but ice chips," Bonnie reported.

"No wonder she's grumpy!" Daniel put a hand on Robert's shoulder. "We can go eat though."

"Oh no. My husband isn't going anywhere. Not until this is all over!"

Robert shrugged, glancing back at Daniel. "Bring me back a cheeseburger and fries." He pulled a five-dollar bill out of his wallet.

The nurse came back in and looked at the printout from the fetal monitor. Robert stood up and looked at the waves being printed. "What's this? It looks like what they use for earthquakes." Robert pulled out a cigarette and his lighter.

The nurse frowned. "You can't smoke in here. You'll have to go to the waiting room. But this machine tracks the infant's heartbeat. If the baby's in trouble, the shape of these waves changes. So far, so good."

Robert put his cigarette and lighter back in his pocket and picked up the printout. "What do these different graphs mean?"

"Well, here, you can see the contractions. You want to see the baby's heart rate return to normal after a contraction. If there's a sudden change, the baby may not be getting enough oxygen and we'll call the doctor in right away." The nurse fingered the paper.

"Fascinating." Robert nodded. He looked back at Debbie. She had her eyes closed. "She doing okay?"

Bernard stood up. "She's been drifting off between contractions since they gave her some pain medication. I'm sure this is tiring. Bonnie, I think maybe we should go home for a little bit. Robert can handle this, right, Son?"

His eyes darted between them, then back to Debbie, who looked peaceful at the moment. "Um, sure. But what do I do when—"

Debbie gasped and leaned forward suddenly, flailing for his hand again. Robert watched how Bonnie got in Debbie's face and began blowing her breath out in accelerating pants, then she slowed her pace when Debbie started relaxing.

"Do that," Bonnie said. "You'll be fine." She kissed Debbie on her cheek. "We'll be back later, Sweetie."

"How long is it between the pains?" Robert asked Debbie. This time she'd dug her nails into his hand, and he rubbed it. "I thought I'd sneak out to the waiting room for a smoke."

She glared at him.

"Or maybe not. I guess I can wait until Daniel is back." Robert ran his hand through his hair.

It took Daniel thirty minutes to return with cheeseburgers, fries, and coffee. The aroma preceded him and forced Debbie's eyes to pop open.

"My God, Daniel, that smell. Onions, I think," Debbie held a towel up to her mouth.

"Oh sorry. That probably made you hungry." Daniel stopped handing Robert his food and moved farther from the bed.

"No, it makes me want to puke!" She located the vomit basin and started to spit into it.

Daniel chuckled and took the food out to the waiting room. Robert looked after him and sighed.

"I guess cheeseburgers are good cold." Robert forced a weak smile.

He had started looking at the printout after every contraction to see if the waves were consistent. The nurse only came in about every forty-five minutes.

"Why are you so interested in that thing?" Debbie yawned.

"Well, I think they said it was brand new. Plus, if it's checking the baby's heartbeat, they don't seem very worried about it. Shouldn't they be watching this all the time? They're checking your pulse and blood pressure and they can see you."

He kept checking the printout frequently while she dozed. The nurse came back in to check on Debbie. "Doesn't this wave look funny? It isn't quite like it was before."

The nurse looked at what he meant. "It does seem different. I'll let the doctor know."

The next wave and the following peaked even more. Robert squinted at the readout. Dr. Hanson appeared again in about twenty minutes. He picked up the printout and Robert backed up.

"Is there something wrong, Doctor?" he asked.

"There are some signs of stress. I'm going to check her again to see if she's effaced any further. You might want to wait outside." Robert grabbed his cigarette and lighter from his pocket. He stopped before he got to the door and leaned against the wall. She'd said he shouldn't leave her.

Debbie groaned as the doctor examined her.

"The good news is that this should be over soon," Dr. Hanson said. "The bad news is we're going to do a C-section. You aren't making progress. I don't want you laboring all day. That isn't good for you or the fetus. We're seeing signs of stress on the monitor which may indicate a problem."

Debbie's lip quivered. "What does that mean? You're doing surgery? I get to sleep through that, don't I?"

"Oh, yes. Once we give you the anesthesia, you won't feel a thing."

"Oh," Debbie relaxed against the bed. "That would be nice."

Robert went back to her side and patted her hand. After a few minutes, there was a flurry of activity, with nurses putting IV bags up, and someone was smearing antiseptic on her abdomen.

Robert stood slack-jawed while they worked around him, and wheeled Debbie out of the room. After a minute he remembered his lunch was out in the waiting room with Daniel.

"What's going on? Are they still checking her?" Daniel asked.

"No, uh, they are doing a C-section. That's what the doc said. They whisked her away." He looked back toward the room he'd just left.

Daniel's brows shot up. "No kidding? Was there something wrong? That's kind of a major surgery where they cut the baby out."

"They surely won't cut the baby? I guess I didn't read that chapter in the library book."

"Here's your cheeseburger and fries. And your change. You'd better save that now. You're about to be a dad." Daniel shook his head.

"They didn't say there was something wrong. What if there's something wrong with the baby?" Robert took his bag of wrapped food from Daniel and set it on a table next to him.

"Maybe you should call your parents. I can call mine if you

want me to. They might want to come and wait with us." Daniel threw his coffee cup and food wrappers away.

The two walked down the hall to a bank of payphones. "You got a dime?" Daniel asked.

Robert fished two out of his pocket and gave Daniel one. Thelma answered after four rings. "Hello, Mama. We at the hospital."

"Robert, Baby, 'dat you?" Thelma said. "Whad happenin'?"

Robert pinched the bridge of his nose. Out of nowhere, tears had welled up and his lips quivered. "It's um Debbie. Havin' the baby." His breath came out in a ragged gasp.

"Robert, what's wrong?"

"I dunno, Mama. It's scary. They took her to the operating room. I ain't sure if they're okay or not."

"You hang on, Sugar. Yo' Daddy and I'll come right away. What hospital?"

He took a deep breath and wiped his eyes. Daniel was still talking to his father. It had to be okay. Debbie and the baby had to pull through. He couldn't believe anything less than that. It was hard enough to imagine he was going to be a father within an hour. He motioned to Daniel he was going down to the waiting room again.

He ate part of his cheeseburger and fries. They tasted pretty bad cold, but he hadn't had any food since early that morning, so he thought he should eat something. Thirty minutes later Thelma and Donovan came in with an apple pie and turkey sandwiches. That nearly made him weep again. But he couldn't be crying like a child. He had to learn to comfort a child now.

Donovan was the first to wrap him in a fierce hug. One of those things Robert had learned from his father was to not waste a hug. You wanna show someone you're with him, hold 'em tight. Thelma was gentler, but she took his face in her hands. He didn't meet her eyes; it was too hard.

"Everything's gonna be fine. You see," his mother said. They sat down, and Robert ate a sandwich and some pie.

Dr. Hanson came into the waiting room. "Mr. Washington?"

Donovan and Robert both looked up.

"Debbie is out of surgery. Everything went well. She'll be in recovery for a little bit, then they will bring her to a room down the hall. They're examining the baby in the nursery, but he seems to be fine too. You can go see him."

"Him?" Robert jumped to his feet. "It's a boy? I have a son?" He let out a whoop before he caught himself.

Daniel came back into the waiting room as Robert charged past him, leading his parents. "It's a boy! We're going to see him!"

Daniel laughed. "Congratulations, Daddy! I'll wait here for my folks. You go ahead."

Robert grinned at him, "Okay, Uncle Daniel."

A nurse spotted them outside the nursery window and motioned for Robert to come in. She put a hospital gown over his sweatshirt and jeans. She picked up the squirming baby swaddled in a blue blanket and placed him in Robert's arms, guiding one of his hands under the baby's head. The infant had tight black curls and big brown eyes and he seemed to be frowning at Robert under his blue knit cap.

"Oh my God. There you are, Little Fella. Aren't you amazing?" he whispered. He walked slowly over to the window to give his parents a better look. Thelma motioned to him to move the baby around to view all angles. Robert returned the baby to the bassinet. "You sure this one is mine?" he asked the nurse.

"Washington? Right? Debbie Washington is your wife?"

"Yeah. It's just the baby looks so . . . light."

213

The nurse smiled. "He'll get darker in a few days or weeks. It has something to do with the ultraviolet rays and the melanin in their skin. White babies often look pink or purple. It's temporary. You'll see."

Robert nodded and went back to the hall with his folks, where they saw Debbie being wheeled into a room. They waited in the hallway until the hospital attendants wheeled the gurney back out and the door was open. Then Robert went in tentatively.

Debbie was shifting and groaning trying to settle into the bed.

"You in pain?"

She panted out a breath and nodded. "They gave me some morphine. It has to kick in. Did you see him? We have a boy!"

"They let me hold him already." Robert stuck out his chest and sat in the chair next to the bed. "He's so handsome, I can't quite believe it."

A nurse brought the bassinet cart in, picked up the baby, and put him in Debbie's arms. "We're going to give you two a little time with him before we let the other family come in to see you."

"Look at him! Wow. André. I think it should be André," Debbie said. She pulled back the baby blanket to look at his little arms and legs. The baby grimaced.

Robert crinkled his brow. "I thought you wanted Adam. Adam S. Washington like the first two presidents. Using Seymour for his middle name."

"I did. But he's going to be his own person. He needs a unique name. André feels right to me. And I know Seymour was the name of your great-granddaddy who was the first free baby born in his county. But how about André Adams Washington? You'd still get the first presidents in there." Debbie studied her husband's face. "Unless you want to name him Robert Junior?"

"Nah, that's my name." Robert smiled. "André it is." He leaned

214

over and kissed the baby's forehead. "And I gotta tell you, Son, yo' mother was absolutely amazing today. Yo' father didn' even show up on time to get her to the hospital, but she was unflappable. Yo' gonna have to be very nice to her after all that pain. I know she was scared, but she came through like a champion."

"You can sweet talk me all you want, Robert Washington. I'm never doing that again."

CHAPTER THIRTY-SIX

January 1974

Debbie had gone back to Dr. Quackenbush for a refill of the diet pills. So far, she had been amazed at how well they were working. She had already lost twenty-five pounds and she was still losing weight. If she lost another ten, she could stop taking them. And she couldn't believe how much more energy she had. Granted, she had many nights when she had trouble sleeping, but she found she didn't need as much sleep and could get more things done. She'd even enrolled in some nursing classes at a community college and could get her homework done while everyone else was asleep.

Debbie, wake up. The kids are awake and I have to go to work. Are you okay?" Robert was dressed for work, staring into her face.

She looked at the clock. It was after seven. How had she slept so late?

"Yeah, I'm up. I guess I stayed up too late last night." She yawned and jumped out of bed wearing a slinky nighty she'd bought last week. She'd never thought she'd fit into a size small. And she noticed her husband noticing too. He watched her flit in and out of the bathroom, even after he said he was headed for work.

"You look fabulous, I have to admit. Very sexy. But I worry you aren't getting enough sleep." He looked at his watch, then reached for her and kissed her longingly. His hands slid down her back to embrace her hips where the nightgown was riding up.

"You'd better get on the road, Babe." She pushed him back with a smile. "I'm fine. I hope the kids won't drive me crazy today." Debbie threw on a bathrobe and went to get the baby up.

An hour later, she was trying to wrangle her four-year-old and twenty-month-old sons into their clothes. She had started attending a YWCA exercise class and she didn't want to be late.

"André, what is wrong with you? You are so slow!"

"NO! I not goin'!" he cried and laid down on the floor whimpering.

"Yes, you are! Stop whining! You aren't a baby anymore!" She tried to pick up the squirming toddler, but he escaped and ran around the dining room table. When she lunged for him, she fell on the floor and he giggled.

Debbie screamed, sat up, and held her knee. "You little demon! Now I probably can't even work out. You're horrible!" She got to her feet and limped to the couch. André came up to check on her and she grabbed him, turning him over her knee to spank him. "Don't ever run away from me. You do that and you get a spanking!" She swatted him, but he started crying, and Jamal waddled in crying too. Debbie stopped and dissolved into tears herself. She soon was cuddling both of them on her lap until everyone's tears ended.

Why did I snap at him like that? He was only being a four-year-old. He rarely has tantrums now, much better than when he was two or three. What's wrong with me? She got up and opened a package of cookies. The boys settled on the sofa with two cookies watching Sesame Street, and she ate ten cookies. Then she felt sick.

CHAPTER THIRTY-SEVEN

December 16, 1981

Debbie was surprised to find Yvonne all alone in her hospital room that morning. Yvonne had delivered twin babies two days before, Jesse and Genevieve. It seemed like she'd had a steady stream of visitors, and Daniel hadn't left her side. Even the babies had been returned to the nursery.

"Yvonne? Sweetie, you awake?"

"Huh? Oh Debs, come in." Yvonne sat up and pushed the button to raise the back of the bed to a sitting position. "Hand me that hairbrush over there, would you? I feel like I'm a mess. I did get to take a shower earlier."

Debbie picked up the brush from the built-in cabinet across the room and took it to Yvonne. "You're lucky you don't have to share a room, especially with two babies."

"They took the babies back to the nursery after breakfast. Did you see them today? They keep changing. I still have to pinch myself to believe it's real." Yvonne pulled the brush through her long brown hair.

"How are you feeling? You should rest up in the hospital while you have plenty of help."

"Oh, Bonnie and my mom are planning to come over once Daniel goes back to work. He had to go into the office for a few hours this morning, but he's been great with the babies so far."

"You've had quite a few visitors. Robert and the boys won't be here until Saturday. You should be home by then. Chantelle is anxious to see the little ones too."

"There's something I wanted to talk to you about. I'm not sure what to do." Yvonne shifted in her bed and glanced toward the open door.

"What is it? You know I have been through this baby thing three times." Debbie sat on the chair next to the bed.

"No, it isn't about the babies. We had some visitors from Daniel's office yesterday. His secretary, Judy, came by. It was nice of her to come; I talk to her all the time when I call his office. But there was someone else, a lawyer they'd recently hired: Michael Conyers."

"Michael Conyers. Why does that name ring a bell?" Debbie squinted.

"I told you about him when I was in college. I dated him during my junior year. He was pre-law when I knew him."

"Oh, the one who was so romantic. He swept you off your feet. He—oh, wasn't he the first guy you ever went to bed with?"

Yvonne raised her brows and nodded. "Exactly."

"He's working with Daniel?"

"I think Daniel hired him to be on his team. They've played racquetball. Daniel called him Mike. I didn't dream it was the Michael I knew."

"And you haven't seen him since college? I mean, that must have been like ten years ago."

"I saw him once last year. He was working at the Attorney General's office in the state capitol. I used to cover the statehouse when I was a reporter. The clerk I was talking to mentioned his name, but I don't think he saw me." Yvonne took a sip from her water bottle.

"What did he say when he saw you this time? Did he know you were married to Daniel?"

"He acted as though he didn't know me. He said it was nice to meet me. But he kept staring at me like he remembered that things had once been hot and heavy between us. I don't know if Daniel picked up on that."

"What did you say to Daniel about Michael?"

"I haven't said anything. That's where I'm stuck. If I tell Daniel that Michael was the guy who broke my heart in college or that he took my virginity, won't that make things awkward between them? I mean it has been a decade. It isn't like we still have feelings for each other. I think Michael was married and divorced in the interim." Yvonne crossed her arms.

"But what if you don't tell him?" Debbie asked. "I don't think you should keep something like this from Daniel. I remember he got pretty upset when he found out I had been lying to him about Robert back in the day."

"I feel like it's better not to tell him. The longer I wait, the more I think I should pretend I don't know Michael either."

"What if Michael tells him? That might make it worse."

"I'm not worried about that. Daniel's his boss, I think. I can't be sure he even remembers me, or at least the specifics. I think he might have had a lot of girlfriends."

The telephone rang. It was a little out of Yvonne's reach, so Debbie picked up the phone and put it on her overbed table.

"Hello?" Yvonne answered. Debbie assumed it was Daniel checking on her. Yvonne's eyes grew wide and she pointed to the phone receiver. She mouthed to Debbie, "It's him!"

"Speak of the devil," Debbie murmured.

"Yes, of course, I remembered you. I didn't know you were working together." Yvonne listened, and Debbie could hear Michael talking but couldn't make out the words. "What do you mean? What did you say about me?"

Debbie stood up and started to leave the room. Yvonne waved her hand and pointed back to the chair telling her to stay. She walked over to the window, trying to ignore Yvonne's conversation, but it was hard to ignore the flirtatious tone creeping into her voice. Yvonne and Daniel had been married for more than seven years. Was it possible she was flattered by another man's attention? No, Yvonne just had two babies. She wasn't in any shape or frame of mind to be . . .

She heard Yvonne hang up. "Well, that's settled, I guess."

"Was that Michael?"

Yvonne nodded. "At least he remembered me. He said, 'how could he forget me?' He doesn't want me to tell Daniel."

"Why not?"

She sighed. "He said he told Daniel something inappropriate about his college girlfriends once when they were drinking. He's afraid Daniel will think he was talking about me and be mad at him. It shouldn't be too hard to act as if we've just met."

"Do you think you should trust Michael after what he did to you in college? It's your choice, of course. But I still think you owe it to your husband to be truthful."

"Forget I mentioned it, Debbie." The nurse brought in the two portable baby cribs with Jesse and Genevieve inside, and both women were immediately distracted by the newborns.

CHAPTER THIRTY-EIGHT

April 17, 1982

It was typical Saturday chaos. Twelve-year-old André was searching the house for his soccer shoes. Jamal, age nine, was chasing their cocker spaniel in and out of the house, and Chantelle, six, was watching Saturday morning cartoons. Debbie was trying to clean up the mess from three children trying to make three different kinds of pancakes. Robert was putting a golf ball into a dustpan in the living room. Every so often the dog would skitter into the ball's path, and the golf ball would go spinning off in a new direction.

When the phone rang, Debbie waited for Robert to stop what he was doing and answer, but he didn't. "Hello, Washington residence," she said, trying to dry her hands on her jeans.

"Thank God you home! Robert there? This's an emergency." Debbie recognized Thelma's voice, but she usually called on Sunday afternoon or evening.

"Sure, Thelma. I'll get him." Worst-case scenarios flashed through her brain. Had Robert's father had some sort of medical problem? Last year, Debbie's father had been rushed to the hospital when he had a heart attack.

When Robert came to the phone, it was hard to tell what was happening from his side of the conversation. Thelma was doing most of the talking. Debbie rubbed her arms focusing on his expressions. He motioned to her to get him something to write on. She pulled out the pad and a pen from a drawer he could have reached himself. Robert rubbed the back of his neck and rolled his shoulders. After what seemed like hours to Debbie, he hung up and slumped onto a stool next to the kitchen peninsula. She watched his face expectantly.

Robert took a slow breath as his eyes narrowed. "My brother, Donald. He . . . he's been arrested."

"Arrested? For what? I thought he was doing so well."

"Shooting a police officer. Right in my parents' front yard." Robert's face was ashen and his hands were shaking when he laid down the pen on the counter.

"What happened?" Debbie laid her hand on his.

"Don't completely understand. Mama was babbling and crying and she wants me to come there to help them. From what I got, Truman's girlfriend and baby were sleeping in the front room. Janel and her kids were upstairs. Truman wasn't there."

Robert rose, walked to the faucet, and filled a glass with water. He took a sip, leaning against the sink. "Somebody lit the grass on fire. Donald came out to investigate and put the fire out with the hose. Then they came back waving guns around, asking for Truman. Donald went back inside and got his Beretta. Mama said the cops showed up. Donald fired once, and the intruders fired several shots into the house. A cop was hit. They think Donald shot him, and he was arrested."

"Oh my God," Debbie said.

"Mama's worried they're going to assume Donald is guilty because he has a gun and learned to shoot in the army. If it was someone besides a cop, it'd be easier."

"It sounds like the cop was hit by mistake."

"I think it was confusing. Dunno what exactly happened. Mama said they all had to leave the house cuz it was a crime scene. They found bullets in the upstairs bedroom where Janel and her kids were sleeping. Donald won't even get a hearing until Monday."

"We need to call Daniel," Debbie said.

"He probably won't know about this yet, it just happened last night."

"Daniel's a defense attorney. He can help Donald."

Robert blinked. "I hadn't even thought of that. But I'm sure Daniel's firm charges a lot of money. Donald's a plumber, he can't afford a high-priced lawyer."

"I'm calling him anyway. I'm sure there's something he can do."

She picked up the phone again. She knew Daniel and Yvonne's number by heart. "Hello, Daniel? How are those babies doing?"

"They're fine, Debs. Do you want to talk to Yvonne? She can give you a blow-by-blow of what they've done every day."

"No, I need to talk to you. You remember Robert's older brother, Donald?"

"Hmmm. He was a medic in Vietnam. He has a plumbing business now. Sure, I've seen him a few times. He came to see the twins in the hospital with Robert's folks."

"He's in a jam. They arrested him last night, I guess. They think he shot a police officer."

"What?"

"Robert, you talk to Daniel. Tell him what your mom said."

Robert took the phone and tried to repeat everything Thelma told him. Debbie went to try to help find the soccer shoe before they had to leave for André's game.

Later that night, after the kids were settled for the night, Robert waited for Debbie sitting up in bed.

"You're still thinking about Donald, aren't you?" she asked.

"Yeah, Daniel called back while you were getting Chantelle down. He thinks it would be helpful for me to go back to Nebraska. The arraignment will be Monday. He was able to see Donald once already. Daniel said the police beat Donald pretty badly."

"What? I don't understand."

"It sounds like the police already decided Donald was guilty of killing one of their fellow officers, and they beat him. He couldn't tell Daniel much since he was still in police custody and didn't want to make it worse." Robert sighed.

"That's terrible. How can they get away with that? Was Daniel able to find out more about what happened?"

"You don't get it, Debbie. They probably couldn't get away with beating a White suspect. They were trying to get him to confess or taking out their anger. They assumed he was guilty because he was Black. Open and shut case." Robert crossed his arms. "As far as what happened Friday night, this gang of roughnecks was lookin' for Truman. There were gunshots. Donald wasn't sure who'd fired on him, when he fired a shot. It must have hit the police officer, and Donald rushed forward to try to save him, and the other cops descended on him like rabid dogs."

"Did Daniel say he'd represent him?"

"I think he got the go-ahead to do that. It's likely to be a high-profile case, which is probably good publicity for Daniel's law firm, even if they don't get their usual fee. Of course, if they lose the case, it won't be good for either of our brothers. There are already protesters outside the city-county building where the jail is. That's one reason I should go, to try to keep the crowds under control." Robert stretched his neck and turned his head both ways.

"Do you want us to come with you? It would cost a fortune trying to make last-minute plane reservations for five people."

"I think you should stay here for now. I hope I'll only be gone a few days, a week at most. I can call and take vacation time or personal leave. The trial probably won't be for months. He might not get out on bail under the circumstances. If it goes to trial, you can all come then. Maybe we'll drive. I don't know. What a nightmare."

Debbie snuggled up against his shoulder, but she felt like there was nothing she could do to ease his worry.

"Debbie, did you read about the riots in Monroe, Georgia, in February? That's less than 200 miles from here." She shook her head. "A Black army private was found hanging from a tree twenty feet off the ground. There were no limbs he could have climbed on, no way he got up there himself. It was obviously a lynching but the coroner's jury ruled it was a suicide. Ol' Ralph Abernathy and one of the Georgia legislators led 2000 Black men marching eleven miles into Monroe to the courthouse to protest. There were 500 Klansmen there shouting, "White Power." As if anyone had to give White men power." Robert shook his head. "I know Lincoln, Nebraska is a far cry from Georgia but this could get outta hand. I hate to see Donald in jail but it also might be safer than back home right now."

"Promise me you won't get in the middle of some brawl." Debbie narrowed her eyes.

"I dunno what will happen. But I have to go defend my family."

"Just don't forget you have a family right here that needs you."

"I know, Baby, I know." He pulled her close.

CHAPTER THIRTY-NINE

May 2, 1970

Nancy Thompson was nursing baby Jennifer in the rocking chair in Debbie and Robert's room. Robert was studying in the basement giving Debbie and Nancy a chance to visit. Four-month-old André was napping in his nursery, the room next to them.

"This room is bigger than I remember it," Nancy said.

Debbie's eyes danced. "Oh yes. My dad, the contractor. When my parents decided we should move in with them, he got to work on a plan to expand the house. Originally, he was going to build Daniel a new bedroom in the unfinished part of the basement. But he added another twelve feet extending into the backyard so Daniel's room would have an attached bathroom. Then that would've made the basement level wider than the first floor so he made the addition to both stories, expanding my room too. Now we have room for a little TV and a table where Robert can study, and the rocker you're sitting in. He made the closet a little bigger too, but Robert keeps some clothes in the baby's room. It was a pain while they were working on it, but now I like it."

"How does Robert like living with his in-laws?"

"He's been great about it." Debbie pushed her hands into the pockets of her jeans and rocked back on her heels.

Nancy laughed, "But? I think there's a 'but' in there somewhere."

Debbie pressed her hand to her mouth. "Sometimes it's a little too close for comfort. Like we have to be super quiet if we're trying to um," she dropped her voice to a whisper, "make love."

"Would your folks be so shocked? I mean they know you have a baby already."

"I know, but knowing about it and hearing it isn't the same

thing. Sometimes, we've snuck down to Daniel's new bedroom in the basement. It has a new queen-sized bed. But I guess we weren't hiding that too well either. My mom told me I had to wash the sheets on that bed after the last time.

"And sometimes they will say something kinda stupid. Like when my mom was making a grocery list, she asked Robert what Black folks eat. Really, he would eat anything, but he told her she had to make him collard greens and grits, soppin' chocolate gravy and biscuits, fried catfish, and red beans and rice. So, my mom called Robert's mom and asked her for recipes for those dishes. Thelma laughed and told her most of them she'd never made. We did have the greens and the catfish; those were good."

Nancy stood up and put baby Jenny on her shoulder to burp her. Debbie heard André crying, so she changed him and brought him into her room.

"At least you and Robert get to live together," Nancy said.

"You're at Terry and Iris's apartment? How's that going?"

"Yes. You know I was surprised when Peter's older brother offered to let me stay with him and his girlfriend until I graduated from high school. Terry has been very sweet to me and Jenny, and I think Iris is jealous. I don't know how long that will last. I've heard them arguing."

"But nothing is going on between you and Terry?" Debbie arched her brows.

Nancy rubbed her nose as though it itched and looked away.

"Is there?" Debbie asked.

"All right, well, don't tell anyone. Terry did kiss me once. It was very nice, better than Peter actually. You know Terry's twenty-two and has more experience."

"Nancy! How did that happen?"

"I only see Peter about three times a week, outside of school, and we're hardly ever alone. Even though we're married, we haven't had sex very often. One night I had taken a shower and Terry came into my room while I was getting ready for bed. Iris works at a bar so she was gone."

"But Terry only kissed you once?"

"It was more than once, but we didn't do what you're thinking. Don't make a big deal out of it."

"You better hope Peter doesn't figure this out." Debbie sat down on the rug and leaned André against her legs. He could almost sit by himself.

"He's getting suspicious, I think. I heard him and Terry yelling at each other last night. I couldn't tell what it was about, but Peter left without saying goodbye to me or the baby."

"Can't you move in with Peter?"

"He's still living at home with his parents and younger sister. I don't know if I told you this, but his family lives on a farm on the edge of town. Peter has to milk cows in the morning and the evening. We only have a month left of high school. We should be able to last that long. After Pete leaves for the army, I'm moving back in with my parents."

"Why don't you do that now?"

"I don't want to. Terry and Iris are more fun. I have more freedom there. If I go back to my folks' house, it will be like I am their little girl again. Don't you feel that way living here?"

"Not completely. I enjoy watching my mom and dad with André. It's like how they must have been with Daniel and me. Of course, watching Robert with André practically makes me cry it's so sweet."

"I know what you mean. Jenny is so excited to see her Daddy." Nancy pulled out a blanket and laid it on the carpet and laid Jenny on the blanket. She sat on the floor next to her. "That's why I couldn't understand Linda having an abortion."

Debbie stiffened. "I don't think I can ever think of Linda the same way after she did that. And Yvonne went with her to Kansas. I didn't hear about it for a couple of weeks. Daniel told me."

"You and I are the lucky ones, aren't we?" Nancy smiled, but her lip quivered.

CHAPTER FORTY

April 18, 1982

Robert scanned the gate at Lincoln Municipal Airport for Daniel. His plane landed at five thirty in the afternoon. Over the years, Robert thought they had developed a mutual respect. At first, Daniel resented Robert moving into his parent's house after he married Debbie, about the same time Daniel left for college in Kansas. When Daniel returned home in November to a brand-new larger bedroom in the basement, his attitude seemed to improve. It took them a while to realize it, but they had a lot in common. For a White brother, Daniel was okay. Heck, he'd even learned how to play chess.

Daniel came up to shake Robert's hand and give him a manly bro-hug.

"Hey White Boy, thanks for doing this," Robert said, using his pet name for his brother-in-law.

"I hate that Donald needs my help at all. It's a terrible twist of fate. We need to talk about Truman though. I'm afraid that's where this all starts."

"Truman?" Robert asked. "I thought he wasn't even home at the time of the shooting." He wasn't sure he wanted to open that can of worms.

Daniel unlocked the trunk for Robert to put his suitcase inside. "He wasn't home. He was in a park on R Street selling coke." Both men got into the car. "He was almost busted by an undercover cop, but when they heard sirens, the deal broke up. From what I heard, the police have been watching Truman for about six months along with some of his associates. He's in some deep shit and with the crackdown on drug trafficking, he could be in the crosshairs."

"Whatchew telling me? My other brother's gettin' arrested too? Jeez Louise, maybe they'll let 'em share a cell." Robert rapped his fingers on his thigh.

"I think Truman's only shot is to get into rehab pronto. Might be too late."

"You're saying he's using too?" As if they didn't have enough to deal with.

Daniel shrugged. "That's better for you to determine. Most dealers are users."

It was only about an eight-minute drive from the airport to the county jail. "Are you ready for this?" Daniel asked. "It isn't going to be pretty."

Daniel and Robert were escorted to a secure visitors' room. Daniel signed in as Donald's attorney. The guard looked at Robert questioningly. "Oh, this is my associate, Robert Wash . . . burn, Robert Washburn," Daniel said.

Robert's eyes bulged when he saw Donald shuffling in wearing restraints. It had been only four months since they'd seen each other, but he nearly didn't recognize him. He was limping, and it was obviously painful to walk. He winced when the guard shoved him in the designated chair. One eye was nearly swollen shut, the other was also blackened. There were numerous lacerations on his forehead and cheeks, and his swollen nose may have been broken. His lip was split and it appeared that one tooth was missing.

Robert pressed his lips tightly together trying to control the rage and nausea vying for his attention. "How're ya doin'?" he finally croaked. *Jesus, he couldn't look much worse and still be upright.* Robert put his hand out to touch Donald's. Daniel shook his head at Robert.

"No touching!" the guard called out. "I thought he worked for you, Adams."

Daniel sighed loudly. "He does, but they know each other. It's difficult to see how he's been injured."

"I heard he put up quite a fight after they brought him in. Not the first guy who thought he could outfight six officers." The guard smirked and flattened himself against the wall like a predatory spider waiting to ambush his prey.

Donald shook his head stiffly. "Thanks for comin', Robert. Sure, um Thelma and Donovan appreciate it."

"What happened?" Robert said.

"Can we have a privileged conversation with our client?" Daniel asked the guard.

The guard attached Donald's handcuffs to his chair. "Bang on the door when you want me to let you out. Forty-five-minute time limit. You've used five already."

Daniel nodded at the guard. He turned to Donald. "Tell Robert what happened Friday night."

Donald's eyes grew tight. "Everyone in bed. Janel put the girls upstairs in her old room. Mom was up wid' them. Dad was practicin' his sermon. Tru not home, but his girl, Karma, she sleeping on the couch wid' their baby. Baby boy nine months now. Holt, dat his name. Dunno where they got dat.

"I hear somethin' outside. Walk to the front porch and see someone throw somethin' on fire on the lawn. Dumb-ass kids, I thought. Ran outside and grabbed the hose and put out the fire. It wasn't dumb-ass kids. Dere were five, maybe six men I didn' know. Gang-bangers maybe. Aks for Tru. Saw one car with Omaha plates. Told 'em Tru wasn't home. Dat's when I saw one of 'em had a piece. Told 'em to go on home now, Tru be back tomorrow. I went inside. They didn't leave, kept walkin' around in front." Donald took a deep breath and his gaze bounced off the floor.

"I got my .38 Beretta, watched them awhile from the window. They started shooting Mama's flowerpots, busted 'em up. Dat woke the house up. I went back to the porch, told 'em again, 'Y'all get on outta here now, Tru ain't home.' Things got crazy then. Heard sirens but the police seemed to jump outta nowhere before the cars got there. I was aiming my Beretta to scare one of the hoods who're waiting fer Tru. But bullets were flying at me right and left. I got off one shot before I hit the deck. Dere musta been at least ten shots coming in my direction. Dunno who fired. Maybe police, maybe the thugs.

"I heard a man call, 'Hold yer fire!' I looked over the wall and there was a cop right by the porch. He bleeding somethin' fierce. Blood spreadin' over his uniform. I didn't think twice. My training kicked in and I dropped the gun and ran to try to help. Rolled him on his back. Bullet went right through his heart. The other cops dragged me off him, I knew it was too late when I saw his eyes. His eyes dead already. I didn't even get to check the house. Everybody else okay, no one hit?" Donald's head bobbed like he might pass out.

"The police report said they've recovered thirteen bullets from two rooms in your house and the porch," Daniel said. "But it appears no one else was hit. They were very lucky. The police only apprehended one of the men who was on your front lawn. The others escaped in the car with the Omaha plates. One of the neighbors saw them drive away while the police were taking you down. Truman hasn't come home yet, at least not as of four o'clock this afternoon."

"Why do they think Donald shot the policeman?" Robert said.

"I assume they pulled a .38 bullet out when they did the autopsy. We might find out tomorrow. The police use .357 hollow-point bullets." Daniel jotted down something in his notebook. "We'll be doing our own ballistics study."

"But it was self-defense. Someone was firing at him." Robert scowled at Daniel, then giving his brother a sidelong look. "Did they say they were the police? Did they order you to drop your weapon?"

"Not dat I remember," Donald said, rubbed his temple, the handcuffs made this awkward.

After a few more minutes, the guard returned informing them the time was up. They told Donald they'd see him at the arraignment.

When Robert and Daniel got outside, they saw a crowd had gathered. Young men Robert recognized from church, held signs saying, "Free Donald Washington." Robert looked at Daniel for a second, then jerked his head. "Come with me," he said.

Robert walked up to a young man with cornrowed bleached hair who seemed to be directing some of the others. "Hey, man. Whatchew doin' here?"

"Organizin', whad it look like?" the kid said. He looked from Robert to Daniel. "You police?"

"No," Robert said. "I'm Robert Washington, Donald's brother from South Carolina. This here's Daniel Adams, Donald's attorney."

"So, you ain't trying to git us to go home?"

"Not necessarily. I don't want there to be any trouble. Don't want anyone else to be hurt or arrested," Robert studied the young man, remembering when he did community organizing at about his age. "Do you know Donald?"

"Sho' enuff, I know him. We all know Donald. He comes 'round the center and plays basketball wid' us. Talks to us afterward. How to stay clean and make a life. He hepped a few guys get jobs."

"This here shit, this ain't right," another young man chimed in. "Donald wouldn't shoot nobody."

A young woman standing near Daniel poked him with her finger, "You gonna get Donald outta this mess, Mister?"

"I am gonna try," Daniel gave her a pinched smile.

"You kids gonna be okay out here tonight? We'll tell Donald you came out for him. But remember, no violence, no property

235

destruction. Are you expecting more people?" Robert asked.

"Yeah, I think some older folks is comin'. Will you talk to the crowd, Brudder?" the first young man asked.

"Yeah, but now I have to go check on my parents. What's your name, Kid?"

"Winston. Everybody calls me Win. I'll be here until ten or so. Gotta make the news."

"Okay, thanks, Win. I'll be back." Robert squeezed Winston's shoulder.

They started back to Daniel's car. "Do you know who's going to be at your parents' house right now?" Daniel asked.

"I dunno. I talked to Mama last night. This ain't good for her heart."

"I need to talk to every person who was in that house on Friday night. I should probably do it right away before the memories fade. I can call one of the firm's associates to meet me there so we can record their interviews."

"I guess Karma and her baby high-tailed it outta there the next morning. You do whatever you think is gonna get Donald free. That kid was right. Donald wouldn't shoot anyone. He was trained to save lives, not take them. I'm sure he feels horrible that the police officer was killed. Hard to tell with his face looking like it went through twelve rounds in Madison Square Garden. You gotta help me keep my mama from seeing him like that." He'd have to keep his mother away from the arraignment.

"His photo may be in the paper tomorrow. Maybe I can find out ahead of the paper coming out. They may use the booking mugshot. I saw that and he hadn't been beaten yet."

When they reached the Washington's house, Daniel grabbed his briefcase as he followed Robert inside. Thelma was crying in Robert's arms before Daniel could step over the threshold. When

Robert eased his mother away, he was caught in a bear hug from Donovan.

Robert swallowed hard. "Mom, Dad, you 'member Debbie's brother, Daniel? He's heading up the defense team for Donald."

Donovan frowned at Daniel. "Being Debbie's brother hardly qualifies you as a hotshot attorney. Have you ever defended someone charged with murder, Son?"

"Yes, sir. We don't have many murder trials in this town, as I'm sure you know. But my firm has handled the majority of them. It isn't like I am working alone if that's what you're worried about. In fact, if you'd let me use your phone, I'd like to call one of my associates to come to help me. I need to take statements from everyone who was here Friday night. We also have an excellent team of investigators. From what I've seen so far, this case may hinge on a thorough investigation."

"You got any Black lawyers at that fancy law firm of yours?" Donovan continued to scrutinize Daniel.

"No, Sir. As far as I know, we've never had a Black applicant for a lawyer position. We do have a Black paralegal," Daniel said.

Donovan nodded. "You won't mind if we bring in somebody the ACLU or NAACP recommends, do you? They're telling me this case could generate a lot of publicity."

"Donald has retained me as counsel. If he wishes to change that, he can." Daniel wrinkled his nose. "If you want to add another attorney, I'll take all the help I can get. I assure you; I'm not doing this for publicity. I don't know Donald well, but my twin sister and my brother-in-law certainly have a stake here. I don't believe Donald is guilty."

Daniel couldn't reach his associate, so he did interviews with Thelma and Donovan himself. Then he talked to Robert's oldest sister, Janel. She was still there, along with her daughters, Natalie, age thirteen, and Delphia, age nine. Daniel asked to go up to the room they had been in at the time of the shooting. Robert went along and sat next to Natalie. There were two twin beds in the room placed at a right angle.

"Is it all right if we talk in front of your girls, Janel?" Daniel asked. He'd taken out a notebook and a tape recorder.

"Sure. I mean, they've been talking about this situation since it happened. It's a good thing you came tonight. We're headin' back to St. Louis tomorrow morning." Janel removed a large satchel from one of the beds so everyone could sit down.

He asked her a few questions about what time they went to bed, and where everyone was. "My mother had come up and she was reading the girls a story from one of her favorite books. We heard raised voices. Then I realized it was Donald. He was on the porch right below this room."

"What did you hear?" Daniel was writing down her words furiously.

"Something like, 'Go on home now, Tru will be here tomorrow.' Then came the hail of gunfire." Janel grimmaced. "We dove for cover but we didn't know where was safe."

"Did the police find any bullets in this room?" Daniel looked at the walls for holes where slugs might have been excavated.

Janel stood and walked around the room. "Here, there may've been one, and here, see where the wood on the headboard was splintered. Natalie's head was about six inches from this spot." Janel shuddered.

"Pooka was shot too," Delphia offered.

Janel smiled and patted her younger daughter's braids. "The bear has some stuffing loose, so she thinks he was hit."

"Can I see Pooka?" Daniel asked.

Delphia retrieved a stuffed Teddy Bear from her suitcase and handed it to Daniel. "See where the stuffing's coming out, he was shot."

Daniel examined the bear, and he could see why she thought so. There appeared to be a hole that was partially covered by a ribbon around the bear's neck.

"Where was Pooka when you heard the shots?" Daniel asked.

"He was right beside me on the pillow," Delphia said.

"No, when we heard noises, he fell off. I remember I picked him up and gave him back to you," Natalie said.

Daniel frowned. "Where did he fall, do you remember, Natalie?"

She pointed to a spot on the floor near the head of the bed Delphia and Janel were sitting on. Daniel put the bear where Natalie had indicated. "Here?"

Natalie nodded. Daniel took a flashlight out of his briefcase and got down on his stomach looking under the bed. There were some shoe boxes stored under the bed which contained old letters. Daniel thought he saw a hole in one of the boxes and pulled it out, then he pushed to a sitting position on the floor.

"What did you find?" Robert asked.

Daniel opened the box and lifted some of the letters. There was a spent .38 bullet resting in the bottom of the shoebox that had gone through some of the letters.

Daniel looked up at Delphia, then at Robert. "Looks like Pooka did take a hit. We're gonna have to make a purple heart for your bear." Delphia beamed. "You know what this means, Robert?" Daniel took out an evidence bag and donned gloves to retrieve the bullet.

"Three bullets missed my sister and her daughters."

"The slugs they recovered earlier were hollow points. This is a

.38. Someone besides the police was firing at this house."

When Robert and Daniel returned to the living room, Daniel said, "I'm sorry we had to talk about this in front of those little girls. It's horrifying that they could've been hit."

Robert scowled at him. "Maybe my dad was right. You don't understand this. Where those little girls live drive-by shootings are a daily event. They can't afford to live in a fantasy world where they think everyone loves them. You've defended Black men before, haven't you?"

"Most of the criminal cases I get assigned involve Black men," Daniel said evenly.

"Of course," Robert scoffed. "Because that's who gets prosecuted. They don't get the cushy probation or plea agreements. Cuz somewhere in the back of y'all's minds is the notion that Black people are guilty and White people are innocent. It's hammered into your subconscious before you hit kindergarten." If Daniel was so clueless, was there any hope that the jury would understand?

Daniel blinked slowly. "Look, maybe I'd better go. You'll want to catch up with your folks. I'll meet you outside the courthouse at eight-thirty."

After Robert went back to the courthouse to talk to the protestors again, he stayed up past midnight waiting for Truman to come home. He finally stumbled in, shoes in hand. The only light was streaming in from the street, but Robert recognized the way his lanky younger brother moved. Robert flicked on a flashlight hoping to keep them hidden from view from the front of the house.

"I see you're still trying to sneak in after Mama and Dad are sleeping," Robert snapped.

Truman gasped. "Robert? What the hell?"

"Don't let Mama hear you talk that way," Robert warned and rose to embrace his younger brother.

Truman's hair was long and unkempt and he wore a bandana around his forehead. He had a beard and mustache, and his dirty clothes looked like they came from the secondhand store. He smelled of sweat, cigarettes, and marijuana.

"She in bed at this hour, right?" Truman said, glancing toward the stairs. "Whatchew doin' here?"

"Our brudder's in a bit of trouble, thanks to you."

Truman sank onto the couch and scraped his face with his hands. "I shoulda known dis was too risky. Settin' up shop so close to home."

Robert stared coldly at him and exhaled. "Yeah, you probably shoulda picked another city to peddle dope."

"You gonna get all on my case now too? None of dat was supposed to go down. I was supposed to get arrested dat night."

Robert wrinkled his brow. "You wanted to get busted?"

"Part of my cover, yeah."

"What the hell you talking about, Tru?"

"If I tell you, you have to swear not to tell anyone. I mean, it's a matter of life and death."

"Seems like we're already way past the life and death stage in this mess. Thirteen bullets were found in this house. Two of them came close to hitting baby Holt."

"I know dat." Truman's shoulders slumped. "I've been working undercover for the Drug Enforcement Agency."

Robert's mouth gaped as he slowly shook his head. "Oh, you trying to leave that baby fatherless, aren't you? Are you serious?"

"I've been doing it for years. Went to training in Des Moines. This gig in Lincoln was only supposed to be for six months, but we're close to making some breakthroughs. Can't talk about dat of course. My boss wanted to pull me out after what happened here the other night, but I think dat would make it worse."

"Why were those guys after you? Did they suspect you were a plant?"

"I dunno. They haven't caught up with me yet. I sent Karma and Holt back to a safe house in Iowa. I have to change the batteries in my pager." Truman laid his head back on the couch. "And grab a shower and some sleep. Anyone crashin' in my old room tonight?"

"I don't know how you can be so cavalier."

"I'm not. I'm exhausted. Can we talk about this tomorrow?"

Robert followed his brother up the stairs and collapsed on the double bed in his old room. When Robert woke up the next morning, Truman was gone without a trace.

CHAPTER FORTY-ONE

The third night of Robert's stay in Lincoln, he stayed at Bernard and Bonnie's house. He'd lived there for four years while he was going to college, and he thought he knew his in-laws pretty well. He had lived under their rules, accepted their generosity when he wasn't in a financial position to argue. After the initial adjustment, they had treated him like a son. They had treated him as Debbie did—as if he was White.

Bonnie had invited Daniel, Yvonne, and their twins, Jesse and Geneviève, nicknamed Gigi, to come to dinner. Daniel had been trying to keep Robert updated regarding Donald's case, so they had spent most of the afternoon together.

"Gosh, those little ones have grown." Robert smiled, taking Gigi and laying her down to take off her jacket. "I don't think Chantelle was ever this small though. It seems like she's been a ball of energy her whole life."

"They're just four months. Mostly sleeping through the night, so we're beginning to feel human again," Yvonne said. "How Debs and your brood?"

"Outgrowing their clothes every month. The kids, not Debbie. She has her hands full though." Robert took Jesse from Daniel to study him. "This one's starting to look like his father already. Sorry, Kid."

Daniel rolled his eyes. "Isn't your nephew, Truman's son, about the same age?"

"Yeah, Holt's a little older. He's a cutie. Tru sent him and his mom out of town for a while."

Daniel studied his face. He seemed to be waiting for more but Robert didn't elaborate.

The dinner was a nice chance to catch up. Daniel and Yvonne left shortly afterward to get their children to bed.

"Robert, you seem pretty quiet. Is there something you want to talk about?" Bonnie asked. He had sat back down at the table, and she laid a hand on his shoulder.

"I was thinking it had been a long time since I stayed at my parents' house. When we come to visit, Debbie always wants to stay here. Next time, maybe we should stay with my parents. The kids could see how I grew up. Maybe visit with some of their cousins."

"Is there enough room there?" Bonnie sat down across the table.

Robert squinted. "There were six kids in my family, so I think we could find room in their five-bedroom house. People sleep on the couch sometimes. You've never been there, have you?" Bonnie shook her head. "And why is that? Debbie and I have been married twelve years and you've never been to my parents' house on S Street."

"I don't know. I guess when you were living here, they came over here."

"Because you were White."

Bonnie's brows shot up. "No, I don't think—"

"And you almost convinced me I was White too. That's what I have been pondering today. How did I convince myself I was as entitled as a White man? Because I married a White woman, because I started living in a White neighborhood? Maybe it was when I chose to pursue an education with mostly White guys. Or stopped trying to talk like I was from the 'hood. Or maybe it wasn't until I accepted a job in aeronautics. And now I think I sold out. Sold my soul to the devil as my dad used to say."

"And who exactly is the devil in this scenario?" Bernard sat back down at the table with Bonnie and Robert.

Robert shook his head. "I talked to some young men outside the jail building. They were trying to organize a peaceful protest in support of Donald. I used to do that kind of thing. They told me they knew my brother, he'd come by and play ball with them, talk to them about their future. He's a good man, Donald. You know he's a plumber now."

Robert studied Bernard for a moment.

"What?" Bernard asked.

"Do you have any Black men on any of the crews in your construction company?"

"No," Bernard said. "Not as far as I know. I know we have one Mexican fella. There aren't that many Black men in this city."

"Have you ever tried to recruit construction workers?"

"No, but it isn't an easy job, roofing, framing, cement work. The hours are long and the work is dirty and back-breaking. Not everyone would want that kind of job." Bernard drummed his fingers on the tabletop.

Robert raised his eyebrows. "Are you saying Black men wouldn't be willing to do hard dirty work? Did I mention my brother's a plumber? That sounds like pretty nasty work to me."

"What are you getting at, Robert? You think we need to have a quota system to hire more Black employees?" Bernard glanced at his wife. "Any coffee left, Hon?" Bonnie retreated to the kitchen.

"I'm trying to have an honest discussion about race. About what's going on right here in Lincoln." Robert watched Bernard's dancing fingers on the tabletop. Bernard couldn't see how his own industry worked.

"Okay. Here's what I see happening," Bernard said. "Ever since the Civil Rights Act was passed, preference has been given to minorities, for job bids, hiring, you name it. It's reverse discrimination. Affirmative action. That hardly seems like it levels the playing field."

"What do you think would level the playing field?" Robert

leaned back in his chair.

"No preference for anyone. Like it used to be."

Robert cleared his throat. "You don't think the way it used to be favored White men? Because White men were the ones with the experience, the ones with the contacts, with the education?"

"No, I don't. Certain things happened for a guy who had the hutzpah to figure out how to get an advantage. Like maybe for some executive jobs, it meant joining a country club, playing golf with some movers and shakers. Or for a guy like me, it might mean meeting a guy for a beer at a local watering hole, or joining the Elks or something to meet more like-minded fellas."

"So how many women or minority folks do you run into at these watering holes or Elks meetings?"

"Not many. I guess I never paid attention. What I am saying is that it's up to the individual to make things happen. The government shouldn't have to step in and tell you who to hire or associate with."

"The government allowed White men to steal land from the Native People when they arrived in North America. The government tolerated the kidnapping and enslavement of hundreds of thousands of Africans, and the subsequent enslavement of up to four million of their descendants. The government denied basic rights to women and minorities given to White men, such as voting, property ownership, or education because the government was made up of White men. And they shouldn't make up for some of those injustices?"

"That has nothing to do with me, or anyone living today. I think I'm a pretty tolerant guy. I mean look at us. My own daughter has children who are half Black."

"Do you want your grandchildren to be discriminated against?"

"Of course not. But what do you think I can do about it? I hardly ever get to see them."

"I think there are things you can do about it. To be fair, there are things I should do myself. It would help to make Blacks more visible here. They need to be able to move to other parts of town. We need to have more Blacks in public office to speak for others. If you want to do something to help the Black community here, talk to my father. He has connections that would be able to help map out ways to improve opportunities."

"What about your brother? What's the status of his case? Is he out on bail?" Bonnie brought in the coffee pot and some cups.

"No, they didn't give him bail. I think the judge thought his life would be at risk if he was out on bail since the victim was a cop." Robert took a sip of the coffee Bonnie poured.

"That doesn't seem right. I thought Daniel was trying to get the charges dismissed because it was self-defense." Bonnie pursed her lips.

"I think Daniel is still trying to get the evidence showing it was self-defense. The NAACP is sending a guy to help him next week. Maybe that will speed up the process."

"I'll tell you what, Robert. You're staying until Friday morning? Why don't you check with your parents and see if we can go to their house tomorrow evening?" Bernard took a deep breath. "I can't change the world or even this town, but maybe there's something I can do to improve housing for the Black community, to try to integrate minorities into other neighborhoods. I don't know why the hell we didn't do this a long time ago, but it's never too late to start."

"You serious, Man?" Robert said jumping up. "I'll go call them right now."

CHAPTER FORTY-TWO

March 1974

Debbie had everything in place for making a grand entrance. The boys were at the babysitter's house until mid-afternoon. She'd curled her hair, and put on more makeup than she had in years, looking like a Maybelline mascara ad.

But the little black knit dress she was wearing was the main event. She'd finally lost forty pounds thanks to those pills from Dr. Quackenbush. She weighed much less than she had in high school. She'd been exercising several times a week and taking the kids for walks. She was happy when she looked at herself in the mirror now and saw how the V-neck dress clung provocatively to her bust then skimmed over her slim waist and hips. The dress was short, but she wore eggplant-colored tights and high heels that lengthened her legs.

It had been five years since the first time they'd gotten intimate. Although it had been clumsy in the beginning, things had taken a sharp turn for the better after their wedding night. They'd realized they could make it better with a little research and hands-on experimentation. Now the biggest obstacle to playing out their fantasies was trying to find time to be together. It wasn't always easy to work in private time with two children, work, and attending school. Occasionally they found time to go dancing.

She was taking no chances today. She'd called and asked Mary Ann to schedule Robert for a lunch appointment and keep his afternoon free, or put a phony meeting on his calendar. But one of her goals was to wipe that smug smile off the face of his assistant, Shelly. She was going to have to compete with Robert's newly sexy wife.

Debbie bit her lip riding up the elevator to Robert's office. Then she remembered she was wearing bright pink lipstick and rubbed it off her teeth looking in the reflection of the brass-plated panel for the elevator buttons. She blew out her breath and inhaled. God, she could even smell the Chanel No. 19 on her wrist.

She strode into the common area where Mary Ann and Shelly's desks were. Both desks were empty. She could see Robert wasn't in his office either, in fact, the other men in the department seemed to be missing as well. This wasn't part of the plan. She looked at her watch. She was a few minutes early compared to the time Mary Ann told her to show up. She walked around looking at the photos of rocket boosters and unfamiliar components framed on the wall. She heard voices coming from behind her.

"Wail, wail, wail. Whadda we have hee-yah" An unfamiliar red-haired man with a serious Southern drawl came up behind her. He almost had his hand on her back before she turned, then he stopped himself. "Tail me y'all hee-yah about the job ohp-nun, and make mah dreams come true."

Debbie's brows rose but she was too surprised to answer. Then there was a balding man in front of her, standing a little too close. This older guy looked familiar and smelled of pipe tobacco. "Has iny-one ev-ah tooold you that you smell as diviiiine as ya look?" he asked her.

She took a step back and stepped on a third man's shoe. She recognized him as one of Robert's co-workers but couldn't recall his name. "Are ya lost, Swatie? This he-ya is Sectah Twenty. What kin we do to hep?"

Mary Ann's throaty laugh rang out, "You boys leave Mrs. Washington alone now. She has an appointment." Mary Ann was sliding into her chair. The three men looked from Debbie to Mary Ann and frowned.

Robert came out of a conference room talking to his boss. He glanced her way, then looked back at his boss and did a double-take.

"Thank you, Gentlemen, ever so much," Debbie said in a breathy Marilyn Monroe voice. They followed her eyes to look at Robert, whose mouth was open.

"Debbie?" He was stopped dead in his tracks. His boss smiled and walked away.

She walked over to him intending to walk him back to his office. But when she got close enough to see the heat in his eyes, she pulled his mouth down to hers in a hungry kiss. Robert wrapped his arms around her back and the other men started cheering and hooting. When he pulled back from the kiss, he scooted her into the relative privacy of his office. He collapsed in his leather office chair.

"Baby. Wow. You look—just wow. What are you doing here? I think I have a lunch meeting and something afterward or I'd—"

She smiled and sat one hip on the edge of his desk, hiking up the short skirt. "Your lunch date and meeting are with me. Mary Ann helped me set it up."

He glanced through the cubicle window at Mary Ann, who nodded.

"Where's Shelly, by the way?" Debbie was enjoying playing temptress now and leaned toward him on one arm flashing a little more cleavage.

"Who?" he said, his eyes dropping from her face to her dress. He swallowed hard.

"Shelly?" She batted her thickened lashes. "The assistant who works with Mary Ann?"

"Oh, her. She quit a few months ago. She wasn't very good at her job. She kept asking me dumb questions."

"Hmmm," Debbie said. *How can men be so gullible?*

He stood back up and took her hand. "If we're going to lunch, we'd better leave. I don't want those wolves out there following us."

The three men were still standing near Mary Ann's desk when they walked toward the elevator. "Mary Ann, I don't think I'll be back until tomorrow," Robert said and the other men chortled.

"This's my wife, fellas, don't get the wrong idea."

When the elevator doors closed behind them, Robert pulled her back into a steamy kiss. She should have tried this a long time ago. Her husband was no longer the skinny boy she fell for at sixteen. Now a handsome man with the same sensuous eyes and the radiant smile he'd always had, he'd started jogging to stay in shape. She liked how he kept fit. And he sure had perfected how to make her melt inside.

They went to one of her favorite garden restaurants and ordered salads and fresh fish. He couldn't seem to stop watching her. "What's this all about? Showing up at my work looking like a vixen."

She smiled. "We're celebrating. I'm five pounds under my goal weight. I'm going to stop taking the diet pills."

His brows puckered. "I think you may have lost a little too much. Your arms look thinner than I have ever seen them." He ran his long fingers up and down her arm above her elbow accidentally brushing the side of her breast and she caught her breath.

"I don't think I have ever been this thin. It feels wonderful. But I'm sure I'll gain a little back. That's why I added a five-pound cushion. But this dress is three sizes smaller than I usually wear. It looks good, don't you think?"

Robert sipped his iced tea. "Oh yeah. It looks good all right. Incredible is more like it. Those idiots at the office were practically drooling over you. I don't think they recognized you from the picnic last summer."

"I wanted to look good for Daniel and Yvonne's wedding in May. And of course, I have to make sure my husband isn't checking out other women."

He blinked quickly several times. "What makes you think I'd ever do that?"

She smiled. "I don't. But sometimes I feel like a frumpy housewife."

"I have never thought so." He kissed her hand. "I'm the one who's become a boring engineer."

"Maybe you can show me an interesting time today." She raised one eyebrow.

"What exactly is this meeting we have this afternoon?" He took a bite of his salad.

"We have to pick the boys up around three. I was planning to meet in our bedroom beforehand." This was as close as she'd ever come to staging a seduction.

Robert stood up abruptly. "I'm done with lunch. You?"

She had arranged the bedroom in advance, with a record ready to play on the turntable and candles ready to be lit. She put on her Barry White album, and they started dancing and kissing.

"What does this remind you of?" Robert asked.

She sighed, "The manse?"

"Good times at the manse. I didn't know what I was doing then. I just knew I wanted you." He pulled down the zipper on her dress. She stepped out of it as he unbuttoned his shirt and pulled off his tie. Then he pulled her back into the dance.

"I think you did all right. We ended up with André, didn't we?"

"I think you should run around in your underwear more." He started kissing her shoulder and running his hand under the cup of her bra.

"I've never thought I looked good in my underwear until now."

He pulled back squinting at her. "Oh, Baby. That's insane. You have always had a beautiful body even when you were nine months pregnant. Maybe I haven't told you enough."

Debbie pressed her lips together. "I always thought I had nice big boobs, but that was about all I had going for me."

He laughed, and unhooked her bra, sliding it off as he pulled her back to study her. "Your boobs aren't nice, they're spectacular. I've known that since the first time we got naked." He slid his hands from her shoulders down her ribcage. "You should uh show them off more often. Maybe not at my office, here at home. And you have a perfectly lovely ass, and um," he shrugged, "everything else too."

Debbie smiled. He was blushing. Robert was educated and articulate about many subjects. But he rarely mentioned her body, and now she saw why. He'd never learned to talk about women. He'd skipped the high school locker rooms, college bars, and military where she assumed men bragged about their conquests. Maybe they still had things to teach each other. She pulled him back to her pushing his shirt off his shoulders in the process so they were skin to skin.

"If you want me to wear less clothing," she said kissing him lightly on the chin, "you're going to have to ask for it. Every time."

He cleared his throat, running his thumbs under her tights and panties. "You're still not naked. Wear less."

CHAPTER FORTY-THREE

April 23, 1982

When Robert came home after five days, he wasn't himself. He was alternately brooding or short-tempered.

"I wish you'd tell me what you're upset about," Debbie began, when they had some time alone. He'd taken an extra day off while the children were in school and they were sitting at the dining table.

When he finally spoke, his voice had a hard edge. "Seems obvious, my brother's in jail waiting for a trial which won't happen for months. My younger brother is the one who brought the War on Drugs to my parents' front yard. I feel powerless to help either one." His fingertips bounced off the edge of the table.

"My parents are nervous wrecks. We were brought up to help our community, to advocate for change." Robert rolled his eyes. "But it's the same ol' shit it has always been."

"You don't think anything had changed in the past few years? What about the civil rights movement?" *Surely, he could see how things had improved. Hadn't he gotten a great job?*

"A bunch of lovely rhetoric. But the institutions haven't changed a bit. Whitey isn't going to let those change. They're designed to protect the status quo." He slumped back, and crossed his arms.

"I'm confused. Now you're talking about politics." Debbie studied him. *Usually, Robert was optimistic. Was he upset about his family's troubles or the world in general?*

"Politics is part of it, I guess. But let's change the scenario." Robert leaned forward and gestured. "Let's say six men showed up in front of your parents' house. Your dad tells them to go away, but they don't. They start shooting up your mom's flowerpots. Your mom calls the police. Your dad goes and gets his shotgun to scare them off. In the confusion when the police arrive, one of them gets

254

hit. The police are going to assume Bernard was defending himself, his home, his wife. Even if the cop dies, the courts are going to give him a pass."

"Why would the six men even show up at my dad's house?" Debbie scoffed.

Robert shook his head, "It doesn't matter. Maybe he fired them off his crew. The point is they'd accept his story and consider it self-defense. He wouldn't be cooling his heels in a cell."

"You're saying Donald is only being tried because he's Black?"

"Yes. He may be found innocent, but he still has to go through the indignity of waiting in jail, which means he's beaten up, he lives in fear, he loses his income, and his reputation. He'll always be labeled as someone who shot a cop, even though Daniel has found evidence the cop may have been shot by one of the hoodlums, or even another cop."

"Wait. Why is Donald still in jail if there's evidence someone else shot the cop?"

"You tell me." His stare was frosty.

Debbie laced her fingers together on the table. "Because he's a Black man. That's what you're saying."

"It feels like the burden of proof is on the defense. The lawyers asked my parents questions about previous incidents I didn't know anything about."

"Such as?" Debbie frowned.

Robert tapped his finger on the table. "Truman was arrested a few times when he was a senior in high school. He was part of a group that harassed the police when they tried to arrest someone nearby. They weren't prosecuted, but the gang of kids got more brazen, and the cops got more annoyed. That was the first time the front lawn was set on fire. It's a Klan tactic. My mother was scared. She grew up in Louisiana and had seen what the Klan did in her home parish.

"Truman moved out after high school and things settled down. There's been an increase in crime and drug trafficking in their area. Stuff I hadn't heard about. Stuff my family should have told me.

"So yeah, I'm pissed. Pissed at them for trying to sweep this under the rug. But mostly pissed at myself for not asking enough questions. I let your parents treat me like I was a White guy. I let my parents hide their problems—"

Debbie stood and took a step back. "Wait just a minute. I can see why you're upset about what's happened. But if my parents treat you like a White guy, isn't that what you want? That means they aren't discriminating; they're treating you like they do me or Daniel."

Robert put his palms up, smirking. "No, they'd never favor anyone the way they do you and Daniel. But what I mean is that they ignore the fact that I'm Black, they try to shelter me from the big bad world. A lot like they tried to shelter you when we wanted to date." He turned to look out the window. "I will always be grateful to your parents. They have tried to do the right thing. They just can't understand because they haven't lived it."

"I guess you think I haven't lived it either." Her blue eyes were steely now.

He looked down and sighed.

"You think I didn't hear the other mothers talking about how nice I must be to adopt an abandoned Black child when I took André to kindergarten the first day? You think I didn't dry Jamal's tears when everyone else in his first-grade class was invited to Sandy Smith's pool party? You think I didn't die inside for my precious daughter when I heard a little blonde girl at the mall ask why she had such funny hair? A little blonde girl who looked just like I used to. I really hope I never said something so thoughtless. No, you're right. I haven't lived it." She crossed her arms and faced the window.

"Debbie . . ." He waited until she turned back to him. "I didn't mean—you're not the problem. I'm beginning to think I am.

"I haven't even tried to find out what's going on in our own community. There must be organized activism with so many Blacks in South Carolina. I need to get involved. Not just for me but for the sake of our children. We ain't in Dixie anymore. This is a perfect place to push for reform."

Debbie narrowed her eyes. "Do you think that's safe?"

Robert stood planting his fists on the table. "I'm tired of being safe. I look at Donald. He goes out of his way to try to help the neighborhood youth. People look up to him, and maybe that made him a target. Truman, who woulda thought he'd try to infiltrate a drug ring? He may be a little nutso but at least he's risking everything for a better future." His eyes flashed in a way she'd rarely seen.

"But me, I'm still playing the White man's game. When I don't get the best assignments at work, I assume it's because I'm the new guy. When cops make me get outta the car for a routine traffic stop, even though I am dressed in a new suit and tie, I ignore it. When little ol' ladies cower when they see me jogging through the neighborhood like I am fleeing from a crime scene in running shorts, I smile and wave. Why are Black men still viewed differently? Why do we allow anyone to treat us that way?"

"So, you're going to resort to violence and reinforce the stereotype?" Debbie pursed her lips.

"No. Violence isn't going to fix this. There's not much I can do alone. I have to work within the system. Find other men and women who are as fed up as I am to bring attention to the problem. Other white-collar folks who have some money and standing. Even that term for professionals, 'white collar' sounds racist.

"The point is, I can't keep doing nothing! Doing nothing means they win!"

He pushed himself off the table and went out to the patio and paced. When he found a forgotten ceramic mug on the outdoor table, he hurled it against the fence. Debbie sank back into her chair and buried her face in her hands.

CHAPTER FORTY-FOUR

April 1974

Debbie stopped taking the rainbow pills from Dr. Quackenbush a few days after she visited Robert at his office. But she was so exhausted by the following day she started taking them again. She called Dr. Quackenbush's office to see if she should taper off the pills. The nurse told her she should come in for an appointment.

"How are you doing today, Mrs. Washington?" the doctor chirped, reading her chart.

"Well, I reached my goal weight and wanted to stop taking the pills. But when I did, I was wiped out. So, I thought maybe I had to do something different, like a smaller dose or something."

"Ah, yes. We can give you a smaller dose. These are prescribed for your weight range. You may not need so much now that you are smaller."

"So how long should I take this new dose before I can stop taking any?" She rubbed her fingers over her eyebrow.

"Well, you could try. But most patients want to continue with some of the therapy to avoid gaining weight back. I don't recommend stopping abruptly."

She took the new packet of pills home. She'd have to wait until the next day to try them as she had already taken some of the old ones. She wondered what exactly was in those pills and why she had to take four different kinds. On the way home, she passed her local drug store, and she went in to talk to a pharmacist.

"Is there some way to determine the chemicals in these pills?" Debbie bit her lower lip. "My diet doctor has given them to me for months but there's no label that I can find."

Mr. Browning, the pharmacist, frowned. "You've been taking pills but you don't know what's in them? Diet doctor, you say? He wasn't the one who was raided last month, was he?"

"I don't know anything about that," Debbie said. "I expected them to give me a prescription the first time, but they have always given me a supply of pills. Of course, the bill I paid covers the pills, I guess. They worked; I lost forty pounds. But now I wonder about continuing to take them."

"Why don't you give me the daily dose of each and I'll have them analyzed. I'll call you when the results come back." Debbie looked at the new instructions and gave him a day's worth of pills. "What's the doctor's name?"

"Quackenbush." She looked at her paperwork. "Arnold Quackenbush."

What did Mr. Browning mean about raids at a diet clinic? She hadn't seen anything in the newspaper. She decided she'd wait until she heard back from him before taking the new pills.

"Debbie, wake up. You've been sleeping for about nine hours. The boys are running around. I fed them already."

She opened her eyes and saw Robert, but her head felt heavy. It had been two days since she'd taken any of her pills.

"I stopped taking the diet pills for a few days. The pharmacist was going to have them tested. But now I feel like a truck backed over me."

"You asked the druggist to test your pills? Didn't he fulfill the prescription?"

She shook her head, then put her hand to her forehead. "No, Dr. Quackenbush provided the pills from his supply." She got to her feet, then sat back down.

"What's wrong? Are you dizzy?"

"I dunno. It looked like the floor was coming up to meet me. Like at a funhouse. It was weird."

"You're sure you aren't pregnant?"

She squinted. "Pregnant? Hmmm. I don't think so. I don't feel the way I did when I was pregnant. But I haven't had a period in uh months. Maybe three months. Not since I started eating less. I'm still taking birth control pills."

She stood again slowly and made her way to the bathroom and got dressed. She was thankful it was Saturday and Robert wasn't going to work. She sat at the dining table drinking coffee but couldn't decide what to do next.

"You should probably eat some breakfast. Want some eggs?" Robert furrowed his brow.

"No. I'll make some toast. No. I guess eggs would be nice. No. I don't want to eat."

"Eat something anyway. It will give you some energy. How about cereal?" He took out a box of cereal and a bowl and spoon and put it in front of her. Then he got the milk out and placed it on the table. She stared out the window.

After about ten minutes, she left the table without eating and went to the living room where her sons were watching television. André was sitting on the couch and Jamal was lying on the footstool. They were watching a Harlem Globetrotters animated show. She sank onto the couch next to André, then laid her head down and fell asleep.

When Robert began shaking her arm, she opened her eyes again. "Debbie, you must be sick. You got up an hour ago and you fell asleep again. Does your head hurt, sore throat, anything like that?"

"I'm so tired. Maybe I should go back to bed."

She slept in her clothes this time until five o'clock. She felt like she was recovering from the flu when she went into the kitchen the second time like she was weak and hadn't eaten. She took the cereal and milk back out and returned to the table. The bowl and spoon were still there.

"The boys and I went to the grocery store. That's a real treat, isn't it? They were constantly trying to grab things off the shelves," Robert chuckled. "Then later we went to the park. It's a beautiful day. Too bad you missed it."

"You think I want to be sick? I don't know what's wrong." She burst into tears. She was as surprised as the look on Robert's face.

He knelt in front of her. "What is it? I didn't mean to upset you."

She shook her head and threw up her hands, "I don't know."

She managed to eat some cereal and part of the hamburger Robert fixed her and took a shower. Robert got the boys to bed and they watched a movie on the couch. She fell asleep leaning on his shoulder.

Robert had never seen Debbie so tired, even during two pregnancies. He called his mother. She had probably seen every kind of illness there was after six children.

"I'm worried about Debbie," he told Thelma. "She usually gets by on seven or eight hours of sleep. Lately, she's stayed up studying until one in the morning and gets up at seven. But today, she can't seem to keep her eyes open. She didn't want to eat breakfast, she went back to bed and said she was exhausted. She ate dinner but then she fell asleep again. Does it sound like mono to you or what?" He poured himself more coffee. How many cups had he had that day?

"Huh. Janel had mono in junior high. She did sleep pretty much all the time for about a week. Could be dat. Debbie got a fever?" Thelma asked.

"I don't think so, she didn't say anything else was wrong."

"Is she pregnant?"

"I asked her that. She didn't think so. But when she was pregnant before she wasn't this tired."

"She's older now."

"She's twenty-two!"

"Could be thyroid. I know a girl at church who was tired all the time after having her first child. She had to take thyroid pills."

"I think Debbie said something about thyroid when she was talking about her diet pills."

"Diet pills? She taking diet pills?"

"Well, she was. She lost quite a bit of weight. I think she said she stopped taking them."

"Withdrawal. She might be addicted. I know my sister's neighbor's daughter had dat happen to her."

"I don't think she's addicted." He rubbed his damp hands on his pant legs.

"No, I'm tellin' ya. This girl, my sister's neighbor's daughter stopped taking them pills and it was like she hit a wall. Boom. No energy at all. Diet pills like speed. Serious drugs."

Robert scowled at the phone receiver. "Debbie ain't hooked on speed, Mama. She's hardly a junkie."

After he hung up, her concerns haunted him. Debbie was sound asleep on the couch still. He'd covered her with an afghan. He went to the bathroom looking for her pills. Not finding them there, he looked in her purse. There was a sixty-day supply from Dr.

Quackenbush's office with dosage instructions. He couldn't tell what the pills were by looking at them, and he found no other descriptions.

Maybe he should take one himself. Better not, they might have some female hormones or something in them. She did say the pharmacist was testing them for her. They'd have to wait.

The next day she seemed better, lethargic but she stayed awake. She started eating meals again. When the boys were napping, he tried to find out more.

"Debbie, when you were taking those diet pills, did you feel like your energy levels were increased?"

"Of course. I've never had so much energy in my life. It was amazing. But the pills were supposed to boost your metabolism and speed up your heart, so that made sense. Maybe my body is adjusting. When I first started taking them, I could hardly sleep at all. This is the other extreme."

"Do you think they might contain speed?"

"Speed? I dunno what that is. I've heard of it, but isn't that a street drug like heroin?"

"Promise me you won't take any more of those pills. At least until we know what they are."

"Okay. But I'm sure it's nothing like speed. I feel a little better today. Kinda achy. You know, maybe I do have the flu. You are tired and achy with the flu." She went to the freezer and opened it. "You know what I am so hungry for? Ice cream! I haven't had any ice cream for months."

"You said you didn't want any ice cream in the house because you were trying to diet."

"I know. But now I lost the weight and I need ice cream. Baskin-Robbins used to have this great lemon custard ice cream. It was wonderful with hot fudge sauce on it with whipped cream and peanuts. I have to have some."

"I don't think there's a Baskin-Robbins in Columbia. The closest is probably in Charleston."

"That'll be a nice drive. I didn't leave the house yesterday. It'll be fun." She started putting on her tennis shoes.

"Debbie, you can't be serious. We can get ice cream at the local grocery store."

"You don't get this. I have been denying myself all sorts of my favorite foods for months so I can look better, so I can be pretty and sexy and look slim for my brother's wedding. I should be able to treat myself once in a while! Why is that so hard to understand?" She choked back tears and fled to the bathroom, slamming the door. Naptime was over abruptly.

The boys were playing with toys on the floor when she came back into the living room.

"Are they ready to go? Did you tell them about the ice cream?"

"Ice cream!" André cried.

"I don't think driving to Charleston for ice cream makes sense," he said.

"All right. Suit yourself. I'll go alone!" She grabbed her purse and headed for the garage.

"Ice cream?" André jumped up and chased after her down the hall, but he couldn't open the door to the garage. Instead, he ran to the large window facing the street and saw her pull the car out. He started bawling when she didn't notice him. "We go get ice cream, Mommy?"

Shit. Robert picked André up and tried to distract him. Was she going to bring some back for the kids at least?

Two hours later she came back in with a pizza box with three pieces missing and two partially melted quarts of ice cream. "Pizza and ice cream! I'll heat the pizza."

Robert walked up to her as she was scurrying around the kitchen. "You seem to have more energy today. Did you get your lemon custard fix?"

She laughed. "Oh, they don't have that this month. I had to get Strawberry Fields Forever with hot fudge and peanuts. I ended up going to Orangeburg instead."

He narrowed his eyes. "You haven't taken any more pills?"

"No. I said I wouldn't. I have had some Mountain Dew. The caffeine helped."

"Soda, pizza, ice cream. I don't think any of those were on the diet you've been so faithful to," he said.

"That's so mean! You're making me crazy! You told me not to take the diet pills, now you don't want me to enjoy eating again! I need a break! Two little kids, the exercise routine, nursing school. At least when I was taking the pills I felt in control. I just ate more calories than I should in two days. It's too much pressure!" She stormed off to the bathroom again.

Robert ran his hands over his close-cropped hair. He had no idea what was wrong with her now. He took two deep breaths and put the boys at the table for some pizza.

CHAPTER FORTY-FIVE

When Robert came home a few nights later, Debbie was staring out the window. Her nursing textbook was open on the dining table. The boys were watching television.

"Studying, I see," he said. There was something off about her, but he couldn't identify it.

She didn't react right away, but finally, she sighed. "I've been trying to read this same paragraph for an hour. I can't seem to focus. Usually, I can get into this stuff, but my mind isn't cooperating."

He frowned. "Any word from the pharmacy?"

"Yeah. I wrote down what Mr. Browning said. I left it by the phone."

Robert found her notes and picked them up and walked back to her. "Digitalis— alters heart electrical impulses. Thyroid— increases metabolism high blood pressure nervousness. Amphetamines— stimulates central nervous system, hypertension. Barbiturates— temporary calming. Make a doctor appointment."

He sat in the chair next to her and ran his hand across her cheek meeting her eyes. "Did he say this was speed?"

She looked away and tried to turn her head but he held it. Her eyes meandered back to his. "I think he said that's what the amphetamines were."

Robert jumped up, bringing his fist to his lips, and turned away from her. "Jesus. My mother was right!" He turned back and saw tears running down her cheeks. Robert exhaled. "Did you make an appointment with your regular doctor?" She nodded. He gathered her up in his arms. "It's gonna be okay, Baby."

"It isn't okay. I can't stop eating. I don't know why. I've gained seven pounds in a week. I want to start taking those pills again but now I'm scared." Her eyes seemed to flit around the room like a trapped moth.

"Let's see what Dr. Wright says. When's your appointment?"

"I took the first one they had. Tomorrow at four-thirty. The babysitter can watch the boys."

"Okay, I'll meet you there."

"No, Robert, you don't have to miss—"

"I'll meet you there."

The next day, Robert went by the pharmacy and picked up the official test results from Mr. Browning. Debbie agreed to bring her pills to the appointment. Dr. Wright performed the usual physical tests and asked Debbie about her symptoms.

"Fortunately, it doesn't appear you have any permanent damage to your heart or your nervous system," Dr. Wright said. "You were lucky you didn't take these drugs for more than six months. Don't be tempted to start these again. We'll have the nurse take some blood to do a thyroid test. I suggest coming back in a month to do that again, as these pills may have affected your hormones. You should start taking a multi-vitamin for at least six months to replace some of the nutrients you may have lost and to restore your hormone balance and your periods. I'm also giving you an anti-depressant for at least thirty days, which should help with some of these side effects you're having, including the overeating."

"Thank you, Dr. Wright," Robert said.

"Both of you are going to need to be vigilant. Withdrawal from amphetamines isn't easy. Some patients report they can't find pleasure in anything, which is why they overeat. They can't concentrate, and they have memory problems. Depression is a big one. These should all be temporary, but you may have to weather the storm. I'd avoid getting pregnant, but I guess you aren't ovulating so that won't happen. Come back and see me in a month."

Debbie heaved a ragged sigh and lowered her eyes.

"There's one other thing. You showed me these drugs, and we have the analysis the pharmacy supplied from a testing laboratory. I can report this to the authorities. In fact, as a physician, I should. We can stop this Dr. Quackenbush from harming other women."

"Oh, but it worked. I mean the pills did what he said they would," Debbie said.

"These drugs aren't approved by the Food and Drug Administration. He's probably violating several laws, which isn't for me to determine. I need your permission to share the evidence with the proper authorities."

Debbie crossed her arms and licked her lips.

"Yes, I think you should report this guy. Debbie, don't you agree?" Robert said.

She put her hands in her lap and looked at them. "I guess. I feel like he took advantage of me."

"That's why you should report him," Robert said. "He shouldn't be pushing illegal drugs to unsuspecting women who are seeking help." Debbie met his eyes and nodded, then looked at Dr. Wright. "Give him the rest of them." She slowly took the envelope of pills out of her purse and handed it to the doctor.

Robert took a deep breath to try to beat back the bile rising in his throat when he saw how hard it was for her to hand over the pills. He wanted a cigarette badly and he'd quit smoking eleven months ago when they moved to South Carolina. Maybe this was how Debbie felt. Hooked.

CHAPTER FORTY-SIX

July 4, 1982

Debbie, Robert, and their three children spent three and a half days driving from their home in South Carolina to Lincoln. Robert insisted they stay with his parents, so they could spend more time with their grandchildren. The trial was set to begin in a week.

Even though she was worried about Robert and his brother, Debbie tried to keep the family calm. Emotional upsets used to cause her to overeat, but she had managed to curtail that bad habit since she had joined a local chapter of Take Off Pounds Sensibly. Now she was within ten pounds of her lowest weight and as healthy as she'd ever been.

On Independence Day, they had the usual barbeque at the Adams house. The extended Washington family had been invited, including Robert's parents and sisters Shaunda, Ruth and their families. Daniel and Yvonne and their six-month-old twins were there, as well as Yvonne's parents, Harold and Connie Edison.

Debbie and Yvonne sat on the picnic table under the crabapple tree, each holding one of the twins. Debbie's three children ran around the yard with Ruth's ten-year-old son, Ivan.

"Are you worried about staying in that house after what happened to Donald? I mean the kids must be running all over in the front yard, back yard, playing with the neighbors," Yvonne asked.

"I was a little nervous about it at first, but Thelma said they haven't had any more trouble. She's more worried about the police cars driving by on the street than any thugs bothering them. Truman went back to Iowa, she thinks, or at least they haven't seen him in months. He calls her every Sunday night."

"Daniel told me Truman has some type of secret job he can't talk about. That must be scary for his mother and father."

"We probably shouldn't talk about it." Debbie lifted baby Jesse and cooed at him evoking a big drooling toothless grin.

"Did your brother tell you we've been getting death threats?" Yvonne pulled a rattle out of her diaper bag and gave it to Gigi.

"What?" Debbie drew in her brows and bounced the baby on her knee.

"Once word got out that Daniel and Hayward Robinson, the NAACP lawyer, were defending Donald, we started getting hang-up calls. Then they started saying nasty things when Daniel was home and answered, and finally, they began threatening our family. We found a dead raccoon on our front step last week."

"You're kidding! Just because Daniel is the defense attorney?"

"Yes. That's why we had to get a second phone number. An answering service picks up the calls on our regular line. I gave you our new non-published phone number, didn't I? Hopefully, we can go back to the first one after the trial ends." Yvonne stood up and put the baby on her hip. "Oh, there's Hay now. Daniel said he'd invited him." She waved over a stocky man with gray sprinkling his nappy hair, mustache, and beard. He looked like he'd played football earlier in life.

"Here's the little princess," Hay said, taking Gigi from her and holding her up to his face. She planted her plump little hand on his broad nose, and he let out a low laugh.

"Hay, have you met Daniel's sister, Debbie? She's married to Robert, Donald's brother," Yvonne said.

"Oh, so you're Debbie, huh? Just as pretty as yo' husband said you were."

Debbie stood to shake his hand, and Yvonne took Jesse from her. She could see why Robert had been impressed with him. He oozed charm and sincerity. He looked into her eyes as though he could see all her secrets as he gripped her hand.

"I know you and Robert are worried about Donald. But I have

seen this before in other cities, other cases. Some of it's for show. Heck, I am here mostly for show. To show that Black folks mean business. Daniel has a good solid case. It's hard waiting when a family member is behind bars. But I have a good feeling about this. Don't tell Daniel that. He's afraid I'll jinx it." Hay laughed aloud again.

"You making moves on my wife, Hayward Robinson?" Robert asked when he saw he was still clasping Debbie's hand.

Hay laughed again and turned to shake Robert's hand. "How are you today, Brother?"

"I'm glad to be here. There's something I wanted to ask you about," Robert said.

"If it's about the defensive strategy, we'd better get Daniel over here." Hay looked toward Daniel in an apron over by the grill.

Robert sat down on the bench pulling Debbie down next to him. "No, it's about South Carolina. I think I told you we live in Columbia. Is there someone from the NAACP who works in the area that I might contact? I'd like to get more involved locally, maybe help with voter registration. According to the newspaper, there are almost 300,000 eligible Blacks who have never registered to vote in my state."

"Of course. I have a roster back in my hotel room. I'll look it up and get you a name and phone number tomorrow."

"Maybe I could help too," Debbie put her hand on Robert's thigh. Her husband nodded.

CHAPTER FORTY-SEVEN

Debbie and Robert were asleep in his old room at the Washington's house. Robert felt someone shaking his arm. He thought the kids were asleep by now.

"Mom, Dad, wake up! There's a man at our window. He says he's our Uncle Tru."

Debbie and Robert both sat upright in bed. André's big eyes glowed in the darkness. Robert struggled to his feet first, wearing only his boxers, and headed into Truman's old bedroom where André and Jamal were bedded down. Debbie followed, pushing André behind her.

When they got to the other bedroom, Truman was perched on a tree branch a few feet from the window, which had been opened about four inches. Robert pushed the sash up as far as it would go and helped Truman through the window.

"You okay, Brudder?" Robert asked.

"Yeah, dat easier when I'se sixteen and snuck in and out. Guess I got bigger." Truman stretched his long thin frame out.

He looked like he'd been living on the streets and smelled like he needed a shower. Debbie probably didn't appreciate him barging in at this hour scaring their sons. She put a protective arm around Jamal who'd kept a silent vigil at the window.

"What're you doin' here?" Robert closed and locked the window.

"Need to talk to you, Man. Who dis? André and Jamal? Been years since I seen 'dem."

Debbie frowned, "You boys get back in bed now. We'll talk to Truman."

She put on a bathrobe over her nightgown, and Robert pulled on his sweatpants and T-shirt, then they went downstairs to the dining room.

"I thought you left town, Truman. What's with the secrecy?" Robert poured water in a coffee mug before he took his chair.

"I've been here since the shooting, Donald's arrest. Went back to see Karma and Holt in Iowa last week. But dere's something you need to check out. Well, da lawyers need to check out."

"What?" Robert yawned. "It's one in the morning. Talk fast."

"They needa look for a second bullet. The policeman who was hit, Jones. Word on the street was he an' his partner, Smitty, getting a kickback from the drug dealers. I heard Smitty shot Jones, to keep him quiet. If dat's true, he should have a hollow point in him. You seen the autopsy report?"

"I think I did. Daniel didn't mention more than one bullet. I think the .38 was in his upper back. Must have gone through his heart if it killed him."

"But you're suggesting it didn't kill him, right?" Debbie said. "There was another wound that wasn't on the autopsy? The coroner couldn't have missed that."

"Not saying he did. Jus' saying dere's somethin' fishy. Will you tell 'dem lawyers?"

"Yes. What about you? Are you staying safe?" Robert pressed his lips tightly.

"Getting' close to the end. Been pulled into this police kickback thing. Tell Adams to watch out. Heard that Smitty has somethin' planned for him."

"What do you mean?" Debbie leaned toward Truman.

"Dunno, jus' heard 'em say he'll get what's comin' to him."

"You have talked to this Smitty guy, the one you think shot his partner?" Robert's eyes narrowed.

"We do business. Part of my gig." Truman shrugged. "Course

he don't know my real name. Gots to go. Anything to eat?" He looked in the refrigerator and found some ham and sour cream raisin pie. He put some of each on a plate and scarfed it down. "These druggies don't eat well. God, Mama's pie is the best."

"You ain't gonna wake the folks up?" Robert wrinkled his nose at the way Truman was shoveling food into his mouth. Their mother would've called him on his table manners.

"Nah, Mama don't want to see me in this getup. I come 'round once this is up. A month tops."

Robert let him out through the back door. He squeezed Truman's shoulder. "Be careful."

"What do you think?" Debbie asked her husband after they got back to bed.

"I'll tell Daniel. I don't see how this will help though."

CHAPTER FORTY-EIGHT

"We've asked for a short continuance," Daniel told the Washington family members gathered at the S Street house the following Friday evening. "We've obtained information that the coroner's report may have been falsified. I reviewed the version of the report with the new coroner, Dr. Jacobs, and he said there is missing information, which led him to believe we have received an incomplete or altered report. I have an investigator in Fort Collins, Colorado, trying to contact the previous coroner, who did the autopsy, and have him look at the version we have to verify its authenticity."

"I don' understand," Thelma said. "Why would you have a report dat wasn't complete?"

"The prosecution is messin' wid you." Donovan poured himself more coffee from the pot on the dining table where they were sitting.

"I don't know. We asked for a new report and the prosecution claims the one they gave us is what they have. They were planning to have Dr. Jacobs present the autopsy report which showed only one bullet hit Officer Jones, a .38. But when we questioned Dr. Jacobs further, he said there should have been more information on the autopsy, at least if he had performed it. So, we're seeking out Dr. Sheen, the previous coroner."

"Do you think the coroner could have gotten away with filing a false report?" Debbie asked.

"I've never had this questioned before. Hay said he's seen it though."

"Oh yeah. A case I worked on in Mississippi. The coroner was bought and paid for by the prosecutor, who was his cousin," Hay chuckled.

"Do you think someone other than the coroner could have messed with the report?" Robert asked.

"I don't know." Daniel rubbed his brow.

"Who do you suspect?" Debbie asked locking eyes with her brother.

"I . . . I shouldn't say more until it's been checked out. But someone may have revised the autopsy report."

"Smitty?" Robert frowned.

Daniel sighed. "We're investigating. That's all I can say." He closed his briefcase on the table. "I wanted you all to know the trial won't start on Monday as planned."

Hayward went back to his motel after the meeting, but Daniel stayed around for a little while to see André, Jamal, and Chantelle. They were engaged in a rousing game of "Sorry!" when Donovan's melodious voice was heard rehearsing his Sunday sermon from the front study.

"Who's that?" Daniel asked.

"Dad," Robert said. "He always records his sermons on Friday night. Then he does some revising on Saturday, but he mostly has it down by Friday night so he can memorize parts of it. He keeps his recordings too. I think he's saved some of them back to when we were kids in St. Louis."

"He records them on Friday night? What time?" Daniel asked.

"Oh, he's startin' early tonight. Usually, he doesn't do it 'til everyone else is in bed and it's quiet," Thelma said.

"He didn't make a recording the night of the shooting, did he? April 16?"

Thelma sighed. "Oh yes. He couldn't listen to dat one though. When the shooting started, he hit the deck, and dat darn tape kept rolling. You could hear it all, the shots, the crying, swearing. It breaks your heart." Her eyes began to mist.

Daniel jumped up. "You're kidding. I have to hear that tape!"

Debbie stood up and put a hand on his arm. "What is it?"

"Don't you see? It could be an important record of what happened."

"If you think it could help, c'mon." Robert and Debbie took Daniel to the study where Donovan was seated at a massive steel desk recording his sermon.

Robert opened the door and waited until Donovan finished his sentence and turned off the tape recorder. "Dad, where's the tape you made on April 16?"

Donovan's eyes clouded. "You don't want to hear it, Son. It has gunshots and all sorts of wailing and screaming. I only listened to part of it and I couldn't take it."

"But Daniel needs to hear it. It might help the case."

Donovan's bushy brows rose. "Oh, well, let's see. I put it in a different place. I didn't want your mother to find it. Bad enough she had to live through that night." He began opening drawers. There were shoeboxes in some of the drawers of the desk with dates printed neatly on them. Then he went to the closet and there were more shoeboxes with more dates shown on the end of them. "Hmmm, where did I—?" He snapped his fingers and pulled open a bottom desk drawer and pulled out a white envelope behind the shoe box. "Here!" he said, opening the envelope. It was neatly labeled "April 16, 1982 shooting." He handed it to Robert.

"This is it?" Daniel asked.

"You want to hear it?" Donovan asked. When Daniel nodded, he popped the tape he was using out of the cassette player and put it near the lamp on the desk. "If you're going to play that, I'm taking the kids outside. I don't want them to listen."

Robert sat in his father's chair when he left and put the cassette in, pushing "play." Robert, Debbie, and Daniel listened to Donovan's sermon. It was for the Sunday after Easter, and he was talking about the Resurrection and the disciples. When they were about ready to push "fast forward" they heard something in the background. Donovan stopped talking on the tape for a moment. There were scuffling sounds, the door banged. There were gunshots. One, then about twenty seconds later, one more. Something shattered. They heard a man's voice shouting, "Y'all git on now! Tru ain't here, I tod 'ja." A chair scraped the floor.

"That'd be Donald's voice," Robert said squinting at the tape.

Robert turned up the volume on the side of the cassette player. They heard sirens approaching and getting louder. More shouting, they couldn't make out the words.

Then came the barrage of gunshots. Debbie gasped. They heard a thumping sound close to the cassette player like Donovan fell to the floor. Then screaming within the house. A woman screaming in a nearby room, a baby crying. Banging, pounding, shouting inside and out. They heard a man's voice yelling, "Hold your fire!" Then more sounds of footsteps running and scuffling on the porch, in the house, hard to distinguish what was happening.

"This is horrible. No wonder Donovan couldn't bear to hear it!" Debbie clasped her hands over her ears.

Robert hit the pause button and stood up to pull Debbie into his arms.

"It seems horrible, but I think I heard something important," Daniel said. He sat in the chair where Robert had been and rewound the tape slightly until he found the part with the gunshots.

Debbie jumped when he played that section again. "Stop playing that, Daniel!"

"Debbie, you can go if it bothers you. Did you hear what I heard, Robert?"

Robert shook his head. Daniel played the whole gunshot segment again. Debbie buried her face in her husband's shoulder.

"I'm no ballistics expert, but I have listened to enough gunshots for trials to think what I hear are Smith & Wesson revolvers. That is the police firing. But right toward the end, you can hear a Beretta 92. If I am right, this proves the police fired first. There is no warning before they started shooting, they just opened fire." Daniel looked from Robert to Debbie and pressed his fingers to the sides of his cheekbones. "I have to get this to my ballistics expert and see what he says."

"But what would it mean?" Robert asked. "We know the police fired at the house, they found spent bullets in the walls. But Donald had a gun pointed at them."

"Not at the police, the thugs, the gangbangers. Those first two shots. Those were different. That must've been when they shot up Thelma's flowerpots. I wonder if they bothered to pull the slugs out of the pots."

Robert scoffed. "I dunno. Mama was mad. She showed me a picture of her pots, blown to smithereens."

"What happened to those pots?"

"Beats me. Let's ask Mama."

In a few minutes, they were in front of the porch, where Thelma pointed to two new ceramic pots with geraniums growing. Daniel had his flashlight in his hand.

"You replanted the flowers? What did you do with the old broken pots?"

"Honey, they was busted so bad, they wouldn't hold water." Thelma fisted her hands on her hips. "I jus' got me some more soil and moved the whole works into these new pots. Lucky for me, the plants hadn't had time to get roots going in April."

"So, the slugs could still be in there?" Daniel asked. "Where were the pots sitting?"

"Right here. Same as now."

Daniel shone his flashlight in the space behind the pots in a crack in the foundation of the porch. "Bingo," he said. He documented the location of the slugs, taking photos, and pulling them out, and putting them in plastic bags. "These probably won't matter, but they help tell the story of what's on the tape. Reverend Washington, is it all right if I take your sermon tape?"

Donovan was sitting in his rocker on the porch. "You go on and take it if you think it'll help Donald. But I may want it back."

"They can probably make you a copy," Daniel said. He put the tape in his briefcase along with the slugs and his camera. He'd already collected Thelma's photos of the busted flowerpots.

"You think this will help, Daniel?" Debbie asked as he started to leave.

"I can't say for sure, but it might prove self-defense. This tape was a lucky find."

Debbie threw her arms around Daniel. "This family needs a break."

"We're trying, Sis. Keep your fingers crossed."

"I'm doing better than dat, Daniel. I'm putting my faith in God. I'll say a special prayer for you tonight too," Thelma said.

"Thank you, ma'am. Like I said, all the help I can get."

CHAPTER FORTY-NINE

It was the first day of Donald's trial. Donovan, Thelma, Shaunda, and Ruth were in the courtroom. Janel was on the potential defense witness list so she wouldn't appear with the family until after her testimony. Yvonne sat with Robert and Debbie.

Debbie scanned the faces of the jury. "There's only one Black juror," she whispered to Robert.

Robert nodded. "This is why voter registration can be so important for minorities. Jurors are pulled from voter lists."

"Yvonne, who's the other man sitting next to Daniel? I know Hayward, but who's the tall guy who looks like a movie star?" Debbie concealed her mouth with her hand.

Yvonne smiled. "That's Michael Conyers. Now do you get it?" Debbie's brows winged up. She got it all right. Any woman would be drawn to those broad shoulders, perfectly styled dark hair, impeccably tailored camel suit, and pleasingly symmetric bone structure. Debbie found herself side-eyeing Yvonne who kept stealing glances in his direction.

The proceedings got underway with the opening statements. Debbie had never seen Daniel in the courtroom. She had already moved to South Carolina when he finished law school. Her eyes flooded when he delivered his opening argument.

"The defense will demonstrate that Donald Washington only brought his handgun out to his parents' porch after he had told the intruders to go away. They were looking for his brother who wasn't at home. When the intruders didn't leave and started shooting up his mother's flowerpots, only then did Mr. Washington threaten them with his handgun.

"Several police officers arrived on the scene, and seeing Mr. Washington with a handgun on his porch, they opened fire on him. We will prove that only then did Mr. Washington fire back, in self-defense, believing it was the intruders who were firing upon him. The police didn't identify themselves to Mr. Washington. While Officer Jones was hit in the melee, he wasn't only hit by a .38 bullet which may have come from Mr. Washington's gun. He was also hit with a hollow-point bullet, the caliber used by Officer Jones' squad. While the .38 bullet hit Officer Jones in the shoulder, the hollow-point gunshot wound was lower and more likely to have been the fatal shot.

"In addition, the defense will show that the neighborhood in which this incident took place has been plagued with armed youths, often high on drugs, roaming the streets, and shooting up property. When Mr. Washington heard shots and felt bullets ricocheting around him as he was trapped in the confines of the stone and wooden porch, he had the impression that his family home was under attack as so many others have been in the past. The police force has failed to protect the citizens of his neighborhood, so as a trained army veteran, he stepped up to assume that duty. It is tragic Officer Jones was killed, but we will show that Mr. Washington wasn't responsible for his death."

There was a recess after about an hour. Debbie roamed around the halls moving to talk to different members of Robert's family. She didn't know either Shaunda or Ruth well, since she and Robert had been in South Carolina for so many years and hadn't always been able to come home for holidays or other family occasions. Everyone was optimistic but cautious.

She went in search of a drinking fountain. The first one she found had a sign on it stating it was out of service. She walked up to the next floor to find another fountain near the restrooms. As she approached a corner, she heard voices. She thought she recognized Yvonne's voice. Maybe she had also been searching for a drinking fountain. She stopped when she heard an unfamiliar man's voice. They were laughing together. Debbie flattened herself against the marble wall and peeked around the corner.

She wasn't sure what she saw. The man had his hand on the wall and seemed to be pushing away from Yvonne. She'd seen that camel suit in court, on the dark-haired man. Had they kissed? She couldn't be sure. The man continued backing away and smiling at Yvonne. Debbie rounded the corner so she was in view.

"Debbie! I didn't think anyone else was up here!" Yvonne laughed. She stepped back and looked at her companion. "Oh, Michael, you should meet Debbie Adams. I mean Washington, Debbie Washington." Yvonne beamed at her. "She's my very best friend in the whole world."

Michael stopped, glancing back at Yvonne, then approached Debbie. He held out his hand to shake hers. "Nice to meet you, Debbie. I'm Michael Conyers. You must be related to the defendant."

Debbie leveled him with her stare. Just because he was good-looking didn't mean he was a good man. What was going on? "Yes, Donald is my husband's brother. And Daniel Adams is my brother."

Michael stiffened and sucked in his breath, then smiled faintly and retreated into the main hallway.

"Yvonne, what the hell are you doing?" Debbie asked.

"It's nothing. Don't worry. He was teasing me. I came up here to use the ladies' and ran into him. C'mon, we'd better go down and see if they're ready to start."

She wanted to trust Yvonne. She hadn't worried when she'd told her about Michael right after her babies were born. No woman would start an affair right after giving birth. But Yvonne looked as beautiful now as she ever had. She'd lost all the baby weight, but her figure seemed to be curvier now. She looked particularly nice today in fact, maybe that was a new navy dress. Her rich brown hair had been styled and bounced as they walked along. She glowed like a woman in love. Debbie hoped her worries were in vain.

The first four days of the trial were the presentation of the prosecution's case. Sometimes it became tedious, and Debbie found herself looking over at the back of Donald's head. This must be torture for him having someone try to prove you are evil. He can't even defend himself or show anger or disgust for fear of making a bad impression on the jurors. Daniel and Hay didn't say much the first few days, other than to make objections and raise procedural questions. Then she'd turn to Robert, who often pursed his lips, crossed his arms, or tapped his foot. Sometimes he'd sigh quietly and look at the floor. She took his hand and tried to comfort him. He'd nod and steal a sidelong glance at her.

Daniel and Hay asked to meet with the family after the prosecution rested its case. The judge recessed the trial in mid-afternoon on the fourth day before having the defense begin. They gathered in the dining room of the Washington house.

"So far all the jury has heard is the prosecution's case. They have to prove Donald is guilty of manslaughter or murder. They proved he fired his weapon. They proved he had a concealed weapon permit. They proved he was a good shot in army training. But I don't think they proved he even shot Officer Jones," Daniel said. "Of course, I'm not on the jury. These people are." Hay opened his briefcase and took out twelve pieces of paper with key facts about each of the jurors. He spread the papers on the table.

"We need to show these twelve people that Donald's a good man," Hay began. "He owns his own business; he works for his community. He cares about his family. The first juror is a Black man. If we can't convince him, we should go home." Donovan laughed loudly and the others chimed in their agreement. "Three of the women work downtown, one in a bank, one at a store, and one for the city. Three White men work in construction, for the electric company, and for an insurance company. The five remaining jurors are White housewives, ranging in age from twenty-two to seventy-four. We have to convince the housewives." Hay looked at Debbie, and the others followed his gaze.

"Why are you looking at me? I'm working part-time as a licensed practical nurse."

"Yes, Sugar," Hay nodded. "But you're White, married and you have children. If you didn't know Donald at all, if he were your neighbor, what would convince you he was a good guy, instead of a cop-killer?"

"Well," Debbie shifted in her chair. She didn't expect to be put on the spot. "If he got on the stand and looked at me with those big soulful eyes of his and told me he was innocent, I'd believe him."

Everyone in the room laughed, even Robert. "It sounds like you have a crush on my brother, Baby!" Robert laughed.

Debbie covered her mouth as the color rose to her cheeks. "No, that isn't what I meant. It's that Donald himself would be the most convincing."

"We can't let him testify, Debs." Daniel stood behind her with his hands on her shoulders. Why did he still do that? As if he was the parent and she the child? "You let a defendant take the stand and you are letting the prosecution take potshots at him. It's not worth the risk in this case."

"What could other people say about Donald that would convince you he was sincere? He can turn those puppy-dog eyes on the ladies in the jury if you don't think it will scare them," Hay said.

"Well, let's see. You could have kids talk about his work at the community center." Debbie picked up a pencil and doodled on some paper on the table.

"Check," Daniel said.

"Someone could talk about his service record as a medic, and his work as an Emergency Services Technician after he was discharged from the army."

"Check," Hay said.

"What if you had some of his customers talk about how he came to their rescue when they had a plumbing emergency?" Debbie said.

Daniel and Hay looked at each other.

"Because housewives would relate to a backed-up toilet or a broken shower or flood in their kitchen. That plumber would be my hero."

"That's a damn good idea! Can you find someone like that, Thelma? You have his business records here, don't you?" Daniel asked.

"Sho' thing. But I can probably tell you a few of those from memory. Who'd ya think answers those frantic phone calls?" Thelma smiled.

"Great. Get me three or four names and numbers and I'll have the office follow up." Daniel rubbed his hands together.

"Debbie, maybe you can help me reach those White housewives," Hay said, squatting next to her chair. "I'm trying to explain to the jury how Donald felt when he saw those bullies out there calling out Truman. I've talked to Donald about this, he says he recognized these boys, not by name, not because they were neighbors or school mates, but he knew their type, he knew what they wanted. It was about drugs, about gang loyalty, about whether Truman was toeing the line or wavering. Donald, he's seen this for years. Here in Lincoln, in Omaha, when he lived in Chicago for a few years. It's a kind of brotherhood of the lawless. Donald knew they was trouble as soon as he spotted them. And he knew Truman wasn't there to protect his family. Truman's baby and his woman were right in the next room. Donald had to step up. He's angry as all get-out with Truman for the spot he put him in, but that's what a brother does. He steps up."

"I think you should say that. Everyone can relate to how far you'd go to protect your family, it's universal," Debbie said. "But it seems like the real problem is you shouldn't have to try to explain to the White jurors what a Black man was feeling, any more than you should have to explain what the police officer was feeling. I mean they must be terrified every time there are gunshots. There should be Black women on the jury. There should be more Black men on the jury. They're the ones who can help enlighten the White jurors.

"I was on a jury in Columbia last year. It was a medical malpractice case. The other jurors listened to me when I had an opinion about something relating to the hospital procedure. But I listened to the Black jurors when they talked about how the victim was discriminated against. I had no idea that was happening today in the health care industry."

"How many Black jurors were on that case in Columbia?" Robert asked.

"Four. There were four Black jurors out of twelve. And Columbia has a high population of Blacks compared to here. The plaintiff was Black, the defendant was the hospital which was represented by White men. But why, especially in a criminal case, can't someone truly be tried by a jury of his or her peers? Why couldn't Donald request to have a jury of at least nine Black people?"

"Debbie," Daniel sighed. "You don't know how this works. We only had one Black jury candidate in the pool of people we were provided."

"And where did the pool come from?" Debbie pursed her lips.

"It comes from voter rolls. And you know in Lincoln, we don't have a large population of Blacks and many aren't registered to vote. It's their choice. You can't force people to sign up to vote. I imagine some people don't want to be drafted onto a jury because they can't afford to lose the wages or they don't have childcare."

"That's the system!" Debbie sniffed. "I say the system is broken. Let's make a new system. Let defendants make some choices as to the jury makeup. Pay jurors to serve. Not twenty bucks a day but a reasonable amount based on the average wages in the town, or the cost of living, whatever. If you have more Black defendants but not a high percentage of Blacks in the population, well first of all, why are so many Blacks getting arrested and tried? But what would be wrong with having a job of being a juror? You could still have a fairly large pool of jurors, say fifty or so, and they'd only be paid when they worked, but they'd become good at it."

Daniel scoffed. "And you're going to let the defendant pick the jury?"

"Not the exact jury maybe, the whada-ya-call-it, demographics. Like, say I was the defendant, and I was charged with hmmm . . . , murdering my lying cheating husband. I'd want a jury of mostly women, preferably divorced women."

All eyes were on Robert. "Don't look at me, I'm innocent!"

Debbie laughed, "Not him, he's a peach." She patted Robert's arm. "This is hypothetical. I'm saying the defendant should be able to choose what a jury of her or his peers would look like. Maybe there'd need to be a backup pool of people who could substitute for the main professional jurors. Like in the Revolutionary War. If you were drafted, you could find another guy to take your place in case you wanted to stay home and grow tobacco or something."

Daniel rolled his eyes. "While this is appealing on some level, we have to deal with reality."

She rose and leaned toward her brother over the table. "We have to change the reality. If not for us, for our children, Daniel."

"Can we table the revolution and get back to the case we're trying on Monday?" Her brother ran his hands over his face.

"No, Daniel, your sister has some good ideas," Hay said. "We might want to interject a little of her idealism into our closing statements. If she can see the need for reform of our justice system, the other ladies on the jury might also. Let's kick that around some more."

CHAPTER FIFTY

On Saturday, Robert accompanied Daniel to the jail to visit Donald. Daniel had been taking Hayward, but this time both attorneys felt Robert should go.

"Ya ready to present my case, Daniel? Or are ya here to ask me 'nother fifty questions?" Donald wrinkled his nose.

"No, if I was here to ask more questions, I'd have brought Hay or one of the paralegals. They're better note-takers."

Robert scrutinized his brother-in-law. "Why did you aks me to come?"

Daniel smiled. "I don't know exactly what is going to happen Monday, but there's something brewing. The prosecutor called me and said they have been doing an internal police investigation which involves the officer who was killed, Jones, his partner, Smitty, and a few other officers. There was another officer they believe was involved who died in an automobile accident last year. My associate, Michael Conyers, used to work in the Attorney General's office and he has been getting hints of this for a couple of weeks."

"What 'dat have ta do wid' me?" Donald asked.

"Well, you know we had a big problem with the autopsy report. It turns out part of it was lost or altered. The previous coroner kept a copy, thank goodness. Otherwise, neither the prosecution nor our side would have gotten a correct autopsy report. Officer Jones most likely died from injuries from a second bullet, a hollow-point, which had to have been fired from one of the officers on the scene. Smith was immediately behind Jones and could have hit him. Granted, it might have been by mistake. Smith was certainly was very vocal about trying you for the crime."

"But you don't think it was an accident?" Robert asked.

"They haven't given me the results of the investigation, but I suspect they were both taking payments from drug dealers to look the other way. I've heard rumors about this. Maybe Smith wanted to make sure Jones kept quiet permanently. If Smith was responsible for Jones' death, it would make sense for him to mess with the autopsy report so it looked like the only bullet recovered was a .38. And by the way, my ballistics expert is planning to testify the .38 slug in Jones' shoulder wasn't fired from your Beretta. The markings on the .38 slug found in the body match the .38 slugs we found behind Thelma's flowerpots. We had trouble getting our hands on the actual bullet since it was part of the state's evidence, but the prosecution is aware of it now. The problem with ballistics is trying to explain it to the average juror."

"You're saying the hoods were still there when the police arrived? They were firing too," Robert said. "Why didn't the police catch them?"

"There's a good question. It's odd. In fact, the state's case is beginning to smell pretty bad." Daniel beamed. "I don't think I'll have to present my defense on Monday. I think I can spend some quality time with my beautiful wife and kids tomorrow."

"You ain't quitting on me now, Counselor," Donald furrowed his brow.

"I ain't a bettin' man, but if I were, I'd bet the prosecution will drop the charges before I get started." Daniel leaned back in his chair and laced his hands behind his head.

"Seriously?" Robert's eyes went wide. "And if that happens, what about Donald?"

"I'd be done, be free to go home?" Donald locked eyes with Daniel.

"I can't be one hundred percent sure. I do still have to be ready to present my witnesses and evidence, but I'm telling you what I think will happen based on what the prosecutor told me a little while ago."

"Would that wipe Donald's record clean? He wouldn't have a

felony charge against him?" Robert asked.

"No, the record would show the charges were dismissed. Which is better than an innocent verdict, by the way, because it proves the evidence didn't support the charges in the first place."

"What about the three months he spent in jail awaiting trial? He lost income; his reputation was damaged. He was beaten for Christ's sake. Can he sue?" Robert set his jaw and raised one brow.

"Let's cross that bridge when we get there, Robert," Daniel said. "Hayward is the civil rights expert. Right now, I suggest you go home to your family and do what they are known for: pray."

CHAPTER FIFTY-ONE

Daniel had asked the entire Washington family to be present on Monday morning for the start of the defense presentation. He even wanted the children to be there, if possible. He told them it was a sign of solidarity. Debbie suspected there was something else going on. She had pestered Robert enough that he admitted they had reason to be optimistic, but he didn't want to get his parents' hopes up yet.

Debbie had dressed André, Jamal, and Chantelle up in their Sunday church clothes and they sat with her and Robert in the courtroom. Janel and her husband, Thomas, were seated nearby with Natalie and Delphia. Shaunda and Ramón, and Ruth, Peter, and Ivan were all grouped nearby.

"This looks like Sunday services," Donovan joked, looking around.

"Gotta keep those prayers coming, to guide Daniel's words," Thelma said. "Dat's why it was important we all come, to show our support and faith in Donald and God Almighty."

"Is the Defense ready to present its case, Mr. Adams?" the judge asked.

Daniel rose automatically. "Yes, Your Honor."

"Your Honor, the State has a request. May we approach the bench?" the District Attorney asked.

Daniel, Hayward, and the D.A. went up to talk to the judge for about three minutes.

Daniel walked back stone-faced, but Hay couldn't contain a smile.

"Your Honor," the D.A. began, "In light of some additional evidence that has come to our way, the state is dropping all charges against Donald Washington."

There was dead silence in the courtroom. The jurors squinted.

The Black juror grinned. The Washingtons let out a collective gasp. Then there was the wild roar of glee.

The judge pounded his gavel for order. "Mr. Washington, will you please stand?"

Donald rose on shaky knees. His lips were trembling and he put one hand up to them. Daniel and Hayward rose with him. Daniel tipped his head back and closed his eyes.

"Mr. Washington," the judge said, "it appears you have been charged with a crime you didn't commit. The court offers its sincere apologies for your trouble. All charges are dismissed and you are free to go."

Debbie couldn't tell who was screaming the loudest. Chantelle covered her ears. Her boys seem to understand this was a celebration and stood on the benches. Thelma was jumping up and down. Shaunda held her arms to the sky and was offering praise. Ruth was hugging everyone in sight. Natalie and Delphia started dancing in the outside aisle. Then Thelma was in Donald's arms spinning around, and Donovan had him in a giant bear hug. Debbie wrapped herself in Robert's embrace, then hurried over to hug Daniel before he escaped.

"You did it, Daniel! I'm so proud of you!" Debbie fought the tears threatening to ruin her makeup.

"Everyone helped put this together. You helped. The family helped. Even Michael Conyers had a secret inside source—" Daniel told her.

Debbie had trouble hearing him over the uproar of the celebration. "Michael told you his secret?"

Daniel squinted at her, "Well yeah, it helped the case—"

"He told you about Yvonne then."

Daniel wrinkled his brow. "Yvonne? No, Yvonne couldn't get off work today."

"He told you he slept with Yvonne in college?"

Daniel's brows shot up and his head jerked back. "What—what are you talking about? Michael Conyers first met Yvonne when we had the twins."

Debbie met his gaze and shook her head slowly. "I thought you said you knew. I'm sorry. Talk to Yvonne." She backed up and ran smack into Donald.

He spun her around in an embrace. "I feel like kissin' everybody! You the first one who ain't my sister!" He locked his mouth on hers so fast, she was breathless. She felt Daniel brushing by her, leaving the courtroom.

Donald let her go as Robert came up to intervene, waving a finger in Donald's face. "I suppose I'll cut you some slack today, considering you haven't had a woman in months, but don't ever try to kiss my wife again!" Donald let out a wicked laugh and hugged Robert, picking him off the ground.

A tall well-groomed man in a suit appeared in front of them. His nappy black hair was cropped close, he was clean-shaven and he wore a big smile, like his brother Robert's.

"Tru! You here!" Donald spun him in a hug too.

"What's going on, Man? You done with your covert operation?" Robert said, accepting a hug from Truman too.

Debbie was then in Truman's arms, but at least he didn't kiss her.

"I'm done, the project's finished. It's up to the local police and D.A.'s office now. And I even earned a promotion. I'll be working a desk in Des Moines for a while anyway. Maybe do some training of recruits. Karma is over the moon. We're even getting hitched."

The party relocated to the Washington's house on S Street. Hayward Robinson was there and announced Daniel had some things to finish on the case but would try to come by later. Thelma sent Ruth and Shaunda to the grocery store, and she started cooking and baking like she was going to feed an army.

"Debbie, I'se gonna need yo' help, Honey. Although I 'spose I should let you off the hook since dat brudder o' yours saved the day."

Debbie smiled but bit her lip. Had she spoiled Daniel's jubilation? "Tell me what I can do, Thelma."

Thelma soon had the food preparation well in hand so Debbie found other ways to help. People kept coming in, giving Donald hugs, shaking his hand, telling him about plumbing jobs they needed. Debbie appointed herself his note keeper, found a three-ring notebook, and wrote down the names and phone numbers of his potential customers. It was a good excuse to meet many of the neighbors and church members she hadn't seen since they moved out of town.

She was so grateful Daniel had insisted the children come to court to see this. They had seen injustice and now the other side: the joy and love overflowing. She almost cried when she saw Bonnie and Bernard at the door.

Chantelle ran up to embrace them. "Grandma, Grandpa, guess what! They let Uncle Donald go! Those White folks finally figured out he didn't shoot nobody!" Bernard picked up the six-year-old and bounced her in excitement.

"Some people are so slow, aren't they? We knew Uncle Donald was right all along," Bernard said.

Bonnie embraced Donald and said something to him Debbie couldn't hear. Then she made her way over to Debbie and wrapped her arms around her. "It's over, Sweetie. You and Robert must be so glad. Where's your brother?"

Debbie glanced back at the door. "Um, he isn't here yet. Hay said he had something to take care of before he could come."

Bonnie and Bernard moved around the room hugging Robert's family members and meeting other well-wishers. The children had moved out to the backyard to kick a ball around or play in the fort which the Washington boys had built twenty years earlier.

The crowd kept coming for hours. Robert introduced Debbie to several young people who had been protesting outside the police station back when Donald was first arrested. Donald seemed particularly pleased to see them.

Hours later, it was down to only family. Bonnie and Bernard asked to take their grandchildren home with them to sleep. Robert was excited to have all six of the brothers and sisters back in the old house one more time. Ruth had sent Pete home with Ivan, and Ramón had left Shaunda there since he had to work early the next day. The siblings were sitting around the living room, and Shaunda opened a bottle of wine. Donald and Tru were drinking beer some of the guests had brought.

Donald sat down across from Debbie and Robert who were snuggled close on the couch.

"I had too much time to think while I'se in jail." Donald balanced his beer can on his knee. "Made me think 'bout what I really want in life. What I been missing."

"What have you been missing? From what I heard, your business was growing, you were helping kids down at the community center," Robert said.

"A woman, a family. Time to quit messin' round. I should be getting' married. Puttin' down roots like y'all. Like you and Debbie, Ruth and Pete, Shaunda and Ramón. Though I can hardly believe she found a man to put up wid her sass."

"So, you're looking for a nice lady?" Debbie smiled.

"I think I've got one picked out. We need to get on wid it now dat I am a free man. I met her about a month before all dis happened. Her name Celia, and she lives in Omaha. We been writing to each other the past few months, and she been to see me when they allowed it. She had to work today, but she be down tomorrow."

"That's wonderful, Donald," Debbie said.

"I hope we can meet her before we head home. We'll figure on leaving the day after tomorrow," Robert said.

They heard a knock on the door, and Debbie saw Daniel's face through the glass and jumped up to admit him. Even in the waning light, he didn't look right. She could smell the beer on his breath when she moved in to hug him. He was dangling a six-pack of beer from one hand, but three cans were missing.

"C'mon in, Sweetie. Thelma and Donovan have gone to bed but the brothers and sisters are still up talking."

"I dunno. Maybe I should stay out here. I wanted to see Donald, to tell him how happy I am for him."

Robert and Donald came out to the porch. It felt cooler with a breeze blowing. Daniel sat on the wide stone sill, reminding Debbie how Donald had done that the first time she'd been there. Daniel opened another can of beer.

"I'm sorry I couldn't get here earlier, Donald. It's been kind of a shitty day, after the court thing. I mean, that was wonderful, and I am so happy they dismissed the charges."

Donald sat down next to Daniel. "Hey Man, you okay? Cuz you don't look okay, and I'se the one who just spent three months in the pokey," he chuckled.

Daniel sighed. "Yeah. Maybe not." He held the cold beer can over his scraped knuckles. "I think I walked out on my wife. Again."

"What?" Debbie moved over to his other side. "What happened?"

Daniel groaned. "I went back to the office and thought I'd confront Michael. I mean I thought there was probably a simple explanation why my co-worker hadn't mentioned he'd been my wife's boyfriend in college."

Robert let out a long whistle.

"He wasn't there. No one in the office seemed to know where he was, they thought he was in court with me. He had been in court with me most of the time on your case, Donald. I decided to go home even though Yvonne told me she had to work today. When I pulled onto our street, I thought I saw Michael's car. I didn't hit the garage door opener because that makes noise. I parked on the driveway."

"Oh no," Debbie covered her eyes.

"They were there all right, but fully clothed, in the living room. The babies were at daycare. I didn't ask questions, I just started swinging."

"You punched Michael? I didn't know you knew how to fight," Robert said.

Daniel scoffed. "I don't. Managed to avoid it until now. Didn't know what I was doing, but my knuckles sure hurt. And his face bled all over Yvonne's new Persian rug, so I guess I did something right."

"Lemme see yo' hand to see if ya broke anything," Donald said, taking Daniel's swollen hand and running his fingers over the top of it. "Debbie, go grab an ice pack from da freezer. Mama always had some handy fo' when one of us did somethin' stupid like dis."

Daniel winced as Donald pushed on his hand. He put the ice pack on when Debbie returned.

"So did yo' wife tell you what's been going on?" Donald asked.

"What's been—" Daniel crinkled his brows at Donald. "You act like you know something."

Donald sighed, "Well, the bailiff's a terrible gossip. Spends all day jus' watching folks in the courtroom. I guess she picked out yo' wife when she came up to talk ta you. Den she heard yo' wife was spotted wid' yo' co-counsel and tod me some shit about to hit the fan."

"Someone saw them? Where?" Daniel gaped.

"Third floor?" Debbie asked.

Donald nodded. "You 'member dat room we used for a meeting during a recess a week ago? Michael was in dat meeting. There was an officer of da court standing guard. He said he saw Michael go into the same room later wid a woman he'd seen in court befo'. Da bailiff put two and two together."

"Oh God," Daniel raked his left hand over his face. "And you, Sister. What do you know about this?"

"Yvonne told me Michael came to visit you both in the hospital after she'd had the twins. She was debating whether to tell you she'd dated him in college. I told her to tell you. Obviously, she didn't. I happened to run into them on the third floor last week during a recess too. Yvonne said it was nothing."

"You believed her?"

Debbie shrugged. "You're the one who needs to know. You must have asked."

"I didn't. I was too mad. She was carrying on about how I was over-reacting, but I didn't care. After I knocked him flat, I left again. Eventually, I went back to the office. I am trying to decide if I can fire him."

"You gonna fire your wife too?" Robert smirked.

Daniel grimaced. "I suppose I'd better have my facts straight before I do anything else."

"Innocent 'til proven guilty, Man. "S'what you tol' me," Donald grinned.

"You want to stay here tonight?" Debbie asked. "It's a giant slumber party. All of Robert's siblings plus Janel's husband and kids. Pancakes for breakfast."

Daniel grunted. "I think I'll go crash and Mom and Dad's."

"Our three kids are sleeping there tonight. But you can pick one of them up and dump them on the couch if they're in your room. They won't care," Robert laughed.

"I doubt I can even pick up a twelve-year-old when he is dead weight, probably not even your skinny ten-year-old. How did you get a twelve-year-old and my kids are only six months old?"

"Oh, you know, it was that accelerated parenting class we took in high school. Quick results." Debbie poked him on his arm with her finger.

Daniel laughed. "I didn't even know it was offered in high school. Guess I didn't sign up."

"No, but then you were the valedictorian dating Yvirgin," Debbie quipped.

"What did you call her, Yvirgin? I've never heard that one." Daniel shook his head. "You didn't call her that to her face?"

Debbie laughed. "No, I think Linda coined that nickname. But seriously, Daniel. Go home. I doubt Yvonne had an affair. She's too strait-laced. And I know she loves you." She pushed a lock of hair off her brother's forehead. "I don't think she would trust Michael again after he broke her heart in college. Maybe she just wanted attention."

"She always wants attention." Daniel studied the floor.

"Sure. But you do tend to get wrapped up helping your clients, you know? Look where you are right now. She's probably worried about you."

Daniel sniffed. "I'm gonna go. You'll still be here tomorrow, won't you?"

CHAPTER FIFTY-TWO

September 15, 1982

Debbie stretched out on the chaise lounge on their shaded patio back home. Robert brought her a glass of iced tea. Their children were playing on a Slip 'N Slide in the backyard.

"That was hot work today, signing up voters. The community center needs better air-conditioning." Debbie gulped half of her glass of tea.

"I think we got close to one hundred though, most of them were minorities. That should help. They also need volunteers to go door-to-door next week." Robert stripped off his T-shirt and wiped sweat from his brow, taking the chair next to her.

"Daddy, Daddy!" Chantelle patted his bare knee below his khaki shorts.

"What, Darling?"

"Are you still my biggest fan?"

He laughed, "Well now that Grandpa isn't here, I guess I am your biggest fan."

"Then watch me! Watch me!" She ran off to play.

"What do they hope to accomplish by knocking on doors?" Debbie asked.

"I guess they're looking for some of the elusive potential voters who have never registered. I suppose some are disabled and don't get out much. Or the opposite could be true where people work two jobs and don't take time to vote."

"But if they aren't motivated or able to vote, what's the point of registering them?"

"Well, we can't register them at their homes. But we can give residents forms and tell them where to turn the forms in. Like if they're going to pick up Food Stamps, they can turn the form in at that office, or the department of motor vehicles. We can give them the hotline number to provide a ride to take them to the polls. It's mainly to assess their barriers to voting or registering. At the same time, we'll be informally surveying people to see what else they need, which may be more important in the end. At least that's what the NAACP is hoping for."

"Robert Washington, I think you're getting into this. Are you thinking of going into politics?"

"I haven't given it much thought. But now that you mention it, why shouldn't the first Black president be named Washington too?" He laughed, as Chantelle screeched flying down the slippery hill on her stomach. "Of course, it might be her!"

Learning To Twirl is Nancy's story. Grab a sneak peek at it on the next page. It will be landing before you know it.

SNEAK PEEK AT *LEARNING TO TWIRL*

September 21, 1968

Nancy was washing the dinner dishes with her mother when she heard a strange noise. It sounded like a motorcycle pulling onto their driveway on Sunrise Road. She looked out the window over the sink and recognized the way the driver shook his shaggy sandy-brown hair and ran his fingers through it.

"What was that?" her father, Darrell, asked from the living room. He went out the front door and stood on the porch.

"Excuse me, sir. I'm looking for Nancy Evans. Is this her house?" Peter Thompson asked, ambling his long lean frame toward the porch.

"It's my house, I'm her father. Is Nancy expecting you?" Darrell fixed the intruder with a tight sneer.

Nancy went outside standing behind her father. "I know him, Dad. It's Peter from my band class."

"Peter what?" Darrell crossed his arms.

"Peter Thompson, Sir." Peter extended his hand closing the distance between him and Darrell. Darrell gave Peter's hand a firm handshake.

"Thompson? I don't think I know that name. Do you attend St. Vincent's?"

"No, sir, we live pretty far northeast. I'm in St. Paul's parish." Peter was wearing a black leather jacket over jeans and a T-shirt and stuck his hands in his pockets.

"Oh, sure. I know Father Henry. How is he doing these days?" Darrell's expression softened slightly.

"Father Henry is amazing for his age. He's there every Sunday."

Nancy's jaw dropped. She had no idea why Peter was at her

house, and how did he know exactly what to say to her father to convince him he was a good Catholic boy who attended Sunday Mass faithfully?

Peter turned and glanced back at the motorcycle. "I came by to talk to Nancy for a few minutes and show her the motorcycle. If that's okay, Sir."

"Nancy, don't you think about getting on that death trap! I guess there's nothing wrong with looking at it. Go on. Don't be long, you've got your studies." Darrell shook his head and went back indoors.

"Thank you, Dad," she sang out as she followed Peter back to the driveway. "When did you get a motorcycle, Peter?"

They were standing looking at the bike, which was slightly dented and speckled with mud. "It's not mine. I borrowed it, so to speak."

"Borrowed it from whom?" she asked.

"Um, it's my brother Terry's bike. He left it at the farm a couple of years ago. I don't think he's ridden it since his accident. So, I tuned it up and decided to take it for a spin."

"He didn't mind?"

"I didn't exactly ask him. I pretty much appropriated it. My parents don't even know I took it."

Her eyes rounded. "Why would you do that? They might be mad."

He shrugged. "They might. I didn't want them to worry for no reason though, which is why I didn't tell them. Your dad isn't the only one who thinks motorcycles are dangerous."

"Peter, how did you even know where I lived?"

"It's on your oboe case. Your name and address are printed on a sticker on the side. Your case is sitting right by your feet where I see it class every day."

"You decided to stop by and show me your stolen motorcycle?" She squinted at him.

He chuckled. "No, that was transportation. I'm not sure how I can explain this. I'm celebrating."

"Celebrating what?" Nancy leaned against the post supporting the carport.

"Don't you notice anything different about me today?" When she gave him the once over, he bared his teeth, then laughed.

"Your braces! You got your braces off! What are you doing to celebrate?" She smiled which made him grin broadly again flashing his straight teeth.

"Well, I've been thinking about it for a few weeks. What could I do that I didn't want to do with braces on my teeth? Mostly I've thought about it sitting next to you in band class."

"What did you decide? Eat caramel popcorn or something like that?"

"No, that isn't what I wanted to try." He looked down at his feet and hesitated. "The thing is, I'm not sure you're willing to try it with me."

"Well, I can't go on the motorcycle. You heard my father."

"No, it's nothing like that. It's more like this." Peter moved carefully toward her until he was right in front of her. Then he lifted her chin with one hand and slowly bent over to take her lips with his. Nancy let out a short chirp of surprise, but didn't move away. After a few seconds, he pulled back and smiled at her. Nancy swiveled around to hug the post she'd been leaning on, laying the side of her face on the post.

"You wanted to kiss someone to celebrate getting your braces off?" she asked.

He smirked. "Not someone. You. I wanted to taste your lips but I didn't want to risk poking you with wires. And It was worth waiting for."

Nancy had no idea he'd been waiting for anything concerning her. She felt her cheeks flushing and started to retreat toward the front door. Thank goodness the carport wasn't visible from the window.

"Nancy, are you okay? You're not mad, are you?"

"I'm fine. I just wasn't expecting—um. I didn't think you thought about me like that."

"Would you go to the homecoming dance with me?" Peter inhaled sharply after blurting that out.

Her brows arched. This guy was full of surprises tonight. Getting those wires off sure gave him a jolt of confidence or something. "Homecoming? Oh, I guess that's in a couple of weeks. I guess so, sure."

"Don't worry. I won't bring the motorcycle. I think I can borrow my dad's pickup."

"Yeah, um good. Hey, I'll see you in band tomorrow. Drive carefully." As she backed up toward the front door, he swung onto the motorcycle, kick-started it, and rode slowly down the drive and up her street. She blinked twice. Had she dreamed that?

She'd known Peter for a year since they both started as sophomores at Capital High, the smallest of the four public high schools. He played tenor saxophone and she played oboe and the band director had arranged the instrument sections in a way that put them next to each other. The band director, Mr. Humphreys, often worked with one group of instruments at a time, and the other students were expected to sit quietly and wait or practice fingering their notes.

She supposed he was nice-looking. His hair was longer than

many of the guys she knew. It fell in shaggy layers like David Cassidy's and ended at his collar. She doubted he'd had it cut by a barber; it was more likely he'd done it himself. He had kind eyes and a narrow face. It was a face she liked.

Sometime last spring, Peter had pulled out one of his spiral notebooks and placed it on his music stand. He would write funny little notes to her when the teacher was working with another section of their class. Sometimes she wrote something back. And they started chatting before and after class when they were putting their instruments together and taking them apart to put in the cases. She'd considered him a casual friend. She didn't think he liked her. Not that way.

But she had noticed him watching her sometimes, if she was honest. More this year. When she put her oboe mouthpiece in her mouth to wet the reeds, he looked at her mouth, which made her a little self-conscious. Had he been wondering what it would be like to kiss her? She hadn't thought about that before. She had to admit the kiss had been pleasant. He acted like he hadn't kissed anyone before but he seemed to have it figured out. As if she would know. The only boy who'd ever kissed her was Tommy McCain in the third grade. And that was only on the cheek.

Peter slipped off his heavy denim coat and rubber boots he wore for his morning milking chores and left them on the chilly enclosed porch. He found his mother, Gwen, making French toast in the warm kitchen. He inhaled coffee and cinnamon.

Mom looks tired. God, maybe not tired, older. When did she get that haggard look on her face? He supposed it had been there since the accident. June 3, 1967: a date that no one in his family will ever forget. The day they all became victims of Trouble, with a capital T. The day they ceased to be the wholesome Christ-centered family who worked hard and reaped the rewards of their efforts and strengthened their bonds with each other. The day they became different people altogether.

"Good morning, Darling," Gwen said. "How did the girls seem this morning?"

"Fine, mostly." He washed his hands in the kitchen sink. "Daisy Mae was fighting me for some reason. I think she might be getting mastitis again."

"You tell your father about that?" Gwen narrowed her gaze on her son.

"Yes, ma'am. He's checking her. But her milk production was down." Peter sank into a wooden chair at the kitchen table with a green Formica top and metal sides. Gwen flipped two pieces of French toast onto his plate, and he doused them with maple syrup. "Bacon ready?"

"On the counter, help yourself. And get the juice and milk out while you're up."

Peter was halfway through his breakfast when his father banged the door entering the porch. He raised his voice to be heard in the kitchen. "You milked Daisy last night, didn't you, Pete?"

"Yes, sir. She seemed okay then before you ask."

"Durn it all. That vet bill is going to kill us." Peter's father, Mark, shuffled through the kitchen mumbling under his breath and picked up the phone in the front hall.

Peter tried to ignore his father's conversation with the veterinarian. Somehow this was going to be his fault; he hadn't paid enough attention to Daisy Mae's udder. This probably never happened when Terry was milking. That was probably what his dad was thinking. Terry was the perfect son. Or he used to be.

Before Mark finished his call, Glenda came to the table and held up her plate for a piece of French toast. Peter gazed at his younger sister, who was fourteen. She used to be a skinny little girl with chestnut braids flying behind her as she rode her quarter horse, Silas. Trouble bullied her too. Since the accident, her parents hadn't had time to take her to horse shows or 4-H events. She withdrew to her room, drawing pictures and eating more than she should until her mother complained she kept outgrowing her clothes.

Yes, Trouble had changed them all. His mother used to be involved in every activity at St. Paul's. She'd helped teach the children's catechism class and had been active in choir and Bible study groups. Then she'd had to spend all of her days at the hospital for nine months, and most of the next six months transporting her oldest son to physical therapy. Now she seemed to be worn out, and disinterested in the things and people she used to enjoy.

His father used to be active in their parish too, organizing a group of teens to go on a mission trip when Terry was a junior. Now that Peter was a junior, Mark no longer seemed to care about things like that. His parents used to have friends come over to play cards once a month, but they no longer made or accepted such invitations.

Peter had been clobbered by Trouble too. He'd understood when he had to take over Terry's chores, but he thought it would at least be temporary. When Terry was a high school junior, he had football, basketball, or track practice almost every night after school. That was when they'd pulled thirteen-year-old Peter into the barn to backfill Terry's jobs. He didn't have to milk in the morning then, his mother usually had part of it done before breakfast. Peter had wanted to try out for the junior varsity basketball team last year. Before he had even asked, he knew he couldn't miss his milking chores. He was lucky they let him participate in marching band.

When his father sat down and filled his plate, Peter cleared his throat. "I asked a girl to go to the homecoming dance with me two weeks from Saturday. I wanted to know if I could borrow the pickup."

"Homecoming? That's happening so soon? Isn't that on a

312

Friday after the football game?" Mark poured syrup over his French toast and dug in.

"They changed it. The football game is on Friday and the dance is on Saturday now."

"Whose lamebrain idea was that?" Mark frowned. "You think you're going to miss milking two nights in a row?"

"I thought maybe Terry could help out on Saturday at least," Peter said.

"He has to work sometimes on Saturdays, you know. And that takes all his energy these days." Gwen sat down to eat some French toast herself after the rest of the family had theirs.

"I can check with him," Peter offered.

"I don't know why they had to change it to a second night. It's been that way for decades. You have the game and everyone is all pumped up over that, then they have the dance." Mark gulped his coffee.

"I think they changed it after some kids were in a car accident last year, Dad," Glenda said. "Margaret told me her sister knew the kids in the accident. It happened when they were coming back to school at ten o'clock."

No one said anything for a moment. Mark stared at Glenda, his eyebrows pulled together in a permanent crease. Then his gaze shifted to Peter. "Go ahead, then. Ask Terry. See if it will work." Then Mark stood up and went back out to the screened porch abandoning his breakfast. Peter heard him pulling on his boots and coat. Mark banged the door again as he left.

Doesn't Trouble know when you've had enough?

ABOUT THE AUTHOR

Claudia Johnson Severin grew up in Lincoln, Nebraska, in the Eastridge neighborhood. She went back to her high school twirler days for this series. Like her main characters, she found hours of practice together developed friendships which led to many adventures outside of school. Along with the seven other twirlers in her high school marching band, she put on a homecoming show using hoops, flags and fire batons. It was probably not as impressive as the one in this book.

Like Debbie, she met her husband at a dance, although in college. Some of the problems described at the first Keentime dance were based on actual events. The events involving police and student teacher misconduct are completely fictional.

This is the second of the Twirler Quartet series, following *Catch It Spinning*, which was Yvonne's story.

Writing about past decades gives the author a chance to rewrite history and gives the characters a chance to benefit from lessons learned in the time since. She loved the 1960s, but wouldn't trade her smartphone for a teen line or her SUV for her old Volkswagen Beetle.

Thank you for reading my book. You can contact me through my website at https://claudiaseverin.net. I would love it if you would add a review for my book on Amazon or Goodreads.

ABOUT THE TIMES

Nebraska's miscegenation law, was passed when Nebraska was still a territory in 1855. It provided that "marriages are void . . . when one is a white person and the other is possessed of one-eighth or more negro, Japanese or Chinese blood." This law was  repealed by the state legislature in March 1963, a few years before the United States Supreme Court banned laws prohibiting interracial marriage in Loving v. Virginia in 1967.

A 1968 Gallup Poll found that only twenty percent of the interviewees from the United States said they approved when asked, "Do you approve or disapprove of marriage between whites and non-whites?" ("Gallup Poll U.S. Nixes Mixed marriages," *Lincoln Journal Star,* Lincoln, NE, November 10, 1968.)

So, how uncommon were interracial couples in 1968? The only White girl I knew who was dating a Black guy was my neighbor. And I only heard about it because her mother was lamenting about it to my mother. I went to the newspaper archives across the country to see what had been written.

"Our biggest problem is people staring at us on the freeway and getting into accidents," Bob, a black man with a white wife, Lois, told writer Nathaniel Freedland. ("Black and White Mixes in Two Directions," *Fort Worth Star-Telegram*, November 17, 1968) He was mostly exaggerating, but he said a car with out-of-state plates once did run into a Santa Monica freeway sidewall while attempting to keep up with them for a better view.

The couple were both high school teachers and reported that while they were dating, some of the faculty became obsessed with race, sending hate letters, packages of garbage, and making obscene phone calls. The harassment ceased once they married.

Freedland interviewed another young interracial couple for the same article, John and Barbara. John reported, "For a while we were getting hassled by the police a lot when we drove around . . .once they flipped a cigarette in my eye and I had to go to the doctor. Another time they stopped me, claiming I had a taillight out and then they pulled me aside and asked if Barbara was my wife or if she working the streets for me. It was better if Barbara did the driving."

Writer Bette Orsini wrote a lengthy feature article, "The Wedding of Black And White," in the *Tampa Bay Times*, August 31, 1969. She noted that nineteen months prior to her article, the supreme court "ordered a Dade County judge to issue a marriage license to a Negro man and a white woman. Up to that time, a Florida judge who issued such a license could be fined $5000 and sentenced to six months in jail."

Her article focused on a Black woman, Pauline, who was married to a White man, John. His father and her mother had reservations about their union. When they bought a house, the seller initially hesitated when John told him he had a Black wife and child. The seller polled the neighbors and found they were receptive, and the sale went through.

United Press International reporter Harry Ferguson wrote a similar article in Tulare, California. ("Spotlight on: Marriage between races," *Tulare Advance-Register*, Tulare, CA, February 17, 1968) He interviewed a black husband with a white wife, who lived in Cambridge, Massachusetts. The husband, Arthur, stated that it was important for his wife to accept that she was part of his black community, and once she became involved, she was treated well. Arthur also said, "One of my sisters resented the idea of my marrying a white girl. For most of the first year of our marriage, she was still rather bitter about it." As for his wife's family, he said, "I know that her parents kept talking to her, urging her to break up with me. By the way, they never talked directly to me about the marriage. They had no contact with me whatsoever. They refused to recognize that I even existed."

A sociologist, Dr. Fred R. Crawford, professor of sociology at Emory University in Atlanta, was quoted by reporter Don McKee as saying, "The polarization of the ethnic groups is actually stronger today than twenty years ago." ("Interracial Marriages Still Rare in the South," *Tallahassee Democrat*, July 24, 1968)

Dr. Crawford also noted, "A controlling factor in marriage is what sociologists call propinquity or nearness, closeness of association. It is entirely possible that the number of interracial marriages will become greater as young people get to know each other."

The last article I looked at was Stefanie Pettit's collection of views expressed by a panel of clergyman in Spokane, Washington. ("Spokane Clergy Express Opinion on Mixed Marriage," *Spokesman-Review*, September 28, 1969) "I believe it's persons over fifty who find interracial marriage revolting. It is also just as tough for a black person whose child marries a white person as it is for the parents of the white person involved. I think the parents of the couple see the marriage as a threat to their security," said the Rev. Alvin O. Mills.

Another minister, Rev. Paul J. Beeman noted, "Everything legal in our society is on the side of integration. This generation of the products of interracial marriage will have it easier than the generation before, and the next generation will have it easier than this one." However, Rev. Clay Cooper stated, "You know, there are white keys and black keys on a piano, and they make beautiful music together. But the black keys are still black and the white keys still white. It's not necessary to blend them to get good music."

These are just a sample of the attitudes one could find when *Twirling Fire* begins.

Please note that in 1968, the news style was to not capitalize names of races, and that has changed.

Made in United States
North Haven, CT
28 November 2021

11666280R00200